HISTORICAL

Your romantic escape to the past.

Wed In Haste To The Duke
Sarah Mallory

More Than A Match For The Earl
Emily E K Murdoch

MILLS & BOON

WED IN HASTE TO THE DUKE
© 2024 by Sarah Mallory
Philippine Copyright 2024
Australian Copyright 2024
New Zealand Copyright 2024

First Published 2024
First Australian Paperback Edition 2024
ISBN 978 1 038 91054 7

MORE THAN A MATCH FOR THE EARL
© 2024 by Emily E K Murdoch
Philippine Copyright 2024
Australian Copyright 2024
New Zealand Copyright 2024

First Published 2024
First Australian Paperback Edition 2024
ISBN 978 1 038 91054 7

Published by
Harlequin Mills & Boon
An imprint of Harlequin Enterprises (Australia) Pty Limited (ABN 47 001 180 918), a subsidiary of HarperCollins Publishers Australia Pty Limited
(ABN 36 009 913 517)
Level 19, 201 Elizabeth Street
SYDNEY NSW 2000 AUSTRALIA

FSC
www.fsc.org
MIX
Paper | Supporting
responsible forestry
FSC® C001695

Cover art used by arrangement with Harlequin Books S.A.. All rights reserved.

Printed and bound in Australia by McPherson's Printing Group

Sarah Mallory grew up in the West Country, England, telling stories. She moved to Yorkshire with her young family, but after nearly thirty years living in a farmhouse on the Pennines, she has now moved to live by the sea in Scotland. Sarah is an award-winning novelist with more than twenty books published by Harlequin Historical. She loves to hear from readers; you can reach her via her website at sarahmallory.com.

Visit the Author Profile page
at millsandboon.com.au for more titles.

DEDICATION

To the Quayistas,
writing buddies through thick and thin.

Chapter One

'What a glorious day for a wedding!'

Angeline Carlow gazed out of the window, little bubbles of excitement bursting within her.

'Aye, it is, miss, but you won't be ready for it if you don't hurry up and change,' retorted her maid.

'We have well over an hour before we need to leave,' replied Angeline. 'Besides, it is not important whether I am ready or not. No one will notice me. Everyone will be looking at the bride and groom.'

'But you will want to look your best, miss, so let's get on with it. Lady Tetchwick asked to see me before she leaves her room,' said Joan, dealing with the fastenings at the back of Angeline's new gown of shell-pink muslin. She added with a sniff, 'Her Ladyship might have her own very superior dresser now, but she isn't above asking her old maid to step in and help with the final touches.'

'Poor Alice, so anxious to show everyone here how fashionable she has become!' Angeline chuckled. 'How fortunate that Barnaby is marrying Meg, who lives in the same parish. It means our sister can show herself off to all her old neighbours. However, what *I* think is more important is that our own people from Goole Park will all be able to come to the church for the wedding. Many of you have watched us grow up. I am sure you all want to come and wish them well.'

'Well, of course we do, Miss Angeline, but there's a deal of work to do before any of us dare leave the house!'

Angeline knew it only too well. She had been up since dawn, smoothing the way. First she had pacified Mrs Penrith. The housekeeper had taken umbrage at the fact that Lord and Lady Tetchwick had brought their four children but only one nursemaid and expected one of the housemaids to fill the gap. Then there had been Cook to placate, Mama having changed her mind on the menu for the wedding breakfast so often that no one in the kitchens knew if they were coming or going. And in the preceding days she had taken on many of her mother's duties, since Mama had been so overwrought by all the preparations for her only son's wedding that she just could not cope with the usual day-to-day tasks.

'There.' Joan stood back at last and gave her mistress an appraising look. 'That's the best I can do for you, Miss Angeline. Pray do not go back into the nursery now, or those children will be creasing your gown or pulling at your hair, and *then* where shall we be?'

Angel laughed. 'We will be in the suds! Off you go now, Joan dear. I promised to look in on Mrs Penrith again before I leave, just to ensure all is in readiness for when the guests return here for the wedding breakfast.'

The maid went out and Angel stood for a moment, enjoying the solitude. Various sounds filtered through her door but nothing that signified alarm. She hoped now that she could relax and enjoy the wedding.

She set off down the grand staircase, but as she reached the landing she noticed a man in the sober garb of a personal servant carrying two portmanteaux and hurrying out of the hall. So their last and most important guest had arrived: Barnaby's groomsman, the Duke of Rotherton.

As Angel ascended the final stairs she saw him. He had already divested himself of his hat and, as he had his back to her, she was able to take in the raven-black hair and tall, athletic figure as he shrugged off his many-caped greatcoat and handed it to the waiting footman. Then he turned and saw her.

'Angel! Good day to you.'

Her heart gave a little skip of pleasure. She was inordinately pleased that he had not forgotten her pet name, only it sounded far more attractive when uttered in that deep, smooth voice. She went towards him, smiling and holding out her hand. 'I hope you had a good journey, Your Grace.'

'Excellent, thank you.' The Duke took her hand and saluted it. 'The roads were good and the weather fine.' He straightened. 'But you used to call me Jason.'

'When you were a grubby schoolboy!' She laughed, trying to ignore the sudden tingle of excitement that had rippled down her spine when his lips brushed her fingers. 'You are much changed.'

'Am I?' He subjected her to a compelling gaze from those slate-grey eyes. 'I recognised you instantly.'

Angel had been a skinny child, so it was hardly a compliment, but she let it go. Her eyes shifted to his severe coat and black neckcloth. He was in mourning for his beautiful wife, tragically killed when her phaeton had overturned, and she needed to say something.

'I know Papa wrote to you, but please allow me to offer my condolences.'

He put up a hand. 'Thank you, but that is not a subject for today.'

'Jason!'

The Duke raised his eyes and looked over her head as Barnaby's voice sounded from the stairs and the next minute her brother was beside them.

'What time do you call this, you rogue?'

'I thought I had made very good time.'

'You should have slept here last night, then I would have been sure of you.'

'As I wrote to tell you, I had business in the north.' Jason spread his hands, a faint smile touching his lips. 'But, as you see, I am here now and at your disposal.'

'You will barely have time to change before we set off for the church!'

'Nearly an hour,' he replied, glancing at the long-case clock. 'I am no dandy who takes all morning to tie his neck-cloth! Adams will be laying out my clothes as we speak.'

'Then I will come with you to your room. We can talk while you dress,' said Barnaby, linking arms with him. As he led the Duke away he looked back. 'Make sure they have sent up hot water for His Grace, will you Angel? There's a good girl.'

She watched them walk off, her brother talking incessantly as they disappeared up the stairs, and a sudden sadness gripped her, much as it had twelve years ago. Jason Darvell had been just fifteen then and mourning his father and trying very hard to bear with his new situation as Duke. Her young heart had ached for him. She'd known how she would have felt if Papa had been taken from them so suddenly.

She had told Jason he had changed, but she thought it was not so much in appearance. He was taller now, of course, his face leaner, the rather hawkish features more pronounced, and his cheeks were dark with stubble. With his colouring, she guessed the shadow would remain, even when he was freshly shaved. But his near-black hair still fell forward over his brow as it had done when he was a boy. No, it was not in looks that he had changed, but the shyness she had noted in the boy had hardened into a cool reserve, she thought, setting off for the kitchens. It was as if he was determined to keep the world at a distance.

It was years since Jason had been at Goole Park, but it was just as it always had been, the faded grandeur of the old house, the cheerful bustle of servants who were efficient but not cowed into silence. Jason was relieved. His happiest memories were attached to this house.

Barnaby ushered him into a large apartment with a dressing room to one side, saying, 'Mama has given you the best guest chamber.' He waved towards the windows. 'You get the best views.'

'I am honoured, naturally, but I would have been very happy with my old bedchamber, near the schoolroom.'

'No chance of that,' Barnaby told him, grinning. 'Alice's brood are in residence up there.' He sobered and went on, 'I am very glad you could come, Jason. I mean, you are still in mourning. It is only six months since Lavinia died. I would have understood if—'

'Yes,' Jason said quickly, turning away from his friend. 'Do you think everyone will be scandalised?'

'No, no, you have buried yourself away from the world for too long. And it is not as if there will be dancing or anything like that while you are here. A quiet ceremony and a couple of days with the family will cause no comment at all.' Barnaby put a hand on his shoulder. 'But how are *you*, Jason? Truthfully, now.'

How was he? Jason considered. He had been stunned, when he'd first learned of the carriage accident that had killed his duchess. Saddened that such a gloriously beautiful and vivacious creature should come to a tragic end. But his main emotion? Relief that his nightmarish marriage was over.

He had loved Lavinia to distraction at first, and been wilfully blind to her greed and selfishness. Later, when it had become impossible to ignore her infidelities, he had chosen to look the other way. He had not been able to bring himself to put them both through the humiliation of a divorce. Everyone thought him a grieving widower and he had done nothing to disillusion them.

He gave a little shrug. 'I am well enough.'

'Aye.' For a moment Barnaby's fingers gripped his shoulder, then he smiled and nodded. 'Come along, then, let's get you changed. You ain't fit to be my groomsman in those dusty clothes! Where's that rascally man of yours?'

The little parish church was packed out with family, friends and neighbours of the bride and groom. When the service ended, everyone moved outside the church and Jason found himself standing next to Lord Goole.

'Never one for weddings,' the Viscount muttered, throwing him a conspiratorial glance. 'Always afraid someone is going to stand up and declare some just impediment, what? But there we are. My only son leg-shackled at last. And Meg's a fine gel…she'll make him a good wife.'

Jason saw the very moment the Viscount realised that he was talking to a recently widowed man, for he coughed nervously and quickly changed the subject.

'Well, well, it's very gratifying to see so many of our neighbours here. I suppose I must go and do the pretty, too, if you will excuse me, Your Grace…?'

He hurried off and Jason moved away from the crowd, content to stand and watch the proceedings. Everyone was now milling around the bride and groom and he was glad his rank precluded strangers approaching him. Since Lavinia's death he had concentrated on business matters, using his bereavement as an excuse to shut himself away. It felt disconcerting to be out in the world again.

At last the carriages appeared, and soon the Duke was travelling back to Goole Park with the rest of the guests invited to the wedding breakfast. Arriving at the house, he escorted an aged dowager duchess into the dining room and they were already seated by the time he spotted Angeline. She walked in, looking neat as a pin in a gown of shell-pink muslin, her dark hair pulled smoothly back and confined by a matching ribbon. She had given her arm to an elderly spinster and it occurred to him that almost everyone took precedence over an unmarried daughter. For all that, when he happened to catch her eye the cheerful smile she gave him seemed to fill the room with sunshine.

The wedding breakfast was finally over. Jason relaxed, knowing he had done his duty. When Barnaby and his bride disappeared to change into their travelling dress he moved out to the great hall with everyone else to wait for them, wondering how soon after their departure he could make his excuses and leave.

Lady Goole had invited him to remain at Goole Park for as long as he wished, but he had only committed himself to two nights. Now he thought even that was too long. Despite this happy occasion he found it difficult to make polite conversation with anyone. He had never been truly at ease with strangers and today was especially difficult. There were too many surreptitious glances and sly hints on the circumstances of his wife's death, a subject that had no place at a wedding.

The chatter in the hall suddenly increased. Jason looked

up to see Barnaby coming down the stairs with his new wife. Summoning a smile, he stepped forward to escort them out to the waiting carriage.

'So glad you could come,' Barnaby said again, as he helped his bride into the travelling chaise. 'And a thousand thanks for the use of your Brighton villa for our honeymoon. Meg is in raptures about it already.'

'I am indeed, Your Grace,' replied the lady, glancing shyly at Jason.

'I never use it now. I shall be glad to think it is occupied.'

Jason touched his hat to them both and closed the carriage door. As the driver whipped up the horses he glanced up at the clear blue sky. It was a fine April day. He had driven here in his curricle, and if he left now he could be back in London before dark.

'Well, thank heaven that is over!' exclaimed the Viscount, taking his arm. 'Come along inside, my boy. Such a long time since you were here…ten years at least! We've missed you, you know. My lady is eager to catch up. We think of you as part of our own family…'

Listening to the kindly words, it dawned on Jason that Lord and Lady Goole would be hurt beyond measure if he suddenly said he was going straight back to town. He could not do it. This went far deeper than duty. The Carlows had welcomed him into their home and shown him such care, such hospitality in the past, that it was impossible to cut his stay any shorter.

'And Brighton, eh?' The Viscount went on as he walked with Jason into the hall. 'Dashed good of you to lend them the house, my boy. Surprised you don't want it yourself, the place being such a fashionable haunt these days.'

'I never go there,' replied Jason. It had been a wedding

present for Lavinia, something she had set her heart on. 'In fact, I am thinking of selling it.'

'What?' The Viscount was scandalised. 'No, no, dear boy, you must not even think of it. It is early days, I know, but you will take another wife and she will no doubt want to enjoy the Brighton society. And don't forget your children. They need a mother.'

'The girls are very well cared for in Kent,' he said shortly. 'And I shall not take another wife.'

Even before he'd married Lavinia she had set up the establishment there for her own daughter, Rose, and when Nell had been still a baby she had persuaded Jason to agree to the child joining her stepsister. Not that he had needed much persuading. His own upbringing had been much lonelier, living at Rotherton with only the servants for company. His duchess had maintained that she could not live with children in the house and Jason, besotted with his new wife, had agreed.

He was glad now that they had never been witness to their mother's profligacy or her lovers.

He felt the bile rising at the thought of his disastrous marriage and suppressed a shudder. Once had been enough.

'Not take another wife?' The Viscount turned to stare at him. 'Now, that, my boy, is out of the question!'

He pulled Jason away into one corner, where they would not be overheard.

'Oh, I know it is early days yet, and you are still in mourning, but you need an heir, my boy. That must be faced, and I would be a poor friend to you if I didn't say so. Surely you do not want that good-for-nothing cousin of yours stepping into your shoes? I am sorry, Your Grace, but it just won't do! Tobias Knowsley is a spendthrift. He will run through your fortune before you are cold in your grave. Not that it is any business of mine,' he added hastily, after a glance at Jason's face. 'But I have known you since you were a boy, and I have only your best interests at heart. I cannot believe you would want Knowsley taking up residence at Rotherton!'

Lord Goole was right. The idea of Toby Knowsley inheriting Rotherton was not something Jason liked to contemplate, but neither did he want to discuss it. He wished he might retire to his room, but a moment's reflection told him that would cause just the sort of comment he most loathed. *Poor Rotherton, the grieving widower.* Or the cuckold. Confound it, he hated being pitied.

He forced himself not to frown and instead summoned up a tight smile. 'You are quite right, sir, and a fount of wisdom, as always.' He waved towards the drawing room. 'We should go in, I think.'

For the sake of his hosts Jason exerted himself to speak with everyone. He liked the Carlows. They were the nearest thing to a family he had ever known. His mother had died when he was a baby and the widowed Duke had little time for his only son. Once he was sent off to school Jason saw even less of his father. The old Duke was rarely at Rotherton for the holidays, and Jason was allowed to spend time at Goole Park with his new friend Barnaby and his happy, loving family.

One protracted circuit of the room was more society than the Duke had experienced for the past six months. He needed a respite. Noting that the long windows leading out onto a terrace had been thrown open, to make the most of the warm spring day, Jason made his way towards them with a nod here, a few words there, until finally he could escape.

There were several people on the terrace and a few more strolling around the flower gardens, but he avoided them all, running lightly down the shallow steps to the lawn and away from the house. No one approached him, but that was no surprise. After all, everyone knew he was still in mourning. What was more natural than that he should wish to spend some time alone?

He was familiar with the gardens and walked on past the rose garden and through an avenue of yews, which led to the shrubbery. It was just as he remembered, surrounded by high hedges and with a well-tended path winding its way between the bushes and with the occasional bench where one might rest. It was quiet, too, which he wanted.

He was just thinking it unlikely any of the guests would venture this far from the house when he heard someone singing. It was a female voice, soft and melodic, crooning a lullaby. Jason had no idea who it might be and, intrigued, he walked around the next curve of the path and came upon Angeline.

She was sitting on a wooden bench and rocking a sleeping baby in her arms. Her head was bent over the child and one glossy dark curl had escaped from its pins and was hanging down over her shoulder. She looked up and he stopped.

'Excuse me.' He felt like an intruder. 'I did not know it was you, I have never heard you sing before.'

She chuckled. 'I rarely do so in company! My little nephew was fractious and Alice needed someone to take him away, because the poor nursemaid was trying to get the others to sleep.'

Her response was so natural that the years fell away. He was a schoolboy again, talking with his friend's little sister.

He sat down beside her. 'Why could Alice not do it?'

'She is required in the drawing room.'

'And you are not?' He frowned. 'Do you *like* children?'

'You sound surprised.' She giggled. 'I like them well enough, and I am content to be out here with the baby, away from all the crowds and chatter. This is quite relaxing after such a busy day.'

'I think you are a very good aunt.'

'I am useful—which makes me of some consequence here, I hope.' That sounded a trifle dispirited, but the next moment she was smiling. 'And how are your daughters, Your Grace?'

His daughters! Jason felt a stab of conscience. His occasional visits to the children were stilted, uncomfortable. His own fault, of course. He had no idea what to do when he saw them.

'I hope you left them well,' Angel said now.

'Yes, they were very well when I last saw them.'

'I am sure they have been a great solace to you this past year.'

He nodded. The girls reminded him too much of their mother, when all he wanted to do was forget.

'Mama and Papa are so happy you came,' she went on. 'It has been such a long time since you visited Goole Park. Why, it must be all of twelve years!'

Jason was well aware of it. After his marriage he had only seen Barnaby in town or at various house parties. He had never brought his wife to Goole Park. Looking back, he knew now he had been afraid of spoiling his happy childhood memories by sharing the place with Lavinia.

He said, 'Well, I am here now.'

'Yes, for a mere two days!' She shook her head at him and he grinned.

'I know, Angel. Hardly long enough to discover everything you have done since we last met.'

'Oh, *I* have done very little,' she replied, 'Save my come-out.'

'Ah, I missed that,' he said apologetically.

'Yes, you and the Duchess were in Paris, I think.'

'That's right. For the short-lived peace.' He did not want to think about that time, when he had watched his wife flirting with every officer in sight. 'How did you enjoy it, all those gowns and parties?'

There was the faintest hesitation before she replied.

'Well enough, but I was a sad disappointment to Mama. I ended the season without one offer of marriage.'

'What? Not one?' He sat back, his brows raised in surprise. 'You did not fall in love with anyone?'

She flushed. 'I did not say that.'

Her arms tightened around the sleeping baby, and there was such a look of sadness in her countenance that he was tempted to ask what had happened.

But before he could speak she had shaken it off and said cheerfully, 'Suffice to say that it cured me of romantic love for ever! I did not go to town again, but I was not sorry for it. It was Lettie's turn the next year, you see, and Alice was increasing.'

He frowned. 'I do not understand…how should that affect you?'

'Because Mama could not be in two places at once. She took Lettie to town while I went off to Shropshire, to stay with Alice. It was not the happiest time. My brother-in-law is very good-natured, but has not an ounce of sense! He fretted so when the baby was born that I wished he had gone off to the races or something with his friends, instead of fussing around Alice and insisting that his own doctor should be present at the birth.' She laughed at the memory. 'I spent most of my time smoothing the midwife's ruffled feathers. She was perfectly competent, but took exception to having her every action questioned.'

'What a horrid situation for you,' he said.

'It was, but I should have disliked London a great deal

more!' There was an engaging twinkle in her brown eyes. 'Lettie was a hit, you see. She received no less than *two* very respectable offers before Marland came along, and would have taken great pleasure in crowing over her achievements if I had been there. You must remember what a little beast she could be, always trying to belittle others.'

He shook his head. 'I remember very little about her, or Alice. To me they were only Barnaby's disapproving sisters. In fact, you are the only one I recall with any clarity.'

'I am?' She blushed, but went on cheerfully, 'I expect that's because I was a nuisance. Quite a little hoyden, Barnaby says. I am sorry if you found me tiresome, but I always enjoyed your visits. It still gives me a great deal of pleasure to look back on them whenever I am in low spirits.'

How could she have enjoyed being teased and scolded for being in the way?

She rose. 'The sun is setting. I must get little Henry back to the nursery.'

'And then will you return to the drawing room?'

'Alas, no. I promised the housekeeper I would help with preparations for supper. One of the kitchen maids has broken her arm and they cannot manage without someone to help carry the food upstairs.' She gave him a little nod. 'Goodnight, Your Grace.'

'Jason,' he reminded her.

For a moment she regarded him, her brown eyes serious and dark as sable now. Then she gave another little nod and walked away.

He watched her, noting the sway of her hips, the way the thin muslin clung to her shapely limbs. He'd been wrong when he'd said she hadn't changed. She was still petite, and she looked younger than her twenty-four years, but there was definitely a womanly figure beneath that pink gown.

When Jason had first visited Goole Park, Angel had been too young to join in their games, but she was clever and quick-witted and hung around them like a shadow, despite their teasing. How old had she been when he last saw her? Twelve? Thirteen? He folded his arms, smiling. By then she was a fearless rider, had a talent for billiards, and she'd also proved a useful extra when they played cricket.

Another memory returned: his last visit to Goole Park. He had just buried his father, and his guardian, an uncle he barely knew, informed him that he would not be going back to school but would finish his education at Rotherton, under the aegis of a tutor. He was the Duke now, his uncle reminded him, and must learn to act like one.

He had been granted one final holiday: a few precious weeks with Barnaby and his family.

When the time came to leave, Jason recalled being assailed by the enormity of the changes to his life. On his way to the drawing room before that final dinner he'd stopped. He'd wanted to turn and run. To hide from everyone and everything. His grief, the sympathy of this kind family, but mostly from the responsibilities that lay ahead for him. He remembered it so vividly now. He was standing outside the door, trying to screw up the courage to re-join the family, when little Angel appeared. She had tucked her hand into his and gone with him into the room.

That was the last time they had met. He had been swept away to take up his new life and never saw her again. Rarely thought of her. Until today.

When Jason finally returned to the drawing room, the wedding guests had departed and only the family were left. This comprised the Viscount and his lady, plus their eldest daughter Alice and her husband Sir Humphrey Tetchwick, who had travelled with their children from their estate in Shropshire for the wedding. The final couple was the Carlows' youngest child, Lettie, and her husband Lord Marland, who lived but two miles away.

Angel had not reappeared. She and Barnaby had been his constant companions on previous visits and he was painfully aware of their absence. His instinct was to withdraw again, but he fought it down and strolled across to take a seat beside Lady Goole.

'We are so pleased to see you here again, Your Grace,' remarked Lady Goole. 'You have been away from Hertfordshire for far too long. I hope you mean to remedy that now.'

'Thank you, ma'am, I shall try to do so.'

'And when you do come again we will hold a little party for you,' declared Lady Marland. 'Nothing too grand. I am sure you must have your fill of ceremony when you are in town! No, this will be a cosy affair, just friends and neighbours.'

'And perhaps a little dancing,' added Alice. 'If you can promise me dancing, Lettie, then we will most definitely come. And I shall bring Sir Humphrey's sisters with me, too. They are both diamonds, in their own way. Young ladies always add lustre to such parties, do you not agree, Your Grace?'

Jason inclined his head but did not reply. He could see the calculation going on behind the lady's smile. She was hoping to provide him with his next bride. When it was clear he was not to be drawn on the subject, the conversation moved on. They began to discuss their plans for the following day.

'I suggest a ride,' said Marland, helping himself to a pinch of snuff from a silver box. 'The fine weather looks set to hold for another day.'

'Oh, what a splendid idea, my love!' exclaimed Lettie. 'I should so enjoy that, but can we mount everyone?'

'Alice and Sir Humphrey can have our hacks,' declared Lady Goole. 'Your father and I plan a very quiet day at home tomorrow, after the rigours of the wedding.'

Alice sighed. 'I would dearly love to ride out with you, but alas little Henry is proving very difficult. Nurse says he is teething, which makes him fractious, and she cannot manage all four children. I told Sir Humphrey we should bring the second nurserymaid but he would not be moved.'

'If my wife had her way we would have hired another coach to accommodate everyone,' replied her loving spouse, laughing.

'Well, I wish we had,' retorted Alice. 'I have not had a moment to myself. Why, I spent a good half-hour in the nursery with the children yesterday, while everyone else was enjoying themselves!'

'Angel can help Nurse while you are gone,' put in Lettie.

'Oh, yes. What a good idea, Sister,' said Alice, much struck. 'The children mind her so much better than I.'

Unable to stop himself, Jason said, 'But surely Miss Carlow will want to ride out too.'

'Oh, no,' replied Lettie, who was, in Jason's opinion, a very managing female. 'Angel is going to distribute the wedding cake to our neighbours. That and helping with the children will fill her day very nicely.'

'There you are, then, it is all settled.' Lord Marland gave his wife an approving smile before turning to Jason. 'You will be joining us I hope, Your Grace? I have a very good second hunter who will be up to your weight. He will give you a good day's sport, I am sure.'

'Thank you, but I have other plans. It is such a long time since I was at Goole Park. I want to reacquaint myself with the grounds here. On foot,' he added firmly, when he saw Lady Marland was about to speak.

'I have had several more paths opened up in the park since you were last here, Duke,' said Lord Goole. 'You will find the vistas from the hill are well worth the walk.'

'Thank you. I shall make sure I go there.'

Soon after that the Marlands' carriage was called and Jason took the opportunity to bid everyone goodnight and escape to his room. He had had enough company for one day, and he was still irritated by Lady Tetchwick's clumsy attempts at matchmaking.

By the time he climbed into his bed, the sheets comfortably warmed beforehand, Jason's ill temper had abated. He lay on his back, hands behind his head, and considered his situation. As a duke without an heir he knew the world would expect him to marry again, but Lavinia had only been dead six months. He had hoped everyone would give him at least a year before they began to throw prospective brides in his way. But it was not only Alice scheming to marry him off. He had already received hints in letters from various members of his family.

He could not deny that he had made a mull of it the first time, marrying for love and against their wishes. And afterwards he had been too proud to admit his mistake in taking for his duchess a widow eight years his senior, a woman with a voracious appetite for lovers.

If Lavinia had provided him with a son, an heir, then perhaps he might have been able to avoid a second marriage, but no more than Viscount Goole did he want to see Toby Knowsley take his place. And if Knowsley predeceased him— which, given his dissolute lifestyle, Jason thought highly likely—then those next in line were no better.

A sigh escaped him. Much as he disliked the idea, it was his duty to marry. He would have to take a bride. But this time it would be purely for convenience. Love would have no place in his next marriage.

Having resolved that issue, Jason thought sleep would come easily, but another source of disquiet intruded. He could not forget the sisters' casual disposal of Angel's time. Not just Alice and Lettie, but Barnaby, too, he thought, recalling how his friend had ordered Angel to make sure hot water was fetched up for their guest. He had barely seen Angel since his arrival, she was always busy with some household task or running errands for her family.

Irritably he turned over and closed his eyes. It was no wonder she looked back so fondly to her childhood. They had turned the poor girl into a drudge.

Chapter Two

Fortune smiled on Goole Park's guests the following day. The sun was shining, although a fresh spring breeze had replaced yesterday's unseasonal heat. The Tetchwicks were in high spirits at breakfast as they discussed their forthcoming outing.

'What time do you expect to return?' asked Angel.

'Oh, Lord, I have no idea,' Alice replied. 'We are riding over to Marland Hall to meet up with Lettie and her husband, and we shall doubtless stop at the Crown for refreshments before we return. Do not expect to see us before dinner.'

'Well, I hope you all enjoy yourselves,' declared the Viscount, as his daughter and son-in-law hurried away. He rose, preparing to take himself off to his study to read his newspaper, but first he turned to the Duke. 'And you, my boy. You said you would be walking the grounds today, did you not? I shall not stand on ceremony with you, Jason. You may come and go as you choose. But if you wish for company I am at your disposal.'

'Thank you, my lord, I am quite happy to explore alone. Unless Miss Angeline would like to come with me?'

Angel felt a rush of pleasure at the unexpected invitation and it was with real regret that she declined, citing her busy day.

Her mother had risen, and was about to follow the Viscount from the room, but now she stopped.

'My dear, I am sure we can do without you for a few hours, if His Grace wishes you to go with him.'

'His Grace is very kind,' replied Angel. 'However, I have other commitments today.'

Her mother gave a soft tut but she did not stay to argue, and Angeline was left alone at the breakfast table with the Duke. She felt a little disappointed that Mama had not insisted she accompany Jason. Everything could have been rearranged with a little effort. But it was clear that the Viscountess saw the invitation as mere courtesy. Which it was, of course.

'It is chastening to think I am of less importance than cake…'

Angeline started. 'Your Grace?'

'I understand you are distributing the bride cake today.'

'Oh…that.' She saw the smile lurking in his rather hard grey eyes and relaxed, knowing he was not really offended. 'Yes, but also I am helping Nurse with the children, and I cannot leave her to cope with four of them alone.'

'No, of course not.' He nodded and put down his napkin. 'I shall leave you to your domestic duties, then.'

With a final nod he left the room and Angel smothered a sigh. The Duke's invitation had come as a surprise, and she would dearly like to have gone with him. However, a moment's reflection convinced her that he had only offered out of kindness. They had nothing in common now. She had no doubt that he would be bored within a half-hour of setting out.

Perhaps an hour, she amended. After all, she was reasonably well educated. Yet there was no escaping the fact that she was a spinster of four-and-twenty, living quietly in Hertfordshire. She cringed inwardly at the thought of the worldly-wise Duke of Rotherton exerting himself to make idle conversation with her. That was something neither of them would enjoy, she decided, and was therefore best avoided.

Jason left the house a short time later, but before heading off on his walk he went to the stables. The head groom there remembered him from his schooldays and was only too delighted to show him the changes, pointing out with some pride the matched pair Lord Goole had recently purchased for his curricle.

'Of course, my lord and lady's hacks are out today, but you'd be pleased with their quality, too, Your Grace.'

'I am sure I would,' said Jason. He walked up to the loose box where a glossy chestnut gelding was looking out, watching him with an intelligent eye.

'And who rides this handsome fellow?' he asked.

'That's Apollo, Your Grace. Miss Angel's horse.'

'She does still ride, then?' He posed the question casually as he scratched the horse's head.

'Oh, aye, that she does. Whenever she can. Your Grace can't have forgotten what a clipping rider she was.'

'No, I haven't forgotten.'

With a final word to the groom Jason set off on his walk, remembering the wild gallops he had enjoyed with Barnaby and Angel, riding across this very park. Such happy, carefree times they had been, before he had become Duke. After that his life had become one of duty and restraint, hiding all emotion.

It was hunger that sent Jason back to the house some hours later. In the past he would have gone to the kitchens and cajoled Cook into finding him something to eat, to keep him going until dinner time. Now, as Duke, he need do no more than lift a finger and his slightest request would be carried out, but he was not inclined to lift that finger. He really wanted to make his way around to the kitchen door and take pot luck there, but he had visions of the kitchen staff being overwhelmed by His Grace the Duke of Rotherton invading their domain. No, that would make them too uncomfortable. He would enter the house the same way he had come out— through the garden door.

He stepped into the inner hall just as Angel was coming down the stone staircase. She smiled when she saw him.

'Did you enjoy your walk, Your Grace?'

'Very much. Have you finished delivering all the cake?'

'Why, yes. I took the gig out this morning for that purpose, and since then I have been in the nursery with my niece and nephews. We did not expect to see you for another hour at least.'

'I was driven back by the need for food.' He grinned as his stomach rumbled. 'I do not believe I can last until dinner time.'

'I should think not.' She indicated the tray she was carrying. 'I am on my way to the kitchens now. I will have something sent up—'

'No.' He put up his hands. 'You do not need to wait upon me. I can easily deal with the matter.'

'But why send another servant running up and down when I am already on my way?'

Jason hesitated. 'Your logic is irrefutable, but by that reasoning I could just as easily go myself.'

'You could indeed,' she agreed cordially. 'If you are that hungry then I suggest you follow me now and we will have you fed in a trice!' She had descended the final few steps and now stood in front of him, smiling. 'We used to raid the kitchens quite often when we were children, so will you come?'

The walk in the sunshine had raised his spirits and her words made him laugh with genuine pleasure, something he had not done for a long time.

'How can I refuse?'

He followed Angel into the nether regions of the house, where she stopped at the servants' hall.

'You had best sit down in there while I take these dishes to the scullery. Poor Cook will go off in a fit of apoplexy if she finds you in the kitchen.'

'Yes, I had thought as much.'

He went into the empty hall and sat down at the scrubbed table while Angel disappeared with her tray. She returned in a very short time with a jug and two tankards, and was followed by a kitchen maid carrying a second, larger tray of dishes.

'Thank you, Maria. Do put the tray down before you try to curtsy to His Grace, there's a good girl.' Angel waited until the maid had left her tray and departed before she set down her own burden. 'I thought you might prefer small beer to quench your thirst after your exertions.'

'And you are going to join me?'

'I really cannot leave you here on your own,' she explained, twinkling at him. 'You would have everyone from the boot boy to the laundrymaid coming to gawp at you and I did not think you would like that. You saw the effect you had on Maria.'

'I was afraid the poor girl was going to faint off.'

Angel laughed. 'She will regale all her friends with the story of how she waited on a duke!' She set the food out before him while he poured the ale. 'There is some of last night's game pie, and a little bread and butter, and cheese with pickles. Simple fare, but you were used to enjoy it.'

'Yes! I remember coming in here with you and Barnaby,

famished from playing out of doors all morning.' He raised his tankard to her. 'Those were good times, Angel.'

'They were, weren't they?' She reached over and stole a morsel of cheese from his plate.

'There is plenty for two,' he said.

'Thank you, but no. I had luncheon with the children, and I am not really hungry, but I could not resist.'

This was the Angel he remembered, her brown eyes shining with mischief and her hair escaping from its pins. They were totally at ease together and conversation flowed, although Jason could never afterwards recall what they talked about. However, he did remember the feeling of disappointment when he had eaten his fill and Angel told him it was time to go.

'It cannot be time to change for dinner just yet.'

'No, but the flowers in the morning room need replacing, and I want to see what pots we have in bloom in the orangery.'

'Surely someone else can do that,' he said, following her out of the room.

'They could, of course, but I *like* to choose the plants.'

'You do too much.'

'I enjoy being busy.'

When they arrived back at the inner hall he stopped her. 'Tell me honestly. Would you not rather be out riding today?'

Jason watched her carefully. He noted the slight hesitation before she shook her head.

'I was needed here.'

'That is not what I asked.'

Angel was subjected to a fierce scrutiny from those rather hard grey eyes and, seeing the stubborn set to his mouth, she knew Jason would take nothing less than the truth. She chose her next words with care.

'I admit I should have liked to be given the choice. But that does not mean I am unhappy—you must never think that.' He did not look convinced and she went on. 'I enjoyed sitting below stairs with you, Your Grace. It was just like we used to do, when you and Barnaby were here for the holidays.'

'Aye. It is a pity we had to grow up.'

There was a wealth of sadness behind his words. Angel wanted to ask him what he meant by it, but the moment passed in a heartbeat and he waved her away.

'I have taken up far too much of your time. Go and choose your plants, Angeline. We will meet again at dinner.'

Jason went up to his room where he found Adams already preparing a bath for him.

'How the devil did you know I was back?' he demanded.

'One of the servants informed me that you were below stairs,' replied the valet.

Jason scowled. He did not need to ask who had sent the lackey, or who had ordered the water to be heated. Angel. From what he had seen so far, she practically ran the household at Goole Park.

If only Rotherton had such a mistress.

The thought caught Jason unawares. He looked about, as if the voice had come from somewhere in the room, rather than inside his own head. Angel considered everyone's comfort before her own, but how would it be if she had her own establishment? If she could please herself over more than the choice of flowers…

'Well, Your Grace, will you bathe now, before the water grows cold?'

'What? Oh, yes. Yes.'

* * *

An hour later he was dressed in his evening coat and pantaloons and making his way to the drawing room when he met Lady Goole, coming up the stairs and looking flustered.

'Oh, Your Grace, I am most sorry to tell you, but Alice and Sir Humphrey have only now returned from their riding expedition. I have just sent word to the kitchen to put dinner back an hour.'

She looked so upset that Jason quickly reassured her he was not inconvenienced in the slightest.

'I can easily amuse myself for an hour,' he told her, and she hurried on, still murmuring disjointed apologies.

'There is already a good fire in the drawing room, if you wish to sit in there.' Angel was standing at the foot of the stairs. 'It is surprising how chill the house can become of an evening.'

'I was thinking I might go to the library and find a book.' He carried on down the stairs, glancing at the apron she wore over her gown. 'What are you going to do?'

'The gardener has brought in several flowering pots for the morning room and I have yet to arrange them.' She waved him away, very much as he had done to her, earlier. 'Go and find your book, but do take it to the drawing room to read. You will be far more comfortable there, and no one will disturb you.'

With a smile she left him, and Jason went off on his quest. But although the Viscount's library was well stocked he could find nothing to distract him from an idea that had been growing within him all morning. It was his duty as Duke of Rotherton to marry again, but the idea of returning to Society's Marriage Mart was abhorrent. Eligible females would be paraded before him and he would be obliged to choose one, but they would be strangers. There was no guarantee of lasting happiness.

How much better, then, to marry Angel, his childhood friend? They understood one another, and neither of them had any illusions of romance. It would be the ideal solution for both of them. What could possibly go wrong?

Angeline was alone in the morning room and surveying a row of Delft pots on a side table. She looked around as he came in.

'I decided upon hyacinths. What do you think?'

'Yes, very pretty. Angel—'

'They are not very showy, but they look well against the blue and white of the pots.'

'Angel, forget about the flowers a moment. I want to talk to you.'

'Yes, of course.' She turned to him, her brows raised. 'Is something wrong?'

'No, nothing like that.' He began to pace the room, trying to order his thoughts. At last he came to stand before her. 'Angeline, will you marry me?'

Her cheeks paled, making her dark eyes look even larger. She said slowly, 'You should ask Papa first.'

'I do not want to marry your father.' He winced at the frivolity of his response, but he saw the slight flicker of her eyelids, a lessoning of tension in her slight frame. He said, 'You are a woman with a mind of your own, Angel. It is what *you* want that matters. I thought…' He searched for the right words. 'I have seen how much you do here for everyone. Too much. You should have a house of your own, rather than running your parents' establishment.'

Silence. Angel had turned away from him and was studying the flowers.

'That is a very kind offer, Your Grace, but…' She straightened one of the pots, moving it barely an inch. 'I do not understand why you should be asking me this. You have pointed out the advantages to *me*, but what about you? What has prompted you to make this offer?'

She turned and fixed Jason with her disconcertingly frank gaze. He remembered as a child she had always been honest and forthright. Nothing missish in her behaviour. He was relieved they could discuss the matter so sensibly.

He smiled. 'You must not think I am doing this purely for your sake. Quite the contrary, in fact. I am being very selfish. I must marry again. I need an heir.' She blushed violently and he said quickly, 'Not immediately, of course. You may be sure I shall not rush you on that! We have always been good friends, Angel, so let me be perfectly honest with you. As long as I have no wife everyone, my family, friends and even complete strangers, will be trying to find one for me. Indeed, it has started already,' he added, thinking of his very first evening at Goole Park. He stepped closer and took her hands. 'I need a wife and I can think of no one I would prefer to have at my side. I believe we would deal very well together, you and I. What do you say? Will you be my duchess?'

'Your Grace does me great honour,' she said, gently pulling her hands free. 'But I regret I must refuse.'

'Refuse! May I ask why?'

'You have been widowed for less than a year. You cannot know what you want yet. You may meet someone else and fall in love again. Someone beautiful and worldly, like your first wife.'

Never! I shall not make that mistake again.

He shook his head. 'No. You have already said you are done with love; I, too, have no wish to suffer from it ever again. Love is a foolish emotion, only designed to cause pain to the unwary. But I am sincerely fond of you, Angel. This would be a marriage of convenience for both of us. You have always been a very practical person. What could be more sensible, more comfortable, than two friends making their life together? I think, no, I am *sure* we can be happy.'

'Are you, Jason?'

It was the first time since he had arrived that she had used his name and he was encouraged by it.

He said, 'I am. Most sincerely. As my duchess you would have my houses to oversee, and the gardens too, if that is your interest. You can be as busy as you want to be, but it will not be all work. You will be able to ride out whenever you please and have your own carriage too, as well as enough pin money to spend as you wish.' He stopped and took a deep breath. 'You would be your own mistress, Angel. You could live the life that *you* want.'

He waited, hoping he had done enough to reassure her.

Angel's mind and her emotions were in turmoil. It was an effort to think, to speak calmly. They had not seen each other since they were children. She knew so little about him. *In your heart you know him very well!*

She quickly squashed that rebellious thought. This was far too important for such childish fantasies. Her own happiness and Jason's were at stake. She was thankful he had not made any pretence about loving her. The hero worship she had felt for Jason as a child was no basis for marriage.

'No,' she said again. 'It would not work, Your Grace.'

'But why? Why do you say that?'

He raked his fingers through his hair, pushing it back from his brow in frustration. It was a gesture she knew well, a reminder of the boy she had known. But Jason Darvell was not a child any longer. He was a man. A duke, no less, with all the responsibilities and obligations the title carried.

'I am very fond of you, Angel,' he said now. 'I always have been. And I think—I hope—you feel the same for me?'

'We were happy enough together as children,' she admitted.

'Exactly! And we can be happy together now. I would not be saying any of this if I was not sure of it. I am offering you independence, Angel. A home of your own. Money, servants, a secure place in society where you will not be the last in consequence. We can travel, if you wish, and there are all the diversions of London to enjoy: lectures, art exhibitions, the theatre. Everything your heart desires.'

Except your love.

Angel was surprised and shocked at her silent *cri de coeur.* Surely she couldn't be in love with Jason Darvell? At least, not in a meaningful way. She was in love with a memory… the boy he had been.

She gave her head a little shake and with a sigh he turned away from her.

'I have seen the way you are treated here,' he said, walking over to the window. 'You are taken for granted. Your sisters want you to be an aunt to their children, your mother wants a companion. Even Barnaby treats you like a servant! I want you to be yourself, Angel. To live as *you* wish and not to be at everyone's beck and call. Rotherton needs a mistress. There would be duties, of course, but you would be in charge. You would have free rein to order things as you wish. The same applies to my other properties. Naturally we would discuss any major changes to ensure we are in agreement, but as my duchess your opinion will be valued. *You* will be valued.' He turned to face her again. 'I shall do everything in my power to make you happy, Angeline, if you will do me the honour of becoming my wife.'

With his back to the light she could not see his expression, but there was no mistaking his sincerity. She felt shaken, un-nerved.

Her eyes shifted to the hyacinths. 'I came in here to ar-range the flowerpots.'

'Would you not rather be arranging your own flowers, in your own morning room?'

She watched him come back across the room towards her. He was dressed with severe simplicity, his shirt and white waistcoat in stark contrast to the black coat and pantaloons. His black hair was slightly dishevelled now, but she preferred it that way. It suited him. She knew some people found him intimidating. He had a commanding presence and a forthright way of speaking, plus those rather harsh, aquiline features, but she recognised the man behind that rather forbidding exte-rior. She had seen the smile lurking in those hooded eyes and the slight lift at the corners of his mouth when he was amused.

Something shifted inside her. He would be a kind, con-siderate husband. They were friends already, and wasn't it possible that might turn to love in time?

'Do you truly believe we can be happy, Jason?'

'I do.' He took her hands again. 'Say yes, Angel. Say you will marry me.'

She swallowed, gripping his fingers to steady herself as the ground seemed to sway beneath her feet.

'Very well.' It was a struggle to speak. Her voice seemed to be coming from a long way away. 'Yes, I will marry you.'

And with that, the darkness closed in.

Jason caught Angel as she collapsed. Going over to the sofa, he gently put her down and sat beside her, chafing her hands until she stirred.

'I beg your pardon.' She struggled to sit up. 'I do not know what came over me.'

'Easy now,' he murmured, pushing her back against the cushions. 'Lie still for a moment. You fainted, that is all.' A rueful smile tugged at the corners of his mouth. 'Not quite the reaction I had hoped for. Do you remember my asking you to marry me?'

'Yes.' She looked up at him shyly. 'Were…were you teasing me?'

'No! How can you think I would jest about something like that? I was in earnest. And you agreed.' He stopped rubbing her hands and held them together between his own. 'But you must be sure, Angel. Did you mean it when you said yes?'

She nodded. 'I did.'

Relief flooded through Jason. Relief and a surprising jolt of happiness. He had thought she would not hesitate to accept him, and her refusal had thrown him completely off-balance. He had then made every effort to persuade her to change her mind—not because she had dented his pride, but because at that moment it had been borne in upon him how much he wanted this marriage. He felt as if the barrier he had built up around himself had cracked a little.

He squeezed her fingers and lifted her hands, one after the other, to his lips.

'You have made me the happiest of men.' He berated himself for not finding a more original response, but at this moment it was all he could think of. 'Shall I fetch you a glass of water, or some wine?'

'No, nothing, thank you, Your Grace.'

'Jason.'

'Jason.' She gave him a little smile. 'You do not need to sit with me. I shall be very well again in a moment. In fact, I should like to be alone, I think.'

'If you are sure… Would you like me to call your maid?'

'No, thank you. I shall be perfectly well if I sit quietly for a little while.'

'Then, with your permission, I will go and find your father, to tell him the good news.' He hesitated. 'Would you object if we announced it immediately?'

'N-no, not at all.'

She was looking a little dazed, but smiling still. He leaned in to kiss her cheek and went off to find the Viscount.

Angeline did not move after Jason had left her. Everything was silent, still. Like the quiet after a storm. She no longer felt faint, but the hope and certainty she had felt when she had accepted his offer had quite disappeared.

She lifted one hand to her cheek. The skin still burned where Jason had kissed it.

'Oh. What have I done?' she whispered to the empty room. 'What have I done?'

Chapter Three

Duchess! I am a duchess.

The words echoed in Angel's head as the carriage hurtled through the Surrey countryside, bowling along lanes where the hedgerows were white with May blossom. She was the Duchess of Rotherton. How was that possible?

It was barely one month since Jason had asked her to marry him. After the initial shock and surprise of their betrothal, her family had risen nobly to the challenge of a second wedding. The Duke had suggested they marry quickly, a quiet ceremony with few guests, but Jason had told Angel they could delay and plan something far more grand if she wished it.

But Angel had not wished it. If Jason wanted a quick, quiet wedding she would be quite content. She had also been happy to go to Rotherton directly after the service. It was, after all, little more than seven months since his first wife had died, and Angel was not ready to be subjected to the gossip and speculation of London.

They had been married that very morning, in the same parish church where her brother had been wed. She was even wearing the same shell-pink gown, although this time her hair was adorned with pink rosebuds and she wore the diamond and pearl necklace that Jason had given her. However, there had been none of the celebrations that had accompanied Barnaby's nuptials, and they had left for Rotherton directly after the service.

The ceremony itself had gone off without a hitch, although Angel half expected someone to stand up and declare that the marriage could not go ahead. Barnaby, perhaps.

Her brother had cut short his honeymoon in order to repay the favour and be the Duke's groomsman. Angel had been very happy to see him and Meg, but her pleasure at the forthcoming ceremony had been dimmed when, the day before the wedding, she'd come out of the library and heard Barnaby and Jason talking.

They were out of sight, on the other side of the grand staircase, and she'd continued towards the stairs, unconcerned, until her brother's voice floated across the hall to her with disastrous clarity.

'Are you sure you want to do this, Jason? Oh, I know Angel is a great gel, and all that, but after Lavinia… Well.' He broke off, then said in a rush, 'My sister is hardly a beauty.'

Angel stopped and drew back, folding her arms across her stomach.

Hardly a beauty! The words hit her like a body blow. There was a console table at one side of the stairs, with a large mirror fixed above it, and she only had to move a couple of paces to see her reflection. Her dark hair was lustrous enough, but she wore it pulled back, smooth and neat. Sensible, if not the height of fashion. Her brown eyes were fringed with dark lashes and her skin was clear. Everything about her was good enough, she thought, but not exceptional. Nothing to set man's pulse racing.

Jason spoke, his tone reproachful.

'That is unkind, Barnaby. And beauty is not always what it seems, my friend.'

Angel would not skulk here any longer, she despised eavesdroppers. Putting up her chin, she walked around the staircase just as Jason laughed.

'Enough of this folly! Angel and I will rub along together very well. There is no more to be said.'

She stepped into sight just as he finished speaking and both men saw her immediately. Barnaby's face was a picture of guilt and confusion.

'Angel! Where the devil did you come from?' He'd glanced up at the grand staircase, knowing as well as she that anyone descending must have heard every word.

'From the kitchens.' She waved a hand back towards the narrow stone staircase the servants used, smiling as if she had not a care in the world. 'Why? Were you looking for me?'

'Oh, no. No. I was, er…'

'But I was,' said Jason, coming forward. 'I thought we might take a little stroll together before dinner.' He pulled her hand onto his sleeve, saying as he walked her out of the house, 'You do not need a wrap, it is a warm day and we shall not be very long.'

They had walked only a few yards across the lawn when he said, 'You heard your brother's remarks, I suppose.'

Angel bit her lip. 'Yes.'

'He is a fool not to appreciate your worth, my dear.'

'But he is right. I am not beautiful.'

'True beauty is not always visible, Angel. It is easy to be misled by a pretty face.'

'Or a handsome one!'

The words were out before she could stop them.

'Ah. The reason you have…er…foresworn romantic love?' he asked lightly. 'Would you like to tell me about that?'

'I would not wish to bore you.'

'I should like to know, all the same.'

He spoke almost casually, but Angel heard the kindness in his voice. She had not even told her family about this, but her conscience argued that if Jason was to be her husband, there should be no secrets between them.

'It was a silly thing, really. A gentleman I met during my come-out. He was handsome, charming... I suppose you would say he swept me off my feet. But I was fortunate. His shallow nature was revealed to me before any harm had been done. He stole a kiss. Nothing more.'

'Not true!' He stopped and pulled her round to face him. 'He hurt you, Angel. That is unforgiveable.'

She gave a little shrug. 'It would have been so much worse if I had married him.'

'And his loss is my gain,' said Jason, bending to kiss her cheek.

It was the merest touch, but it struck her like a lightning bolt, shaking her to the core. She'd put one hand against his waistcoat. 'Oh, Jason, are you quite sure you want to marry me? I have *nothing* to offer you. I am a country mouse. I have been to London but once in my life and know so little of society.'

'Then it will be my privilege to introduce you! Not that we shall spend all our time in society. Rotherton will be our main residence and I am eager to show it to you.' He covered her hand, holding it against his heart. 'Believe me, Angel, you are all I want in a wife. You are honest and practical, infinitely kind, and sensible, too.'

Yes. Sensible Angeline. That thought was enough to steady her racing pulse. Neither of them wanted to suffer more heartbreak, so it was far better that they marry as friends.

Even so, as they strolled on Angel could not forget her brother's words any more than she could forget that Jason had not suggested taking her to the villa at Brighton, the one he had loaned to Barnaby for his honeymoon.

Again, she tried to be sensible. His first marriage had been a love match. To see another woman in the villa might bring back unwelcome memories for the Duke.

As the carriage rattled on, she could only hope the same would not be true at Rotherton, since that was to be their home.

The coach slowed to negotiate an imposing entrance.

'Look, Angel, that is Rotherton, set out below us. What think you of your new home?'

The Duke's question brought an end to her daydreams and she turned obediently to look out of the window.

The drive wound downwards in a wide arc, affording her a good view of the house. It was a palatial building, created in the baroque style. The creamy stone façade of the east front boasted at least a dozen long windows between embedded columns stretching out on either side of the main entrance with its grand portico. She already knew that this huge stately pile had been the seat of the Darvell family for three centuries. In that time it had been much altered and enlarged, and now looked dauntingly grand, even for the daughter of a viscount.

The Duke was watching her, smiling faintly. 'Well, Duchess?'

'It is considerably larger than Goole Park.'

He laughed. 'It is, but you will very soon be at home in it.'

She thought that doubtful, but said nothing.

The carriage rattled on through the elegant park and came to a halt at the shallow steps of the portico. A liveried servant was waiting on the drive to open the door and the Duke jumped out, acknowledging the man's bow with a nod before turning to offer his hand to Angel. When she had alighted he did not release her fingers, but pulled them onto the sleeve of his coat.

'And here is my butler, on his way to greet us,' he remarked, as a soberly dressed figure came down the steps towards them. 'Good day to you, Langshaw.'

'Welcome home, Your Grace. To you and the new Duchess.'

Angel nodded, and hoped a smile would suffice. She felt so nervous she was not sure her voice would work.

'Langshaw has been butler at Rotherton since my father's time,' said Jason cheerfully. 'Anything you need to know, just ask him—isn't that right, Langshaw?'

'I will endeavour to answer any questions Her Grace may have,' replied the butler, allowing himself a little smile that made him suddenly look far less intimidating. 'However, I am sure Her Grace will find Mrs Wenlock a much better informant on domestic matters, having been here even longer than I.'

'Ah, yes.' Jason nodded. 'Our excellent housekeeper, who runs Rotherton with a rod of iron! Where is she?'

'In the Marble Hall, Your Grace, where the staff are gathered to greet their new mistress.'

Jason nodded, and ushered Angel inside. The formidable Mrs Wenlock was indeed waiting for them—only the housekeeper was not at all formidable. She greeted the Duke with the same warm affection Angel had noted in the butler, and was at pains to put the new Duchess at her ease, while an army of servants looked on. A few were brought to Angel's attention, but there was no attempt to introduce every one of them. The housekeeper remarked shrewdly that no one could be expected to remember all their names in one go, and they were quickly despatched about their duties.

'The baggage coach arrived some time ago and all your

luggage has already gone up,' the housekeeper informed them. 'I will have hot water taken upstairs shortly, but in the meantime I have had refreshments carried into the Yellow Salon.'

The Duke was in the act of removing the cloak from Angel's shoulders and she felt him pause. Glancing up, she saw he was frowning. It was gone in an instant, and when he replied to the housekeeper his tone was perfectly calm.

'Thank you, Mrs Wenlock. There will be plenty of time for Her Grace to see the rest of the house tomorrow, but I suppose we might as well start with the Yellow Salon.'

He shrugged off his greatcoat and handed it to a waiting footman before leading Angel across the hall. At the salon door Jason hesitated, then gestured for her to precede him.

Angel walked in and stopped to look about her. Tall windows overlooked the drive and the parkland beyond, and the room was as large as the drawing room at Goole Park. However, unlike the worn and slightly faded glory of Angel's old home, everything here was startlingly new and decorated in every shade of yellow, from the creamy walls to the straw-coloured silk on the chairs and sofas and the butter-yellow damask curtains.

'What a…a cheerful room,' she managed at last.

Jason poured two glasses of wine and handed one to her.

'Aye.' His lip curled in sardonic amusement. 'Very *yellow*, ain't it?'

'Possibly because all the furnishings are so new.' She sat down cautiously on one of the sofas and ran a hand over the rich fabric.

'True. This room has hardly been used since it was refurbished. It was my first wife's decision to decorate it thus, to match her portrait.'

He waved towards a large canvas hanging on one side

of the chimneypiece and Angel obediently looked at it. She had seen the painting the moment she had come in. It would have been impossible not to do so.

Encased in a richly carved and gilded frame, the life-size depiction of the Duke's first wife dominated the room. A statuesque and golden-haired goddess, gowned simply in flowing white muslin, her blue eyes stared out of the painting as if she were gazing at the park, visible through the windows opposite. She was standing on a carpet of wild spring flowers, predominantly white and yellow blooms, and cradling an armful of daffodils.

Angel swallowed before saying in a hollow voice, 'She is very beautiful.'

She glanced at the Duke, but he was not looking at her. His eyes were fixed on the painting.

'I commissioned it soon after our wedding.'

He fell silent, and after a few moments she tried again. 'The setting is Rotherton, I think. Is that not the house in the background?'

'It is—although the wild flowers are never so abundant as that in the park. The deer see to that!' Another silence, then he said bitterly, 'She is depicted as Persephone, the goddess of spring. And, ironically, of the dead.'

He raised his glass and took a sip while Angel remained silent and still. She did not want to interrupt his thoughts, whatever they were. A moment later he shook off his contemplative mood and turned to her.

'If you have finished your wine I will escort you up to your room. Your maid should have everything ready for you by now. On the way I will show you the drawing and dining rooms, so that you will know where to find them.'

'Thank you, that is very thoughtful.' She rose and put her

fingers on his proffered arm. 'I think it would be very easy to get lost in this house!'

He covered her fingers where they rested on his arm.

'You will soon grow accustomed.'

His words and the gesture were reassuring, but as he escorted her out of the room Angeline looked back at the beautiful woman staring out from the portrait. She felt an icy finger running down her spine. How could dark hair and a petite figure ever match the golden beauty of Jason's first wife?

Having given his new bride into the care of her maid, Jason went to his own room, his brow furrowed. Adams was waiting for him, but after one look at his master's face he did not speak, merely went on preparing the bath for the Duke to wash off the dirt of travelling.

Jason barely noticed his man's silence. His thoughts were dark and not altogether happy. The day had passed off as well as he could have hoped, but now he was here at Rotherton with Angeline, doubts were setting in. He could not forget Lady Goole's look of concern as he took his leave of her.

'Take care of Angel, Your Grace,' she had begged him. 'I thought she might never recover from the disappointment she suffered at her come-out, but I am glad she has. She deserves to be happy.'

Why on earth had he been in such a hurry to marry again? He should have courted Angel properly, not proposed within days of her brother's wedding. But he had been so incensed at the thought of leaving her at Goole Park, little more than a servant for her family, that he had determined to carry her off at once and give her a new life of ease and comfort.

He should not have rushed her into marriage, and such a small, private affair at that. He had convinced himself he was doing it for her benefit. Now he realised it had been an act of pure self-interest on his part.

He had not seen Angel for years, but almost as soon as they'd met again it had been as if they had never been apart. She challenged him, teased him. She made him feel more relaxed and at ease than he had done for years. But that was no reason to marry without giving her time to consider. What if she came to regret tying herself to a man she did not love?

He recalled his short visit to London before the wedding, and a visit to his club, where he'd announced to his acquaintances that he was getting married. They had been surprised, but he remembered one of them saying, with a laugh, 'Well, good luck to you, Your Grace. If you do change your mind I suppose you can always get an annulment!'

He had laughed at that, along with everyone else, but was it such a nonsensical idea? He had no qualms about consummating the marriage, but what of Angel?

Jason took in a sharp breath as Adams tipped the final jug of hot water over his head, but it did not distract him from the unpleasant truth. Confound it, there were plenty of women ready to marry him and give him an heir, but by marrying Angeline he risked losing her friendship, and only now did he realise just how precious that was to him.

'I should never have done it!'

'Your Grace?'

His man was standing by the bath, holding up Jason's robe and regarding him with a questioning eye.

'Talking to myself,' he muttered, pushing himself up out of the tub.

He slipped his arms into the robe and took the proffered cloth to wipe his hair, but even as he dried his body confusion continued to rage in his mind. Finally, as his man tenderly eased him into his new blue coat and settled it across his shoulders, the question that was bothering him the most burst out.

'Damn it, Adams, was I a selfish brute to marry her out of hand?'

His valet was the soul of discretion, and Jason expected him to maintain a dignified silence. He was more than a little surprised when Adams responded.

'It is not my place to comment, Your Grace. But, since you ask, from what I have seen and heard of the lady, I think she will suit you very well.'

Jason stared. Adams had been with him ever since he'd become Duke at the tender age of fifteen, and he had never before heard the valet express an opinion on anything other than the cut of his coat or his choice of footwear.

'Confound it, 'tis not about whether she will suit me,' said Jason. 'Will I make her happy?'

'As to that, I cannot say, Your Grace. But I think it very likely.'

Adams gathered up the discarded towels and carried them away, leaving his master to digest those words as best he could.

The evening sun was pouring in through the drawing room windows when Jason walked in. Angeline was already there, inspecting the paintings. She was wearing a cherry-red silk gown with a fine cream shawl arranged about her shoulders. Her dark hair was pinned up and confined by a red ribbon, and when she turned towards him he saw she was wearing the demi-parure of pearls and diamonds he had given her as a wedding gift. She was a picture of simple elegance, and Jason thought he had rarely seen anything more beautiful.

'You have some fine works of art here,' she commented.

It took him a while to realise she was speaking. He had to give himself a mental shake before he could answer.

'Yes, my grandfather brought most of the landscapes back from his Grand Tour.'

'The portraits, too, are very good.'

'They should be. The Dukes of Rotherton only ever commissioned work from the finest artists of their day.'

He watched her move around to stand before a large painting of a family group on the right of the chimney breast.

'Is this your grandfather?'

'Yes. The Fifth Duke and his duchess with their three children.'

'The boy, then, is your father.'

'That's right.'

'And this is he as Duke?' She moved across to the far side, gesturing to the couple staring out from the gilded frame on the left of the fireplace.

'Yes.'

'You are very like him.'

'Am I?' He studied the bewigged figure dressed in velvet and lace, staring out so haughtily. 'I hardly knew him.' He saw that Angel was regarding him, her brows raised, and he shrugged. 'My mother died soon after I was born and my father rarely visited Rotherton. I lived in the nursery wing here until I went off to school at eight years old.'

'Oh, how sad!'

He looked at her in surprise. 'I never thought so. At least, not until I met Barnaby and spent my holidays with him at Goole Park.'

'Our family must have come as a shock to you!' She laughed. Then she asked, 'When will I meet the children?'

'The children?'

'Your daughters. Will they be coming down to join us before dinner?'

'They are in Kent.'

'Oh, are they visiting family?'

'No, they live there. I beg your pardon, I thought you knew.'

Angel looked shocked. 'I assumed they lived here, at Rotherton.'

'No. You are frowning. Is there aught amiss with that? The nursery here has been woefully neglected. Their present accommodation is much more suitable for two young girls.'

'Oh. I should have thought…' Her voice trailed off, then she said brightly, 'It is no matter. If we mean to make this our home we can refurbish the nursery and bring them to live with us.'

'Why? They are perfectly happy with Mrs Watson.'

'But they are your daughters, Jason.'

He flushed and found himself repeating the argument Lavinia had used. 'You would find it a dashed nuisance, I am sure, having them in the house.' He added, 'I thought you would like to settle in here before anything else.'

Under her steady, thoughtful gaze he felt uneasy, but at that moment the butler came in to announce that dinner was ready, and Jason gave a rueful smile.

'I am proving a very poor host! We were so busy discussing the artwork I omitted to serve you with a glass of wine. Would you like Langshaw to send word to the kitchens to delay our meal?'

'Oh, there is there is no need for that,' she said quickly. 'I am perfectly ready to go in to dinner.'

He detected an odd note in her voice and he said, as Langshaw withdrew, 'Is something wrong, Angel? Are you unwell?'

'No, no,' she assured him. 'I am a little tired, I think, that is all.'

'Yes, of course.' He was relieved. 'It has been a long day. A good meal will revive you, I hope.'

'Yes, I am sure it will,' she agreed, laying her fingers on his arm and going with him to the dining room.

Crossing the hall with Jason, Angel knew it was not exhaustion that was weighing down her spirits. It was the thought that Jason did not care about his family. She was sure that was not his true nature. He had been very young when he'd first married, and had scandalised society by marrying a widow so much older than himself.

Angel remembered Barnaby telling their parents all about it, quite forgetting that his fifteen-year-old sister was in the room. Jason had stood firm against the wishes of his family, and even his guardian, and insisted that he would marry the love of his life, who was already carrying his child. Angel also remembered her mother's disapproval when the society pages had reported that the Duchess had returned to London very quickly.

'The fact that the baby was born just four months after the wedding is neither here nor there,' Lady Goole had explained to her husband. 'These things happen. But to leave her baby with only the wet nurse and servants so soon after her confinement—it would not do for me, I can tell you!'

It was not unusual to put children to a wet nurse, Angel knew that. She could understand why the Duke, only eighteen himself, would have had little interest in a baby, or in his eight-year-old stepdaughter.

But surely now the children would be a comfort, thought Angel. They would be a link with the wife he had loved so much. The wife she was very much afraid still held his heart.

They reached the dining room and Angel put these thoughts aside as a liveried servant jumped forward to open the door. It was her first dinner at Rotherton with Jason and she would not spoil it with vexing questions.

'Good heavens!'

She could not help exclaiming when she saw that one place had been set at each end of the long dining table and the space between covered with a vast amount of silverware.

Jason, coming to a halt beside her, gave her a questioning glance.

'It, it is very impressive, Your Grace, but.' She hesitated. 'Do we really have to dine like this, when there are only the two of us?'

He raised his quizzing glass and surveyed the table.

'It is rather daunting, isn't it?' he replied, the trace of a laugh in his voice.

She said slowly, 'Do you always dine like this when you are here?'

'Er…no. The little parlour downstairs suits my purposes very well when I am alone. There are, in fact, several rooms set aside for use by the family, although the rest of them have not been used since my parents' time.' He looked back to address the butler, who had followed them into the room. 'I shall sit at Her Grace's right hand tonight, Langshaw. Pray have everything moved there for me. And in future, when we are dining alone, the Duchess and I will use the small dining parlour.'

'Very well, Your Grace.'

'I think they are eager to impress their new mistress,' Jason told her, escorting her over to one side of the room while they waited for everything to be rearranged. 'Ain't that so, Langshaw?'

'It is, Your Grace. We were all anxious that Her Grace should not find anything wanting at Rotherton.'

'Everyone has been to such a lot of trouble to make me welcome and I am most obliged to you all for your efforts,' Angel addressed the butler, smiling. 'This is a very elegant room, and everything looks most impressive, but His Grace and I will not put you to the trouble of all this when we are dining *à deux*.'

'Very well, Your Grace.'

'I do hope I have not offended,' she murmured, as the butler made his stately exit.

'Not at all, you were very gracious. You are mistress here now, and must order everything as you wish.'

'As long as you will be happy dining in the small parlour?'

'Aye, it will be much cosier. And it is closer to the kitchens, too, so it will suit everyone better.'

Dinner progressed slowly, for Cook also wanted to impress the new Duchess. There was such a multitude of dishes on the table that it was almost impossible to try every single one. Angel did her best, taking minute quantities from each until finally she could put down her knife and fork and sit back in her chair.

'I am replete,' she declared. 'That is the finest meal I have ever enjoyed!'

She knew her words would find their way back to the tyrant who ruled the kitchens, and she hoped it would ease her path as she took charge of the household.

The covers were removed. Sweetmeats and dishes of nuts and sugared almonds were brought to the table, and Langshaw placed decanters of wine at the Duke's elbow before following the other servants out of the room. At last they were alone.

Jason picked up one of the decanters. 'Madeira?'

'Yes, thank you.'

'Did you really enjoy your dinner?' he asked, filling her glass and serving himself with port.

'Very much. I am looking forward to spending the morning with Mrs Wenlock. I have a great deal to learn about Rotherton and I know it will take time. I hope she will bear with me.'

'I have no doubt she will, but she will also remind you that you are mistress here now. I want you to be comfortable at Rotherton.'

She chuckled. 'We will not be very comfortable if I upset all your servants!'

'Oh, I doubt you will do that. But there must be changes you wish to make.'

Angel thought about suggesting once again that they invite his children to Rotherton, but decided now was not the time.

She said instead, 'Certainly, but not yet. I shall not rush into anything.'

'Not even redecorating the Yellow Salon?'

'Certainly not that. It would be the height of extravagance to change the furnishings in that room upon a whim.'

'You are free to order things at Rotherton just as you wish, Angel. Even *"upon a whim"*.'

'Thank you, but spending money for the sake of it is not my way,' she replied firmly. 'I do not intend to make any changes at all until I am more familiar with the house.'

'So I shall not come back to Rotherton in a month's time to find you have remodelled the whole?'

She did not notice the teasing note in his voice.

'You are going away?'

'I am.'

He was no longer looking at her, but intently studying the glass held between his long fingers.

'I spoke with my steward Simon Merrick earlier. There are a number of business matters concerning my estates that require attention. It will involve talks in town with my lawyer, and with Telford, my man of business, then I must also go north to one or more of my other properties before returning to London. My going now to deal with these matters will give you time to settle in and become acquainted with Rotherton. And you will be busy with morning calls.' He grimaced. 'The ladies of the neighbourhood will call and you will visit them in return, but you do not need me for that. In fact, I should be very much in the way!'

'Oh.' She tried to digest this news. 'When do you propose to leave?'

'Tomorrow.'

'Tomorrow?'

'I am sorry. I should have told you before.'

'Yes, you should!' She set down her glass with a snap. 'You are in a tearing hurry to be gone from me, sir.'

'No, Angel, you misunderstand me.'

'Do I?' She stared at him. 'We were married *this morning*, and you propose to leave me after just one night...' Something about his manner, the way he kept his eyes averted, made her uneasy. She even felt a little sick. 'Or are we not even to have that?'

She and Jason had exchanged nothing more than a chaste kiss so far, but Angel knew what was expected of a bride and had been preparing herself to do her duty in the bedroom.

He looked uncomfortable. 'I said I would not rush you. I want to give you time to grow accustomed to your new position.'

'Alone?'

From everything she had learned or observed from her sisters, Angel did not anticipate much pleasure in the experience, but to suddenly discover the Duke had no intention of taking her to his bed was a cruel blow.

Jason saw the suspicion of tears in her eyes and cursed himself for a fool. There had been so little opportunity for reflection in the past month that he had thought she would welcome some time alone. For his part, there was indeed business to be dealt with, but it could have been avoided if he had really wished to do so. He was using the excuse to get away from Rotherton…to give them both a little time to consider their situation.

He was haunted by the Viscount's final words to him, declaring how relieved he and Lady Goole were to have Angeline so comfortably settled at last. Jason wanted to be sure she had not been coerced into this marriage.

'Angel—' He reached across to touch her hand where it rested on the table, but she snatched it away.

'Am I *that* repulsive that you c-cannot even bring yourself to c-consummate our marriage?'

'No, that's not it at all!' He jumped up and caught her arm as she left her seat. 'Angel, please. Let me explain.'

She resisted for a moment, then sank back down onto the chair.

'Well, Your Grace?' Her tone was arctic. 'What is it you want to explain?'

Jason resumed his own seat. He had to make her understand, but he must be careful. He could not afford to get this wrong.

'Everything happened so quickly,' he said at last. 'It was only when we left the church, man and wife, that I realised how much I had rushed you into this. I know, too, that your parents were eager for the match, and that must have weighed with you. There was no time to reflect upon whether we were doing the right thing.'

She maintained a stony silence and Jason forced himself to go on.

'All this…' he waved a hand '…this *grandeur* can be daunting. I thought you might be regretting your decision to marry me. If that is the case, then it is not too late. The marriage can be annulled.'

Angel was very pale, her dark eyes troubled.

'Is that what you want, Your Grace? Do you *regret* marrying me?'

'No, not at all. But I have been wed before. I know what marriage entails. You are an innocent. A maid. It would be no wonder if you were a little frightened of…what lay ahead.'

Her cheeks flamed. 'If you are referring to the…the marriage bed, I have two married sisters, sir. I know something of what is required of a wife.'

'But I fear you may not know what is required of a *duchess*, Angel. I have duties, obligations, and so does my wife. My houses and estates require a mistress.'

He stopped, recalling Lavinia's reaction when he had said something similar to her.

'I cannot live my life at Rotherton, darling Jason. It would destroy me. I will not be a prisoner in that cold barrack. Or in any of your houses!'

He shook his head, trying to block out that disdainful voice.

'There is the townhouse, of course, but the other properties cannot be ignored. We cannot live in London all year.'

'You think that is what I want?' She leaned towards him. 'I enjoy living in the country, Jason. I am prepared for my life to be different, for it to be hard work. I am not daunted by any of it.'

She was gazing at him so earnestly that he felt a constriction around his heart. It would be so easy to take her to his bed, to bind her to him, but the doubts persisted. He must be honest with her.

'If that were the only thing! You do not know me well enough yet, Angel.' He shrugged. 'I am not at ease in society. I dislike fuss and grandeur. I have been told I am cold-hearted. Morose, even. And I can be overbearing. I have a temper.'

'Is that all?' she replied with a faint glimmer of a smile. 'You are not cold-hearted, Jason. And I have a temper myself—as you witnessed when we were children. I do not believe it will be a barrier to our happiness.'

He was grateful for her attempts to alleviate the gloom, but he would not trap her into a marriage she might later regret. He knew only too well what hell that could be.

'No, Angel, we cannot make light of this. I shall leave at dawn. You will have time to become familiar with Rotherton, time to reflect upon everything this marriage entails. When I return, if you are of the same mind, then we shall begin our married life.'

'And you will be gone for a month?'

'At least. Perhaps a little longer.'

He waited. Some of the colour had returned to her face and he hoped now that she understood he was doing this for her sake.

'Very well.' She pushed aside her half-filled glass. 'Then I shall bid you goodnight, Your Grace.'

'Allow me to escort you to your room.'

He expected her to refuse, but she nodded and he pushed back his chair, holding out his hand to help her up.

Angel was silent as Jason escorted her from the dining room. This was not how she had imagined her wedding night.

She did not doubt Jason believed he was being kind, giving her the chance to reconsider her decision. However, his proposal had been too persuasive. He had pointed out to her the disadvantages of her life at Goole Park and shown her a vision of something far better. A future she had never dreamed could be hers. She would not change *her* mind, but despite the Duke's protestations she suspected he was having second thoughts.

Her heart sank at the idea, but if that was the case then it was better to delay consummating the marriage. Far more sensible.

And that was what he had called her, was it not? *Sensible.*

'Here we are.' Jason's voice interrupted her thoughts. 'There is a connecting door between our rooms, but it is locked at present. The key is on your side, so you need have no fear that I shall impose myself upon you.'

'Oh.' This was a wretched start to their marriage. She stifled a sigh and said quietly, 'Thank you…you are very kind.'

'I hope you will sleep well, Angel. And you must feel free to do what you will with Rotherton while I am away. I know I can trust you not to dispose of all the family treasures!'

She could not bring herself to respond to his attempts at a jest, and after a moment he went on.

'Order the household as you wish. I really, truly, want you to be happy here.'

'Do you?' She looked up, straining to see his face in the shadowy light.

He did not answer.

She put her hand on his chest, feeling the strong beat of his heart through the fine silk waistcoat. It sent the blood pulsing through her own body. Daringly, she leaned a little closer. He hesitated only a moment, then lowered his head and kissed her.

It was not a chaste brush of the lips, as on previous occasions, the kind of kiss she had been expecting. This time his mouth crushed against hers, demanding a response, and Angel's heart pounded against her ribs. His arms came around her and he teased her lips apart, his tongue darting and dancing, making her bones melt. Hitherto unknown and unimagined sensations rippled through her and she clutched his coat. She breathed in the musky scent from his skin. She felt light-headed, almost faint, and there was an unfamiliar ache low in her body, a yearning for more. Much more.

She was about to slip her arms about his neck when he broke off the kiss.

'Enough now.' His voice was ragged. He caught her hands and held them firm against his chest. 'I shall be gone before you wake in the morning, but I wanted to kiss you goodbye. Something to remember while I am in London.'

Remember? That kiss was burned into her heart. She would never forget it.

He squeezed her fingers before turning to open the door of her bedchamber. 'Goodnight, Angel.'

She could not move, shocked to the core by the feelings he had aroused. Silently she watched him walk away, heard the faint scrape as he opened his door. When he looked back at her, his face was no more than a pale smudge against the darkness, then he was gone.

It had been a long and exhausting day, but Angel was so on edge she knew she would not sleep easily. She was glad Mama had said she might bring Joan with her as her dresser—one familiar face in a house full of strangers. The maid helped her into her nightgown and tucked her between the warmed sheets, but after tossing and turning for several long minutes Angel slipped out of the luxurious feather bed.

She padded across to the windows in the south wall and threw back the heavy curtains.

A pale half-moon shone down on a blue-grey landscape. She stared at it for a moment, before the chill night air drove her back to her bed. The wedding and the drive to Rotherton had taken its toll, but Jason's hard, searing kiss and the exhilaration she had felt for those few precious moments after his lips met hers, threatened to keep her awake all night.

Chapter Four

The sun was just rising as Jason's travelling carriage bowled away from Rotherton. He yawned and leaned back against the silk squabs, looking out at the familiar landscape. He had barely slept, conscious that only a wooden door separated him from Angel. He had told her this was a marriage of convenience, but he knew now it was anything but that. If he was honest, he had known it when she had swooned and he had caught her up. How good she had felt in his arms. How *right*. Light as a feather, her warm body resting against his chest, she had aroused his protective instincts, but also something much more primal. That goodbye kiss last night had confirmed it, and it had taken every ounce of his will-power not to carry her off to bed there and then.

More than once during the long night he had been tempted to go to her, but he had fought it. He had endured one disastrous marriage and was determined not to bind Angel into life with a man she did not love.

Angel woke to a chorus of birdsong coming in through the open window. She sat up and looked towards the connecting door. Before returning to her bed last night she had unlocked it, hoping Jason might change his mind and come to her, but he had not. She reached for her wrap. It was very early. If he had not yet left then she must speak to him. It was important to tell him she had no regrets about this marriage. That she would never change her mind.

Even as she scrambled out of bed she heard the sound of a carriage. She ran over to the windows that overlooked the drive and was in time to see the carriage pulling away, the coat of arms on the door glinting in the early-morning sunshine.

She stood watching until the carriage disappeared amongst the trees. Jason had said his trip was for business, but she thought of him in London, amongst his friends, in the company of beautiful ladies. Perhaps he had a mistress. Many men did.

Angel shrugged and turned away from the window. The idea of Jason with another woman provoked a stab of jealousy like a physical pain, but there was nothing to be done about that now. Or, at least, she amended, not at present. She was his wife, his duchess, and she had no wish to change her mind.

She could only pray that Jason would not change his.

Determined not to mope, Angel did not return to her bed but rang for her maid. She was mistress of Rotherton now, and there was much to learn about her new domain. The Duke had told her she might order everything as she wished, but she would defer to Mrs Wenlock until she was more familiar with this house and its ways.

She set to work directly after breakfast, joining the housekeeper for a tour of the house. This took some time, because once Mrs Wenlock realised that her new mistress was interested in the whole house she became expansive. She detailed everything she knew of the history of Rotherton and its traditions, and Angel drank it all in.

They began in the attics and the topmost rooms, which were set aside for servants and children, then the smaller bedrooms that Mrs Wenlock explained could accommodate single gentlemen if all the other guest rooms were in use.

Angel listened closely, taking in as much as was possible. Upon her arrival she had experienced the grandeur of the drawing and dining rooms, but even that did not prepare her for the magnificence of the public rooms on the first floor—especially the two state bedchambers, renamed after a royal visit forty years ago. They were lavishly appointed, with gilded furniture and elaborately plastered ceilings, and the state beds were curtained with magnificently embroidered silk hangings.

'The late Duchess commissioned them to replace the originals,' explained the housekeeper. 'They are perfect replicas in every detail.'

Angel shook her head and sighed. 'It seems a pity to go to all that trouble when no one ever uses these rooms.'

'Oh, they have been used, ma'am. When—' The housekeeper broke off, her cheeks flushing scarlet, then went on in a rush, 'But I shouldn't be rattling on like this when we have so much more of the house to see. If you'll come with me, Your Grace?'

Angel was tempted to ask Mrs Wenlock what she had been about to say, but the housekeeper was already hurrying away, and she was obliged to follow her down the stairs.

There were several rooms on the ground floor that were set aside for the family, all very elegant but with none of the opulence of the public rooms. These included the small dining parlour Jason had mentioned, which had double doors leading to a family drawing room. Also a sunny morning room and a small, booklined room that Mrs Wenlock told Angel was the Duke's study.

'And is there a duchess's sitting room?' Angel enquired as she followed the housekeeper across the hall. 'Somewhere I might sew, or read, or write my letters?'

'Why, yes, Your Grace, this one.'

She threw open a door and Angel found herself in the Yellow Salon, where Jason had brought her on their arrival yesterday.

The housekeeper gave a little cough, her glance straying to the portrait of the last Duchess. 'I am sure His Grace would not object if you wished to make a few changes.'

'No. no. I do not think we should do that,' Angel disclaimed quickly. 'This is a most elegant room and…and quite perfect for welcoming guests. However, I should be comfortable with something a little less…grand.'

'There *is* a smaller room, ma'am, but it is presently unfurnished.'

'May I see it?'

Angel followed the housekeeper to a door tucked away beyond the dining parlour.

'Here we are, Your Grace.'

Angel stepped into the room. It was small, but windows on two sides made it very light. The walls and oak panelling were all painted in the palest cream, and it reminded Angel of a blank canvas, waiting to be used.

'This was the cabinet room in the old Duke's day, ma'am. Full of papers and maps. They were all moved to the library early last year, when the late Duchess decided to decorate. Sadly, it was not to be.'

Angel walked around the room. It was on the northwest corner of the house, with a view of the drive and the park from one window, and from the other she could see out over the formal flower garden to lawns that swept down to a lake.

'It will suit my purpose admirably.' She turned back, smiling. 'Mrs Wenlock, I noticed a great deal of furniture in the attics… May I see what we have to furnish my new sitting room?'

* * *

Within days the Duchess's sitting room was complete. Not only had Angel found sofas and chairs in the attics, but also a pretty little writing desk and a bookcase. It was all furniture that the housekeeper informed her had been set aside when the Yellow Salon had been decorated. Mrs Wenlock also showed her a trunk, in which they found suitable window curtains, and a further search unearthed a rug that would fit perfectly in the room.

Angel had helped to clean the furniture, brushing the dust from the padded chairs and sofa and polishing the wood until it gleamed. She'd enjoyed the effort, and now she gazed at the result with no little satisfaction. The flowered fabrics were a little worn, and the colours faded over the years to soft greens, pinks and whites, but the effect was charming. The little writing desk had been placed beneath the window, so she could look up from writing her letters to gaze out at the lake, and the bookcase was already home to the selection of favourite books she had brought with her from Goole Park.

She only wished Jason could be there to see it.

Setting up her own room had encouraged Angel to make more changes. When Mrs Wenlock had taken her to the nursery wing Angel had been surprised to discover it was not in such poor condition as she'd expected. As well as bedchambers for children and their attendants, there was a schoolroom, a dining room and a small suite of rooms for a governess or tutor. She took it upon herself to have them all cleaned, but gave instructions that the battered cupboards and worn but comfortable chairs in the nursery should not be removed. It was just the sort of room where children could enjoy themselves without worrying about damaging anything precious.

Not her children, of course. At least, not yet. But there was the Duke's daughter, Lady Elinor, and his stepdaughter Rose Haringey to consider. She did not think it right that they should be living in a separate establishment if their father was going to make his home at Rotherton, and she was formulating a plan to remedy that. It was a rather daring one, and she was not sure she should do anything until she had spoken to Jason.

However, the arrival of an express shortly after dinner gave her thoughts another direction altogether. With a trembling hand she took the letter from the butler, fearing something had happened to Jason. Then she saw that it had come from Hertfordshire, from her sister, and she tore it open, expecting bad news about her parents.

'Oh, dear!'

She put a hand to her mouth as she scanned Lettie's hasty scrawl. Taking a deep breath, she looked up at the waiting butler.

'Langshaw, will you send Mrs Wenlock to me, if you please?' She added, as cheerfully as she could, 'Visitors will be arriving tomorrow evening. We must prepare!'

Her sisters descended upon Rotherton, declaring that they had set out as soon as they heard she was alone. Angel was relieved to find that their husbands had not accompanied them, apparently preferring to visit when the Duke was present.

'We can only stay for four nights,' Lettie told Angel. 'Marland is taking me to Brighton later this month, but Alice and I just had to come and keep you company.'

Angel had ordered refreshments to be served in the Yellow Salon. She thought it far less comfortable than her own little sitting room, but she knew her sisters would be impressed. As she'd expected, they exclaimed in delight at the bright magnificence of the room.

'But what on earth is Rotherton about, Angeline, leaving you here while he goes off to London?' demanded Alice, helping herself to one of the little fancy cakes.

'He has business in the north, too,' replied Angel. 'It means a great deal of travelling.'

'But surely you could have arranged to meet up with him in town?' said Lettie.

'I did not think of it.'

'But the Duke should have thought of it. Is he ashamed of you?'

'Ashamed!' Angel blushed. 'No, not at all. You will recall it was agreed, before we left Goole, that we will be going to town for the winter.'

'One has to admit you are not quite ready for society,' said Alice, casting a disparaging glance at the apricot muslin day dress her sister was wearing. 'You will need *dozens* of new gowns. Everything must be worthy of a duchess.'

'Precisely. Which is why I could not accompany the Duke at such short notice. Mama is ordering pattern books for me to take to Madame Sophie. She is the local seamstress in Middlewych, and highly recommended by my neighbours. They say she is very good.'

'Yes, but is she good *enough*?' countered Lettie.

Angel frowned. It had not occurred to her that Jason might be ashamed of her.

'Did you know the late Duchess?' she asked, glancing up at the painting beside the chimneypiece.

'We saw her in town, of course,' said Lettie, 'but we were not acquainted.'

'And does this portrait do her justice?'

It was Alice who replied, saying airily, 'It is a good likeness, but nothing can compare with the original. She was a glorious creature—there is no denying it. Men could not keep their eyes off her.' She laughed gaily. 'Even Humphrey was captivated. Said she was the handsomest woman he had ever seen. And always so gay, so vivacious!'

Angel thought of her staid, rather pompous brother-in-law and her heart sank a little. Lavinia must indeed have been quite dazzling.

'No one ever refused an invitation to one of her parties,' Alice went on. 'She was famed for her entertainments. Everyone was shocked when she died in that carriage accident.'

'You told me most of the ladies breathed a sigh of relief,' Lettie remarked, smirking. 'Especially the married ones.'

Alice threw her a frowning look before turning back to Angel.

'Let us not talk of the past. Instead I shall say what a treat it is to be here with you, Angeline. How soon may we look over the house? If it is all as impressive as this room, then it must be magnificent!'

'The state rooms are indeed splendid,' agreed Angel. 'However, the family rooms on this floor are far more comfortable. We will be dining in the small dining parlour tonight.' Angel ignored their murmurs of disappointment and went on, 'However, I have put you in the state bedchambers.'

The change in both her sisters at this news almost overset Angel. Their looks of dissatisfaction were replaced by such beaming smiles that she almost giggled.

'Can you imagine what Marland will say when I tell him I have slept in a royal bed?' declared Lettie, clapping her hands. 'I should not care if it was hard as a board!'

Angel laughed 'I hope it will be more comfortable than that. The rooms were very recently refurbished. On the orders of the late Duchess,' she added, determined to be scrupulously fair to Jason's first wife.

Lettie snorted. 'In readiness for the Prince of Wales to call, no doubt— Now what have I said?' She raised her brows at Alice, who was frowning at her across the table. 'You told me yourself everyone save Rotherton knew that she and Prinny—'

Alice broke in quickly. 'No, no, you must have misunderstood me.'

The atmosphere in the Yellow Salon had grown very tense.

Angel looked from one sister to the other. 'Are you saying the Prince of Wales stayed here?' she said slowly. 'That she was his *mistress*?'

That would certainly account for Mrs Wenlock not wishing to disclose who had used the state bedchambers. Now it seemed only too obvious.

'Goodness, Angel, how you do take one up!' declared Alice, much flustered. 'I have no idea if Prinny ever visited Rotherton. There was never anything more than rumours. Let us talk of something else.'

'But I should like to know.'

'Of course you would,' agreed Lettie. 'One forgets that you have been incarcerated at Goole Park all these years, and I doubt Mama or Papa would talk of it.'

'They never listen to tittle-tattle,' retorted Angel, sitting up very straight, 'And they brought us up to think unfounded gossip quite reprehensible.'

'Yes, of course,' said Alice hurriedly. 'And the poor lady is dead now, so it can have no relevance.'

'Perhaps not.' Angel's hands were resting in her lap, and she had to work hard not to clasp them tightly together. 'However, I will be sure to hear of it when I go to London. Tell me what they were saying, if you please.'

'I know nothing, only hearsay,' Lettie declared. 'Marland and I spend far less time in town than Alice.'

'And Sir Humphrey and I were never part of the Duchess's closest circle,' said Alice, looking a little uncomfortable. 'It was clear the Prince of Wales was very taken with the lovely Lavinia, but there is always gossip and speculation about persons of high rank, Angel. Especially princes.'

'And dukes,' giggled Lettie. 'Once you are in town, Angel, you will discover that for yourself. Just the fact that Rotherton chose the incomparable Mrs Haringey at his duchess was enough to cause a scandal. Although you were still in the schoolroom then, and will not remember.'

Angel said nothing. She *did* remember, and had thought it highly romantic that Jason should fly in the face of his family's opposition to marry the woman he loved.

'If it was a love match then it did not last long,' said Alice, as if reading her thoughts. 'After the first few years they were rarely seen together. The Duchess held court in London, and invitations to her lavish entertainments at Darvell House were much sought after.' She leaned forward to say in hushed tones, 'She was notorious for her...*flirtations*. Her name was linked to any number of gentlemen.'

'And what of Jason?' Angel forced herself to ask. 'Did he have any number of mistresses?'

'My dear, if he did you must not blame him,' said Lettie, giving her a condescending smile. 'It is the way of the world.'

Yes. Angel was well aware of that. A man like Jason, titled, rich and handsome, would be impossibly attractive.

'But you must not let that upset you, Angeline,' said Alice, determined to be practical. 'Jason has made you his duchess. That puts you in a very strong position.'

It would, if we were truly married.

Angel swallowed the thought. It would not do to let this conversation unsettle her. Jason had married her and entrusted Rotherton to her care. That must be enough. For the present.

'You need to assert yourself, Angel,' Alice went on, glancing up at the portrait of Lavinia. 'You should start by removing that painting.'

But this Angel would not allow. 'The room was decorated to match it and its absence would be noticed.'

Her sisters argued but Angel stood firm, saying finally, if not quite truthfully, 'A likeness of the late Duchess does not trouble me.'

'Well, it should.' Alice was blunt. 'She was a beauty. Which you are not.'

Angel shrugged. 'She is dead, which I am not.'

She knew this calm response would irritate her sister. But she was as yet unsure how Jason felt about his late wife, and until she knew that she would not make any changes to the Yellow Salon.

Alice huffed. 'I still say you would be well advised to remove it, if you do not wish the Duke to make the obvious comparisons.'

Angel inclined her head, acknowledging the point, then turned the conversation.

The little party broke up shortly after. It was clear that Lettie and Alice were eager to see their bedchambers, and Angel rang for the housekeeper.

'Mrs Wenlock will show you to your rooms,' she said, excusing herself from this duty. 'She will be able to answer any questions better than I. We shall meet again at dinner.'

'Oh, I almost forgot!' exclaimed Lettie, as she was leaving the salon. 'Papa asked us to bring your horse. He is in the stables.'

That news brought a genuine smile to Angel's face.

'Oh, thank you, Lettie! I shall write to Papa and thank him for his thoughtfulness in sending Apollo so quickly.'

Her sisters went off with the housekeeper, leaving Angel alone with her thoughts. However, she did not want to dwell on what they had said, and turned her mind to planning some diversions for their stay.

With an hour or so before she needed to change for dinner, she decided to visit the stables. She had not yet done so, and not only could she see her beloved hack, she could also find out what vehicles were at her disposal. The weather looked settled for the moment, and she thought her sisters might enjoy a drive through the park or the surrounding countryside.

Stopping only to change her shoes, Angel walked briskly to the stables, where she sought out Thomas Crick, the elderly groom who was in charge. When she explained her mission he was happy to show her where Apollo was being housed, and after Angel had made sufficient fuss of the horse Thomas accompanied her around the rest of the stables.

'Are there any other horses suitable for a lady?' she asked him, thinking that perhaps her sisters would like to ride.

'Alas, ma'am, no. Her Grace's mounts were sold off when she died,' he told her. 'Every last one of them.'

'Oh! How many did she have?'

'Well, there was the grey…' Thomas began to tick them off on his fingers. 'That was her favourite. Then there was the black mare—part Arab, she was. Then the chestnut mare. And a hunter, which she never rode.' He coughed. 'They was all of them bought for their looks, ma'am, if you'll excuse my saying so. Having seen that gelding of Your Grace's, I doubt they would have suited you. Showy creatures, they was, like the pair she bought for her phaeton. His Grace was quick to sell 'em all off after Her Grace's accident. He did keep the carriage horses, though.'

'Oh? Did the late Duchess have her own carriage?'

'Aye, ma'am. Would you like to see it?'

'Yes, please!'

Angel hoped it would be an open carriage that she and her sisters might use to drive around the countryside when the weather was fine, but when they reached the carriage house Thomas led her over to an elegant travelling chariot.

He opened the door and Angel looked inside. The padded seats and squabs were covered in blue and yellow silk, with matching blinds at the windows. However, there was only one bench seat.

'It was a wedding present from His Grace,' Thomas explained. 'The very latest design. Her Grace used it a lot. Always gadding around the country, she was. Mostly without the Duke.' She heard a note of disapproval in the old man's voice. 'The last few years we saw very little of Her Grace here at Rotherton.'

Angel stepped away from the chaise, saying, 'Sadly it will only hold two people, so it is not what I require. I was hoping to take my sisters out to see the countryside, if the weather holds.'

The old man grinned at her. 'In that case, Your Grace, you'll be wanting the landau.'

The four days passed swiftly, despite Angel's misgivings. She was glad of her sisters' company when her neighbours made their morning calls, and they were loud in their praise of her new home, but when Lettie or Alice pressed her to make changes she held firm.

There was some respite from their attempts to interfere when they spent a whole day driving out in the landau. Its luxury and elegance, and the ducal crest emblazoned on the sides, were everything that Lettie and Alice desired. They thoroughly enjoyed themselves.

The visit had gone better than expected, but Angel felt only relief as she waved them off. She had not allowed her sisters to bully her and, heartened by this small success, she turned her mind to the matter that had been niggling away at her since her arrival at Rotherton.

The very next day she went in search of the Duke's steward. He was surprised when she entered his office, and he quickly rose from his desk to welcome her.

'Your Grace! Is there anything amiss? How may I help you?'

He pulled out a chair and invited her to sit down.

'No there is nothing amiss, Mr Merrick. I simply wish to make contact with the children.'

'Children?'

'Yes.' She nodded. 'The Duke's daughters. I believe they have their own establishment in Kent?'

'That is correct, Your Grace. Near Ashford. They are in the care of Mrs Watson. A widow, and a most genteel and capable person. His Grace and I have both called there, and I can assure you that they are most comfortably settled.'

'I do not doubt it, Mr Merrick, and I should like to write to Mrs Watson. Today.'

'I see…'

She did not miss the slight hesitation.

'Perhaps it might be better to wait until His Grace has returned,' he said.

'Alas, we do not know quite when that will be. Unless you have heard from him?'

She looked hopefully at Simon Merrick, but he shook his

head. 'The Duke's plans were extensive, Your Grace. His last letter said he was on his way to London, but I believe it will take another three weeks at least for him to conclude all his business.'

That would be a full six weeks since he had left Rotherton. Angel's heart sank a little, but she refused to be downhearted and summoned up a smile.

'His Grace left so suddenly that we did not have time to discuss everything.' She paused. 'He told you I have his blessing to do as I wish, did he not?'

'Yes. Yes, he did, ma'am. But…'

'Excellent!' She beamed at him. 'Then if you will furnish me with Mrs Watson's direction, I shall leave you in peace!'

Chapter Five

It was midnight when Jason arrived back in London and he fell into bed, exhausted. After his initial visit to the capital he had spent most of the past three weeks visiting his estates in Hereford, Nottingham and Yorkshire. Abandoning his chaise in town, he had elected to travel by horse for speed, and made the most of each day, concluding his business as quickly as possible and hurrying back to London for a final meeting with his lawyer.

For the first time in years he was eager to return to Rotherton. He couldn't help wondering how Angel was faring without him.

When Adams came in with his morning cup of coffee, Jason opened a bleary eye and reached out for his pocket watch.

He sat up. 'Ten o'clock! By heavens, Adams, why did you not wake me earlier?'

'I thought it best to let you sleep, sir, after your jauntering all around the country.'

Jason heard the minatory tone in the valet's voice and felt a smile growing. 'You are in high dudgeon because I would not take you with me?'

'In no way, Your Grace. You explained at the outset that you did not require my services during your travels.'

'Quite. I had a lot of miles to cover and no time to wait for a baggage coach to catch up with me.' He grinned. 'And you would have been damnably uncomfortable riding everywhere, Adams. Just think of the affront to your dignity!'

His valet afforded this with no more than a look and went back to laying out his master's clothes.

'I suggest the new Bath Superfine, Your Grace. With the dove-grey waistcoat, if you intend to visit the city this morning.'

'Aye, that will do.' Jason sipped his coffee and leaned back against the pillows. 'Although I might put off seeing Telford until tomorrow.'

He yawned. Perhaps his business could wait another day. The rest would be very welcome after all the miles he had ridden recently.

He took his time dressing and went down to break his fast in the dining room, where he found a small pile of letters awaiting him on the table. That, too, could wait. At least until he had consumed a sustaining meal of eggs, ham and cold beef.

Having satisfied his appetite, Jason began to look through the assortment of invitations, calling cards and letters, which he tossed aside. The familiar handwriting on one letter, however, caught his attention.

'Now, what would Simon be writing to me about?' he murmured, breaking the seal and unfolding the crisp paper.

He scanned the short note, his brow contracting. Then, with an oath, he stormed out of the breakfast room, barking orders as he went.

Three days later Jason was back at Rotherton. He jumped out of the carriage almost before it came to a stand on the sweeping drive and ran up the steps into the house. Langshaw was crossing the hall, but stopped at the sight of his master, startled for once out of his stately demeanour.

'Y-Your Grace!'

'Where is she?' Jason tossed his hat and gloves onto a bench. 'The Duchess,' he barked, seeing his butler's blank face. 'Where will I find her?'

'I believe Her Grace is on the north lawn, sir.' Langshaw had recovered himself a little now. 'Shall I send—?'

'No,' said Jason, grimly. 'I will go myself.'

He strode off through the house, cutting through the rooms to take the most direct route and going out via a garden door in the north front. A terrace ran the length of the house, with shallow steps to a small flower garden, and beyond that the lawns leading down to the lake.

A carriage rug was spread out on the grass and there were signs of a picnic, although no one was in sight. Then he heard voices and laughter coming from beyond the willows that screened some of the water from view. Quickening his pace, he moved on past the trees and soon discovered the reason for the merriment.

Angel and the girls were on the lake in a small boat.

He stopped, a chill running down his spine when he saw Rose, his stepdaughter, plying the oars with her young sister facing her. Angel was sitting in the bow, giving commands between peals of laughter.

'What the devil do you think you are doing!'

His voice thundered across the water. The laughter stopped immediately and the two girls looked up in alarm. Angel, sitting with her back to him, twisted around quickly.

'Oh! Y-Your Grace! I didn't think you would be back yet.'

'No! Don't stand up—'

His warning came too late. The little boat rocked alarmingly, Angel lost her balance and tumbled headlong into the water.

Jason swore, but even as he ran along the small wooden jetty she emerged from the water, coughing and laughing at the same time.

'No, no, I do not need rescuing,' she called to him as he unbuttoned his coat, ready to dive in. 'You see, it is not too deep here. I can walk to the bank. Although… Rose, dear, I think perhaps you had best row back to the jetty now.'

'You had indeed,' barked Jason.

'Pray do not be cross with them, Jason,' Angel begged him. 'It was my idea.'

He bit back a cutting retort and turned his attention to securing the boat and helping the girls to alight. They were both looking very frightened, and since Angel was in no immediate danger he took a moment to reassure them that he was in no way angry with them.

'Where did you learn to row?' he asked Rose, all the time keeping one eye on Angel, who was wading through the water.

'The Duchess has been teaching me.'

'She was going to teach me, too,' Elinor piped up, her face crumpling with disappointment.

'Another day, Nell,' Jason told her.

He could see Angel moving steadily towards the jetty. It was too high for her to climb out of the water and he knew he must help her, even though part of him—a very ignoble part—wanted to leave her to struggle.

'You two had best go back to the house.'

Rose hesitated. 'But what about the Duchess?'

'I will deal with the Duchess.' He hoped his calm tone was reassuring, even if he could not quite manage a smile. 'Off you go now. Take your sister indoors.'

He waited until they were running off to the house before turning back to the lake. Angel was at the jetty by this time, and he reached down to lift her out of the water.

'Thank you.'

'Damned foolishness! You don't deserve that I should rescue you.'

'If you had not bellowed at us I should not have fallen in!'

She was glaring at him, trying to look dignified and failing miserably. She was wet through, her dark hair hanging in tangles about her shoulders. As for her summer gown… the thin muslin clung like a second skin. Jason could see every contour, the soft swell of her breasts, the tiny waist and long, shapely legs.

Suddenly, the blood was thundering through his body. All he could think of was stripping off her wet clothes and running his hands over every inch of that dainty body…

With a growl of frustration he grabbed her hand. 'Come along, let's get you back to the house.'

He set off quickly, trying desperately to ignore the heat inside him…the strong desire to pull her down onto that carriage rug and kiss her senseless. Confound it, this was no time to lose his head over his own wife!

Angel stumbled and Jason slowed his pace. She was shivering, her bare arms resembling goose-skin.

'We need to get you warm.' He scooped up the rug. 'Here, put this around you.'

Her teeth were chattering now, and once he had wrapped her in the rug he swept her up into his arms.

'No, don't fight me,' he said, ignoring her protests. 'We will be much quicker this way.'

She stopped struggling, and after they had gone a few more yards she put her arms around his neck.

'I beg your pardon, Jason,' she murmured, resting her head against his shoulder.

'So you should. You are a dashed nuisance.'

'The gardener told me the lake is quite shallow at this end. I thought it would be safe enough.'

'Safe enough for you, perhaps. What if little Nell had fallen in?'

'I would have rescued her. I can swim, you know.'

This information did not lessen his irritation one bit. He said savagely, 'If there is any justice you will contract a severe chill and perish horribly!'

This retort elicited nothing more than a small chuckle, and he glanced down at her.

'You should be quaking in your wet little shoes, madam!'

'No, I shouldn't. You used to say just such things to me when we were children. Your bluff and bluster has never frightened me.' She raised her head. 'But it might make Rose or Nell anxious. They do not know you.'

That put an end to his softening mood.

He said, defensively, 'Yes, they do. I make regular visits to Kent to see them.'

'Once a month at most, they have told me. It is not enough, Jason.'

He was about to say it was none of her concern, but they had reached the house and Mrs Wenlock was at the door.

'Oh, good heavens, Your Grace! Bring the poor mistress in, sir. Miss Rose told us what had happened. I have had hot water taken up to Her Grace's room and hot bricks put in the bed. Peter and Samuel are here, and ready to carry her up the stairs.'

Jason glanced at the hovering footmen and his arms tightened. He would not allow anyone to relieve him of his burden, even if she *was* the most annoying female he had ever encountered.

'No! I will do it.'

Angel breathed a little sigh. There was something tremendously comforting about being in the Duke's arms. He had lifted her from the water as if she weighed no more than a feather, and although he had been furious with her she had never doubted that his anger was borne of concern. Wrapped in the rug, and with his arms holding her firm, she found the trembling had soon subsided. She was still cold, but not dangerously so. She felt quite well enough to make her own way to her rooms and would have done so, rather than have the servants convey her to her room. However, she was content for Jason to carry her. He was holding her against him, his arms strong and secure around her, and a little thrill went through her. A frisson of happy anticipation for what might happen next.

She kept her arms about Jason's neck and her cheek against his shoulder as he followed the housekeeper up the stairs. He was still in his travelling clothes, and she could smell the dust of the road on his coat, but there was also a faint trace of musk and sandalwood that made her feel lightheaded. His hair brushed against her hands, soft as silk. He wore it slightly longer than was fashionable and she closed her eyes, imagining what it would be like to run her fingers through those raven locks while he kissed her until she was dizzy…

'Here we are, Your Grace.'

Mrs Wenlock's voice dispelled Angel's pleasant daydream. The housekeeper opened the door and Jason carried Angel into her bedchamber. It was bustling with maids and warm from the hastily kindled fire. A hipbath had been placed before the hearth and the rising steam was scented with roses.

'There.' He put Angel on her feet, but retained his hold for a moment. 'Can you stand?'

Oh, she was so tempted to say no! What on earth was wrong with her? She was always so independent—why would she now want to behave like some poor weak creature?

'Yes, thank you, Your Grace.'

'You should remain in your room for the rest of the day.'

'I am very well now,' she assured him, risking a smile. 'I shall join you in the drawing room before dinner.'

'I shall look forward to it,' he said coolly.

Angel's giddy excitement faded when she glanced up at his hooded eyes. There was no warm glint in their slate-grey depths. They were hard and dark as stone.

He had not forgiven her for bringing the girls to Rotherton.

Jason left his wife to the ministrations of the maidservants and went off to change out of his own travel-dusty clothes, wondering what the devil had been going on at Rotherton in his absence. An earlier letter from his steward had warned him that Angel intended to write to Mrs Watson, but Merrick's subsequent letter had come as a severe shock. He had not expected Angel to bring the girls to Rotherton without consulting him. Now he asked himself what other mischief she had been about in his absence.

Well, he had only himself to blame, he thought wryly. After all, he had given her free rein.

But if that was not enough, she had frightened him half out of his wits by falling into the water. She had then completed his downfall by standing before him like some water

sprite, ready to drive him to distraction. He cursed silently.
It was years since he had felt so out of control!

'I must fight this.' He stopped at the door to his own bedchamber and closed his eyes. 'I lost my head over one woman.
I am not about to let that happen again!'

He went in to find his valet waiting for him, apologising
for the lack of hot water.

'I have managed to procure you half a pail, Your Grace,
but the water in your bathtub is barely lukewarm. All the
rest has been diverted.'

'I am well aware of that,' Jason snapped, throwing off his
clothes. 'It doesn't matter, a cold bath will suit me very well.'

Refreshed and rested, Angel made her way downstairs to
the family drawing room at the appointed time. The Duke
was already there, staring out of the window. She stopped
in the doorway, wishing that this room did not overlook the
lake. It would remind him of her folly.

He turned and came towards her, fixing her with a frowning gaze.

Trying not to feel daunted, she smiled at him and carefully closed the door upon them.

'Mrs Watson and the girls have been joining me here each
evening, but I thought tonight it would be better if they took
their dinner in the nursery.'

'They will take their dinner in the nursery every night for
the rest of their visit,' he snapped. 'You will see to it, madam.'

She lowered her eyes. 'As you wish, Your Grace.'

'I do wish it!'

She heard his sigh of exasperation.

He said, 'You showed some good sense, at least, in bringing Mrs Watson with the children. How long have they been here?'

'Only four days.' She sat down and folded her hands in her lap. 'After calling upon Mrs Watson, I invited them all here for a short visit. A few weeks, nothing more.'

'I am glad to hear it. Their home is in Kent.'

'Their home should be here, with us.'

'*Us?* I did not think the matter of our marriage was quite settled yet!'

Angel did her best to hide her dismay at his icy tone.

'I have already told you, Jason, I made my decision when I married you.' She glanced down at the plain gold band upon her finger. 'If, however, *you* have changed your mind then pray tell me.'

'Of course not! I beg your pardon, Angel, it's just that I was taken by surprise, seeing you and the girls together.' He looked at her, a reluctant smile tugging at his mouth. 'Not quite such a shock as I gave you, it seems.'

'I did not expect you to return for at least a se'ennight.'

His scowl returned. 'You should have written, madam, to inform me of your intentions.'

'Asking your permission? You would have refused.'

His eyes narrowed but he did not contradict her.

She went on, 'I did not mean to surprise you, Jason. I know Mr Merrick corresponds with you regularly and thought he would tell you.'

'Simon informed me that you were *writing* to Mrs Watson. Then he sent an express saying the children had arrived. *That* was enough to have me concluding my affairs in London!'

'Are you very angry with me?'

'Only for trying to drown yourself.'

'I would not have drowned. I told you—I can swim.'

'I did not know that at the time!' He frowned at her. 'When

did you learn? I cannot recall that Barnaby and I were ever that lost to all sense of propriety.'

'No, no.' She blushed. 'I discovered our governess could swim and persuaded Mama to allow her to teach us. Alice, Lettie and me, that is. We used the sheltered end of the lake at Goole Park. I thought it most unfair that Barnaby should be the only one to learn.'

Jason nodded. 'And you can row, too.'

'Of course. *You* taught me that, do you not remember?'

'I remember having some tiresome brat pestering me.' The frown lifted. He threw himself down upon the sofa beside her. 'How long ago that seems now.'

'A lifetime,' she agreed. Angel waited a moment, then said quietly, 'You were very patient with that tiresome brat, Jason. I am sure you could do as well by your own children.'

Immediately he stiffened. 'Rose Haringey is *not* my daughter.'

'But she is your stepdaughter. And she is not really a child, either. She is seventeen, old enough to go into Society.'

'Mrs Watson will see to that.'

'Her mother was your duchess, Jason. I also understand that Rose is not penniless.'

'No. She will inherit a substantial sum from her father's estate when she is five-and-twenty.'

'Even more reason for us to bring her out.'

'No.'

'Why not?'

'Because.' He stopped. 'Because it would be too much of a burden for you. As my new wife, you will have enough to do once we reach town.'

'I am aware of that, Jason, and I am prepared for it. I shall need to buy new gowns in London, gowns more suited to a duchess. We could buy some for Rose at the same time. What is to prevent us taking both the girls with us to London? Mrs Watson, too, of course,' she added quickly. 'Then it would not be nearly so much work for me.' She paused, and when Jason remained silent she went on cheerfully, 'I should enjoy taking the girls to the museums and the parks, and Rose could be introduced to Society under your aegis. She will be eighteen in December, is there any reason why we should *not* bring her out?'

'No.'

'There, you see,' declared Angel. 'We could even take them to Astley's Amphitheatre. Or *I* could,' she added, teasing him, 'if you think it beneath your dignity.'

'I mean no, it will not do. I will not take Rose to London.'

'But—'

'Enough, madam!' He jumped up. 'We will talk no more about it, if you please. Neither will we discuss bringing the children here to live. Once they have finished their holiday Mrs Watson will take them back to Kent. That is the end of the matter.'

'The end of the matter.' Angel rose slowly to her feet. 'Is this how it is to be? Your word in this house is law?'

'In this instance, yes!'

'But you told me I could order things as I wish. That I have...how did you phrase it?...free rein.'

'In the running of my household, yes!'

'*Your* household?' She drew herself up, although she still had to look up at him. 'Is that all I am to you, Duke, some sort of *housekeeper*?'

'No! Of course I don't mean— Confound it, madam, do not take me up so!'

For a long moment they glared at one another. Angel thought of several choice ripostes. She was also tempted to storm out, slamming the door behind her, but that would achieve nothing. Instead she merely nodded.

'Very well, Your Grace. It shall be as you wish.' She resumed her seat and after a moment she said, 'Pray come and sit down, Jason. You have not yet told me what you have been doing while you were away.' She waited until he had joined her on the sofa then went on chattily, 'I trust your trip to town was successful, and you achieved everything you wished to do?'

'Angel...' There was a note of warning in his tone but she ignored it.

'You visited your other estates too, I believe. Mr Merrick told me about them. I particularly liked his description of the hunting lodge in Nottingham. I hope you do not mean to keep it all for yourself. And the house in Hereford. Darvell Hall, is it? I believe that dates back to Tudor times.'

'Angel, stop!'

'Is anything wrong, sir?'

He frowned at her. 'I am not going to change my mind about this, madam!'

'About what?' she asked innocently.

'Stop it, Angel, *now*!'

She turned to look at him, her eyes wide.

'You used to do this when you were a child. If Barnaby and I refused to let you join in with our games, you pretended to accept the situation.'

'I was *obliged* to accept it. You were both older than I. Stronger, too.'

He regarded her for a moment, then his frown disappeared and he leaned into the corner of the sofa, stretching one arm along the back.

'And you were a minx!' he told her. 'Instead of having a tantrum or bursting into tears you would chip away at us, little by little. Wheedling and cajoling.'

'Surely not!' She saw his lips twitch and tried not to smile.

'Wheedling and cajoling,' he repeated. 'Until we gave in.'

Angel laughed. 'No, no, I was never so devious.'

'Oh, you were, my sweet torment.' There was a gleam of cynical amusement in his grey eyes now. 'And you still are. I know your game, Angel, and your wiles will no longer work on me!'

His hand brushed her neck and a little thrill ran though her. She had dressed her hair loosely, because it was still damp from her soaking, and now she felt his fingers playing with a stray lock. She was filled with unfamiliar sensations that excited and frightened her in equal measure.

Angel sat very still. The air in the room seemed to press in upon her…heavy, expectant.

'My *wiles*, sir?' She attempted to speak lightly. 'I do not understand.'

'No? I could almost believe you fell into the water deliberately.'

He was curling the lock of hair around his fingers and Angel's spine tingled. She felt she might melt with pure longing!

'Why…' She swallowed, folding her hands together in her lap to stop them shaking. 'Why would I do such a thing?'

'Because you knew that when I pulled you out your body would shine through that gossamer-thin muslin.'

'No!'

'Yes. You looked like Venus, rising from the sea.'

His words flowed over her, warm and soft as velvet.

'Oh!' Angel felt herself blushing with pleasure. Now she was too shy to look at him at all! She stared down at her clasped hands. 'I had no idea. What, what a lovely thing to say to me!'

He had moved closer. His fingers were no longer playing with her hair. They were on her back, holding her close.

He caught her chin and gently turned her face up to his. 'I missed you damnably while I was away.'

Her heart leapt at his words, at the heat in his look. She dared to tell him the truth.

'I missed you, too, Jason. I hope you won't leave me again. At least not yet.'

There was a flash of fire in his eyes that set her heart pounding, then his mouth descended on hers and set her body alight.

His kiss was hard, savage and thrilling. Tiny arrows of fire darted through her body, from her head to her toes, sending the blood fizzing through her veins, and she clung to Jason as he dragged her onto his lap. He continued to kiss her until she was almost swooning with desire. She drove her hands through his hair, revelling in the silky feel of it against her fingers. Every sense was enhanced. She was acutely aware of his hard body pressed against hers, the soft wool of his coat, the cool linen at his neck. The smell of his skin was intoxicating, the faint woody scent mixed with something very masculine, very arousing.

Finally, he raised his head.

'We should stop.' His voice was rough, ragged, as if he was labouring under a great strain.

Angel sighed and clung to him. 'I do not want to stop.'

She wanted him to scoop her up into his arms and carry her upstairs. Her body was crying out for him to continue the pleasurable caresses, to bring this to its inevitable conclusion, and her disappointment was severe when he eased her from his lap and onto the sofa beside him.

'Ah, Angel, you are too sweet, too innocent. I cannot take such advantage of you.'

He was slipping away from her. She grasped his hands, wanting him so badly it hurt.

'You are *not* taking advantage! I am your *wife*, Jason, I want this as much as you.'

She spoke calmly, but inside she was begging for him to kiss her again.

'No.' He shook his head. 'We will do nothing we might regret later.'

He was rejecting her. Again. The recent heat in her body was replaced by an icy chill, as if she was back in the lake. Only this time it was much, much worse, because he had pushed her.

'That *you* might regret,' she retorted. 'I have already told you I consider our marriage vows binding.'

'They will be, once the marriage is consummated.' He freed his hands from her grasp and rose to his feet. 'Then there is no going back. Think, Angel! We would be bound together for the rest of our lives, however unhappy. We could end up hating one another. Believe me, I know it!'

He had walked away to the window and Angel stared at his back. There was tension in every line of him, the broad shoulders tense and unyielding. An old saying came to her: *Marry in haste, repent at leisure*. He had married her because he was lonely. And perhaps out of pity for little Angeline Carlow, who had been fading into an old maid. Of course he regretted it.

Tears stung her eyes and she fought them back. She was a duchess now. Duchesses did not weep. They made the best of their situation.

She rose and shook out her skirts. 'We married too soon. You need more time to grieve for your dead wife.'

'No. Angel, I—'

'You have no need to explain.' She cut him off. He might be in control of himself, but she was not. She needed to get away before she collapsed in a puddle of tears and frustra-

tion. 'We will forget this ever happened and carry on as we
have been. As we agreed.'

Only she had *not* agreed to this sham marriage!

She looked around her, suddenly feeling a little lost.

'Perhaps you will excuse me if I do not dine with you tonight. I, I have a headache.'

Jason heard the soft swish of skirts as she moved across
the room and the gentle click of the door closing behind her.
He rubbed a hand across his eyes. What a mull he had made
of that! Angel was right. He did need more time. But not to
mourn Lavinia.

He had expected marriage to his childhood friend to be
one of convenience. Finding himself suddenly lusting after
his own wife was something he had not foreseen, and it was
mightily *inconvenient*!

Chapter Six

Angel went downstairs the next morning in some trepidation. Despite telling Jason they would go on as before, she was not sure if she could do so after that kiss. She had found it too intense, too searingly wonderful to forget it. However, it *must* be forgotten. She needed to act naturally, especially while the children were at Rotherton.

Everyone else was at the breakfast table and she hesitated in the doorway, unsure how to proceed.

Jason rose to greet her. 'Good morning, my dear.'

His smile was reassuring, but she suddenly felt quite shy, although she could not think why a mere smile from him should cause her any embarrassment. He held the chair while she sat down, and when his hand rested briefly on her shoulder it was as if a net full of butterflies had been unleashed inside her.

He was trying to be kind, to put her at her ease. Angel appreciated the gesture, but it only made her even more sorry that he had not taken her to his bed. She had spent the night tossing and turning, imagining how that would be. But there was still hope. She just needed to be patient.

There was surprising little constraint at breakfast. Rose and Nell chattered away to the Duke, who was at pains to draw them out.

Watching them, Angel wondered again why he should be so against having them to live at Rotherton. Mrs Watson was an admirable governess and companion for the girls, but Angel knew from her own childhood that there was no substitute for living in a home with kind and loving parents.

'And what are your plans for the day, Angeline?'

Jason's enquiry interrupted her thoughts.

'I was going to visit Madame Sophie, today, to choose a new gown and possibly do a little shopping. I thought Rose might like to come with me.' She smiled at the girl.

'I should like that, very much,' said Rose.

'But Papa is taking us out on the lake today,' Nell announced. 'He is going to teach me to row.'

'I thought since I...er...interrupted your lesson yesterday, it was the least I could do,' said Jason. He met Angel's eyes across the table. 'There is room for four in the boat. I thought we might all go.'

It was clearly an olive branch, but having mentioned the dressmaker to Rose, Angel could not disappoint her.

She said, 'It shall be Rose's decision. If she would like to go boating then we shall drive into Middlewych tomorrow.'

But it was clear the lure of a dressmaker and shopping appealed to Rose far more than spending another day on the water. They split into two parties and Angel went off to order the carriage.

Jason enjoyed the time with Nell far more than he had expected. His suggestion that he teach her to row had been made on the spur of the moment and he had instantly regretted it. He knew nothing about children—especially girls. As an only child he had grown up very much alone, except for his visits to Goole Park, where he had seen little of the older sisters. It was only Angel, the youngest, who had followed him and Barnaby around, making a nuisance of herself.

No, he corrected himself. She had not been a nuisance. She had been happy to fetch and carry for the boys and eager to learn. He remembered that in the later holidays she had also been good enough at cricket and battledore to join in, despite being four years their junior.

It was not until they were on the lake that he realised Nell was too young and too small to row proficiently, but when he pointed this out her disappointment tugged at his heart. He helped her with the oars, praising her efforts, and when she grew tired he took over and rowed her around the lake. He pointed out to her the hidden nests amongst the rushes, rowed towards the shallows to search for wading birds, and showed her the best places to look for dragonflies.

In spite of his initial doubts the hours flew by, and the afternoon was well advanced when he carried a tired Nell back to the house and handed her over to Mrs Watson, who was waiting for them in the schoolroom.

'Well, Your Grace, it was very good of you to give up your day like that.'

'It was a pleasure,' Jason replied, surprised to discover he really meant it. 'We will do it again, if the weather holds.'

'Oh, yes, please, Papa!'

Nell's obvious delight was gratifying, and he went back down the stairs, still smiling.

It was not yet time to change for dinner and Jason went off in search of Angel. He wanted to share with her the amusing things Nell had said, to describe the girl's attempts to handle the oars and the unexpected pride he had felt at her brave efforts.

When he was informed that the Duchess had not yet returned his disappointment was stronger than he had anticipated, but he put it aside and went off to see Simon Merrick and distract himself with estate business.

'I beg your pardon. I hope I did not keep you waiting.'

Angel entered the family drawing room a good twenty minutes after the appointed hour, the apology tripping off her lips.

'Not at all,' said Jason, politely and inaccurately. He had been impatient to see her. He threw aside the *Gentleman's Magazine*. 'Are the girls not coming downstairs?'

He went over to the side table to pour wine for them both.

'They have dined with Mrs Watson, as you decreed.'

Decreed! Jason stopped, the decanter in mid-air. 'I am glad to see my wishes still carry *some* weight in this house, madam.'

She smiled, not a whit perturbed by his acid tone.

'Pray do not be so tiresome, Jason. I would not deliberately flout your orders.' She sat down on the sofa and arranged her skirts before looking up at him again, her lips curving into a mischievous smile. 'Well? Are you going to stare at me all night or shall we take wine together?'

The anger that had been building vanished and Jason gave a crack of laughter. He filled the glasses and carried one over to her.

'How was your shopping trip?'

'Oh, we had a splendid time! Madame Sophie is an excellent seamstress. She showed me several garments that she is working on at the moment, and I have ordered a new morning gown and a walking out dress. But perhaps I should spare you the details.'

'Please do!'

He handed her a glass and she took it, glancing up at him.

'I also ordered a new gown for Rose. I hope you do not mind, sir?'

'Not at all,' he replied. 'Will it be finished in time for me to see her wearing it, or will we have to send it on to her in Kent?'

Angel took a sip of wine before replying. 'Their visit could always be extended.'

'No, it could not. The children need to get back to their routine.'

'Rose is hardly a child any more, Jason.' She had clearly observed the crease furrowing his brow and smiled. 'But let us not quarrel. Tell me about your day. I visited the schoolroom before coming downstairs and Nell can talk of nothing but the lake. There is no doubt that *she* enjoyed herself!'

'I am very glad about that. I did my best, but you know I have no experience of children.'

'She said that with your help she rowed across the lake. She is so proud. Before today, I believe she was more than a little in awe of you.'

'I cannot think why that should be.'

'Can you not? Rose told me that before coming to Rotherton she and Nell had never spent more than an hour or two in your company.'

Her tone was even enough, but it did not prevent Jason experiencing a small flare of guilt. Had he been wrong to leave the children in Kent? Surely they were safer there. Happy and secure. He did not want their vision of their mother tarnished by gossip. He wanted to protect them from the truth. At least until they were older.

'They want for nothing. Mrs Watson is an excellent guardian. They do not need me.'

Her shoulders lifted a fraction.

'You disagree?' he challenged her, on the alert for her next assault.

She hesitated, as if weighing her words carefully.

'You are their father, or stepfather, in Rose's case,' she amended. 'How are they to learn by what standards to measure a gentleman if you are never there to set the example?'

He wanted to believe her, but he had shirked his responsibilities towards the girls for too long. It was too late to change now.

He shook his head. 'Very flattering, ma'am, but you will not persuade me to change my mind. The children will return to Kent and there's an end to it.'

The entry of Langshaw at that moment prevented any further conversation. Jason escorted his wife to the dining room and the subject was not mentioned again, but he was not fooled. He knew Angel too well to think it really was the end of the matter.

Angel had certainly not forgotten Rose and Nell. The Duke was a kind man at heart, she knew that, but his upbringing had been very different from her own. He had been reared by servants and clearly saw no reason why his children should be treated any differently. Angel thought it might not be too difficult to persuade him that Nell should live with them, but his stepdaughter was another matter. Judging by the portrait of Lavinia in the Yellow Salon, Rose looked very like her mother. The idea that this reminder of his dead wife was too disturbing for Jason sent a chill through Angel that was hard to dispel.

Last night's kiss, which had set her body tingling, had clearly not affected the Duke the same way. That strengthened her suspicion that he was still in love with his first wife, and she could understand that to have Lavinia's daughter living at Rotherton would be a constant, painful reminder of what he had lost. But that would not stop her trying to change his mind.

When they sat down to dinner Angel engaged Jason in light-hearted conversation on a number of unexceptional subjects. That and the excellent food did much to restore the easy camaraderie between them, and after the meal Angel was pleased and surprised when Jason said he would take his brandy with her, rather than keeping solitary state at the table.

'And I believe you have a new sitting room,' he added, as they went through to the drawing room.

'Yes. Oh, dear, I beg your pardon, Jason. I should have told you.'

He shook his head at her. 'There is no need to look so guilty. We have been distracted by our visitors.'

'I suppose we have.' She hesitated. 'Would you like to see it now?'

She led the way into the little corner room she had taken for her own. It was glowing with the evening sunshine and she was pleased that he was seeing it at its best.

'I hope you do not object? The room was empty and Mrs Wenlock said there were no plans for it. She helped me to find all the furniture and the curtains from what was stored in the attics—'

'Hush, hush!' he interrupted her, laughing. 'You do not need to justify anything to me, Angel. I gave you carte blanche to do what you wished at Rotherton and you have turned this into a snug little lair for yourself. My only criticism is that it has cost me nothing. I recognise everything here, the faded chairs, for example, and that old writing desk.'

'But I do not need anything new,' she assured him. 'This is a room in which I can be comfortable.'

'I believe you can.' A heartbeat of hesitation, then he said, 'And will you allow me to join you, sometimes?'

'Of course, whenever you wish.' A little rush of happiness bubbled up and she added, 'We might sit here now, if you like. I could ring for Langshaw to bring in your brandy, and a glass of wine for me.'

When the wine had been served they sat together and talked. Angel asked him about his visit to London and the country estates before entertaining him with a description of her sisters' visit.

Jason sipped his brandy and watched her, observing how her hair gleamed like polished mahogany in the evening sunlight.

A feeling of quiet contentment stole over him. He remembered sitting on this very sofa years ago. It was still comfortable, despite the covers being a trifle worn. He could not recall when he had last felt so at home in his own house.

The sun had finally disappeared below the horizon and the shadows were lengthening when the butler came in with a lighted taper.

Jason put down his glass and jumped up. 'Thank you, Langshaw, I'll do that.'

He took the taper and made his way around the room, taking no small satisfaction in replacing the evening gloom with the soft glow of the candles.

'You know,' he remarked, 'Rotherton feels very different from how it was when I went away.'

'I have made only small changes, and done nothing without consulting Mrs Wenlock or Langshaw.'

'No, no, I am not complaining, I like it. The house is more...comfortable, somehow. More like Goole Park.'

'Mayhap that is because of the children. I did not wish them to be confined to the nursery wing.'

He chuckled. 'Aye, that would be it. They leave their

mark wherever they go…cushions disturbed, furniture out of place.'

'But they do no harm, Jason.'

'No, I know that.'

'Then why not allow them to make their home here?'

He paused before lighting the last candle.

Because I want you to myself. Selfish, I know, but I don't want to share you!

'No.' He blew out the taper and sat down beside her, searching for more excuses not to have the children there. 'It would be too much work for you. They would consume all your time and energy.'

She laughed. 'With so many servants they consume very little of either. And Mrs Watson would most likely come and live here with them. How can that be too much work for me?'

'It will be. Trust me on that.'

Jason tried to convince himself he was right. What did either of them know of raising a family? Lavinia had been a mother: she had made it plain to him that children were better off in their own establishment. He could still hear her explaining it to him, shortly after Nell was born.

'Believe me, Jason, children demand far too much of a mother's time. She has no leisure to think of her husband's needs…'

Something twisted inside. It was ironic that shortly after she had told him this he'd discovered how rarely she thought of her husband or his needs.

He turned to Angel, sitting beside him. She was gazing at him, a shy smile in her eyes, and he ran a finger down her cheek. The dark lashes fluttered and her lips parted a little, inviting him to kiss her. It set his pulse racing, but he knew it would not stop at one kiss. She filled his senses. It was difficult to think of anything except taking her to his bed and exploring every inch of that creamy, soft skin.

She touched his arm. 'It would take very little to refurbish the nursery wing, Jason.'

'No!' He caught her hand. 'Stop this now, madam.'

He saw her flinch, as if he had slapped her. The hurt in her eyes caused a sudden constriction in his chest.

She said quietly, 'Can we not even *talk* about it?'

His breath hitched as those dark eyes searched his face. Was she really so innocent that she did not know the effect she was having on him?

He said brusquely, 'We *have* talked, and I have given you my final word. I will not countenance it.' He pushed himself to his feet. 'It is growing late. I will escort you to your room.'

He braced himself for a scene. Tears had been Lavinia's weapon. Her blue eyes would glisten like sapphires and she would look more adorable than ever. The boy he had been had succumbed, time and again, giving way to her on every point. It had taken him years to realise it was all a sham... that she had never truly loved him.

It was a lesson he had learned well, he thought as he held out one hand to Angel. 'Well, madam, are you ready?'

He hardened his heart, steeling himself as he waited for her to weep or rail against him. Or to sulk.

Instead she took the proffered hand and allowed him to pull her to her feet.

'I am perfectly ready, Your Grace.'

Angel accompanied the Duke silently up the stairs. He had withdrawn from her as soon as she had mentioned bringing the children here, yet moments earlier he himself had spoken about them quite comfortably. They stopped at the door of her bedchamber.

'Are you still at odds with me?' she asked, noting his frown.

He started, as if his thoughts had been far away. 'No, no. I…er… I was thinking of something. Business I need to finish.'

It seemed a poor excuse and she did not really believe him. She searched his face for some sign of warmth, but his eyes were shuttered. Hard and indifferent, as if they were strangers. She wanted him to talk to her—about the children, about his dead wife—but she knew that was not his way. Not yet, at least.

She gave a little smile, a slight lift of her shoulders, and eased her hand from his arm. So be it.

He opened her door and stepped back for her to enter. 'Goodnight, madam.'

With a quiet 'goodnight' Angel walked past him into the room. It would take time and patience to bring out the kind, loving man she was sure lurked behind his cold exterior,

Having said he must work, Jason went back to his study and sat down at his desk, but it was impossible to concentrate on the ledgers spread out before him. He could not forget the way Angel had looked when he had left her. The enigmatic glance…the cool way she had wished him goodnight.

She confused him. No tears, no tantrums. The thought that she did not care for him occurred, only to be rejected. Angel was not like Lavinia. She was too sweet, too innocent to use her feminine allure to get her own way. At least not deliberately.

Jason shifted restlessly on his chair, recalling how good it had felt to hold her, to kiss her. He had been lost the moment he'd taken her in his arms. After Lavinia, he had not believed he could feel such an all-consuming passion for another woman, but it seemed he was wrong, and it disturbed him.

Two hours and a few glasses of brandy later, Jason slipped into his own bed, but sleep would not come. He tossed and turned, his mind wandering constantly to the woman in the next room. Was Angel asleep, or was she, too, lying awake, her body aching for his touch? He almost groaned at the thought, but he would not give in. He had promised himself he would be strong for both of them. His marriage to Lavinia had turned into a living hell because he had rushed into it. He was not about to make the same mistake again.

Shortly after dawn Jason gave up trying to sleep. He threw on his clothes and went out to the stables for an early-morning ride. The exercise and fresh air helped him to clear his head, and a couple of hours later he was able to join everyone for breakfast with at least the semblance of calm.

Angel was the first thing he noticed when he entered the room. She was very pale, as if she, too, had not slept well. She was talking calmly enough with Mrs Watson, and joking with Rose, but when he addressed a remark to her she avoided his eyes as she made her reply.

He knew then, without any doubt, that his coldness last night had upset her. His conscience smote him, he could not bear to see Angel unhappy. He needed to talk to her. Alone.

At the first break in the conversation he said, 'It is such a lovely day, Duchess, I thought we might go riding together. The ground is firm, but not too hard. Perfect for a gallop.'

'Oh…' A gratifying blush suffused her cheeks. 'But you have already been riding today.'

'Which is how I know it is the perfect morning for going out.'

She gave a tiny shake of her head. 'That is very kind of

you, Your Grace, but Rose and I are going into Rotherton to collect her new gown. Perhaps another day.'

Mrs Watson earned Jason's eternal gratitude by saying, 'If that is all, ma'am, I would be happy to go with Rose in your stead.'

'An excellent idea!' He turned back to Angel. 'Well, Duchess, what do you say? I have yet to see you put that handsome chestnut gelding of yours through its paces.'

Still she demurred. 'I would not want to take up your time. I know Mr Merrick has business matters to discuss with you.'

'There are always business matters to discuss, but they will wait.' He waved away her arguments. 'I will see Simon later. It would be a pity not to take advantage of this good weather.'

She was going to refuse. He saw it in her face and he waited to hear what excuse she would come up with next. Then help came from an unexpected source.

'Do go, Angel,' Rose urged her. 'I am sure Mrs Watson would enjoy a visit to Madame Sophie. And Nell has not yet been to Middlewych,' she added. 'She could come with us, too.'

'Well, if you are sure…'

'Good. I shall send word to the stables immediately,' declared Jason, before Angel could come up with any more excuses. 'Mrs Watson will take the girls into Middlewych.' He turned to smile at the widow. 'You must stop at the Rotherton Arms, ma'am. It is on the high street, and when you have finished your shopping they will provide you with a luncheon!'

'There appears to be nothing more to be said on the matter,' murmured Angel.

She was looking a little bemused, but she was at least smiling.

Jason grinned at her. 'Exactly. I shall tell Thomas to have our horses ready in, say, half an hour. Will that suit you?'

'Yes, thank you. If you will excuse me? I will go and change.'

Angel quickly donned her riding habit of tawny wool with its matching curly brimmed hat. It was not new, but it fitted her like a glove, making the most of her slender figure. Half an hour later she was holding up the voluminous skirts and hurrying down the stairs again.

The Duke was waiting for her in the hall and he smiled as she approached. 'Shall we go?'

They stepped out into the warm sunshine and made their way to the stables, where their horses were ready and waiting. Apollo was a little restive at first. However, by the time he had settled down any awkwardness she'd felt at being alone with Jason had evaporated.

'You did not ride that mare earlier this morning, I presume?' she remarked, nodding towards the rangy black hunter he was riding.

'No, I took out Major. He's an old boy now, but still enjoys a gallop.'

'I am surprised you wished to ride out again so soon.'

'As I said, it is a shame to waste such a day as this.' He glanced across at her. 'And I wanted to have you to myself for a while.'

His words and the glinting smile that accompanied them caught her off guard. She felt herself blushing, but Jason had already ridden ahead and she urged Apollo into a canter. The ground was not unfamiliar—a groom had accompanied her for a few gentle rides while the Duke had been absent from Rotherton—but this was different. Riding out with Jason, pushing Apollo to keep up with him. she felt like a child again, eager to prove she was his equal in the saddle. And when they eventually drew rein and he complimented her, she felt the same flush of unalloyed joy that she had done all those years ago.

'I am not offering you Spanish coin, Angel,' he told her. 'You are an excellent horsewoman. It was neck or nothing over those hedges.'

'That was all Apollo,' she said, leaning forward to pat the gelding's ruddy neck. 'Papa thought he might be too strong for me, but Barnaby persuaded him otherwise.'

'Yes, because he knows how well you ride. Do you remember how you used to steal off on his horse and go careering across the countryside? Without a lady's saddle, too!'

'Stop, stop!' she cried, laughing. 'I am ashamed to think I was such a sad romp!'

'Don't be,' he told her. 'I have always admired your spirit.'

His words took her by surprise. They pleased her, too, for it was a compliment of no mean order, although Jason appeared unaware of it. He was already looking to the far hills.

'There is a good viewpoint beyond the woods. If we push on we should be able to reach it before we need to turn for home. What do you say?'

Angel readily agreed and they set off again, cantering across the open ground and slowing only as they rode through a small area of woodland that covered the lower slopes of the hill.

When they reached the viewpoint, Jason came to a halt. 'Well, what do you think?'

'It's beautiful.'

While Angel gazed at the patchwork of fields and woodland spread out below them Jason took the opportunity to study her, thinking how well she looked on horseback. Her back straight, hands lightly holding the reins, she looked completely at home. Her figure showed to advantage, too, in that habit. It was the rich yellow-brown of autumn leaves and contrasted well with the glossy mahogany of her hair, peeping out beneath that fetching little hat. The mannish jacket fitted perfectly, accentuating a waist so small he thought his hands might well be able to encircle it. In fact, his fingers itched to try.

'Do we have time to walk for a little while?'

Her warm brown eyes were fixed on him, and it took a few moments for Jason to register what she had said and answer her.

'As much time as you wish!'

Having tethered the horses to a bush, Jason lifted her down, holding her for a fraction longer than was necessary.

'What is the joke, sir? Why are you smiling like that?'

She was looking up at him, her brows raised, and he felt the smile deepen inside like a warm glow.

'I had been wondering if I could span your waist with my hands. Now I know.'

She blushed adorably, and with a laugh he pulled her hand onto his sleeve.

'Come along, let us walk!' He led her to the edge of the escarpment, where the land fell away steeply. 'You can see Rotherton from here,' he said, pointing. 'Look for Middlewych first, over there. Then follow the river. Do you see? The house is just visible on the rise beyond the woods.'

'Yes, yes, I see it. I had not realised we had come so far.'

'Was it worth the ride?'

'Oh, yes, very much so.' She turned to him, her eyes glowing with pleasure. '*Thank* you, Jason, for suggesting it.'

'You are very welcome.' Something shifted inside him as he gazed down at her smiling, heart-shaped face. 'But I had my reasons for wanting to ride out with you. I needed to talk to you alone. To atone for my boorish behaviour yesterday.'

Her smile faded. She looked away from him and stared out across the landscape.

'You were angry with me. For suggesting Rose and Nell should live at Rotherton.'

'Yes, I was angry, and it was wrong of me. I should have explained why I will not have them at the house. It is for purely logical, practical reasons.'

They were the reasons Lavinia had given him, but that did not make them any less true. At least, that was what he had always told himself.

He went on. 'Children are noisy and disruptive. It is their nature. And they are forever getting under one's feet. If they lived with us then before long we would resent having them in the house. These are early days in our marriage. Their presence would cause arguments and possibly ill feeling between us.'

Angel turned to stare at him, a crease furrowing her brow. 'Who has told you this, Jason?'

'You have visited the establishment in Kent,' he said, ignoring her question. 'You cannot deny that Rose and Nell are very happy with Mrs Watson. Why move them?'

Angel did not reply but she looked down, hiding her thoughts from him.

He gave a hiss of exasperation. 'Why is it so important to you that they should live at Rotherton?'

'Why is it so important to you that they should not?' she countered.

'I have told you. They would destroy our comfort. Neither of us is experienced in rearing a family.'

'But we could learn, Jason. Will you not even consider it?'

'I *have* considered, and decided it will not do.'

'Not even for their come-out?'

He hesitated. 'Nell, perhaps, can be presented in London. But not Rose.'

She looked troubled at that, and he frowned.

'What? What is it, Angel? Out with it!'

'I wondered.' She stopped and Jason noted how tightly she was gripping her riding crop. 'Rose looks so very like her mother. I thought…the memories, your loss. I thought seeing her might be too painful for you.'

She was right, it *was* painful, Jason admitted to himself. But not for the reason she thought.

A shadow crossed her countenance. She said gently, 'It is true, then. She reminds you too much of your lost love.'

Jason knew he should tell her the truth. He wanted to tell her that it was not love he felt for Lavinia but rage and disgust. He was also fearful. If Rose turned out like her mother she would be a determined flirt. Then again, she was an innocent, and such a beautiful young woman would be the target of every rake in London. He was afraid he would not be able to protect her. He wanted to say all this, but it was as if the words were locked somewhere inside and he did not have the key.

He scowled in frustration. 'That is nonsense.' He waved one hand dismissively. 'Rose is a very pretty girl. Beautiful, even, but that is not why I am against her living at Rotherton.'

Angel did not look as if she quite believed that, but there was no judgement in her dark eyes. She merely wanted to understand him, and she deserved that he should at least try to explain.

He turned away and walked a few paces along the ridge, fighting against his reticence, the defensive wall he had built around himself. He must say something.

'If you want the truth,' *Well, part of it, at least...* 'I am afraid of not living up to their expectations. I.' *Deep breath, man. Tell her!* 'I do not know how to go on, how to behave, with children.'

'You managed very well with Nell,' Angel reminded him. 'She loved her time on the lake with you. It is now *Papa this,* and *Papa that* at every turn.' She chuckled. 'You have become quite a favourite.'

'I am glad. I do not want her to be afraid of me.' He looked back. 'But that does not mean I will allow the girls to be uprooted from Kent!'

'If it is because you feel ill at ease with them, that will change once you are better acquainted.' She came closer and touched his sleeve. 'You should give them a chance to get to know you.'

He shook her off. 'Dammit, Angel, why will you not let it be? We all went on very well before you started interfering!'

She said gently, 'We both know that is not true.'

He gave a sigh and stared out towards the horizon. 'You are quite right. It isn't true.'

He could feel his defences crumbling. 'Perhaps we could extend their visit,' he said at last. 'See how we all go on together.'

'That is a good idea.' She slipped one hand into the crook of his arm. 'Rotherton is a very large house, Jason. The girls need not trouble you.'

'No, well... We shall see.' He glanced at the sun. 'It grows late. We should be heading back.'

They walked to the horses in silence and he threw her up into the saddle, holding on to the bridle until she had Apollo under control.

'Thank you.' She smiled down at him and he shook his head.

'I make no promises about the girls,' he warned her as

he sprang up onto the hunter. 'You will say nothing to them about making their home with us!'

'But of course not, Your Grace. The decision to have Nell and Rose live with us at Rotherton must be yours and yours alone.'

Her meek tone made him frown suspiciously, but she met his gaze with such wide-eyed innocence that he did not challenge her further.

And yet, as they made their way down the hill, he had the feeling that he had already lost that battle.

Chapter Seven

By dinner the following day Mrs Watson and her charges had been invited to remain for another month. The Duke had also given instructions that they should dine together *en famille* in the little dining room.

Angel was surprised at this sudden change of heart and said as much, although she waited until Mrs Watson had taken Rose and Nell up to bed before broaching the subject.

'How kind of you to suggest they should all stay a little longer.'

They were alone in the drawing room and Jason was pouring them both a glass of wine.

'I could hardly do anything else after your cajoling yesterday.'

She saw the glint of amusement in his eyes and laughed. 'Perhaps not, but I had not expected you to act quite so soon.'

'It seemed...expedient.' He sat down beside her. 'I put the idea to Mrs Watson this morning and she thought it would be especially beneficial for Rose. Before they left Ashford she had been attracting a great deal of attention from the local beaux.'

'That does not surprise me. Rose is exceptionally pretty.' She slanted a glance at him. 'As I told you, she is no longer a child.'

'She is only seventeen.'

'But not too young to go into society a little.'

'Perhaps not.'

Angel waited a moment, then she said slowly, 'There is an assembly at the Rotherton Arms on Thursday next.'

'Surely you are not suggesting we take her?'

'Why not? I am sure it is perfectly respectable.'

'I would not know. I have not attended a dance there for years. You know I was never one for such occasions, Angel.'

She turned slightly to look at him. 'Did you never take your duchess to an assembly there?'

'At first, yes. But in later years…' His jaw tightened. 'We were rarely at Rotherton together.'

Angel hid her surprise. She recalled her conversation with her sisters and the rumours concerning Lavinia and the Prince of Wales. Could it be Lavinia had played the Duke false? Perhaps they had both looked elsewhere for their pleasures.

She quickly pushed the thought aside.

'Well, I shall make enquiries,' she told him. 'If reports are favourable then I shall take Rose to the assembly. It will give her a chance to show off her new gown. There will be no need for you to trouble yourself, Your Grace. Mrs Watson will come with us.'

But this Jason would not allow. 'If you go, then I must go with you.'

'But why? You have just said you dislike going into company. And after London I am sure you will find a provincial dance deadly dull.'

She could not keep a slight edge from her voice and he heard it.

'I was in London for business, madam. I did not attend

any balls,' he retorted. 'However, it would be my duty to accompany you to your first assembly at Rotherton.'

Ah, yes, duty. Her spirits dipped.

'Also,' he went on, 'I need to show the young bucks of Rotherton that Rose is under my protection and not to be trifled with.'

'Then we shall be very glad of your company,' replied Angel, rising. 'Now, if you will excuse me, I shall go to bed. No, don't get up, sir. You have not yet finished your wine and I am quite capable of finding my way to my room.'

With that she went out, closing the door gently behind her. This was definite progress. Even if he had only agreed out of a sense of duty, Jason had relented on extending Rose and Nell's visit and he had also declared he would accompany them to the assembly.

As she went up the stairs Angel's heart gave a little skip at the thought that he might even be persuaded to dance with her.

Alone in the silent room, Jason sat back and exhaled, long and slow. Why the devil had he said he would go to the Rotherton Arms? It was bound to be a tedious evening. He did not like assemblies. It was bad enough being obliged to stand up with a succession of elderly matrons or simpering debutantes. Even worse would be the stares and sly glances. The rumours shared in quiet corners.

He rubbed his chin. There really was no need for him to go for Rose's sake. The mere fact that she was his stepdaughter would ensure no one tried to take advantage of her. And he was confident that Mrs Watson would not allow her charge to indulge in anything but the mildest of flirtations.

But what about Angel? Who would protect her from the

whispers and the gossip? Or indeed from any roguish fellows bent on mischief?

'By heaven, I will go!' he exclaimed to the empty room. 'And I will stand up with her myself for every dance if necessary!'

He was startled by his sudden outburst, but amused too. Angel would never countenance such behaviour. He could almost hear her chiding him if he refused to dance with any other lady. Most unbecoming of a duke to snub his neighbours like that!

He finished his wine and set off for his bedchamber, but at Angel's door he stopped. Should he go in? Would she welcome him?

He reached out but stopped short of grasping the handle. She had made it perfectly plain she did not want him to accompany her. And their conversation had been all about the children.

His hand fell and he walked on.

Angel had no interest in him at all.

On Thursday evening Angeline left her room at the appointed time, arrayed in an evening gown of cerulean blue silk net embroidered with gold thread. She had ordered it from Madame Sophie at the same time as choosing new dresses for Rose, and she hoped that Jason would approve.

She made her way down the grand staircase to find the Duke was already in the hall and looking very handsome in his black evening dress. He was conversing with Mrs Watson, but broke off when Angel appeared and came towards her.

'Ah, there you are at last.'

He was smiling, and she was tempted to ask what he thought of the gown, but decided against it.

'I hope I have not kept you waiting?'

'No, no. The carriage is at the door, but the horses will take no harm for a few more minutes.' He took the silk cloak from her and began to arrange it around her shoulders. 'Rose has not appeared yet.'

'I am sure she will be here soon,' said Angel. 'I sent Joan along to dress her hair.'

At that moment Rose came down the stairs, wearing her new gown of white muslin.

'And I am here now.'

Angel looked up as Jason's hands gripped her shoulders. His eyes were fixed on Rose. He was very pale, and a muscle twitched in his cheek. He looked as if he had seen a ghost.

Angel's spirits plummeted, but the next moment he had released her and moved forward, smiling and holding out his hands to his stepdaughter.

'You look charming, my dear. You will be the belle of the ball tonight, I am sure.'

Rose blushed and disclaimed. 'Th-thank you, Your Grace. Do you not think Angel looks very well in her new silk gown?'

'I do. I think she looks beautiful.'

Angel had looked away and was busy tying the strings of her cloak.

'Pray, do not go on,' she said, forcing a little laugh. 'You will put me to the blush. Now, if we are ready, shall we go?'

Even to her own ears her cheerfulness sounded strained. Jason was looking keenly at her, but she avoided his eyes and hurried out to the waiting carriage.

The assembly rooms at the Rotherton Arms were already crowded when Jason escorted his party to the ballroom, although the dancing had not yet commenced. It was a warm evening and the ladies' fans were in play. A happy buzz of voices was filling the room, but the chatter sank to near silence when they walked in. The noise quickly swelled again and Mr Burchill, the master of ceremonies, hurried across to the newcomers, exclaiming at the honour His Grace was bestowing upon their humble gathering.

Angel had been very quiet in the carriage, but Jason was relieved to see she had quite recovered her spirits. As he exchanged a few words with the master of ceremonies he watched her responding to the Squire and his lady, who had come up to greet them. She was quite at ease and he relaxed a little. A country mouse she might be, but she knew how to go on in company.

The musicians struck up for the first dance and Jason prepared himself for the coming ordeal. He was naturally reserved, but he knew what was expected of him.

Burchill presented him to a dowager viscountess for the first dance, and then he stood up with the Squire's wife. His next partner was Lady Kennet, a rather alarming widow who still lived in the family home and tyrannised her son and daughter-in-law. She had known the Duke since he was a boy and took great pleasure in reminding him of the fact.

'So you have married again,' she remarked as the music ended. 'I met your new duchess at the little party Lady Whalton gave to welcome her to Rotherton. You were away at the time.'

Jason did not miss the faint note of censure in her last words. He said mildly, 'Yes, I had business that could not wait.' He gave her his arm to escort her off the floor. 'But I am here now, and mean to remain for some time.'

'I am glad to hear it. Everyone at Rotherton was surprised to find you had wed again so soon, but your new duchess is a charming gel. She will do very well for you.'

He inclined his head and said drily, 'I'm glad you approve, ma'am.'

'I do,' she replied. 'I also like the look of your stepdaughter. Very pretty manners. She is bidding fair to be a beauty, too. Like her mother.' She released his arm. 'Let us hope that is the only thing she has inherited from the late Duchess!'

On this parting shot she walked away, and Jason took himself off to the refreshments table to recover his composure. He had known coming here tonight would be a trial, but he had hoped no one would mention Lavinia to his face. Now he could not wait for the evening to end!

He was standing by the punchbowl when Angel came up to him.

'You are taking a second cup?' she asked, smiling. 'Oh, dear, is it as bad as that?'

The laugh in her voice instantly soothed his ill temper.

'I am rewarding myself for spending the first half of the evening doing the pretty on the dance floor with my neighbours.'

He filled a fresh cup and handed it to her. 'It really wasn't that bad. I am just out of practice at exchanging niceties with my dance partners.'

'Then dance with me next. You do not need to be polite to me.'

She was sipping at her punch and gazing away into the distance, as if his answer did not really matter to her.

He frowned. 'Have we ever danced together? I cannot remember it.'

'I was still in the schoolroom the last time you came to Goole Park,' she reminded him. 'You were fifteen and despised dancing. We never stood up together.'

Jason grinned. 'Then it is high time we rectified the matter!'

'Yes, isn't it?' Her eyes twinkled in response. 'Although

I believe it is highly unfashionable to dance with one's husband.'

'Do you care about that?'

The twinkled deepened. 'Not in the least.'

'Very well then.' He put down his cup. 'The next set is forming. Shall we join them?'

They danced two country dances together, then the Duke persuaded her to dance a reel, after which she begged to be allowed to sit down and he accompanied her to a couple of empty chairs.

Angel sat back with a sigh and closed her eyes. 'That is better. I am so hot I can scarce breathe!'

Taking her fan, he opened it and waved it to and fro, making the tiny curls around her face dance.

'There, is that better?'

'Yes, thank you.' Angel smiled. 'How pleasant it would be to sit here with you for the rest of the evening, but it cannot be.'

'Why not? We are Duke and Duchess. We can do as we wish.'

She chuckled. 'You know that is not so. Your neighbours all wish to speak with you, and you will want to look out for Rose, too.'

'Will I?'

'I thought you had come to make sure no young men became too familiar with her.'

'It was clear to me from the start that Mrs Watson is more than capable of looking after Rose.' He glanced around the room. 'At present my stepdaughter appears to be part of a large group of young people. She has made friends very quickly.'

'I took her to visit some of the families in the area as

soon as she arrived, so she is already acquainted with several of them.'

'You are very good to her.'

'Why should I not be?' She looked at him, surprised. 'I am very fond of Rose. And Nell, too.'

'Many new wives would resent their stepdaughters. And some new husbands might resent their bride giving so much attention to anyone but themselves. Not that that applies to me!' he added hastily, remembering his earlier selfish thoughts.

'No. Of course.'

Was that a note of disappointment in her voice? Did she *want* to spend more time with him?

Jason was about to ask but Angel was looking past him, and he turned his head to see a portly gentleman bearing down on them.

He clicked his tongue in annoyance. 'And here comes Burchill to carry you off again. He takes his duties very seriously. Shall I tell him you are indisposed or merely wave him away?'

'Neither,' she muttered. 'Hush, now, or he will hear you.'

'Ah, Your Grace.' Mr Burchill's corset creaked as he made a very low bow to Jason. 'What a splendid evening this is turning out to be! You have been most obliging, Your Grace, most obliging. And I know you will not object if I steal your good lady away from you once more. There is someone here very desirous to meet her. And if Her Grace will be so kind as to honour the gentleman with her hand for the next dance…'

Jason cast a teasing glance at Angel. 'Alas, sir, I fear my wife is feeling the heat somewhat—'

'Nonsense, I am quite recovered now.' She flew out of her chair and bestowed a brilliant smile upon the master of ceremonies. 'I shall be delighted to dance again, Mr Burchill. Lead on, sir!'

'Ah, you are too kind, ma'am, but with so many gentlemen begging for the honour of dancing with Your Grace, I fear we will not be able to accommodate them all.'

Jason had also risen and he touched Burchill's arm.

'One more thing before you go. The Duchess is at liberty to dance with anyone she wishes this evening. Except for the final dance.' He looked at Angel. 'That, madam, I claim for myself.'

His tone was deliberately autocratic and he wondered how she would respond. Her head came up and the flash of fire in those dark eyes was a mixture of surprise, anger and amusement. Then she snatched her fan from his hand and, with a look that promised retribution for his teasing, sailed off to meet her next partner.

Having sent his duchess away to dance, Jason discovered he did not want to stand up with anyone else. He feared he would not be able to give his partner sufficient attention. His eyes would be following Angel, anxious to see just how much she was enjoying another man's attentions. He remembered only too well the agony of watching his first wife flirting with her dance partners and did not wish to experience that hurt again.

Not that he had ever allowed anyone but Lavinia to see how much he cared.

At first she had laughed it off and soothed his ruffled feathers. Later he had discovered it was not only on the dance floor that she enjoyed other men's company.

Looking back, he could not recall precisely when his jealousy had faded, leaving only anger and outrage at her behaviour. He only knew that at some time, long before she had broken her neck in that carriage accident, he had ceased to love his wife.

Jason saw Rose going down the dance with Kenelm Babberton, the son of one of his neighbours. The boy was clearly enraptured. He could not keep his eyes off his partner and Jason did not blame him. At seventeen, Rose was already bidding fair to rival her mother, with her golden hair and that bewitching smile. She would break hearts, he knew it, but she would also attract any number of rogues.

Not that Babberton was a rogue, thought Jason, regarding the young man's honest, open countenance. He was more likely to need protecting from voracious females!

Nevertheless, Jason decided he should make it plain that he was keeping a watchful eye on his stepdaughter. He wandered across the room to join Mrs Watson until the dance ended, then he would stand up with Rose himself.

Angel did not sit down again for the rest of the evening. The master of ceremonies had not lied about the number of gentlemen wishing to stand up with her. Thankfully, she loved to dance and enjoyed herself immensely, but deep inside a little fizz of anticipation was building as the evening drew to a close.

Had Jason been serious when he had claimed the last dance from her? A slight shiver ran through her when she remembered his haughty tone and the hot, possessive look in his eyes as he had spoken.

He was making it plain to the world that she was his.

The sizzle of excitement increased. Did he also intend to make it clear to her, later, by taking her to bed?

Angel laughed and talked with her partners, but all the time she was aware of the Duke. His tall figure was easy to spot as he made his way around the room, with a word here, a smile there. Then she saw him dancing with Rose, and for one dreadful moment her heart stopped.

This was how it must have looked when he and Lavinia had danced together. The Duke broad-shouldered and straight-backed, a commanding presence on the dance floor, and his duchess a dazzling golden beauty at his side. Angel forced her eyes away. The black, raging jealousy she felt for a dead woman was foolish and illogical. She must not give in to it.

The evening was almost over and Angel slipped away to a shadowy corner of the room to avoid Mr Burchill, whom she knew would want her to dance again. There was an open window nearby and she moved across to it, looking down into the dark street below. She felt tired, even a little deflated, and wanted to save her remaining energy for her dance with Jason.

She had been looking forward to it so much that she was afraid that it might not live up to her expectations. It was only one dance, after all. Did she hope to impress him? At eight-and-twenty, the Duke was no stranger to society. He had danced in the finest ballrooms and with the most beautiful and accomplished dancers. Her own performance must surely compare most unfavourably.

'Well, madam, are you ready for our dance?'

Angel turned quickly. The Duke was standing beside her, as immaculate as when they had arrived. Other men were looking a little dishevelled, and some of them distinctly red-faced, after the evening's exertions, but not Jason. His raven hair was still neat, the blue-black coat lay smoothly across his broad chest and the snowy linen of his shirt and neck-cloth were immaculate. Looking at his face, she noted that save for the shadow of stubble on his lean cheeks he looked cool and composed.

Which was more than she could say for herself. Just the sound of his voice had set her heart racing. She felt hot, anxious, and she was obliged to breathe deeply before she could take his hand and accompany him onto the dance floor.

They took their places in the set. The music started and her nerves steadied a little. They skipped, circled, crossed and twirled as if they had been dancing together for years rather than just this one evening. The Duke was smiling at her, which made Angel's heart soar, and when they were separated by the movement of the dance their coming together again was joyous. By the time she made her final curtsy and walked off on Jason's arm, Angel was bursting with happiness.

As soon as the dancing concluded there was a rush for the doors, with everyone making their way to collect cloaks and change shoes.

'I think we would do well to wait a little,' said the Duke, holding back.

'Very well.' Angel was content to wait with him until the crush had died down.

The servants were already clearing the ballroom and smoke from the freshly snuffed candles clouded the air. Jason guided Angel across to the open window. The shadows were deeper here, and they could hear the noise from the dispersing crowd.

'Tell me,' he said. 'Tell me about this man who broke your heart.'

Angel closed her fan. She had told no one of the pain and humiliation she had felt, but perhaps it was time. She could do this if she kept her tone light.

'It is a familiar story. We met at Almack's. He was very handsome, very charming, and I was flattered by his attentions. I was smitten, and truly thought he loved me. He gave me to understand he would be making me an offer, but then...' She was obliged to take a breath, to swallow the hurt and humiliation that had never quite gone away. 'Then a new debutante arrived in London. A fair-haired beauty who had all the gentlemen vying for her attentions. My beau was the one who won her hand. I first learned of it one night. At Almack's.'

She was so lost in the past that she jumped when Jason put his hands over hers and removed the fan from her fingers.

'You have broken the sticks,' he said gently.

A shudder ran through her, ending in a long sigh. 'It is the first time I have spoken of that night.'

'I am sorry if I have upset you.'

She glanced up and saw his face was full of concern.

'Please don't be sorry. I am glad I have told you. It was a long time ago and deserves to be forgotten.'

'And I am honoured by your confidence. Do you know where this fellow is now?'

'Why do you ask?'

'Because I want to run the villain through!'

He vehemence surprised her. She gave a shaky laugh.

'Then I am glad I did not divulge his name! He married the beauty, but sadly they were both far too extravagant, and soon their debts were such that they were obliged to go abroad to escape their creditors.'

'Leaving you with a broken heart,' he muttered, throwing the mangled fan aside.

'I thought so, at the time. But I have recovered now and I am much the wiser for it.'

He hesitated. 'You told me once that the villain had stolen a kiss from you.'

'Did I?' she looked at him, surprised. 'It is of no consequence now.'

'It has not given you a distaste for kisses?'

'Not in the least.' She blushed and looked away, saying shyly, 'I like it when you kiss me.'

He put his fingers under her chin and she felt their gentle pressure, lifting her face up, then he gently lowered his head. Angel did not wait for his lips to reach hers. She stretched up and captured his mouth, slipping her arm about his neck. What followed was a long, lingering kiss.

They were oblivious to the servants clearing the room, the squeaking chandelier chains and the scrape of chairs being moved, until one of the footmen noticed the couple in the shadows.

'Oh! Beggin' your pardon, sir, madam. I didn't see you there!' he muttered, hurrying away.

Jason lifted his head, but kept his eyes on Angel. There was no mistaking the glow of pleasure in her face.

'I just wanted to be sure,' he murmured, happiness spreading through him like a flame. 'Allow me to escort you home, ma'am.'

'Well, I think that went very well!' declared Mrs Watson when they were all in the carriage and travelling back to Rotherton.

'Oh, yes!' Rose gave a loud sigh. 'I had the most wonderful time. I danced almost every dance!'

'I am glad you enjoyed it,' replied Angel. She turned to Jason, who was sitting beside her. 'I hope you did not find it too tedious, Your Grace?'

His glowing look almost melted her on the spot. He caught her gloved fingers and raised them to his lips.

'On the contrary, it was far better than I expected.'

He continued to hold her hand and she felt quite dizzy with delight as the carriage rattled along the lanes in the early-morning light.

The rest of the journey passed in near silence. Mrs Watson was dozing in her corner and Rose gazed out of the window, most likely reliving her evening, and Angel was happy to sit quietly, her fingers snug in the Duke's warm clasp.

Could anything be more perfect?

Jason held on to the small hand, trying not to crush it. The evening had been a revelation. He had no doubts now that Angel would make him a perfect wife. He had heard nothing but compliments all evening. She won everyone over with her kindness and her gracious manners. He had seen her dancing with his neighbours, dull dogs like the crusty old General Appleton and young Lord Kennet, as well as a floridly handsome buck that Jason did not know, but whom he disliked as soon as he saw him stand up with Angel. He had watched the pair keenly as the music started, ready to step in if the fellow should become too forward, but Angel treated him with the same smiling good humour she had shown to all her partners. She was friendly, cool, and composed.

Until that final dance. Jason's pulse quickened when he remembered standing opposite her and seeing that becoming flush on her cheeks. There was an added sparkle in her eyes, too, and she gave him a beaming smile that he had not seen her bestow on anyone else that evening. His body had responded to that look. It set his pulse racing and he wanted to drag her away into the night and kiss her senseless.

Now, in the darkened coach, with Angel beside him, he had to breathe deep and slow in order to stay calm, reminding himself that they were not alone. *Not yet*, he thought, desire rapidly increasing. But they would soon be back at Rotherton, and tonight he fully intended to make Angel his wife—in every sense.

When they reached the house Jason jumped down from the coach and turned to hand out the ladies. Angel was first, but instead of hurrying away indoors she stood aside, shaking out her skirts while he helped the others to alight. Mrs Watson and Rose moved towards the door, but his heart leapt when he saw Angel was waiting for him.

He closed the door and the carriage moved off.

'Well, madam?'

She came closer and slipped her hand onto his sleeve.

'Well, Your Grace?'

In the dawn light he could see the smile lilting on her lips and he bent to brush them with his own. 'Shall it be my room or yours?'

'Either.' A very wicked gurgle of laughter escaped her. 'Perhaps both?'

Elation surged through Jason. He smothered a laugh and whispered, with mock outrage, 'I thought I had married an innocent maid!'

'I am certainly a maid, sir, but I have two married sisters. One…hears things.' She squeezed his arm. 'We should go indoors, Jason.'

Curbing a desire to pick her up and carry her to his bed, Jason walked her towards the house. As they approached the open door he could hear raised voices coming from the hall, and they stepped inside just as Rose gave a small shriek. She and Mrs Watson were standing with the young nursemaid, who was wringing her hands and looking agitated. All three were talking at once.

'What the devil is going on here?' His voice cut through the chatter.

'It is Nell, Your Grace,' said Mrs Watson. 'Edith says she has a temperature and has thrown out a rash.'

'She has been a little quiet for a couple of days,' said Angel, going forward and casting her cloak onto a bench as she passed. 'Has the doctor been summoned, Edith?'

'N-no, ma'am.' The maid wrung her hands even harder. 'I was going to ask Mrs Wenlock to send someone for the doctor when we heard the carriage. Miss Nell's burning up now something terrible.'

Rose gave a sob and started for the stairs. 'I must go to her!'

'No!' Angel caught her arm. 'She might be infectious. It would be better for you to stay away from your sister until the doctor has examined her.'

'But I must see her! What…what if she does not get better?'

'She will get better,' Angel told her. 'We shall make sure of it.'

It was clear to Jason that this news, following the excitement of the evening, was too much for Rose, and she began to weep. When Mrs Watson tried to comfort her she clung to her, crying even harder.

'Take Rose to her room and look after her, if you please, Mrs Watson,' said Angel, moving towards the stairs.

The older woman hesitated. 'But what about Nell, Your Grace?'

'I will go to her. But we need to send for a doctor.' She glanced towards the footman hovering at the side of the hall. 'You will arrange it, if you please.'

The servant shifted from foot to foot and looked indecisive. Jason recognised him as one of the footmen Lavinia had hired for their stature and handsome faces rather than their intelligence. Angel was already heading up the stairs, but when the man did not move she addressed him again, more sharply.

'Send someone for the doctor, *now*!'

'I will go,' said Jason. He turned back towards the outer door, barking an order to the hapless lackey as he passed. 'Find Adams and tell him to bring my riding boots out to the stables for me!'

With that he left the hall at a run. Whatever amorous intentions he had planned for this evening must wait. It was clear that Nell needed Angel far more than he did tonight.

Chapter Eight

$\mathcal{A}$ngel sat beside Nell's bed, occasionally bathing her forehead with lavender oil. The little girl was sleeping now and Angel had sent the nursemaid away to get some rest. Silence had descended on the house and the morning light was growing stronger. There was no clock in the room, but Angel thought an hour at least must have passed since Jason had set off to fetch the doctor. The window was open and she was on the alert for sounds of an arrival. All she could do until then was wait.

It was impossible to stop her thoughts from wandering. If Nell had not been taken ill she might now be lying in Jason's bed. Would there be another chance? He had warned her the children would consume all her time. He might not forgive her for putting Nell's needs before his own.

She shook her head, refusing to believe that Jason could be so selfish, but in her tired mind the sly voice of doubt would not be silenced. After all, he had resisted having the children here. He had warned her how it would be. Perhaps he would put her aside now. Annul the marriage and find himself a duchess more suited to the life he wanted.

Perhaps she should have waited until their marriage was secure before bringing the children to live with them. Now she would not just be losing Jason, she would be losing the girls, too, and she had grown fond of them.

These dismal thoughts were interrupted by the unmistakable sound of a carriage. Moments later she heard voices. The door opened and Jason came in, followed by a stocky man who introduced himself cheerfully as Dr Granger.

'Now then, what have we here?' he said, divesting himself of his hat and gloves and coming over to the bed.

Angel was aware of Jason leaving the room, but she had no time to dwell on it. She quickly explained the symptoms as she knew them to the doctor, then stood back while he made a thorough examination of the sleeping child.

'Your Grace is concerned it might be scarlet fever?'

'That is my biggest fear, Doctor, yes. I had a mild case of it as a child.'

He pulled the sheet back up over Nell.

'I have my doubts, but we must wait a few days to be sure. You will be aware that it is highly infectious. No one should leave the house until we know for certain. I think it would be best if the rest of the household kept away from this room, too.'

'It shall be arranged. The maid Edith and I can look after Nell, if you tell me what to do.'

'Sadly there is very little we can do. Time will tell. I am not in favour of blood-letting in cases like this. Keep her temperature down and get as much liquid in her as you can. Lemonade and barley water are particular good for soothing the throat. And a little soft food or broth, if she can manage it.'

'Thank you. I am sure we can do that.'

'Very well.' He picked up his hat and gloves. 'I will call again tomorrow and see how she goes on.' He looked back at the bed. 'The child looks healthy enough, and if it is not what you fear then she should recover quickly.'

* * *

Jason spoke briefly with Dr Granger before he left and, after giving his instructions to the butler, he went to bed. The doctor had assured him there was nothing more to do now but wait.

It did not surprise him to learn that his duchess had taken charge of the sickroom. That was typical of Angel. The momentary thought that she might be doing it to avoid him occurred only to be dismissed as unworthy of him. He resolved that, in the morning, he would do whatever he could to help her.

'Well, here's a to-do.' Having brought the Duke his morning coffee, Adams was now pouring hot water into the bowl on the washstand. 'Everyone is buzzing with the news that Lady Elinor is at death's door. I left Mrs Wenlock dealing with one of the housemaids, who is in hysterics because she cannot visit her family today, you having given orders that no one is to leave the house.'

'The devil she is! I thought I had explained everything clearly enough to Langshaw before I went to bed.'

'I am sure you did, Your Grace, but with the Duchess choosing to nurse Lady Elinor herself… Well, you know what servants are like.'

'Thankfully I do not!' Jason threw back the covers. 'Dr Granger is not yet certain if it is scarlet fever, but until he *is* sure we must be cautious.'

'Of course, Your Grace. I will visit the servants' hall and do my best to make sure everyone understands that.'

Jason found only Mrs Watson at the breakfast table, and saw immediately that she was looking unusually anxious.

'This is a sad business, Your Grace. I wish that the Duchess had not taken the nursing of Lady Elinor upon herself, and with only young Edith to help her.'

'Her Grace has nieces and nephews, Mrs Watson, and she has some experience of the sickroom,' he reassured her. 'And someone must look after Rose. I hope she is not still distressed?'

'No, sir, but she is so exhausted by the events of yesterday that I left her to sleep.' She paused. 'Her Grace has instructed that we move out of the nursery wing, and I wondered if you would prefer me to take Rose back to Kent? With scarlet fever in the house...'

'The doctor is not yet certain that it is,' he replied coolly. 'Your leaving might unsettle everyone even more.'

She looked relieved. 'I am pleased to hear you say so, Your Grace. Rose would be very unhappy to leave her sister, and I would not wish to go until I know Lady Elinor is out of danger. Families are such a worry, Your Grace, are they not?'

Jason was about to reply that he knew nothing about the matter, but that was not true any longer. After having the girls at Rotherton these past weeks he realised that he had grown accustomed to them being in the house. He liked the lively atmosphere, the cushions out of place, doors left open. The sudden giggles and laughter that echoed through the stately rooms and corridors. The house felt warmer. More alive.

'Yes, they are, Mrs Watson.'

He smiled at her, acknowledging that he was anxious about the girls. And Angel, too.

His family.

After breakfast Jason busied himself in his office, but he could not settle. He was waiting for the doctor to give his judgement upon Nell's illness, as was everyone in the house.

Jason missed Angel damnably. He wanted to know how she was coping, to talk to her. To be of some use. Most of all he wanted to hold her. All he could do for the moment was to go about his business and help to calm the nerves of his household.

It was late on Sunday afternoon when Dr Granger called again. He was taken directly to the sickroom, where Angel was waiting for him.

'Well, Your Grace, Lady Elinor…' He bowed to the little girl, who was propped up against the pillows, looking pale and hollow-eyed. 'At least you are awake for me today!'

Angel liked his cheerful, no-nonsense manner and she managed a smile.

'Nell is a little better, I think, Doctor. She says her throat is very sore, but she has managed to eat a slice of bread dipped in tea this morning. And last night she ate some of the excellent lemon syllabub that Cook prepared especially for her.'

'Well, well, that is good news. We can't have you fading away to a wraith, my lady, can we?'

Angel stood back, watching, as the doctor examined Nell. He continued to talk to her, and although Nell made no reply she did give the doctor a faint, wavering smile when he took his leave. Angel followed him out of the room and they stopped on the landing for him to deliver his verdict.

'I cannot rule out scarlet fever, Your Grace, so we must not relax our guard just yet. You are keeping her isolated?'

'Yes, Doctor. Only Edith and I come into the sickroom, and we keep our distance from the rest of the household.' She saw his brows rise a little and added, 'We take all our meals in the schoolroom, and I am making use of one of the bedchambers in this wing. No one else comes any further than the top of the stairs.'

'Good, good.' He nodded. 'I hope such precautions will not be necessary for very much longer, but the child's temperature is still high, and the rash has not subsided. I will send over a draught to calm her when she grows restless. However, that sore throat worries me. You might try a sage gargle twice a day, and continue to bathe her whenever she grows too hot.' He donned his hat and began to pull on his gloves. 'I shall call again in two days, but do not hesitate to send for me if you are concerned.'

'Thank you, Dr Granger.'

He nodded, and said with a twinkle, 'A message from you at any time, day or night, will fetch me. I've no fear you will disturb me unnecessarily, ma'am!'

With that he ran lightly down the stairs, leaving Angel to return to her charge.

For the next two days Angel and Edith nursed Nell, who was by turns fractious and listless. Angel was heartened though, that the angry red rash was fading, and when Dr Granger called again he declared himself almost sure that Nell was not suffering from scarlet fever.

'However, while there is the slightest doubt we must continue with the precautions,' he warned Angel. 'No visitors, and you and the nursemaid should continue to avoid the other members of the household.'

'For how long, sir? I know Nell's sister is anxious to see her.'

'Well, now…' He stroked his chin. 'These lesser infections sometimes last no more than a week. I will call again on Saturday to see how you go on.'

With that Angel had to be satisfied. She went over to the window and saw Jason on the drive, talking with the doctor. By Saturday it would be a full week since she had spoken with the Duke and she missed him terribly. But what played most on her mind was that he might *not* be missing her.

It was gone nine o'clock when Edith came in to relieve Angel, and she went into the schoolroom to eat the meal that Cook had sent up for her. The tray was already on the table, and as she sat down she saw a folded paper pushed beneath one of the dishes.

It was a note from the Duke, asking her to meet him. Angel's throat dried as her eyes scanned the paper.

Dr Granger confirms it is safe to meet out of doors, as long as we keep our distance. When you have dined, you will find me waiting on the south lawn.

How was she to understand this? The wording was formal, even a little cold. Was he going to rebuke her? Or was it possible that he wanted her company?

'Well, you will only know once you have spoken to him,' she said aloud.

As soon as she had finished her meal Angel went down the back stairs to the garden door. This brought her out on the far side of the house, but the walk in the fresh air helped to clear her head. It was nearly midsummer, and the sun had not quite set, although it cast long shadows across the formal gardens. The air was warm and she breathed in the fragrance of the summer flowers blooming in the borders.

When she cut through the rose garden the scent was particularly heady. It was an ideal spot for a romantic assignation, she thought, before reluctantly pushing aside such a notion and walking on.

She saw Jason as soon as she reached the south lawn and her stomach flipped over.

'Dr Watson told me the fever had broken,' he said, stopping while they were still some distance apart.

'Yes.' She longed to run to him, to feel his arms about her. 'Nell is a little better. I left her sleeping.'

They began to walk, keeping a wide space between them. Too far even to reach out and touch hands.

'I was afraid you would not come,' he said. 'I know how tired you must be.'

'It is not so very bad. Edith is proving to be very capable. She is sitting with Nell now.'

He nodded. 'Dr Granger said he is hopeful that these restrictions need not last much longer.'

'He does not think it is scarlet fever, but wants to be sure.' She burst out, 'I am so sorry! I should have spoken with you before going off to look after Nell.'

'There was no time. Everything was in uproar and someone had to assume responsibility.'

'And you rode for the doctor yourself,' she said. 'That was very good of you.'

'It is nothing compared to what you have taken upon yourself.'

Angel stopped. 'I did not mean this to happen. I did not mean to abandon you for the children.'

'Hush, now. It could not be helped.'

'But this is not what you wanted!'

'I certainly did not want Nell to be ill, but I am glad that it happened at Rotherton. Granger is an excellent doctor. And he has told me he has the utmost faith in you.'

'That is very gratifying, Your Grace.' She twisted her hands together and said in a rush, 'Once Dr Granger says there is no fear of infection there is no need for you to stay at Rotherton. I am sure you have much to do elsewhere.'

* * *

Jason felt aggrieved that she could think he would walk away from his responsibilities, even though it was what he had done in the past.

'Do you think me so heartless that I would leave my daughter at such a time? I am not so uncaring.'

'I know that, but what I mean is, you must be dreadfully bored here. You might go to London. Visit your clubs. And your friends.'

He dismissed this with a wave of his hand. 'I am not bored, Angel. There is plenty here to occupy my time. And I will not leave Rotherton while Nell is sick. That is why I wanted to see you. To tell you I am here to help, in any way I can.'

'How kind of you…'

He was concerned for his daughter. That was as it should be and she was glad of it. But her spirits, dragged down by lack of sleep, slumped lower before she gave herself a mental shake. It would be foolish and very selfish to want anything more.

'Thank you, Your Grace.'

Jason heard the tired note in her voice and his heart went out to her. He wanted to cross the space between them and wrap her in his arms.

I miss you, Angel. I wish I could take you to bed and kiss away that sad look.

If only he could voice those words! It was something he had never learned—how to talk about his innermost feelings. Jason had never known his mother, and his father had discouraged displays of emotion. He had implanted in his son a belief that a nobleman should never display any sign of weakness or self-doubt.

Only once had Jason managed to overcome his natural reticence, and that had been with Lavinia. He had been infatuated, unable to see or think of anything but her happiness, her desires. He had not realised she was totally incapable of loving anyone but herself. He had laid his heart at her feet and she had trampled it into the ground. The restraint instilled in him as a boy had returned, reinforced by her cruel contempt. Now it was solid as steel. Unbreakable.

Not that Angel would want to hear such maudlin rubbish. She needed practical help from him now, and that he could give her.

'We must tempt Nell's appetite. I shall order the choicest fruits to be sent up from the glasshouses,' he told her. 'And send word to me if there is anything else you think she would like. We must get her well again.'

'Thank you, Your Grace. You are very good.'

She sounded a little surprised at this, and it pricked his conscience. He went on, 'And do not fret about Rose. Mrs Watson is looking after her, and I take her for the occasional airing in my carriage. There can be no harm in driving out, as long as we do not stop.'

'An excellent plan.'

There was still a listlessness in her voice that concerned him. He said, 'But I am keeping you from your rest. Off you go to bed now, Angel.'

She nodded. 'Goodnight, Your Grace.'

He watched her walk away, wishing he could do more, vowing that when this was over he would make it up to her. Somehow.

Over the next few days Jason was encouraged by news that Nell's condition was improving, and when Dr Granger called he declared himself satisfied that she was no longer infectious. However, he cautioned that Nell's recovery might be slow, and she would still need careful nursing.

After that, the Duchess was able to join the rest of the family for dinner each evening, but Jason was quick to note her subdued manner and the dark circles beneath her eyes. It was understandable, of course. Angel had been relieved of much of the burden, but Nell became fractious if she was away for too long and she still spent hours each day in the sickroom. She was exhausted, and Jason ruthlessly suppressed his own desires while he gave her time to recover.

As for Angel, emerging from the nursery wing after a week of constant nursing duties, she felt thoroughly dispirited by the Duke's behaviour. The easy camaraderie between them had quite disappeared. She found she could not confide in him and explain that Nell's recovery was proving quite as draining as her illness. Angel now only attended the nursery during the day, but her time was spent soothing Nell when she was tearful or trying to find ways to entertain her.

The Duke's warning that the children would consume all her time had been proved correct. Not that he reminded her of it. Whenever they met, Jason was invariably polite but he had withdrawn from her. At dinner he entertained her with light conversation, helped her to the choicest cuts and delicacies on offer and was solicitous of her care, but at the end of every evening he was keen to say goodnight, giving her the barest peck on the cheek before leaving her to go to her bed alone.

Angel wanted desperately to talk to him, but her tired brain could not find the words, and beneath it all was the fear that he might finally say what she already suspected. That he no longer wanted her for his wife.

* * *

Towards the end of the second week Nell had improved sufficiently for Mrs Watson to resume her duties in the nursery. Rose was also allowed to visit, amusing Nell with games and books as well as passing on to her all the messages and little gifts that had arrived at Rotherton from their kindly neighbours.

Angel knew she should be happy that she was no longer needed in the sickroom but, strangely, it only added to the depression that was clouding her spirits. She could not shake it off and when, a few days later, she went up to her room to change her gown she sat down at her dressing table, looking at herself in the mirror and wondering what the future might hold.

She and Jason had been getting on well until the night of the assembly. Since then they had been more like polite strangers. Not that she could share these dismal thoughts with anyone… So she put on a brave smile as she went downstairs to join the family in the garden.

The gentle breeze carried their laughter across the lawn to Angel. Mrs Watson was sitting on a chair in the shade of a large chestnut tree. Rose and Nell were on rugs at her feet and Jason was sitting beside them. He was very much at his ease with the girls now, and that at least was a good sign, thought Angel, determined to be cheerful.

As she approached the little group, Mrs Watson waved to her.

'Ah, there you are, Duchess! Would you like this chair? I can easily have another fetched.'

Angel declined, smiling. 'Thank you, but no, ma'am, I am very happy to sit on a cushion,' she said, suiting the action to the words.

This was such a lovely spot, with the lawns stretching

down to the lake that sparkled in the sunshine and everyone gathered together so comfortably. Angel felt some of the
tension easing out of her. Perhaps things were not so bleak
after all.

Jason had watched Angel as she walked across the lawn,
his insides twisting with desire. He wanted to jump up and
go to meet her, but he knew if he touched her he would not
be able to let her go, and he was uncertain of her feelings
for him. Travelling back from the assembly, everything had
seemed so right. She had been happy, laughing, but he had
barely seen her smile since that night. She looked cheerful
enough now, but there was no light in her eyes. Her face was
pale and drawn, and guilt smote him.

She had exhausted herself, looking after Nell. By marrying her so precipitately he had placed the burden of his
family on her shoulders and, being Angel, she had accepted
it without question.

Ironic, he thought bitterly. He had no doubts now that he
wanted Angel as his wife, but he was no longer sure of what
she wanted, and her happiness was paramount.

'What do you think, Duchess?' exclaimed Rose, breaking
into his thoughts. 'Papa Duke is sending us all to Brighton.'

'We are discussing it,' Jason corrected her quickly. He
glanced at Angel, but could read nothing from her face. 'You
will recall I have a villa there. It has been standing empty
since your brother's visit. I suggested Mrs Watson should
take Nell and Rose to Brighton for the rest of the summer,
rather than returning directly to Kent. A little sea bathing
will benefit Nell's recovery.' He picked a few dried leaves
off the rug. 'I think you would enjoy it too, Duchess. You
have worn yourself out with all the constant nursing. You
deserve a rest and a change of air.'

* * *

Not by the flicker of an eye did Angel react, but she felt as if a splinter of ice had lodged itself in her heart. There could be no misunderstanding his words. He was sending her away!

'It would be much better if you came too, Papa,' said Nell. 'Do come with us!'

'Alas, I have important business here that requires my attention.'

'But it cannot be more than fifty miles,' argued Rose. 'That is not too far to ride in a day. You might at least come and visit us.'

'Sadly that will not be possible. But I am sure you will all enjoy yourselves equally well without me.'

Angel listened in silence as the conversation swirled around her: the delights of Brighton in the summer, the drives they might take, the shops and libraries.

Inside, she was protesting vehemently.

Do I have no say in this? Are my wishes of no account?

Then, as if her thoughts had reached Jason, he turned to her.

'You are very quiet, Angel, what think you of the plan?'

'I think it is an excellent idea,' declared Nell happily. 'I shall take care of the Duchess and look after her, just as she looked after me!'

'Hush, Nell.' Rose was watching Angel, her blue eyes shadowed with concern. 'Her Grace might prefer a little time away from us.'

Angel could not allow the girls to think that. She said quickly, 'Nonsense! I love being with you all. How soon…? That is, when are you proposing we go to Brighton?'

'A week today,' said Jason. 'If Dr Granger approves.'

'You have everything arranged, then.' She felt brittle as glass, but summoned up a beaming smile. 'Well, well. Sea bathing, girls. How exciting.' She scrambled to her feet. 'Excuse me. I have just remembered something I need to say to Mrs Wenlock.'

She hurried away, blinking back the tears that threatened to blind her.

'Angel.' She heard Jason's voice close behind her. 'Angel, what is wrong? Is aught amiss?'

She walked faster. 'Go away, Duke. I am too angry to talk to you!'

He put his hand on her arm but she pushed him off. *'Leave me alone!'*

She almost ran towards the house, not stopping until she had reached the seclusion of her own bedchamber. It was blessedly empty and she walked quickly up and down, taking deep, shuddering breaths. She did not know if she most wanted to lash out in anger or to weep.

She had no time to decide before Jason came into the room. He closed the door. 'Are you angry with me, Angel?'

She rounded on him. 'How dare you! How *dare* you arrange everything without a word to me?'

'If you mean the visit to the coast, I told you we were merely discussing it. Nothing is settled.'

She gave a furious huff of disbelief.

'It did not sound like that to me! You are packing us all off to Brighton in a week's time. Out of your way.'

'That is nonsense.'

'Is it?' She began to stride back and forth again. 'Family life has been everything you warned it would be. Noisy, disruptive, all-consuming. Inconvenient!'

'Yes, but—'

'I am not surprised if you have had enough of us.' She threw the words over her shoulder as she continued her angry pacing. 'But why did you not talk to me first?'

'I barely see you, save at dinner,' he retorted. 'And even then our conversation consists of the merest commonplace remarks!'

'Yes.' She dashed a hand across her eyes. 'Because you c-cannot bear to be in my company!'

'That is not true.'

'You have come up with the most elegant solution, have you not?' she went on bitterly. 'Sending everyone off to Brighton is the perfect excuse to rid yourself of a wife you no longer want in your house!'

'You have that all wrong!' He stepped in front of her and caught her wrists, forcing her to stop. 'I am sending you away because…because…confound it… *I want you too much!*'

Chapter Nine

Angel was staring up at him, eyes glittering with rage. Jason was still holding her wrists and he gave them a little shake.

'Do you understand what I am saying, Angel? I want you. Too. Damned. Much.'

He struggled to get out those last words. He was painfully aware of her breasts pressing against him every time she took a ragged breath. The heat of her body, the flowery perfume she used. She was irresistible. He bent his head and captured her lips, subjecting them to a bruising kiss. For a moment Angel did not move, then she whimpered, deep in her throat. He should stop, pull away, but she confounded him by leaning into him, her mouth working against his.

She was giving him back kiss for kiss and there was no anger now, only white-hot passion. Jason swept her up into his arms and carried her across the room. They tumbled onto the bed, lost in a frenzy of kissing and caressing, tearing off the clothing that prevented them from exploring each other fully. Angel's eager, innocent responses inflamed him. The gasps of pleasure as he kissed her breasts heated his blood. She responded eagerly to his touch and stroked her hands over his skin until he was a heated mass of pure need.

It was over all too quickly. A rapid, urgent coupling when her cries mingled with his. And then they were lying together, spent and exhausted. Angel gave a long, shuddering sigh and he gathered her into his arms.

'I hurt you. I am sorry.' He rested his cheek against her hair. 'It was your first time. I should have been more gentle with you.'

'No, it was not painful. At least, not very much.' She pressed a kiss on his naked chest. 'I did not know what to expect. Certainly not such…such incredible *pleasure*.'

'Truly?'

She pushed herself away a little, so she could look at him, and he saw that her eyes were shining with happiness.

'Truly.' She blushed and hid her face in his shoulder.

Smiling, Jason pulled her close again.

'You understand that there is no going back now,' he murmured. 'Our marriage is binding. For life.'

'Are you sorry about that, Jason?'

His arms tightened around her.

'No, Angel, I am not sorry.' He dropped a kiss on her hair. 'I am not sorry at all.'

When Angel woke she found Jason propped up on one elbow and looking down at her.

'Time to get up,' he said. 'We must find the family and tell them you will not be going to the Brighton with them.'

'We could all go. I should like to see the villa.' She added daringly, 'Barnaby and Meg said it is perfect for lovers.'

She had expected Jason to laugh at her remark, but instead she had the impression he had turned to stone. His expression was inscrutable and her brow furrowed with concern.

'Jason?'

The hard look disappeared and he dropped a light kiss on her nose.

'Another time,' he said lightly. 'For the present I want to

keep you at Rotherton, all to myself.' He rolled away from her. 'Come along now, Madam Duchess, we must get dressed.'

Angel followed him off the bed and said nothing more, but she could not help thinking she had touched a raw nerve.

When the children learned that Angel would not be joining them they were disappointed, but this was overridden by their excitement for the forthcoming treat, once Dr Granger gave his full approval of the plan.

A week later, Angel and Jason waved off the rather ancient berline, which was large enough to carry Mrs Watson, Rose and Nell, as well as the maid Edith and a large quantity of baggage.

Once the carriage was out of sight Jason turned to Angel. 'Would you like to walk down to the lake with me?'

'I thought you were meeting with Mr Merrick?'

'Not for an hour yet.'

She smiled. 'Then, yes, I should like a walk.'

He pulled her hand onto his arm and they strolled off towards the lake.

'At last, we have Rotherton to ourselves!'

'Have the children been too much of an inconvenience?' she asked him.

'I have to confess there have been times when their presence has stopped me from carrying you off to bed!'

Angel blushed. Just thinking of the nights she and Jason had spent together during the past week turned her bones to water.

'However, despite that,' he went on, 'I was thinking that perhaps the children should make Rotherton their home. What do you say?'

Her heart skipped a beat. 'I say it is a wonderful idea, Jason. You know I have long thought so.'

'I would not arrange anything without consulting you.' He gave her a quick, glinting smile. 'I do not want you flying into a temper again, as you did over my suggestion you should go to Brighton.'

'Pray, do not remind me of that!'

'The quarrel did not end so very badly, though, did it?' He stopped and pulled her round into his arms. 'In fact, I think it is resolved most satisfactorily.'

Angel felt the now familiar tug of desire curling inside her, and when he bent his head to kiss her she responded eagerly.

It was several minutes before they could resume their walk, and as they did he remarked, 'Do you know, you blush most delightfully?'

'Hush!' she begged, a laugh trembling in her voice. 'You are only increasing my confusion.'

'Well, you may take comfort from the fact that there is no one near enough to see you. Which is why I have…er… "packed the children off" to Brighton, as you phrased it. Although it was not the only reason.'

Angel waited for him to continue, wondering where this was leading.

'You may recall that Rose was quite a hit at the assembly. You were in the sickroom, and may not have heard, but several posies of flowers arrived for her the following day. I thought little of it at the time, and with all the concern for Nell I forgot all about the flowers. However, Mrs Watson tells me that whenever she takes the girls into town there are always numerous young fellows wanting to speak with Rose. I even found one young rascal loitering in the lane, and was obliged to tell him he would not be welcome at the house.'

Angel chuckled. 'I am surprised it was only one young man lying in wait for her! Rose is a very pretty young lady. I doubt it will be any different in Brighton.'

'True, but there are other diversions in Brighton—the sea bathing, for one thing. And Mrs Watson has been charged to keep a close eye on her.' He swung his cane at a weed that had dared to spring up in the grass. 'She is too young to be thinking of marriage.'

'She will be eighteen in December, Jason. It is quite natural that she should be thinking of it. And she must meet young gentlemen at some time, you know.'

His jaw tightened. 'And what if she takes it into her head to elope?'

'Goodness! Why on earth should she do that?'

'Because she is her mother's daughter!' He beheaded another weed with a flick of his cane. 'It concerns me.'

'Yes, Rose is bidding fair to be a beauty, is she not?' Angel hesitated. 'That is why I think it would be better if the girls made their home at Rotherton. Between us, I am sure Mrs Watson and I could ensure that Rose is never without a chaperon.'

She said no more. It was better that Jason should take his time to consider the idea.

They strolled alongside the lake for another half-hour before turning back to the house.

'What do you propose to do with yourself today?' Jason asked her when they reached the hall.

'I have arranged to take the carriage into Middlewych at twelve, to do a little shopping, including collecting a few things for Mrs Wenlock.'

He glanced across at the clock. 'It is gone eleven now. I am sorry if I kept you.'

'Not at all.' She added shyly, 'I enjoyed it.'

'So too did I.' That glinting smile appeared again. 'Of course, we could send word that you no longer need the carriage.'

A little shock of excitement rippled through Angel at the thought, but she shook her head.

'Mr Merrick is waiting for you, Your Grace.'

'I am sure I can fob him off.'

Angel laughed at that. 'No, indeed. I would not have you neglect your duties. And your housekeeper is relying on *me* to fetch her shopping.'

'What a cruel woman you are, Duchess. Very well, then, but one final kiss before we part.'

He drew her to him, kissing her so thoroughly that she was very tempted to change her mind about going to Middlewych. At last he put her away from him, but he kept his hands on her shoulders for a moment and looked at her with narrowed eyes.

'How the devil do you expect me to concentrate on estate matters after that?' he demanded.

She blushed and stepped away from him. 'Go you about your business, sir, and let me go to mine!'

With that she hurried away up the stairs to change, but her heart was singing.

Arriving at Middlewych, Angel left the carriage at the Rotherton Arms and was soon walking along the high street with her maid. First she would fulfil Mrs Wenlock's request for cotton and thread at Chapmans, an establishment that combined the offices of a haberdasher and a draper. Having been there before, she knew that the shop would be bursting with every sort of sewing aid, from needles and thread to bolts of material. It left little space for customers, and when she reached the shop, she suggested Joan should wait for her outside.

It being a warm day, the door had been propped open, so no bell announced her entry, but Angel did not mind this.

She was not yet accustomed to the deference the townsfolk considered was due to a duchess. There was no one behind the counter, and a display of muslins, worsteds and calicos obscured Angel's view of the back of the shop, but she could hear voices, suggesting that there were ladies gathered there, waiting to be served.

Angel moved further in to inspect a pretty patterned chintz. She still could not see the other customers, but their conversation floated clearly across to her. She recognised one of the voices as that of Lady Hutton. They had met a few times, but Angel had been warned that the woman was a notorious gossip and she had not pursued the acquaintance. She was glad of it, too. She could hear the lady holding forth, blackening the character of some unfortunate creature.

'Did you see them dancing together at the assembly? So diverting! He scarcely took his eyes off her the whole time they stood up together.'

'But then, why not?' replied a second voice. 'She is quite as beautiful as her mother.'

Lady Hutton snorted. 'I must say I thought it most unbecoming.'

'Aye, quite scandalous.' Someone tittered. 'His own step-daughter, too!'

Angel froze. She stared at the brightly coloured material in her hand as the voices continued relentlessly.

'My maid saw the carriage driving by this morning.' Lady Hutton's voice again. 'The girls and their chaperon are off to Brighton, I understand.'

'Yes, that is what I heard, too. No doubt the Duchess insisted upon it. Trying to nip the affair in the bud before it gets out of hand.'

'Oh, I do not accuse His Grace of anything of *that* nature.' Lady Hutton disclaimed hastily. 'I do not say he is *enam-*

oured of the chit…merely that the girl's likeness to her late
mama must bring it all back to the poor man. Such a lovely
creature. He was devoted to her, you know. How it must
grieve him to be constantly reminded of what he has lost.'

There could be no doubt now of the subject of their conversation. Angel forced her numb fingers to release the
chintz. She must put a stop to this. But she needed to breathe
deep and compose herself before her limbs would move, and
the gossip continued on the other side of the display.

'He must be regretting his hasty wedding now.' This was
a third female, her voice full of spurious sympathy. 'Not that
his new duchess isn't a most agreeable lady, and I am sure
she is very good at keeping house, but she is no beauty, compared to his first wife…'

Angel stepped into view and the words trailed off into
silence. She kept her chin up, regarding the three women
with as much hauteur as she could manage. She recognised
them all: Lady Hutton, her widowed sister Mrs Pole, and
Mrs Nisbet—pillars of the community and stalwarts of the
church. Hypocrites, every one of them, she thought angrily.

The three ladies goggled at her, then they each dropped
a deep curtsy, muttering embarrassed greetings.

'Your Grace!' Mrs Chapman came bustling out of the
backroom, her arms full of boxes. 'Oh, dear…oh, dear. I beg
your pardon, ma'am. My serving maid has gone off somewhere or I would have come out immediately!'

'It is no matter.' Angel turned her back on the three now-
silent crones. 'I shall return later. Pray deal with your other
customers.'

Then, without a backward glance, Angel sailed out with
her head held high.

She collected Joan and they walked briskly back to the
Rotherton Arms. She had been looking forward to spend-

ing a happy hour browsing the shops, but now her pleasure was at an end. She wasted no time on the contemptible hints that Jason might be attracted to Rose. Not for one moment did she believe that. But she did believe that he was still in love with Lavinia. She remembered now his reluctance to take her to Brighton. The villa there had been a present to his first wife, and it was clearly too full of treasured memories to share with his second.

Angel fought down a painful stab of jealousy and reminded herself that Jason had never pretended to love her. Theirs was a marriage of convenience, and it was naïve of her to expect anything more. She had spent most of her four-and-twenty years living quietly in the country. She knew so little of the real world, or of men. And as for love, her one experience of that had ended in bitter disappointment and heartbreak.

'And you would do well to remember that,' she told herself. 'Don't fall in love with a man who cannot love you back. One, moreover, who prefers beauty to every other womanly quality.'

But in her heart Angel knew it was already too late.

When they reached the Rotherton Arms, Angel bespoke a private parlour. She treated her maid to a glass of lemonade and for herself she ordered coffee. It was hot and strong and she sipped it slowly while she composed herself. Gossip of any sort was abhorrent, and she was determined to forget all about it. On Sunday she would be obliged to attend church, and she had no doubt the three crones would be there. She would say nothing and ignore them, which was all the attention they deserved. For now she could only hope that they were as mortified as she was by today's encounter.

After a suitable time Angel sent Joan back to Chapmans to buy the items required by Mrs Wenlock while she remained in the private parlour. She had quite lost her appetite for shopping.

It had turned sultry by the time she returned to Rotherton. A storm was brewing. The air was very still, and heavy clouds were bubbling up on the horizon as she hurried into the house. Angel's head ached, and she sent her maid to the housekeeper with her purchases while she went to lie down in her room.

She had hoped to sleep, but her mind would not rest. She stared up at the carved tester, going over and over what she had heard in Chapmans. How ever much Angel told herself that it was mere gossip and should be ignored, she could not forget Lady Hutton's words. True, she was no beauty, like his first wife, but that did not mean Jason was unhappy with her. Or that he regretted marrying her. Angel clung to that thought.

She needed to tell someone about the encounter, and who else was there but Jason? He would most likely laugh when she told him about the gossip. He would take her in his arms and kiss away her fears. Wouldn't he?

Eventually she dozed, and woke later to find the room growing quite dark as the storm clouds gathered. She went over to her dressing table and sat down to tidy her hair. She was not at all refreshed from her sleep. She felt dull, listless. The encounter in Chapmans was still preying on her mind and she knew she would not be easy until she had spoken with Jason about it.

Downstairs, she found the butler in the Marble Hall. He was standing at the open door, looking out at the empty drive.

'Langshaw, is His Grace still with Mr Merrick in his office?'

'No, madam, they rode out to visit Holts Farm.' He glanced up at the black rain clouds and a shadow of concern flickered over his usually impassive countenance. 'We must hope they return before this storm breaks.'

Even as he finished speaking the first fat drops of rain fell, splashing on the gravel and quickly turning into a steady downpour.

'It's very likely they have taken shelter somewhere until this passes,' he went on, closing the door. 'Is there anything I can do for you, Your Grace?'

'No. No, thank you.'

Angel was disappointed that she would have to wait to see Jason, but decided against returning to her room. Better to find something to do until it was time to change for dinner.

Her first thought was the library, but when she went in the grey skies had made the room so dark and uninviting that she quickly changed her mind and wandered back to the hall. It was empty now and she walked around it, too restless to settle to anything. Then, finding herself at the door of the Yellow Salon, she went in.

The bright colours were somewhat muted by the heavy clouds and the rain, but that only seemed to enhance the colours in the portrait of the late Duchess. Angel stood before it, looking up at the beautiful creature with her golden hair and blue eyes. Lavinia gazed out over Angel's head, a faint smile curving her red lips. She was an alluring figure, confident and enchanting. Triumphant.

Angel's spirits were already low, but now they fell into an abyss. Compared to such a goddess she felt plain and insignificant. Jason could never love a woman whose talents, such as they were, amounted to an ability to run his houses. Perhaps that was why he had married her. Because she posed no threat. She would arouse in him no aching desires.

With a sob, Angel turned away and covered her face in her hands. What a timely reminder not to give her heart to a man who did not want it.

* * *

'Home at last!'

Jason cantered through the gates with his steward beside him. He had never been more glad to see Rotherton. They had already turned back when the heavens had opened, but they were still both soaked to the skin.

There was a sudden flash, and a loud clap of thunder exploded above them.

'We need to get under cover,' declared Merrick.

As they slowed to trot past the house a movement in one of the windows caught Jason's eye. Someone was in the Yellow Salon. He looked again and saw a figure, head bowed and shoulders drooping.

He stopped. 'Simon will you take Major back to the stables for me?'

'Of course.'

Jason jumped down and handed over the reins, then he ran into the house.

'Ah, you are back at last, Your Grace.' Langshaw came hurrying across the hall to greet him. 'I saw you on the drive and I have already sent word to Adams…'

'Yes, yes, I will go up in a moment.'

He thrust his hat, gloves and riding crop into the butler's hands and strode off to the Yellow Salon. Even as he opened the door he heard a sob.

'Angel! What is it? What is the matter?'

She jumped at the sound of his voice but did not turn towards him.

'N-nothing. I am being foolishly melancholy,' she said, hunting for her handkerchief. 'Forgive me. Please go away and forget you have seen me thus. I shall recover in a very short while, I promise.'

But he had already crossed the room. He took her shoulders and gently turned her around to face him.

'I cannot leave you while you are so upset.' She was still searching for her handkerchief so he pulled out his own. Thankfully it was dry, unlike most of his clothing. He handed it to her. 'Come. Sit here with me and tell me who or what has upset you.'

He guided her to the sofa and pressed her gently down, searching to say something that would cheer her.

'Are you missing the children? Is that it?' he asked, kneeling before her. 'We agreed this morning that they should live here, and if Mrs Watson will agree to come, too, then she will be able to look after them. I am sure that between us we can prevent Rose from making any undesirable acquaintances. At least until we go to London. There—does that make you happy?'

'It does, of course. I am sure it is the right decision.'

She finished wiping her eyes and then sat silently, gazing down at the crumpled handkerchief between her fingers.

'But that is not why you were crying.'

'No.'

'Then tell me. I have never seen you like this before, Angel. I want to help you.'

'You cannot help!' She jumped up and moved away from him. 'Forgive me, I am being very foolish. I overheard someone gossiping in the town.'

He watched as she walked across to the window and stared out at the rain-soaked landscape.

'And what did you hear?'

'That you are still in love with L-Lavinia.'

Jason flinched, waiting for the punch in the gut that always occurred when he heard that name. It did not come. Rage, regret and mortification were all there, but they were muted, superseded by an overwhelming need to comfort Angel.

'Not that I care for myself,' she went on, raising her chin a little. 'But the gossip made me think that perhaps we were wed too quickly. Six months was not time enough for you to grieve properly. I would quite understand if you were regretting our hasty marriage.'

He desperately wanted to deny it. The words were screaming around in his head, but he could not bring himself to say them. He had always envied the way Angel and her family could speak so freely with one another, laugh or cry, confide or argue with equal frankness. He had been reared to believe it was his duty to lead the way—not to show fear or doubt. Not to show any emotion.

He wanted to explain that it was his first marriage that he regretted, not this one, but he could not. His eyes strayed to the portrait of his first duchess. Words had come easily with Lavinia. Protestations of love and devotion had often tripped from her lips. But in her case it had never been true. And for himself…? Looking now at that beautiful face, he realised it had been a youthful passion that had soon burned itself out, only he had been too proud, too foolish, to see it. Even now he could barely admit it to himself.

And yet he must speak! Angel was distressed. She needed reassurance. She needed *him*.

He walked over and wrapped his arms about her, resting his cheek against her hair.

'I regret many things, Angel, but not marrying you,' he murmured. 'Never marrying you. You are my wife, my duchess. I would not want any other.'

Jason turned her about and put his fingers beneath her chin, gently urging her to look up at him. She was so dainty, so fragile, that he was almost overwhelmed by the need to protect her, to keep her safe. To make her happy. He kissed her eyes, tasting the salty tears on his lips before trailing kisses down her cheek. He captured her mouth and she trembled for a moment, then she was responding, giving him back kiss for kiss.

Reassured, he lifted her into his arms.

She gave a shaky laugh. 'What are you doing?'

He dropped another kiss on her mouth. 'Taking you to bed, madam.'

He saw the flash of fire her eyes before she buried her face in his shoulder.

'You are very wet.' Her voice was muffled.

'Then the sooner I am out of these clothes the better,' he declared, carrying her out of the room.

'But the servants…'

'Damn the servants!'

Jason went up the stairs two at a time, Angel held firmly in his arms. When they reached her room he somehow managed to open the door without dropping her and stepped inside. Joan, her dresser, was at the linen press and turned quickly, surprise and alarm in her face when she saw Jason.

'Leave us,' he said, kicking the door closed behind him. 'No, not this way. Go out through my room. And take Adams away with you.'

Joan stared at him. 'But he has p-prepared your bath, Your Grace!'

'Excellent. Tell him I will deal with it from here. Now, off you go.'

He waited until the woman had hurried away through the adjoining door, then lowered Angel to her feet. She was shaking and he held on to her, afraid she was too distressed to stand, but when she looked at him he saw she was laughing through her blushes.

'Poor Joan. I have never seen her so nonplussed!'

His lips twitched. 'She had best get used to it.'

He took her hand and led her through into his room, where a steaming bath stood before the fireplace.

Angel cleared her throat. 'J-just the thing if you have had a soaking in the rain,' she remarked, clearly trying to act as if this was an everyday occurrence.

'Yes, isn't it?' he replied. 'Will you help me out of my wet clothes?'

'I…um…'

He pulled her around into his arms again. 'Perhaps we should both undress,' he suggested. 'After all, I made your gown quite damp when I carried you up the stairs.' He saw her glance towards the bathtub and went on softly, 'It is large enough for the two of us. Trust me.'

She looked up at him, her eyes shadowed, and for a moment he thought she was going to make her excuses and leave. Then her fingers were unfastening the buttons of his coat and elation soared through him.

Silently they undressed one another, leaving their discarded clothes tangled together in a heap on the floor. Jason left Angel's shift until last, drawing it slowly over her head and tossing it aside. Then he gazed at her, standing naked before him.

'By heaven, but you are lovely!'

Angel's spirits soared. The blood sang in her veins and she felt like a princess, a goddess, when Jason helped her into the bath. She breathed in the heady spice-scented steam as Jason followed, folding his long limbs around hers in the confined space of the tub. He ran his finger down her breast and caressed one hard, rosy nub. She drew in a ragged breath and her body tingled. This was intimate. Exciting and daring.

'Comfortable, Duchess?'

'This is very…decadent.'

'Not at all,' he murmured, sliding his hand down her body. 'It would only be decadent if we had wine, and if the floor was strewn with rose petals for my lady to walk on.'

She closed her eyes, trembling deliciously at the idea. 'I think I should like that.'

'Next time.' He leaned forward to kiss her.

Angel gasped as his fingers slipped gently between her thighs. She moved against his hand, feeling the waves of pleasure building inside. She could feel the hard, knotted muscle beneath the skin as she gripped his shoulders. Every nerve was tingling, her breasts felt hot and full, and she pushed against him, almost swooning with the dizzying excitement of his touch.

Jason groaned. 'Damme but this tub is not big enough for all I want to do with you!'

Angel laughed, a low, seductive sound that surprised and pleased her. She might not be as beautiful as his first wife but she felt alluring, desirable. He rose and held out his hand to help her up. The sight of his glistening muscled body, his unmistakable arousal, made her throat go dry. He pulled her to her feet and her breasts tightened as they grazed his chest. Her whole body was now a mass of desire.

'Enough. I cannot wait for you a moment longer.'

Jason dragged her into his arms and Angel's body responded instantly to his kiss. Her heart was thudding so loud she was sure he must hear it as he swept her up and carried her over to the bed. Impatiently she reached out for him, pulling him down beside her and covering his freshly scented body with kisses. She explored him with her mouth, excited by the crisp smattering of hair on his chest and the smooth plane of his stomach. She had no idea if what she was doing was right, and when she heard him gasp she hesitated.

'No, no, don't stop, Angel.' He drew her back against him, his voice low and unsteady. 'You are driving me wild.'

He whispered encouragement and she followed his lead, kissing, touching and stroking, moving against him and exulting in her growing sense of power. Until he flipped her onto her back and began to kiss her. His caresses sent her body quite out of control. She writhed and twisted beneath him, weeping with the sheer pleasure of his touch.

She was almost beyond thought when he entered her and they moved together as one, slowly at first, then faster, more urgently. Something was building inside her…a wave of pleasure lifting her higher, higher. Jason shuddered and she clung to him as he gave one final thrust. The wave crested, flooding her body, and she tumbled into unconsciousness, her mind shattering into a thousand jagged pieces.

It was several moments before Angel recovered sufficiently to think coherently.

Jason was holding her. He brushed his lips against hers. 'How was that?'

'I… I hardly know… Wonderful.'

She felt him relax a little and he said quietly, 'I cannot stop the gossip, Angel, but it is not true, believe me. It is not easy for me to tell you what I feel, but I hope you will know. I hope I have shown you just how much I…value you.'

'Thank you.'

He *valued* her. The word sounded mundane, sensible. She snuggled closer, stifling a sigh. She should be content with that, but she was aware of doubt gnawing away at her.

Angel thought Jason had gone to sleep until he said suddenly, 'The portrait will be removed from the Yellow Salon. We will find something else to go in its place.'

For a moment Angel was too surprised to answer him. Then she said, 'But the whole room is designed around it.'

'Then we will redesign it. You shall decorate it as you wish.'

'Oh, that…that is so kind, so generous of you, Jason. But… where would we put the painting?'

'The long gallery, perhaps. We have family portraits there going back generations.'

'I do not think we should move it. At least not yet.'

He raised himself on one elbow and frowned at her. 'I do not understand. I found you crying in that room.'

'But not about the painting!' Angel was not prepared to admit she was jealous of Lavinia. She said gently, 'It is a portrait of the girls' mother, Jason. They have told me she was this…this glorious, beautiful creature who would descend upon them, bringing gifts or taking them out for special treats. She was their mama, and that room, the portrait, is all they have left of her.'

'They saw little enough of her in life!'

'But they have memories.'

'No. It upsets you, and I will not have that.'

His concern warmed her heart. That wayward lock of black hair had fallen across his brow and she reached up to push it back.

'It is only a painting, after all.'

He lowered his head and brushed his mouth over hers.

'You are an Angel indeed,' he murmured.

When he kissed her again her body responded instantly, pushing against him as their naked limbs tangled together.

'We should stop,' he murmured, his lips against her cheek. 'It must be almost time for dinner.'

'Oh…' Angel's eyelids fluttered as he laid a trail of kisses down her neck, then began to kiss her breasts, and she moaned softly. 'I have quite lost my appetite.'

'Well, that is most fortunate, because I have, too.'

He shifted his position and began to work his way down her body. He trailed a line of butterfly kisses over her belly before easing himself between her legs. He set to work with his tongue on the hot space between her thighs and her body arched. She clutched at his shoulders.

'Oh, Oh! What…what are you doing?'

He broke off and glanced up at her. 'I am pleasuring my duchess. Do you want me to stop?'

She saw the black fire in his eyes and her breath hitched.

'No.' She forced the word out. 'Oh, no, Jason, don't stop now!'

When Angel woke up the rain had stopped and the house was very quiet. She stretched, catlike. In fact she almost purred.

Jason was asleep beside her. She could hear his steady breathing, feel the warmth of his naked body next to her. She turned towards him and he stirred, gathering her against him before sinking back into a deep slumber.

Chapter Ten

For Angel, the summer months alone with Jason were almost idyllic. They enjoyed a delayed honeymoon at Rotherton, riding or driving out together and spending the evenings companionably indoors, talking and laughing. The nights were equally blissful. Jason was a skilful lover, and Angel tried not to be anxious. If Jason was still in love with his late wife there was nothing she could do about it. She told herself she was content to know that Jason cared about her.

She wrote to Mrs Watson, informing her that the Duke had decided to move the girls to Rotherton permanently and asking her to join them and continue as governess and companion to her charges. The widow replied by return, expressing her pleasure at the idea, and Angel set to work refurbishing the nursery wing. It needed little more than fresh paint on the walls, and she'd have everything ready by the time Mrs Watson and the girls returned to Rotherton at the beginning of September.

Angel and Jason were strolling through the gardens at Rotherton the night before the Brighton party were due to arrive when he surprised her by saying, 'It is Nell's tenth birthday this month. I think we should give her a pony. Mrs

Watson arranged for the girls to learn to ride in Kent, but only on hired hacks. They had no horses of their own.'

'An excellent idea,' she exclaimed, heartened to see Jason taking such an interest in his daughter.

'Good. I will set Thomas to work finding a suitable mount for her.'

'And we might do the same for Rose on her birthday in December,' said Angel. 'Although if we are all going to London this winter, she might wish to wait until we return.'

He turned his head to look at her. '*Are* we all going to London?'

She gave him a sunny smile. 'I very much hope so, Jason.'

His reply was nothing more than a scowl and Angel held her peace. For now. She was confident now that Rose would have her London come-out and she hoped that at some point Jason would tell her why he was so against it.

The arrival of the Brighton party brought a change to Rotherton. Jason might grumble at the noise and disorder in the house, but secretly he was delighted to have his family back with him.

His family!

Rose and Nell's joy that Rotherton would henceforth be their home pleased him greatly. He thought a little disruption a small price to pay for having them here. He was also pleased that Mrs Watson was happy to remain as their governess and chaperon. It meant that Angel need not devote all her energies to the nursery.

He was honest enough to admit that he wanted her to himself, at least some of the time.

Nell was ecstatic to be presented with a pony for her birthday, and spent a great deal each day at the stables with her new acquisition. Jason appointed one of the senior grooms to look after her and take her riding whenever he or Angel were not available.

Rose appeared to accept her sister's good fortune with equanimity and declared herself content to wait for a horse of her own. In the meantime she was happy to borrow Apollo, and to walk or drive out in the carriage with Edith beside her, if there was no other chaperon.

By October the weather was turning and Angel began to make her preparations for London. The Duke had still not agreed to Rose being presented in town, and he avoided her every attempt to discuss the subject. She could only hope that he would change his mind.

Jason had spent the morning at Home Farm, discussing plans for improvements to the drainage and new farming methods. The meeting had gone surprisingly well. As he was riding back to Rotherton he noticed the changes to the distant hills. Soon, for a few short weeks, the wooded slopes would blaze with gold. He sat up straighter in the saddle and looked about him with a satisfied eye. He had forgotten how much he loved autumn.

It was not only progress on his estates that accounted for his good mood. He was enjoying life at Rotherton far more than he had for a very long time. He had known things would change when he married Angel, but he had never expected it to be like this. He had guessed she would be a good house-keeper, but it was in bed that she surprised him. Angel was a revelation, eager to learn, and matching him for passion. Their nights together were exciting, fulfilling.

But it was even more than that, he thought now. She filled the house with laughter. He enjoyed her company, their con-versations and even their occasional disagreements. She had reunited him with his family and whenever he was away from her, for any time, he could not wait to get back. Just like today.

Jason spurred his horse on and hurried into the house just as Angel was coming down the stairs.

'Are you going out?'

Even before he had finished speaking he was laughing at himself. The answer was obvious. She was wearing a walking dress that admirably suited her slender figure and there was a straw bonnet tied with a jaunty bow covering her dark curls. When had shy little Angel in her practical gowns changed into this enchanting creature whose very presence could turn him into such an idiot?

She continued down the stairs, her eyes twinkling. 'As you see. I am going to visit Mrs Elnet in the village. Her little boy is sick and I hope a few treats will restore his appetite. I have asked Cook to include some thick broth and a jar of Gloucester Jelly. I have also added a late peach or two from the glasshouses, I am sure we can spare them.' She gestured towards the window. 'It is such a fine day I thought I might take the open carriage. I hope you do not object? I was about to send word to the stables before I go and collect the basket—'

'Yes, yes, but let me take you in my curricle.'

She looked surprised. 'But you have just this minute come in.'

And I should very much like to go out again. I shall drive you.'

Twenty minutes later they were bowling along in the Duke's curricle, pulled by a pair of handsome matched bays.

Sitting up beside Jason, Angel sighed happily. She loved driving out with Jason, especially alone like this, without even a groom.

She turned her face up to the sun. 'It is such a fine day, it might almost be summer,' she remarked.

'Make the most of it. I was at the Home Farm this morning and old Ted was telling me there is bad weather on the way.'

She chuckled. 'Country lore, Your Grace?'

'Ted is a shepherd. He has lived out of doors all his life and is rarely wrong about these things.'

'Well, the harvest is in now, is it not?'

'Yes. And it is a good one. I looked in the barns before I left the farm this morning.'

She asked him more questions and they whiled away the rest of the journey discussing his plans for the estate.

When they reached Mrs Elnet's neat little cottage Angel climbed nimbly down from the curricle.

'How long do you expect to be?' asked Jason, handing her the basket.

'No more than fifteen minutes. Twenty at most. Mrs Elnet will not wish me to be under her feet for longer than that.'

'Then I shall walk the horses on to the crossroads and return for you.'

She thanked him and watched him drive off before making her way to the cottage door.

Her visit was soon accomplished and Angel left the cottage just as the Duke's curricle bowled into sight. The bays were coming to a halt as she walked up the path, and it was then she noticed Jason was not alone.

'Rose! What on earth—?'

'It will be a crush, but it cannot be helped,' said Jason, reaching across his stepdaughter to help Angel up into the carriage.

'No, no, there is plenty of room.' Distracted, Angel squeezed herself into the remaining space on the seat. She glanced anxiously at Rose's flushed countenance. 'But what has occurred? I thought you had taken a walk with your maid.'

'She sent Edith off to visit her family in the village.' Jason ground out the words. 'I found her flirting with a damn-dashed scoundrel!'

'Kenelm Babberton is not a scoundrel!' exclaimed Rose angrily.

'He is for keeping a tryst with you.'

'What else can we do when you have banned him from calling at the house?'

Angel was surprised at the uncharacteristic vehemence of Rose's response. She saw the Duke's jaw tighten and said quickly, 'I do not understand. Who is this Mr Babberton?'

'The damned scoundrel lying in wait for Rose when her sister was still in the sickroom!'

'You met him at the assembly, Angel,' said Rose. 'Mr Burchill presented him to you before we danced together.'

Angel searched her memory. 'Ah, yes. A fresh-faced young man with a shock of curly hair. I had forgotten. Coming home that night to find Nell so ill drove almost everything from my mind. I am very sorry.'

'No need to be sorry,' Jason snapped, whipping up his team. 'I have forbidden Rose to see the fellow again!'

Rose was about to retort, but Angel gripped her hand and squeezed it hard.

'We can discuss all this when we get back,' she said firmly. 'For now, Your Grace, pray look to your driving. You frightened that poor oxcart driver by cutting in too close.'

There was more than a hint of gritted teeth when he answered her.

'I am perfectly capable of handling this team, madam!'

'Pho,' said Angel, not a whit intimidated by his sharp

retort. 'You have already jerked on the reins twice. Look to your horses, sir, before you ruin their mouths!'

Jason bit back the words that sprang to his lips. She was right, damn her. He was angry. Furious, in fact, but it would not do to take it out on the bays.

He drove on in silence, determined to give his duchess no further cause to criticise his driving. Steadying his breathing, he concentrated on getting the equipage swiftly but safely back to the stables, and by the time they approached Rotherton he had his temper under control. He drove through the gates at speed and saw from the corner of his eye that Angel was gripping the side rail. He allowed himself a moment of ignoble satisfaction and pulled up at the house with a spray of gravel.

A servant ran out to help the ladies alight, and Jason drove the curricle to the stables. He returned to find Angel had left word for him to join her in the family drawing room.

'Rose has gone up to her room,' she said, when he came in. 'The poor girl is very distressed.'

'She deserves to be. Conducting herself like a hoyden.'

Angel nodded. 'Yes, she told me you called her that. She tells me she and Mr Babberton were just talking.'

'They were arm and arm in the lane. With their heads together!'

'Is that all?'

'*All*, madam? Anyone might have seen them flirting. They were making themselves the subject of gossip!'

His anger flared again and he paced the room, unable to keep still.

'It was very wrong of her to send the maid away,' said Angel, after a moment. 'But Rose is no longer a child, Jason.

She tells me it is the first time she has met Mr Babberton alone and admits that it was imprudent.'

'Imprudent! It was damned irresponsible!'

'It was,' Angel agreed, trying to calm the situation. 'You are right, and I hope I have made it clear to Rose that concern for her welfare made you act the way you did.'

Jason nodded.

Angel went on, 'Rose is anxious about Edith, too. She thinks you will dismiss the poor girl.'

'Damme, she is right!'

'I told her I will not allow that.' Angel carried on calmly, as if he had not spoken. 'That is the way to ensure that gossip spreads. I am certain your anger frightened Edith out of her wits and she will not neglect her duties again. Besides, she was very useful when Nell was sick. I shall give her another chance.'

He said stiffly, 'You are in charge of the house servants, madam, you must do as you see fit.'

He waved a hand, dismissing the maid from his mind. But Rose was his stepdaughter, it was his duty to keep her safe. The devil of it was that he knew nothing of dealing with young people. His upbringing had not prepared him for this. He was out of his depth, like an inexperienced swimmer struggling to find a way out of stormy waters.

'Damme, I should have left the children in Kent!'

'The same thing would have happened there,' Angel told him. 'Rose is a very pretty young lady, Jason. She is bound to attract the attention of local gentlemen.' She paused. 'She says she and Mr Babberton are in love.'

'Hah! That is absurd. They are both children. They do not know their own minds.'

'She is nearly eighteen, Jason.'

Jason walked over to the window. He looked for solace

in the landscape and found none. He had made the most disastrous decisions at that age.

He said, 'Babberton is not much older.'

'Mr Babberton is one-and-twenty.'

'The fact that he was willing to meet her so clandestinely shows he is not a fit companion for her!'

'If he is in love he might well act foolishly.'

'Love—hah! If they met at the assembly then they cannot have known each other all that long. We were all confined to the house after that.'

'Only for a week.' Angel rose and crossed the room to join him at the window. 'Rose told me they met again by chance on her first outing to Rotherton. And since then they have met at the circulating library, or when Rose has been visiting her friends. Your neighbours, Jason. Surely Mr Babberton would not be allowed into their houses if he was not respectable?'

'Oh, he is very respectable.'

'Then why has he not called here?'

'Because I caught him loitering outside the house and made it clear that he was not welcome.'

'Oh.' She digested this. 'Is he so ineligible, then?'

'Not at all. His father is Lord Winchcombe, and he will inherit a very pretty little property in due course. But that is not the point.' He turned to face her. 'They are both far too young.'

'You were no older when you defied your family and married Lavinia.'

'I forbid you to mention her name!'

Angel went white and recoiled.

Jason rubbed a hand over his eyes. The reminder had caught him on the raw.

'I b-beg your pardon,' she said, while he was still struggling to speak. 'I did not realise just how much you still...'

'No!' He took a step towards her. 'Confound it, you have it all wrong!'

She retreated, shaking her head. 'We will continue this another time. Excuse me, I n-need to change.'

She almost ran to the door.

Call her back, man. Explain yourself.

But the words would not come. He was left with nothing but remorse for his own weakness.

They met again at dinner. Angel appeared to be quite herself, save that she would not meet his eyes. Rose came in, pale and subdued, and returned only monosyllabic answers to his attempts at conversation. Eventually he gave up, leaving it to Angel, Nell and Mrs Watson to keep a flow of small-talk going throughout the meal.

When dinner was finished, Jason took his obligatory glass of brandy alone in the dining room before joining the others in the family drawing room. The atmosphere was still strained, and after half an hour Mrs Watson bade Nell say goodnight before she carried her off to bed.

Rose jumped up. 'I shall go with you.'

'Would you not like to stay for a little longer?' Jason made a last attempt to make peace. 'We have not yet seen the tea tray.'

Flushing a little, Rose shook her head and hurried out of the room. Jason was left alone with his duchess, who ignored him and bent her head over her embroidery. He went across and sat down beside her on the sofa.

'I have made a mull of everything today, Angel, have I not?'

'She will come around in a few days.'

'I did not mean Rose. I meant with you.' Her head bent

lower over her work as she set another stitch and he went on, 'I beg your pardon. I did not mean to fly at you.'

'I am sure I, too, will come around.'

'I…' He sat forward, hands clasped, elbows resting on his knees. 'I apologise, Angel. You said…you *did* nothing wrong. I reacted badly when…' He drew in a deep breath. 'When you mentioned… Lavinia.'

She did not reply, but he saw her fingers hesitate before she pushed the needle into the fabric again. He forced himself to continue.

'I have never said…never spoken about her with anyone.' She had stopped sewing, he noted. 'Hearing her name brought everything back again.'

She touched his arm. 'Oh, Jason, I am very sorry. I know how hard this must be…losing someone dear to you. If it is still so painful perhaps it is best that we don't talk of it.'

He knew he should correct her. Describe the pain, the anguish of falling out of love. The humiliation of discovering that the goddess he'd worshipped was nothing but a spoiled, heartless beauty.

Then he heard his father's voice, echoing down through the years.

'Never show weakness, boy.'

He could not do it. He was the Duke. He cared too much for Angel's good opinion to confess how weak he had been to be deceived by a traitorous woman.

'Let us talk instead about Rose,' said Angel.

'Rose?'

'Yes.' Angel began to pack up her embroidery. 'She is in the throes of her first love affair. Most likely it will come to naught, if it is allowed to run its course, but you will not persuade her to believe that. Any attempt to prevent her meeting Mr Babberton could make her rebellious, but I have explained to her that no guardian would countenance an engagement before a young lady has had her come-out. I believe I can persuade her to come to London with us, if you will agree to it. After all, what girl would not want to be brought out in town, to acquire a little town bronze before she settled down?'

'I have already given you my views on taking Rose and Nell to London.'

'Yes, but that was before they made their home with us.'

The shy twinkle had returned to her eyes and the last remnants of his anger faded.

He laughed. 'You have me there, madam!'

'I am glad you think so,' she responded cheerfully. 'But, Jason, you are much better acquainted with your family now. You know they are not the onerous responsibility you expected. And think how much they would both enjoy the sights and entertainments of the capital! Think what pleasure *we* would derive from that.'

'Nonsense. I can think of nothing more tiresome!'

But his resistance was weakening, and Jason knew she had seen through his bluster.

'Then Mrs Watson or I will take them out,' she said. 'You may go about your business and we will tell you of our outings when we see you. Oh, do say they may come, Jason! Rose will go on much better in town—there will so much more to occupy her mind there.'

'And until then? What of Babberton?'

'I think you should allow her to meet him, as long as there are no more clandestine assignations. There will be ample opportunity for them to see one another in company, and Mrs Watson and I will be much more on our guard now. We must hope that if we do not oppose the friendship they will discover it is just that. And once Rose is in London there will be any number of town beaux to divert her attention.'

'There will also be any number of rakes and rogues, ready to take advantage of an heiress,' he warned.

'But when it is known she is under your care, very few will attempt to go too far.' Angel folded her embroidery and put it on the table at her elbow. 'Well, sir, do you wish to consider further? Or will you let me give Rose the good news that she and Nell are coming to London with us?'

With a sigh he threw himself back on the sofa. 'Do I have any choice?' he said.

'Of course you do, Your Grace. It is for you to decide.'

He turned to look at her, his eyes narrowed. Angel was regarding him, her hands folded in her lap and with a look of such innocence that another laugh escaped him.

'Very well, madam, it shall be as you wish. We will take the girls with us to town. It will at least remove Rose from Babberton's company for a few months.'

'And may I tell her that if, by the time we return to Rotherton, she is still of the same mind, you will not object to Mr Babberton as a suitor?'

'No, you may not.' She raised her brows at him and he released his breath in a long hiss. 'You may say that we will discuss it at that time.'

Immediately she beamed at him. 'Thank you, Jason. I shall go upstairs, and if Rose is still awake I shall tell her of the treat in store!'

With that she hurried away and Jason was left alone, wondering what had just happened. He had quite decided that Mrs Watson would bring Rose out quietly, in Kent. Certainly he had been determined she would not be presented in London, where she would hear gossip about her mother that would upset her. Old rumours would be unearthed, old scandals recalled. He had lived through it all once and had no wish to do so again. Yet it seemed that now he would have to, and to protect Rose, too.

He turned his eyes to the ceiling. Angel made so few demands upon him, no tears or tantrums. She did not wait until she was lying in his arms, beguiling him with her kisses and caresses, to ask for favours, but for all that he had given in to her on almost every point.

How the devil did she do it?

Chapter Eleven

London. Angel had only visited the capital once, for her come-out, when her parents had hired one of the smaller properties in Hanover Square for the season. Now she was on her way the Duke's neo-classical townhouse overlooking Green Park.

They reached Darvell House shortly after noon. The travelling carriage drew up at the door and Angel looked out at the building that was to be their home for the next few months.

'It is not as impressive as Spencer House,' said Jason, helping her to alight. 'Nor as large as Cleveland House, but it has a pleasant garden adjoining the park.'

'I like it very much.' Angel glanced back as the commodious berline turned the corner. 'Here come Mrs Watson with the girls now. We shall see what they think!'

An army of servants were gathered in the hall, and Angel was glad of Jason's hand on her back, supportive, comforting.

'This is Marcuss,' he said, leading her up to a stately figure standing a little apart from the liveried servants. 'He has been in charge here since before my time. Anything you need to know, just ask him.'

'Welcome to Darvell House, Your Grace.' The butler bowed low. 'Perhaps you will allow me to present your household to you?'

Reassured by the man's kindly smile, Angel nodded. The formalities were cut short by the entrance of Mrs Watson and her charges and the arrival at the door of the baggage coach.

The Duke and Duchess's personal servants came in quickly, followed by the trunks which needed to be distributed to the various bedchambers. Jason carried Angel away from the chaos to the morning room, ordering refreshments to be brought into them.

'That's better,' he said, closing the door upon the noise and bustle. 'We will stay here until everything has settled down.'

He took her pelisse and threw it over a chair while Angel looked around her at the silk-lined walls and Carrara marble chimneypiece.

'This is a very elegant apartment.'

'Aye, one of the more restrained rooms of the house. The most splendid apartments are on the first floor. Due to a number of distant relatives dying without heirs, the Darvells inherited several large fortunes, which enabled them to build this house and decorate it to impress.'

'It will certainly do that.' She bit her lip. 'I confess I find it all a little daunting.'

'No need—you will be a splendid mistress. You are the most capable woman I know.'

Angel looked away from the glow in his eyes. Capable, yes. Sensible Angeline. How she wished he would call her beautiful!

Thankfully, the servants entered at that moment with their refreshments and she did not need to reply.

After they had finished a glass of wine, and Angel had been persuaded to nibble on one of the fancy cakes brought in for their delectation, the Duke suggested it would be safe now to go upstairs.

'I should very much like to see the rooms prepared for

Rose, Nell and Mrs Watson,' she told him, as he escorted her from the room. 'I want to assure myself that they are comfortable.'

'Of course, if you wish. We shall do that first. I should have known you would put their comfort before your own.'

'But not before yours, Jason!'

She cast an anxious look at him and was reassured by his smile.

'No,' he murmured, bending to kiss her cheek. 'Not before mine.'

They set off up the grand staircase and had reached the landing when Adams appeared.

'Your Grace, if I might have a word with you...'

'Not now, Adams.' Jason waved him aside and guided Angel towards the plain staircase leading up to the second floor. 'I must admit I am curious to see the children's apartments for myself. I have not been in those rooms for years.'

'I hope you will not be disappointed. Sometimes places feel smaller once we are grown.'

'That would be an advantage. These nursery apartments always seemed too large for an only child.'

Angel's heart tightened at his bleak tone, and she tucked her hand into his arm in silent sympathy.

Mrs Watson and the girls were happily settled in their rooms, which appeared far more comfortable than Jason remembered. Angel, too, was content with the arrangements, and after agreeing with everyone that they would convene in the drawing room before dinner she was ready to see her own bedchamber.

'I shall draw up a list of things to entertain the girls,' remarked Angel, as he guided her back through the corridors and down the stairs. 'It is a pity we are nearing winter, so there will be no military reviews in the Park, but Rose is old enough to visit the theatre, and I think they would both enjoy a visit to the British Museum. Oh, and Astley's Amphitheatre, of course. You might like to join us there?'

'I might, indeed! But you must not run yourself ragged over the children. You will be presented to the ton as my duchess and you must be prepared. There may be…talk.'

'Because you did not wait a full year's mourning before marrying me?'

'Yes.'

She nodded. 'I am aware there will be gossip, but I shall not mind it if you are with me.'

He kissed her cheek. 'I shall do my best to support you.'

'I know it,' she replied, smiling at him in a way that lifted his heart. 'The Queen is not holding her drawing rooms, which is understandable while the poor King is so unwell, so at least we do not need to prepare for that ordeal! But there is Almack's.'

She stopped, and Jason sensed a reluctance to think of it. He asked gently, 'Does that evoke unpleasant memories for you?'

'Yes, a few,' she admitted. 'But Rose will want to go. I am sure the hostesses will not refuse vouchers to a young lady brought out under your aegis.' She hurried on, 'Of course it will not be necessary for you to go with us if you dislike it so.'

He did dislike it. He hated the place with its intrigues and gossip. but he would be there to look after his duchess.

'Of course I shall come with you.'

She squeezed his arm. 'Just once, then, Jason.'

Her understanding struck him like a heavy blow. He would not leave her to face the ordeal alone. And he would do all he could to protect her. Not only from the gossip but from her own unhappy memories.

'I shall accompany you whenever I can, but there are other matters that require my attention, too. The sale of the Kent house, for instance, since it is no longer required.'

'I understand that, and I shall not expect you live in my pocket, as they say. Besides, Mama is coming to town in a few weeks, and she is going to see to the purchase of gowns for myself and Rose. But, Jason, I know these events are horrendously expensive. I hope you will advise me how much I may spend?'

Jason relaxed a little. He was far happier to discuss money than the necessary social events they must attend.

He said, 'You must spend as much as you wish.' They had reached the Duchess's bedchamber and he threw open the door. 'I trust you not to ruin me!'

The happy smile she gave him before preceding him into the room warmed his heart.

'Oh!'

She had taken only a few steps inside the room and Jason, stopping beside her, felt his blood run cold.

Rich red silk still adorned the walls, but the tester bed with its satin hangings was gone, along with all the original furniture. Lavinia had turned the room into a sumptuous private boudoir. He even imagined a trace of her scent lingering in the air.

How the devil had he forgotten about this? And how the deuce was he to explain it to Angel?

Then, unexpectedly, he heard her laugh.

It is either laugh or cry, thought Angel.

The first sight of what was supposed to be her bedchamber had shocked her, but she was also amused by the dazzling brashness of the room.

All the furniture had been painted gold. The window was

framed by rich golden curtains and a large dressing table and mirror stood before it. To one side of the marble fireplace was a daybed with scrolled and fluted ends, its sides and seat deeply padded, and everything was covered in the same gold silk damask as the curtains. The red walls were hung about with mirrors, all of them in wildly ornate and gilded frames. Even the ormolu clock on the mantelshelf was flanked by a pair of Chinese vases with bronze-gilt banding.

Taking up most of the room was a bed unlike anything Angel had ever seen before. It had no canopy, and she saw the four corner supports were carved into the shape of quivers, presumably for the benefit of the Cupid perched atop the footboard and looking across at a naked goddess draped artistically across the carved and padded headboard. The space between these figures boasted fat, gold-embroidered pillows and a scarlet coverlet exquisitely embroidered in gold thread.

Angel thought it all far more suited to a courtesan—or at least what she imagined a courtesan's room might look like—than a duchess.

She heard the Duke swear quietly.

'I beg your pardon, madam. I had not… I would have thought—' A sound from the corridor made him turn. 'Adams—wait!'

He strode away to the valet, who had stopped at the door of the Duke's room.

'Is this why you wanted to speak to me?' Jason waved one hand in the direction of the bedchamber behind him.

'Yes, Your Grace.' Adams replied woodenly. 'I only discovered it when I overheard Her Grace's maid complaining to the housekeeper.'

Angel saw the valet shift his gaze to somewhere beyond Jason's shoulder.

'I am informed that it was decided, since Your Grace

made no mention of the room, that you wished it to remain as it was.'

'Remain?' Jason had lowered his voice, but every word was audible to Angel, still standing in the doorway. 'Why the devil would I want it to remain like that?'

No, thought Angel with a sigh, *you would not.*

She had known from the moment she saw the room that it had not been prepared for her. She went across to a concealed door in the wall and peeped in. Her dresser was unpacking her trunks there, a look of the utmost disapproval on her face. Joan opened her mouth to speak, but Angel shook her head and retreated as she heard Jason come back into the bedroom.

'Angel, this is not what I intended.'

Having shut the door to the dressing room, Angel ran her hand along the back of one of the gilded chairs.

'No, I am sure it is not,' she said, with admirable calm.

He raked a hand through his hair. 'I had quite forgotten. I—'

'Yes.' She put up a hand to stop him, all desire to laugh gone. 'You have no need to explain. I quite understand.'

She saw a dull flush darken his cheeks.

He went on, 'Everything should have been restored. I did not expect it to still be like this. I am very sorry, Angel.'

'It is no matter. I am sure there are plenty of other rooms I may use.'

She looked around the room again, taking in the garish luxury. This was a room for lovers, she thought. Her eyes moved from the extravagant bed to the couch and back again. She did not know whether to rage at him or to weep.

'It should have been attended to!' he exclaimed angrily. 'My people should have known what needed to be done.'

'Oh, Jason,' she said, her voice mocking. 'You married me

within six months of becoming a widower, which argues a man violently in love! If you sent no instruction to the contrary, what did you expect them to think?'

'Angel, let me explain!'

He came towards her and she flinched away. She would dissolve into tears if he touched her.

'Oh, there is no need for that,' she said with brittle cheerfulness. 'Perhaps you would have a guest room prepared for me until this is put right? In the meantime, the dressing room is very well appointed, and there is plenty of room in there for me to change into my evening gown.' She walked back to the concealed door. 'We will meet again at dinner, but we will not refer to the matter, if you please. I am sure we will both find it highly amusing. In time.'

'Angel, wait—' Jason put out his hand, but the door had already closed behind her with a snap.

'Hell and damnation!'

He walked over to the fireplace and stood staring down into the empty grate, one booted foot resting on the fender.

How could he have forgotten?

In the white-hot passion of his early years with Lavinia he had agreed she might do as she wished with his properties, not caring as long as she was happy. But this transformation had happened much later, and he had only seen it once before, when he had come to London in the weeks after she'd died. He had known immediately she had done it to punish him. She'd no longer had the power to hurt him with her lovers and her outrageous behaviour, so she had sought to do so by turning the room into something resembling a bagnio.

It had been a calculated insult to his family, and as such she would have known he would feel the desecration deeply. His mistake had been to walk away. Not by a look or a word had he revealed to his staff his displeasure. He could hardly blame them now for thinking he had wanted it left that way.

He rubbed a hand over his face. 'You have had your revenge, then, Lavinia!'

He heard a soft cough and looked up to see his valet in the doorway. There was no one Jason trusted more—and, by heaven, he needed to speak to someone!

'I am in the suds now, I fear, Adams.'

'Yes, Your Grace. Is there anything I can do?'

'Have the Blue Room prepared for the Duchess, if you would. Send out today for a new feather mattress for the bed in there, no matter what the cost. Make sure it is in place before she retires tonight.'

'Very well, Your Grace. And this room?'

Jason looked about him, grimacing at the gaudy ostentation.

'Have it all put back as it was. Everything. No, wait, you will buy a new mattress for here, too. My duchess deserves only the best!'

It was some hours until dinner. Angel knew she could not hide away in the dressing room until then, but neither did she want company. She changed from her travelling clothes into a warm day dress and matching pelisse of holly-green and went out to explore the garden. High railings separated the garden from Green Park, but shrubs and trees provided an effective screen and she was able to wander the paths without fear of being spied upon by strangers.

The Duke's obvious chagrin at finding the bedchamber just as he and his first wife had left it went some way to assuaging her anger with him. She could even find it in her heart to sympathise. It must remind him of his lost love. She recalled how he had looked when his father had died, and he'd visited Goole Park for the last time as a boy. Angel's young heart had ached for Jason as he'd tried to act normally, to do his duty. He was so brave, yet always so alone.

The crunch of footsteps on the gravel path broke into her reverie. The Duke was coming towards her.

'What can I say, Angel?' He hurried up to her and took her hands. 'I am more sorry than I can tell you for this.'

'Pray do not make yourself unhappy over it, Jason. I unders—'

'No, you don't!' he interrupted her, his grey eyes stormy, troubled.

She waited while he appeared to wrestle with himself.

Then, 'I need to tell you, if you will listen?'

'Of course.'

He nodded and fell into step beside her.

'I had not seen that room for years.'

'There was no reason for you to do so if she was sharing your bed.'

'That's just it.' His jaw tightened. 'She was not. At least, not so much after Nell was born. Lavinia kept putting it off. At first it was on the doctor's advice, then there were other excuses… Until she wanted something from me, that is. Then she would be so sweet, so loving, that I would succumb to her blandishments. Then, some years ago, I came to London unexpectedly to join her and she was here. With her lover. Or rather, one of them.'

'Oh, Jason!'

'After that, if I was obliged to come to town when Lavinia was at Darvell House, I stayed at my club and left my duchess to hold court here. My only demand for keeping up the pretence of our marriage was that neither she—nor any of her lovers—should ever enter the Duke's bedchamber.' His mouth twisted. 'I no longer had any interest in entering hers.'

Listening to the tragic tale, Angel felt a hollow ache growing inside her. 'Did,' she swallowed. 'Did my brother know of this?'

'Call it pride, if you will, but I could not bring myself to tell anyone, even Barnaby.' He shrugged. 'The ton does not expect husbands and wives to appear often together, but there were rumours.'

'I am so sorry.'

She could only guess how difficult it was for him to go into public with such gossip swirling about him. She squeezed his arm and he nodded, briefly putting his hand over hers.

They strolled on in silence for a few moments before he spoke again.

'This is a wretched start, Angel, I would not have had it so. I have ordered the room to be put back as it was in my parents' time, for now, but believe me, you may make any changes you wish to the furnishings.' He glanced down at her. 'I am sure you will exercise a little more taste.'

She was heartened by the glimmer of a smile she saw in his eyes but she made no reply. It was one thing for Jason to criticise his dead wife, quite another for her to do so.

'So now you know it all,' he said. 'I should have told you at the outset. I apologise.'

And do you still love her, Jason?

Angel could not bring herself to ask him that question.

He went on, 'The Blue Bedroom is being prepared for you now. I hope it will only be a night or two before your own bedchamber is restored.' He paused. 'Or, of course, you might share my bed.'

She stepped in front of him.

'Is that what you wish?' she asked, searching his face.

'Yes.' He pulled her into his arms. 'Oh, yes, I want that. More than anything.'

He lowered his head and kissed her then, and Angel responded.

She was his solace, his comfort. His practical duchess and that would have to suffice.

But it did not stop her yearning for more.

Once it was known the Duke and Duchess of Rotherton were in residence morning callers arrived, and the inevitable invitations. Jason was not always available to accompany Angel, but friends of her family and of the Duke were quick to make themselves known, and before long her circle of acquaintances had grown sufficiently to ensure that she rarely found herself completely amongst strangers. But she still found going into society a challenge.

She was aware that she was being compared to Jason's first wife and made no effort to try and outshine her. With her dark hair and slender figure Angel would never be a voluptuous, dazzling beauty, like Lavinia, but she refused to be daunted. She restyled her hair and bought several more gowns. The finest modistes in town were eager for custom from the new Duchess and put aside their other commissions in order to rush through her orders.

Her latest purchase had arrived in time for her to wear it to Lady Tiverton's ball. It would be the most glittering occasion, and she was very glad Jason was coming with her. Once she had changed into the gown—a daring creation in deep coral silk embroidered with gold thread—she went downstairs to join him in the drawing room while they waited for their carriage to be brought around. His look of admiration when she walked in warmed her immensely.

'You do not think it is a little too…grand?' she asked him, looking down at the brightly coloured skirts.

He grinned. 'You are a duchess—how could it be? And you have a new way of dressing your hair, too. It suits you.'

She blushed, pleased beyond measure that he had noticed.

'You do not object?' she asked shyly, putting a hand up to the topknot. 'The coiffeuse told me it is becoming all the fashion.'

'Not at all. I like it. Very fetching.' He kissed her cheek, sending a flutter of pleasure running through her from head to toe. 'Now, shall we go?'

Tiverton House was bustling when they arrived. Torches flared at the entrance and liveried servants were waiting to help guests from the carriages as they pulled up. Jason escorted Angel into the ballroom, where the dancing had already commenced.

'By heaven, this is a sad crush,' he muttered.

'That means it is a success,' replied Angel, smiling and nodding to an acquaintance. 'We need not stay too long.'

Their hostess came up and carried Angel off to meet some especial friends. This resulted in several invitations to dance, and it was not until supper time that she was free to look for the Duke. She had last seen him dancing with a dashing redhead in an emerald gown spangled with gold. Now, as she looked in vain for his tall, imposing figure, she felt a small stirring of unease. The redhead had been gazing up at him in a way that could not be described as anything other than inviting…

Then he was there, moving through the crowd towards her.

'I was looking for you,' she said, almost dizzy with relief.

'I have been doing my duty on the dance floor.'

'Yes, I too was doing my duty.' She hesitated. 'I hoped you might dance with me.'

He said, a hint of a smile in his eyes, 'Do you really wish to dance with your husband?'

'But of course!' She opened her eyes at him. 'You dance better than anyone I know.'

Flatterer!' He laughed. 'Come along then, madam. Two dances and then I shall take myself off to the card room.'

They were just leaving the dance floor when Angel spotted a familiar face in the crowd.

'Barnaby!' She hurried towards him. 'But this is a surprise! I did not know you were in town.'

'I arrived earlier today. I have an appointment tomorrow with my man of business.' He leaned forward to kiss her cheek before turning to the Duke. 'Jason.'

'Good evening, Barnaby. Is your wife with you?'

'No, alas. It is a very short visit, just a couple of days, and not worth subjecting her to the journey.' He grinned and said, colouring a little, 'She is in an...*interesting* condition. We thought it best she should rest.'

'Oh, Barnaby, how marvellous!' exclaimed Angel, beaming at him. 'I shall write tomorrow, to congratulate her.'

'Yes, do. She will be delighted to hear from you.' He looked past her. 'A new set is forming for the Scotch reel. My favourite! Will you stand up with me, Sister?'

'Why, yes, gladly.' She threw a mischievous glance at the Duke. 'Unless you wish to claim this dance, sir?'

'No, no, I am off to play cards. Go and enjoy yourself.'

'I shall join you after this dance,' Barnaby called after him as he led Angel away to take their places in the set. 'By Jove, Sis, you are looking very well. That orange gown is very stylish. You are dressing your hair differently, too.'

Angel beamed at him. Jason was not merely being polite, her looks must be improved if her brother had noticed them! They leapt and skipped their way through the reel and then

Barnaby carried her away for a glass of punch before heading off to the card room.

When he had gone Angel went back to the ballroom. The dancing had not yet recommenced, and it was more crowded than ever. As she moved between the guests she heard her name. The speaker, a woman, had her back to Angel, but she immediately recognised the red hair and the green and gold gown. It was the lady she had seen Jason dancing with earlier. The redhead was part of a little group of ladies and gentlemen, and Angel heard her say, in a voice dripping with scorn, 'I could not believe it when I heard that Rotherton had married again. How could he, after the ravishingly lovely Lavinia?'

The backs of two large gentlemen in the group provided a convenient screen for Angel. She knew she should walk on, but she could not help herself. More ladies were joining in, their disdainful voices carrying with disastrous clarity.

'I saw them dancing earlier. She is well enough, I suppose, but when one remembers his last duchess there can be no comparison.'

'Indeed! Poor Rotherton. Whatever can have possessed him to settle for such an ordinary little thing when he might have had his pick of the London beauties?'

'Perhaps that was the point.' It was the redhead again. 'Lavinia led the Duke a merry dance with her tantrums and her lovers! From what I have seen of the new duchess, *she* is unlikely to cause him any heartache...'

Angel made herself move away. She could no longer hear them, but she could not forget their words. She moved aimlessly through the crowd, her thoughts bleak. How drab and dull she must look, compared to the late duchess. It would be no wonder if Jason began to regret that he had married her.

'There you are.'

The Duke's voice at her shoulder made her jump.

'Oh… Jason. I could not see you!'

Well, I am here now, and I have come to take you down to supper,' he said, pulling her hand onto his sleeve.

'If you do not object, I would much rather leave.'

He gave her a searching look. 'You are pale. Has anyone upset you?'

'Of course not. I am a little tired, that is all.'

He stopped. 'Would you really like me to take you home?'

She hesitated and he went on, with a smile.

'Pray do not say you want to stay for my sake. I have had quite enough society for one night.'

'Then, yes, please, Jason. I should like to go now.'

In a very short while they were in their carriage, bowling through the darkened streets towards Darvell House, and Angel could no longer ignore the question that was lodged in her head.

'Who was the lady you were dancing with, Jason? A pretty matron with red hair.'

'Mrs Sharrow. An acquaintance, merely. Lavinia knew her better than I. Why do you ask?'

'Oh.' She waved an airy hand. 'I merely wondered who she was.'

He pulled her closer. 'Jealous?'

With his arm around her, and that teasing note in his voice, she felt much better. Well enough to chuckle.

'Not at all.'

'Good. You have no need to be, you know.'

'No, I know that.'

But the hollowness inside her persisted.

She was not jealous of any *living* rival.

Angel was her usual smiling self at breakfast, but as Jason drove to the city to see his man of business he was haunted by the sadness he had seen in her face at Tiverton House last night. She had told him she was tired, but she had seemed more out of spirits—which was certainly not warranted by the occasion. He had seen the admiring glances she had received, accepted any number of compliments on her behalf, and knew that she deserved them all. She had been a hit, but she was so modest, so unassuming, that perhaps she did not realise it.

'Damnation, man, you know women like to be told these things!'

His outburst surprised his groom, sitting beside him in the curricle, and he felt obliged to explain.

'I was talking to myself, Ben. You know I've never been one for making pretty speeches, but I think perhaps I need to make the attempt with the Duchess.'

'Women's like horses, Your Grace,' opined the groom, sagely. 'Unpredictable, but most of 'em respond to a kind word. Although, if you'll forgive my saying so, sir, I have always found Her Grace very easy to talk to.'

'You have?' Jason threw a frowning look at his groom. 'I didn't know that.'

'Aye.' The groom sat back, folding his arms across his chest. 'She came to the stables regularly while we was at Rotherton, to see that horse of hers and to talk with the stable hands. Very keen that the younger ones should learn their letters, she is, and to make sure everyone has comfortable quarters.'

Jason gave a bark of laughter. 'I am sure Crick has something to say about that! He's not one to endure anyone interfering in his domain.'

'Well, that's the thing, Your Grace,' said Ben, rubbing his chin. 'Old Thomas don't mind it at all. He won't hear a word against the new mistress—especially since she had the roof mended and new windows put in the loft.'

Jason digested this. Angel had asked who maintained the outbuildings at Rotherton. He had told her to speak with Simon and then forgotten all about it.

'In fact,' Ben continued, 'the stable lads think the world of her. She has a pleasant word for everyone, and time to listen to their worries.'

Jason felt a stab of conscience that he had not known of this. He had told Angel to run his houses as she wished, and she did, not bothering him with details. But confound it, he *wanted* to be bothered. Clearly he should spend more time discussing these things with his duchess.

His business with Telford was soon completed and Jason drove directly back to Darvell House. He was impatient to see Angel, to talk to her. To make sure she realised how proud he was of her, and how well she had been received last night.

He drove to the front door and jumped down, leaving Ben to take the curricle away to the stables. He ran up the steps and hurried inside just as an elegant figure in a dove-grey suit and a curly brimmed beaver hat was strolling across the hall.

Jason stopped, his mouth twisting with dislike. 'Knowsley! What the devil are you doing here?'

'Dear me, Cousin, you are devilish impolite today.'

'Is there any reason why I should be polite to you?' Jason retorted. A glance showed him that the footman had closed the door and disappeared, but he still lowered his voice. 'I say again: what is your business here?'

Knowsley waved one hand towards the morning room. 'I have been paying my respects to your new duchess.'

Jason stiffened. 'The devil you have!'

'Yes. As behoves a close relative and…er…your heir.'

Jason's temper flared at the smug look on that handsome face but he curbed it, schooling his own features into a look of indifference.

He said coldly, 'Then, if you are done here, I will not detain you.'

Jason went to pass him, but his cousin raised his elegant silver-topped cane and barred his way.

'Do you not want to hear my verdict on your new bride? Can't hold a candle to Lavinia, of course, but pretty enough. I don't doubt she'll fulfil her purpose and give you a son to cut me out.'

Jason snatched the cane and Knowsley stepped back quickly, holding up his hands and laughing.

'No, no, Rotherton, don't call me out. That would cause the sort of scandal you'd most abhor! I meant no harm, I assure you.'

'Then you had best leave now.' He thrust the cane back at Knowsley and turned away.

At that moment there was a burst of girlish laughter from the landing, and Jason swung back to see Rose and Nell at the top of the stairs. What damned ill timing!

Knowsley had dropped his cane but he quickly scooped it up and was already walking towards the stairs.

'Lady Elinor and Miss Haringey, if I am not mistaken,' he drawled, touching his hat. 'Good afternoon to you. I am Tobias Knowsley, your cousin.' He threw a mocking glance at Jason. 'Well, to be accurate, I am the Duke's cousin—but that makes us all somehow related, what?'

The girls had reached the hall by this time, and he bowed first of all to Nell, who was regarding him silently.

'Lady Elinor.'

He turned to Rose.

'Miss Haringey.'

Jason noted the searching look, the faint hesitation before he inclined his head to her. 'You are very like your mother.'

'Why, thank you, Mr Knowsley.'

'No, no, I will not have such formality! You must call me Toby. I hope we are all going to be great friends.'

This jovial declaration received nothing more than uncertain smiles from the young ladies, and Jason stepped up, determined to put an end to this charade.

'Rose, Nell, you will find the Duchess in the morning room. Off you go now. I will show Mr Knowsley out.'

'Charming girls,' observed Knowsley, when they had run off. 'I look forward to our being better acquainted.'

'I will not hear of it.'

'No? You may scoff, Duke, but I am quite sincere. I am of an age now to understand the importance of family.'

'You will stay away from this house, Knowsley, and from my family. Do you hear me?'

'Oh, yes,' he said softly. 'I hear you, Cousin.'

He touched his hat and Jason watched him saunter out, not at all convinced by his cousin's sober tone and demeanour.

Jason went into the morning room, where he found Angel, Rose and Nell about to begin a game of spillikins. He was invited to join in, but declined.

'I shall sit and watch, if I may.'

'I do not think it will take long,' said Rose. 'Angel is very good at this!'

He sat down on one of the sofas to observe the play. How long had it been since this house had echoed to the sound of so much laughter? How long had he lived such a lonely life?

It was not just since Lavinia's death. It had started years

before that. When Nell was born, in fact. Lavinia had hated carrying a child, bemoaning the damage to her figure, but it had taken him a long time to realise why no more children were forthcoming. And even then she had assured him that the poisons and potions she used had been necessary to protect her own health.

He had believed her at first, so besotted had he been. But not any more.

A cheer roused him from his dismal reflections. The game was over, and Rose and Nell were congratulating Angel.

'Do let us play again,' cried Nell. 'Then Papa Duke can join in!'

Angel laughed and shook her head. 'I think not, I want a little time to savour my victory. Besides, it is very nearly time for your walk.'

Both girls protested but after a glance at Jason Angel was adamant. 'We can play again before dinner, if you wish, but off you go now and find Mrs Watson.'

She shepherded them out of the door and closed it with an exaggerated sigh.

Jason smiled. 'You are very good with them.'

'They are delightful,' she said, coming to sit beside him. 'Mrs Watson has brought them up very well. She is truly fond of them.'

'What did Toby Knowsley want?'

She blinked at the sudden change of subject. 'To introduce himself. He was most apologetic for calling when you were not at home, but thought, as your cousin, there would be no objection.'

'You saw him alone?'

'Why, yes. Was I wrong to do so?'

She was looking up at him, her dark eyes so innocent that Jason felt himself relaxing.

'No, but I would not want him running free in this house.'

'You do not like him? He appeared to be very pleasant.'

'As a weasel may appear harmless!' She frowned and he added, bitterly, 'Knowsley was Lavinia's lover.'

Chapter Twelve

Angel gasped. 'I—I cannot believe it!'

'Why not? My cousin is handsome, charming and sociable. He has a great deal of address.' Jason scowled at the carpet. 'He is everything that I am not!'

Angel did not agree with him, but she was still taking in what he had told her about Mr Knowsley.

'Lovers!' she said. 'B-but how? I mean why did you…'

'Why did I not put a stop to it?' He shrugged. 'He was not the first. I had given up caring by the time I discovered the truth.'

Angel felt sick at heart for Jason. She wanted to take him in her arms and kiss away the darkness she saw in his face. Instead she put her hand on his sleeve.

'I think perhaps you cared too much.'

'No. Not about them. I cared only for my family's name.'

She said quietly, 'I do not believe that, Jason.'

'No?' His lip curled. 'While she was discreet, I was prepared to put up with her infidelities.'

'That must have been very painful for you.'

'It was not so bad. After I discovered the truth about her and my cousin we lived separate lives.'

Angel bit her lip, thinking of the gilded boudoir upstairs. He said, as if reading her mind, 'She redecorated that bedroom to spite me, but I do not believe she used it often. There are servants here who have been with the family since before I was born. I have no doubt they made it clear what they thought of her behaviour.' A pause. 'The villa in Brighton, however, was another matter.'

'Is that why you will not go there?'

She read the answer in his face and her hands clenched into tight fists as she fought down her anger at his own cousin and the spoiled woman who had caused him so much pain.

'I will instruct the servants to tell Mr Knowsley we are not at home if he calls again. But if we meet in public...?'

'A nod will suffice. You need not acknowledge him.' He sighed. 'The devil of it is that now he has met Rose. He was very taken with her.'

'Do you think that will be a problem?'

He shrugged. 'He might think she is like her mother.'

Angel shook her head. 'Rose is not like that at all. She is a very kind, sweet-natured girl. But, Jason, I do not wish to spoil her memories of her mother. Would you object if we do not tell her anything of your cousin, save that you do not get on?'

'If you think that will suffice.'

'I hope so. We can tell Mrs Watson the same. We will none of us pursue Mr Knowsley's acquaintance.'

He nodded, the darkness lifting from his countenance.

'Are you sure you would not like Mrs Watson to take the girls back to Kent?' he said, coming back towards her. 'I have not yet sold the house.'

'No! They are your family, Jason. They are our responsibility. Also, I feel Rose will be much safer under our eye.'

'Bless you.' He pulled her to her feet and into his arms. 'Dearest Angel, would you have married me if you had known we would have such problems?'

'Of course. You are…' *You are my whole world.* 'You are a duke, sir. That outweighs everything!'

It was not what she wanted to tell him, but she had her pride, too. He had never sought her love and she could not bear to have him reject it.

It took a full week for the servants to return the Duchess's bedchamber to its former order, and even in that short time London life became even busier than ever. More families arrived in town for the winter and the number of invitations increased, not only for Her Grace the Duchess but also for Rose, who was quickly making friends amongst other young debutantes.

There might be whispers about her mother, but if the Duke of Rotherton and his new duchess supported the lovely Miss Haringey, then fond mamas with daughters to launch into society saw every advantage in befriending her. Angel and Mrs Watson accompanied Rose whenever they could, but they also allowed her to attend parties of pleasure with only her maid to escort her, if they were sure a responsible chaperon was present.

When Jason was dealing with business matters Angel had her household duties, plus morning visits and charitable causes to occupy the days, and she was always careful to hide her disappointment if he could not accompany her to the routs, soirées and parties that filled her evenings.

It was not fashionable for a husband and wife to be constantly in each other's company. Theirs was a marriage of convenience and Angel could never forget it. She did not want Jason to think she could not manage quite well without him, although in truth she found little amusement in going out alone.

* * *

Jason, however, was wishing that his wife would show just a little less independence. If he was engaged to dine out with friends he could not help but wonder what Angel was doing. He began to drop in at the parties and balls she attended, arriving late but always in time to claim a dance with his wife and accompany her back to Darvell House.

Coming in earlier than usual one evening, he was disappointed to discover that Angel had already gone out.

'Her Grace has escorted Miss Haringey to an engagement,' Marcuss informed him. 'Mrs Watson being a trifle under the weather.'

'Oh, yes. The Westberes' evening party. I recall they were talking about it at breakfast.'

Nodding, he went on to his room. He knew the hosts slightly. They had come to town with three daughters to marry off and were forever inviting other debutantes and eligible bachelors to their evening parties. Jason was sure it would be a dull affair, but he missed Angel and decided he would change and go there rather than wait at home for her to return.

He arrived at the Westberes' just before supper and went in search of Angel, whom he found sitting with a group of matrons at one side of the ballroom. His arrival caused a stir amongst the ladies—as he remarked when he eventually managed to draw Angel away.

'I thought they would never stop talking,' he muttered. 'I was hoping to dance with you, but it is too late for that now.'

'You cannot blame them,' she said, a laugh in her voice. 'Dukes are something of a rarity. I am not sure any of them has met one before. It will give them something to talk of for weeks to come, I should imagine.'

'You speak as if I was a freak!' He grinned down at her.

He added, looking around the room, 'I suppose Rose is on the dance floor?'

'Yes, but there is no need for us to wait for her. She is having supper with Mrs Westbere.'

'Better and better. I shall have you to myself!'

Angel went down to supper in the best of spirits. They found a quiet corner, and although any number of eyes were turned upon them, no one was brave enough to interrupt their *tête-à-tête*. Angel enjoyed herself immensely, and she was surprised when she heard the musicians striking up again.

'Goodness, the dancing is recommencing. I did not realise we had been here so long.' She laughed and looked around her, saying guiltily, 'Nearly everyone else has gone upstairs.'

Jason rose and offered her his arm. 'And I suppose we must join them.'

Together they went back to the ballroom, where a lively reel was in progress. The throng was too great for Angel to see over the heads of those watching the dancing, but the Duke had no such problem and she was glad to have his tall, imposing presence at her side to carve a path through the crowd.

When he stopped, Angel glanced up and saw that he was staring at the dancers.

'What is it?' she asked. 'Jason?'

'Is this why you were happy to keep me at supper, madam?'

He looked down at her, all trace of humour gone from his eyes. They were now as hard as slate.

'What is it?' she asked him again. 'What can you see?'

He said grimly, 'My cousin is here, and he is dancing with Rose.'

A chill ran through Angel. 'Mr Knowsley? I had not seen him…'

'You were too busy enjoying yourself!'

She flushed. 'That is unfair, Jason. I did not know he was here.'

'Rose is your responsibility tonight,' he retorted. 'It is your duty to make sure she is safe.'

'She is hardly likely to come to harm dancing a reel!'

She tried to pull her hand free but he clamped it to his arm.

'Oh, no, madam. You will not disappear now. We need to sort this out as soon as the music ends!'

'That is what I intend to do!' she retorted. 'Pray remember that we decided Rose need be told nothing about Mr Knowsley. You cannot blame her for standing up with him.'

'I do not blame her. I blame *you*, madam!'

Angel bit her lip. She accompanied Jason through the crowd, ready to meet Rose and Mr Knowsley when they finally walked off the floor. Rose was looking flushed and happy after the exertion of the dance, and when she saw the Duke she beamed at him.

'Your Grace! I did not think you would come tonight.'

Her greeting was quite unaffected. Angel thought that should tell Jason that Rose was innocent of any intrigue, but she answered quickly, before he could speak.

'Nor I. Is it not the most delightful surprise?'

She smiled up at him, holding her breath and praying that he would not lose his temper.

'No, I had not planned it.' He nodded to his cousin. 'Perhaps you will give me a few moments of your time.'

Toby Knowsley was looking wary, but he could hardly refuse the Duke.

Angel stepped across to Rose and linked arms with her. 'Yes, let us leave the gentlemen to their talk and we will go and sit down. I vow you have been so busy this evening I have scarce seen you!'

She led Rose away from the dance floor, heading for the side of the room, away from the crowd.

'Is the Duke angry with me?' Rose asked her, when they had found two empty chairs in a window embrasure.

'Now, what makes you think that?

'He was frowning so heavily when he looked at me. He looked most displeased.'

'Not with you, my dear. He had not expected to see you dancing with his cousin, that is all.' Angel took a moment to rearrange her skirts while she chose her next words. 'The Duke would not wish it known, but he, he does not quite approve of Mr Knowsley. His manners are not those of a gentleman.'

'Oh.' Rose digested this. 'He is always very friendly, but I have never felt quite at ease with him.'

'You have met him before tonight, then?'

'Oh, yes. We have met several times, in various shops, and in the library, for instance. But now I think of it, it has always been when you or Mrs Watson were absent. He was at Almack's last week, when Mrs Westbere took me there with her daughters. I only stood up with him to be polite, because he said we were as good as cousins.'

'You do not like him?'

Rose shook her head. 'No. Jane Westbere thinks he is very handsome and charming, but he stares at one so.'

Angel hid her relief.

'You are free to refuse him the next time he asks you to dance,' she said, patting Rose's hand. Although she thought it was unlikely Toby Knowsley would ask again, after this evening.

They remained at the side of the room until Rose's next partner came looking for her. Since it was young Mr Westbere, the son of the house, Angel sent her off with a smile, but she herself moved closer to the dance floor, from where she could do her duty as chaperon.

She was still there when Jason came back into the ballroom. She saw him making his way towards her. In repose, his expression was naturally reserved, even a little forbidding, and it was impossible to read his mood until he was much closer. Then she saw the cold, angry light in his eyes.

'Where is Mr Knowsley?' she asked him.

'Gone.' He noticed her anxious look and added, 'We did not come to blows. I merely warned him what would happen if he came near any of my family again.'

'I am glad.' She took his arm. 'Let us walk a little. Rose will come to no harm while she is dancing with Mr Westbere.'

She cast a glance up at him as they began to stroll about the room.

'I beg your pardon. I shall not forget my responsibilities again this evening.'

'So that rankled, did it? It was as much my fault, for carrying you off to supper with me.'

She acknowledged this with a slight nod, much encouraged. Her husband was not one to readily admit he was at fault.

'Rose has told me she does not much like Mr Knowsley.'

'Then she is a better judge of character than I thought.'

'You hardly know her, Jason.' She hesitated. 'I told her you did not approve of Mr Knowsley's manners.'

'An understatement!'

'I know, but I believe it was enough. Rose knows now you will not be offended if she refuses to dance with him again.'

'Thank you.' He looked down at her, his face relaxing into a rueful smile. 'I am not yet experienced in the role of guardian.'

She squeezed his arm. 'It is only right that you are cautious where your ward is concerned.'

He looked over her head. 'I shall be more than cautious where Tobias Knowsley is concerned!'

A few days later, at the beginning of November, Lady Goole arrived at Darvell House.

'I can stay only a few weeks,' she told Angel, when she joined her to take tea in the morning room. 'Meg is increasing—but you know that. She told me you saw Barnaby when he was in town recently. They are coming to Goole Park for Christmas, because Barnaby wants the baby to be born there.' As Angel handed her a cup of tea she said, 'I was wondering, perhaps, if *you* had anything to tell me, my dear...?'

'No, Mama. Not yet.' Angel felt a blush stealing to her cheeks and she busied herself filling her own cup.

'Ah, well, it is early days.'

Angel quickly changed the subject. 'I have put you in the Blue Room, Mama. It overlooks the park, so it is blissfully quiet at night, and the bed is very comfortable.' She added airily, 'It has a new feather mattress.'

'Goodness, I hope you did not go to such an expense just for me!' exclaimed Lady Goole.

Angel shook her head, but did not explain. She had no wish to tell her mother just how that particular purchase had come about.

She said, 'Mrs Watson has taken Rose and Nell on an outing to Green Park, but they will be back in time to see you before dinner.'

'Ah. I hope the children are not taking up too much of your time?'

'Not at all. They are very well behaved. And Rose is nearly eighteen. She is very good company.'

'And the Duke?' Lady Goole sipped at her tea. 'Is he good company?'

'Why, yes. He is very attentive. Although I do not think he is comfortable going into society. There are too many reminders of his first wife.'

'Ah.'

'People make…comparisons. Between me and the late Duchess.'

'That is understandable, my dear. You must not let it upset you.'

'I do not. Well, not much.' Angel bit her lip. 'But… I cannot bring myself to like the late Duchess. Her behaviour…' She tailed off, unwilling to confide everything to Mama. 'It is not merely jealousy. I cannot like the way she convinced Jason it would best to set her daughters up in their own establishment.'

'You must remember, my dear, that Jason was brought up in very much the same way,' reasoned Lady Goole. 'His parents were rarely at home with him. He would see nothing wrong in it. But all that has changed now, I believe?'

'Why, yes. We are all pleased with the arrangement.'

'And you still have Mrs Watson to look after the children.' Her mother nodded. 'That means you have more time for your husband when he needs you.'

'Yes.'

Angel hoped she did not sound unsure about that. She knew Jason wanted her, that he found comfort in her arms. And she was useful, but did he really *need* her?

Lady Goole was watching her closely. 'Are you regretting marrying the Duke, Angeline?'

'No. Oh, no. It is just… I wonder if *he* regrets marrying *me.*'

'Oh, my poor girl! Did he tell you he was in love with you?'

'No, of course not. I never thought, never expected…'

Lady Goole put down her teacup. She said delicately, 'I hope he is not unkind?'

'No, no! Jason is the very kindest of men. And attentive. Generous, too.'

'Does he have a mistress? Oh, do not colour up so, my dear. That would not be unusual for a man such as Rotherton.'

'I know that, but I am almost sure he does not have a mistress.' Angel plucked at her skirts and said, in a burst of confidence, 'I think he is still in love with his first wife.'

'I see.' Lady Goole sighed and shook her head at her daughter. 'Life is not a fairy tale, Angeline. You have an exemplary husband. Many women would envy you your good fortune. Give Jason time, my dear. It has been just over a year since his wife's untimely death. Let him grieve and mourn. As his wife, you are well placed to win his affections when he is ready. In the meantime you must show the Duke that you are the perfect partner for him!'

She gave Angel a smile of reassurance and drained her cup.

'Now, tomorrow we shall go shopping. I need to buy some new gowns to take home with me, and I am sure you could do with more.'

'Oh, no, Mama, I have already purchased any number of gowns!'

'Nonsense. A duchess can never have too many. We shall visit the finest modistes in London. Oh, my dear, I am so looking forward to going out and about with you! We must make a plan. But first let us have more tea!'

With Lady Goole in London, Angeline found her days became very full indeed. There were trips to silk warehouses, plus visits to linen drapers, modistes, mantuamakers and hosiers. Angel might protest that she could not possibly wear so many new clothes, but her mama was adamant.

'A duchess attracts attention every time she ventures out. You will be scrutinised from head to toe. Every detail will be noted and discussed.'

Angel gave a wry smile. 'I think that happens already.'

'So you must always look your best. Now, there is a very good shawl and linen warehouse in Fleet Street that we must visit, but because of its proximity to the prison I think we should take along a second footman when we go, don't you?'

It was not only shopping that kept the ladies busy. Lady Goole was anxious to be out and about as much as possible, and Angeline accepted far more invitations than she had done prior to her mama's visit.

Thankfully, she was growing accustomed to hearing talk of Lavinia. Without exception it was agreed that for beauty she had no equal, but Angel soon discovered that not everyone had been enamoured of the late duchess. There were rumours of excessive gambling, even hints of her numerous lovers, although Angel already knew about that. What she had not heard before was that Lavinia had been high-handed and demanding with those she considered inferior—until Joan informed her of it.

'Not that one should always believe everything one hears below stairs,' added Joan, after she had passed on yet another instance of the late Duchess's petty tyranny. 'But I have been told enough, and from several sources, to believe at least *some* of it must be true. Don't you think so, Your Grace?'

'Very possibly,' Angel agreed. 'But we will not repeat any of this outside this room.'

'Oh, no, indeed, ma'am. I wouldn't dream of it,' replied Joan, much affronted. 'I just thought you should know, seeing as how you might be thinking your predecessor was such a paragon.'

Touched by Joan's loyalty, Angel thanked her and said they should now put it from their minds. However, she could not forget. It saddened her to think Jason still worshipped such a flawed goddess.

When an invitation arrived from the Countess of Cherston, Angel took it immediately to her mother.

'She has invited us to her masquerade tomorrow night, Mama. She apologises for the late notice, but says the card slipped down behind her desk and she has just this minute found it! I do not think it would be suitable for Rose, but I should very much like to go. I have never been to a masked ball. What say you?'

Lady Goole tapped her lip. 'These affairs often turn a little rowdy after midnight…'

'We need not stay late, Mama. And there could be no harm in it if you were to come with me.'

Lady Goole sighed. 'It is a long time since I attended a masquerade. But where would we get costumes at this late date?'

'Do we need them? I believe many people simply wear a domino over their evening clothes.'

'Yes, it would be easy enough to purchase dominos, I suppose. And masks.' She laughed. 'What fun it would be!'

Before making a final decision, Angel asked Jason for his opinion.

'I have never been to a proper masquerade,' she told him. 'Mama held one at Goole Park once, but it was only for our neighbours and I recognised everyone immediately, despite their masks.'

'How disappointing! Then go, if you wish. I have not

seen Cherston for years, but I recall he was ever a dull dog and very respectable. I have no objection if Lady Goole is going with you.'

'Would you not like to come?'

He grimaced. 'Not unless you especially wish it. And besides, Westbere has invited me to join him for a dinner at Boodle's tomorrow. I thought it would be politic to attend.'

She chuckled. 'Yes, you owe him that after we left their party so precipitately. Very well, Mama and I will go, and I shall tell you all about it when we get back!'

Jason watched her trip away, thinking that if he hadn't accepted Westbere's invitation then he might well have gone with her, just to share her pleasure in the novelty.

He frowned. This growing desire to be in his wife's company was concerning. Angel might be nothing like his first wife, but he still did not want to lose his head over her!

No, he thought, setting off to join Westbere the following evening. Far better that he did not follow her everywhere.

Besides, there was no need. Angel would have Lady Goole on hand to look after her.

Angel adjusted the hood of her domino and checked that her half-mask was in place before stepping down from the coach. She accompanied her mother into the house, where all was bustle and noise. There were a number of black dominos on display in the ballroom, but these only enhanced the colourful and garish costumes of most of the guests.

'Heavens, I had forgotten how abandoned these affairs can become!' exclaimed Lady Goole. 'But then, I only ever attended masquerades with your father. Perhaps you should have pressed Rotherton to come with us.'

'Yes, perhaps.' Angel quickly moved back as a shepherd

and shepherdess barged past her, laughing immoderately. 'I do not think we will remain here long.'

'No, I agree. We shall certainly leave before midnight,' said her mother. 'Until then, we must stay together.'

But this was not possible. They were pressed to dance and, as Lady Goole remarked, it would have been extremely ill-humoured of them not to join in.

'We will meet here, by the door, at a quarter to twelve,' she assured Angel, before being whisked away by a jovial Falstaff.

The room was still cool enough to make skipping around in an enveloping domino possible, and once on the dance floor Angel began to enjoy herself. Everyone was very jolly, if a little loud, but so happy and good-natured that she had no qualms about standing up with strangers.

As she glanced at the large ormolu clock on the mantelshelf she felt this was like a fairy tale, where she must be gone by midnight.

At Boodle's the dinner was good, but Jason found himself one of the younger members of the party. Talk meandered between politics and sport, but when the gentlemen began to discuss the merits of various blends of snuff his mind began to wander. Only to be brought back when he suddenly heard a name he recognised.

'I've no doubt there will be some of the more exotic mixtures available at the Cherstons' ball tonight,' remarked his host. 'I understand the Earl thinks himself something of a connoisseur, but it's all an affectation. He himself favours taking snuff from the wrist of his latest paramour.'

'Cherston?' Jason's brows went up. 'I thought he disapproved of mistresses—or has he changed now he is in his dotage?'

'Good God, Your Grace, where have you been?' laughed someone further down the table. 'The old Earl has been dead these two years or more. No, I mean his son. A very rakish fellow. And his wife is no better.'

Jason picked up his glass. He was out of touch. His visits to town had been purely for business in recent years, and while Lavinia had been alive he had made a point of avoiding their friends and the gossip pages of the newspapers.

He said casually, 'What exactly is happening tonight?'

'They are hosting a masquerade,' Westbere told him.

The man beside him laughed. 'That's what they call it! But knowing Cherston and that trollop he married there'll be plenty of high-flyers present, and any number of young bucks. It will be a dashed romp by midnight, mark my words!'

Jason pushed back his chair.

'Anything wrong, your Grace?' enquired his host.

'No, no,' Jason replied, trying to remain calm. 'Just remembered something I need to do tonight. Excuse me!'

It was not far to Portland Square and Jason set off on foot, striding through the dark streets and ignoring the icy wind that cut at his cheeks. If what he had heard about the Cherstons was correct, it was possible that Angel and her mother would already have left, but he could not risk wasting time going back to Darvell House to find out.

The square frontage of the Cherstons' hired mansion was illuminated by torches, and the windows glowed with candlelight, but no carriages waited outside.

And nor would they, he thought grimly. It was not yet midnight, and no one would leave before the unmasking.

The ballroom was growing warmer and Angel decided she would sit out the next dance. She walked around the edge of the room, enjoying the spectacle. Her mother was dancing with an ageing Harlequin and laughing so much that Angel smiled. Mama rarely came to London and it was good to see her enjoying herself.

When the musicians struck up for a Scotch reel, Angel knew it was likely to be the last dance before the midnight unmasking. She had already refused two gentlemen, both of whom were clearly inebriated, but stood up with a third, whose plain coat suggested a certain sobriety.

The music started, the tempo very quick, and soon everyone was reeling and skipping. Such was the energy that before long Angel's hood came free of its pins and slipped back, but she hardly noticed, too busy keeping pace with the dance. It was extremely fast, everyone was whooping and laughing, and Angel was enjoying it immensely.

They had reached the final movement of the dance when her partner took her hands to spin her about, only instead of releasing her at the required time he clung tighter and spun her away from the dance floor. Angel was off balance and could do nothing but try to keep her feet. Those watching fell back, screeching with laughter, as he pulled her through an open doorway and into an inner hall.

Angel tried to free her hands but her partner held on and pushed her backwards into the shadows.

'This is no longer amusing, sir,' she told him, too angry to be afraid. 'I insist you let me go.'

He fell against her, pinning her to the wall. 'Not before I have claimed my prize, fair maid.'

His hot breath was on her cheek. Angel was no longer a shy debutante, and she gathered herself to fight, but then, quite suddenly, she was free. A tall figure in a black cloak had pulled her would-be attacker away.

The man squawked ineffectually as he was lifted off his

feet and thrown aside like a rag doll. The cloaked figure followed and stood over him like a dark knight, tall and menacing.

'Get up,' he ordered savagely. 'Stand up, you dog. We will finish this now!'

'No!' Angel knew that voice. 'No. I am not hurt!'

She ran across and caught the Duke's arm. She could almost feel the rage radiating from him, and beneath his sleeve the knotted muscle was hard as steel.

She said again, 'I am not hurt, sir. Pray, take me away from here.'

Jason felt the red-hot anger cooling. Angel's hand had slipped down and wrapped around his clenched fist. She was unhurt, and still masked.

'Cover your head,' he ordered. 'We might yet get out of this without being recognised.'

When she had pulled the hood up he took her arm and escorted her quickly back through the ballroom. Thankfully everyone was too drunk to take any notice of them.

'Are you very angry with me?' she asked him.

'Furious!'

Although mainly with himself for not taking better care of her.

'I did not need your help,' she said, her little chin raised defiantly.

'Hah!'

'It is true! I was about to send him about his business when you came blundering in.'

He stopped. 'My *blundering*, as you call it, madam, saved you from being mauled by that rogue!' Her eyes glittered through the slits of her mask and he added savagely, 'I have told you, I know how to protect my own!'

He looked so menacing that Angel shivered. Beneath his reserve she detected a wild spirit in her husband that made him very dangerous.

But not to me. Never to me.

Aloud, she said, 'We must find Mama.'

'I met her when I came in and told her to wait by the door.'

'You must not blame her, Jason.'

'I don't.'

She sighed. 'You blame me.'

He stopped. 'After what you told me about your previous visit to London, I should have thought you would have more sense!'

'I do!' she retorted, bridling. 'Since then I have always made sure my hairpins are long and sharp. As you will discover if you keep glaring at me like that!'

Jason's eyes narrowed, and Angel braced herself for a stinging retort, but instead he set off again, keeping a tight grip on her arm.

She said suddenly, 'Your domino smells of camphor. Where did you get it?'

'There was a drunkard in the square. He did not require it any longer.'

'If he is still there when we go outside you can return it.'

He laughed.

It sounded harsh, but even that was better than his remaining stubbornly angry with her.

They found Lady Goole pacing by the ballroom entrance.

'Oh, my dear! I would never have brought you here if I had known how it would be!' she cried, taking Angel's hands. 'And then I could not see you! There were so many people milling around, blocking the way.'

'Pray do not upset yourself, Mama. I have enjoyed myself prodigiously.'

She threw a challenging look at Jason, which he met with a scowl.

'It is growing rowdier by the minute,' he muttered. 'Time to be going.'

'I have summoned the carriage,' said Lady Goole as they made their way downstairs. 'It should be here by now.'

They found their town coach waiting at the door and Jason handed the ladies in.

'Wait!' Angel put up a hand as Jason jumped in and began to close the door. 'You must return that cloak to its owner.' He hesitated and she added, 'If for no other reason than it smells so atrociously.'

She thought he might explode, but a sudden grin replaced the irritation in his face. He disappeared, coming back a few minutes later to announce that he had given the domino to one of Cherston's servants.

'The fellow is gone, but he can collect his property tomorrow. If he can remember where he left it.'

It was a subdued party that returned to Darvell House. Lady Goole went up to her room immediately, but Angel hesitated, looking at the Duke. He was abstracted, a slight crease in his brow, but then he looked up and saw her waiting.

'I beg your pardon. My thoughts were elsewhere.'

'I wondered if we might take a glass of wine together,' she suggested.

He shook his head. 'Alas, no. I have business that requires my attention.'

'Immediately?'

'Yes. And you must be tired after your…exertions.' He took her hand and lifted it to his lips. 'Goodnight, Angel. Sleep well.'

'Goodnight, Your Grace.'

She made her way up to her bedchamber, her spirits droop-ing. He had dismissed her. Not in so many words, but she knew he would not come to her room tonight. He was still angry at having to rescue her from a scrape—not that she had needed rescuing!

The sudden spurt of rebellion died away. How she wished that she had never gone to that silly masquerade. But it was too late for regrets. Jason was disappointed in her and that was not at all what she wanted.

Almost before Angel had said goodnight Jason turned and went into his study. He had shut the door on the sight of her walking up the stairs, but he could not shut her out of his mind. He had told her he was furious, but it was not anger he had felt when he'd learned the sort of masquerade she was attending. It was fear. Ice-cold dread at what might happen to her in such company. And when he'd found that scoundrel trying to molest her it had roused all his protective instincts.

He walked over to the side table and poured himself a glass of brandy. Damnation. His worst fears had been re-alised. He had vowed he would never lose his head over a woman again and here he was, just as besotted and even more in love than he had ever been.

Chapter Thirteen

Returning to Darvell House from a morning visit to a new acquaintance, Angel was glad Mama had insisted she buy a fur-lined pelisse to wear beneath her cloak. It helped to keep out the icy November wind that whipped through the London streets and even permeated the town coach.

She hurried into the hall and heard a merry laugh coming from the morning room, followed by the murmur of voices.

'Oh, do we have visitors?' she asked as she removed her bonnet and gloves.

She realised the waiting servant was another of the handsome but slow-witted creatures Lavinia had taken on, and when he gave her nothing more than a startled look she smothered a sigh.

'No matter. I will go in directly.' She shrugged off her pelisse and handed everything to the hapless footman, saying, 'And, no, I do not need you to announce me!'

Really, she thought as she hurried towards the morning room, *I shall have to talk to Jason about turning the man off.*

But all thoughts about the unfortunate lackey fled as soon as she opened the door.

'Mr Babberton!'

The young man was sitting on the sofa with Rose beside

him. They both jumped to their feet as she came in, Kenelm Babberton flushing to the roots of his curly brown hair.

Angel shut the door quickly behind her. 'What is the meaning of this? You know you should not be here. Alone, too.'

'We are not alone,' said Rose. 'I mean, Lady Goole was here.'

'Well, she is clearly not here now!'

'She w-went off to speak to someone…' Rose twisted her hands together and threw a despairing look at Mr Babberton.

He turned to Angel. 'I beg your pardon, Your Grace. I know we agreed not to see one another, but I could not stay away any longer.'

'Evidently.'

He flushed and spread his hands, searching around for the words to express himself.

'When Rose went off to London I felt… It was as if part of me was missing! I—'

He stopped as Lady Goole rattled the doorhandle and came in, saying, 'There, that is settled— Oh! You are back, Duchess.' She smiled brightly, but not before Angel caught her look of guilty dismay.

'Did you admit Mr Babberton, ma'am?' Angel demanded.

'Why, yes,' replied Lady Goole, adopting an innocent demeanour. 'Rose said he was an acquaintance from Rotherton.'

'And it is true!' declared Rose. She reached out and took the young man's hand. 'We are *very* good friends!'

Angel's heart was touched, but she said, trying to keep her voice calm, 'I think, sir, it would be best if you left before the Duke comes in.'

Mr Babberton pulled himself up straighter. 'I am not afraid to meet His Grace, ma'am. In fact, I should very much like to talk to him.'

'That may be so, but not today,' she said firmly, imagining Jason's reaction if he found the young man in his house. 'Pray go now. I shall talk to the Duke on your behalf.'

'You, you will?' said Rose.

'You have my word.' Angel nodded. 'If Mr Babberton is staying in town then the Duke must be informed.'

'Of course,' he said quickly. 'That is why I called today— to see him. But I was informed His Grace was not at home.' He stopped, looking a little uncomfortable. 'And then I asked for Miss Haringey.'

An awkward silence fell over the room. Lady Goole was regarding the young couple with every appearance of sympathy, but Angel knew it would not do. She walked across to the chimneypiece and tugged at the bellpull.

'I suggest you go now, Mr Babberton, and you must not contact Miss Haringey again until you hear from me.'

'But, Angel—'

'No, Rose. That is how it must be. At least until I have spoken with the Duke.'

'But you will plead my case for me?' asked Mr Babberton, his blue eyes fixed upon Angel.

'I shall do my best. Now, go, sir, and wait until you hear from me.'

The footman was at the door. Kenelm Babberton threw one last, longing look at Rose before he recovered himself, bowed formally to the ladies and went out.

No one moved. They listened to his booted footsteps crossing the hall and the clunk of the street door. Rose gave a sob and Angel went over to take her hands.

'There really is no need for you to weep, Rose. The Duke has already agreed to discuss the situation when we return to Rotherton.'

'But that will not be until the spring! It is too cruel when we are in love!'

Angel's heart went out to the girl, but Rose was the Duke's ward, not hers, and she dare not raise false hopes.

As if reading her mind, Rose gave a little cry and ran out of the room.

'Ah, the poor dears!' Lady Goole sank down onto the sofa. 'Was I very wrong to leave them alone?'

'I am afraid you were, Mama,' said Angel. 'They formed an attachment while we were at Rotherton and the Duke was furious when he discovered it. Mr Babberton was forbidden to come to the house. That is in part why Jason allowed the girls to come to London. We neither of us expected Rose's swain to follow her. I thought, with time and all the distractions of the capital, she would forget him.'

'And now I have spoiled all that.' Lady Goole sighed and shook her head. 'I am very sorry, my love, but it was a genuine mistake. When the footman asked if we were at home to Mr Babberton, Rose looked so pleased that I assumed he had called before. If I had known...'

'How could you know, Mama? Pray do not torment yourself. Rose should have told you, although I cannot find it in my heart to be angry with her when she thinks herself so much in love.'

Lady Goole said nothing. She spent a few moments smoothing out her skirts then she said, without looking up, 'Far be it from me to criticise the Duke, but I have always thought it unwise to keep young people apart. It is far too easy for them to convince themselves that they are star-crossed lovers. Much better to let them get to know one another. They very often discover that they are not in love at all. In some cases they do not even *like* one another very much! But that is only my opinion, of course.'

'It is mine too, Mama, but Jason thinks differently and he is Rose's guardian.'

'Well, you must talk to him,' said her mother. 'Rotherton is not an unreasonable man. I am sure you can persuade him to let them meet. As long as they are supervised, of course.'

'Of course.' Angel nodded. 'I shall speak to him at the earliest opportunity.'

Not that she could be sure when that would be. She had seen very little of Jason for the past week. Since the Cherstons' masquerade, in fact. He had taken to spending most of the day at his club, or locked in his study not to be disturbed. If he joined the family for dinner he was quiet, preoccupied.

Angel suspected he was still angry with her. Disappointed, perhaps, that she had shown such a lack of judgement in attending the masquerade. However, she must speak to him about Rose and Kenelm Babberton before he discovered for himself that the young man was in town and jumped to his own conclusions.

The following morning, therefore, she went to his study as soon as she had finished her breakfast, entering upon the knock.

'May I speak to you, Your Grace?'

'Can it not wait?' He scowled at her and waved at the documents spread out over the desk. 'I have an appointment with Telford and I need to finish these papers first.'

'It will not take long.'

She sat down across the desk from him and quickly explained about Rose and Mr Babberton.

'Are you telling me the young devil had the audacity to come to Darvell House?' he demanded, when she had finished.

'Yes. I believe he really did want to speak to you, which I think, in the circumstances, was very brave of him.'

'It was damned foolish! I expressly told him he must not see Rose.'

'I think they might truly be in love, Jason. Will you not reconsider—?'

'No!' He slammed his hands on the desk. 'I will not countenance it, madam! It was you who suggested she should have a London season.'

'Yes, and I still believe it is the right thing to do. Is there any harm in allowing her to see Mr Babberton while he is in town? After all, you cannot prevent him from being here.'

'I can and I will!'

She shook her head, smiling a little. 'What, will you become a tyrant, Jason? I think not.'

Jason almost ground his teeth at that. How did she always manage to find his weakness. Of course he was no tyrant!

She went on. 'I believe Mr Babberton was sincere when he told me he called here with every intention of speaking with you. Surely it is better to let them meet? Under strict supervision, of course.' She hesitated. 'If you do not trust me to do it, then there is Mrs Watson, and also Mama. Now that she understands the situation I am sure she would agree to play chaperon sometimes.'

'Good God, woman, will you not let it be?' he exclaimed, jumping to his feet. 'I have said no and I mean it. Be warned, madam: I won't let you coax and cajole me this time.' He glared down at her. 'Have you not done enough damage already? Not content with bringing the children to live at Rotherton, you have now thrust them into the London house! Confound it, you have done nothing but turn my ordered world upside down! I should never—'

He broke off, turning away from her with an angry growl.

Angel pressed her hands to her chest, trying to stop the fearful thud of her heart.

She finished the sentence for him. 'You should never have married me.'

She blinked rapidly and fixed her eyes on the Duke's broad back, stiff and yielding under the black coat. It was true, then. She had long suspected it, but now she knew the truth.

She drew in a deep breath. 'Perhaps you are right, sir. I have certainly not done well by Rose, have I? First I allowed your cousin to dance with her when I should have prevented it. Although Mrs Watson and I have seen Mr Knowsley at several balls and parties since, and even if he does stare a great deal at Rose, he has made no attempt to approach her. But I beg you, Jason, do not let your anger with me cloud your judgement. Allow Rose and Mr Babberton to meet. Watch them together and judge their affection for yourself.'

Jason stared out at the street. Marrying Angel was the very best thing he had ever done, so why did he not say so? Why could he not bring himself to tell her?

He was on the edge of a precipice.

To admit how much he cared was to risk everything he had struggled for years to repair. Everything Lavinia had destroyed. His life, his happiness. His heart.

Angel went on, the unhappiness in her voice slicing into him.

'I will say no more. I am clearly not the best person to act as advocate for the young couple. However, I thought it important you were informed that Mr Babberton is in London. I would not have you think that anyone in this house is trying to deceive you.'

There was a pause, then he heard her sigh.

'Excuse me. You have business in the City today and I have taken up too much of your time.'

He heard the click of the door and swung round, but she had gone. All that was left was her perfume…a faint trace of summer flowers.

It was gone noon when Jason left Telford's offices and he made his way to a nearby tavern. After a gruelling interview with his man of business he felt in need of sustenance, and a little quiet reflection.

The lowering sky matched his mood, which had not improved since he had quit Darvell House that morning. The encounter with Angel concerned him. He was frustrated that he could not explain his true feelings. He had always struggled with a natural reserve, but these past few years it had become an almost physical barrier. He had worn his heart on his sleeve for Lavinia and her betrayal had left deep scars. Pride had stopped him denouncing her, and they had continued with their sham marriage until her death, when he had withdrawn from Society to lick his wounds.

Jason knew he would be hiding away still if Angel had not rescued him. She had coaxed him back into the world, brought his family to Rotherton and filled the old house with warmth and laughter. He owed her so much, and she deserved a great deal more than his morose reticence. He should have told her everything about his first marriage…how his first wife had broken his heart. Perhaps then he might have been able to tell her that she had mended it.

Confound it, he was a fool of the highest order!

And now Telford had shown him just how much of a fool he had been. And not just over Lavinia.

When they had married, Jason had been content for Lavinia to retain control of her properties, including the house in Kent, which she told him she would settle upon Rose. He had trusted her word, and it had come as a shock today to find that it was mortgaged to the hilt. Its sale would bring in only a pittance.

Galling as he'd found this news, it was not financial matters but Angeline who was uppermost in his mind as he sat in the tavern. He had arrived at Goole Park for Barnaby's wedding troubled and angry, but she had soothed his soul. He'd found peace in her company and had married her for purely selfish reasons.

The first glimmer of a smile lightened his spirits as he finished his meal and poured more ale into his tankard. Yes, she had turned his world upside down, there was no doubt about that, but it was for the better. She endured his moods with patience and good humour, and she had even taken on responsibility for Rose and Nell. Compared to Lavinia, Angel gave so much and asked for very little in return.

Jason drained his tankard. By heaven, he might not be able to *say* the words, but he could show her how much he valued her. A grand gesture was required, and he knew just what to do.

Jason made his way to his bankers on the Strand and was shown into an inner office, where one of the elderly partners was waiting to do his bidding.

'I want you to fetch the family jewels from the Darvell vault.'

'Of course, Your Grace. Which ones?'

'All of them,' said Jason.

'All?'

'Yes, of course.'

'As Your Grace wishes.'

The man bowed and left the room and Jason sat down to await his return. The only jewellery he had given Angel was his wedding gift—a few paltry diamonds and pearls. Now she should have her choice from all the family jewels. He was only sorry that he had not thought of it earlier.

Just what was in the collection he could not recall. There were pieces going back several generations, plus the jewellery that he had lavished upon his late duchess. Jason had instructed that all the jewellery should be sent to the bank for safekeeping when she died, and then he had forgotten all about it.

He wondered which of the family pieces would best become Angel. Rubies, perhaps. Or sapphires. Some of it would be unfashionable now, but the stones could be reset if Angel liked them. He had a vague memory of seeing a parure of emeralds set in gold that would look magnificent against Angel's creamy skin...

The door opened and the senior partner came back with several velvet boxes in his hands. He was accompanied by a minion carrying a large jewel case.

'Here we are, Your Grace.'

The clerk withdrew and the elderly partner spread the boxes over the desk and began to open them. In the large box Jason recognised the garnets that his grandmother had worn: a necklace, earrings and a pair of bracelets all set in gold. There was also his mother's necklace of blue jasper cameos, linked with gold chain.

Soon the whole desk was glittering with gold and silver jewellery set with seed pearls and diamonds, emeralds and rubies. The last box revealed Jason's wedding present to Lavinia—a diamond and sapphire necklace with matching eardrops and bracelets.

'I must say I was a little surprised that Your Grace wished to leave all these pieces in our vaults,' remarked the banker. 'No doubt some of the more recent additions have sentimental value for you.'

'No, none at all.' Jason was surprised to find how little he cared about the money he had lavished upon Lavinia. His only regret was that he had allowed her to manipulate him for so long.

The banker continued. 'Some of the gems are extremely well-made—one would hardly know they were paste.'

Jason looked up. *'Paste?'*

A shadow of concern flickered over the man's face.

Jason picked up one of the necklaces and studied it, then another. Fine, tell-tale scratches on the stones revealed that they were imitation.

He fixed the banker with a hard, steady gaze. 'What the devil has been going on here? What has happened to my family's jewels?'

The banker sat down. 'There are *some* genuine pieces here, Your Grace. The blue jasper, for example. And the garnets. Also some of the early sets, pieces that have remained in the bank since your father's time.'

'And all the rest are paste?' Jason dropped the necklace he was holding back onto the table.

'Why, yes, Your Grace. It was assumed you knew of it.'

'The devil I did! Tell me.'

The old man gazed down at his clasped hands and said in a colourless voice, 'The late Duchess came in to collect them, Your Grace. Not all at once, you understand. She made several visits to the bank over the years. I remember the first occasion most particularly, because I checked the records myself, to make sure that you had signed the necessary permissions.'

Jason felt a chill hand clutching at his insides. Yes, he remembered now, all too clearly, putting his seal and signature to a letter. In those early days he would have given his new wife anything she asked for.

The sombre voice continued. 'I was also present when your secretary brought all the jewellery into the bank last winter and I made a full and detailed inventory of all the pieces.' The old man paused and added gently, 'Your secretary signed for them all, Your Grace. Perhaps you would like to see the ledger entries?'

'No, that will not be necessary.'

Jason rubbed a hand over his eyes, thinking of the receipts Simon had brought him. He had sent his man away and stuffed the papers in the drawer without a second glance. How could he have been so stupidly naive? Even the stones in his wedding gift to Lavinia had been sold and replaced with cheap replicas.

He had given her a very generous allowance, refused her nothing, but it had clearly not been enough.

Chapter Fourteen

Jason left the bank, anger and depression weighing heavily on his spirits. It was growing dark, and he hunched himself into his greatcoat as he set off to walk back to Darvell House.

How had he allowed himself to be so deceived? And how would he tell Angel?

He could buy her new jewellery, of course. He would take her to Rundell and Bridge and beg her choose whatever she liked. But at some point he would have to explain to her what had happened to the family jewels.

As he turned off St James's Street he thought it would not be such a bad thing. He wanted no more secrets between them. She needed to know the truth. About everything.

He quickened his step, eager now to see Angel. Perhaps, at last, they could put the past behind them and start again.

He turned the corner and Darvell House was there before him. His mood lightened, just knowing Angel was in there, waiting for him. Looking up, Jason saw the golden glow of candlelight shining through the thin under-curtains in the morning room window. A shadow fell upon the muslin: a woman's figure.

Angel, he thought, smiling. His wife. His duchess.

He saw a second shadow, a man this time, and as he watched, the two joined together in an embrace.

The world tilted. Jason shook his head and looked again at the window, but the image had not changed. There could be no mistake. Angel was kissing a man, a lover. Under his own roof!

Cursing under his breath, Jason crossed the road and strode into the house, tossing his hat, gloves and cane at the footman before taking the stairs two at a time. He burst into the morning room, his hands bunching into fists.

'Take your hands off her, damn you!'

The couple jumped apart, staring at him in alarm. Only it was not Angel he saw in front of the window, but Rose.

'Jason, pray do not be angry. It is not what it seems!' Angel had been standing by the fire but now she came hurrying across to him, hands held out.

He said icily, 'I am quite capable of seeing what is going on, madam.'

'No, no! Mr Babberton is going back to Surrey. His father has broken his leg and he is needed at home.'

She was standing before him, shielding the errant lovers from his wrath.

Kenelm Babberton stepped forward. 'I set out for Winchcombe Lodge in the morning. Her Grace was kind enough to allow me to come in and take my leave of Miss Haringey.'

Jason snarled. 'You were doing a dam—dashed sight more than that when I came in!'

Babberton flushed a little and inclined his head. 'I beg your pardon. I was overcome by the violence of my feelings.'

'We are in love!' cried Rose, taking his hand. 'You cannot blame Kenelm for his actions, Papa Duke. No one with a heart would blame him!'

Jason was almost grinding his teeth. Now there were two females standing between him and Babberton! Confound it, did they think he was going to run the man through in the morning room?

He breathed deep and, with an effort, unclenched his fists.

'I should leave.' Babberton picked up his hat. 'I have booked a place on the morning mail and have yet to pack.'

He turned to Rose, taking her hand and bowing over it. He gave her a brief sustaining smile before releasing her and turning to Angel.

'Goodbye, Your Grace. And thank you for all your efforts on my behalf.'

'I am only sorry that it could not have turned out better,' replied Angel, as he bowed low to her. 'Pray, give our regards to your mother, and wish Lord Winchcombe a speedy recovery.'

'Thank you, ma'am, I shall.' Then he bowed to the Duke. 'Your Grace. We shall speak again when you return to Rotherton.'

With that, he went out, leaving a heavy silence behind him.

'Well,' muttered Jason. 'You have to admire his nerve.'

Rose glared at him, her eyes sparkling with unshed tears. '*He*, at least, behaved like a gentleman!'

Angel saw Jason frown and quickly stepped forward.

'It is time to change or we shall all be late for dinner. Have you forgotten, Rose? We are going to the Westberes' soirée tonight.'

She ushered the girl out of the room and watched her run up the stairs before closing the door and turning back to the Duke.

'Poor child. I doubt we shall see her at dinner.'

'Do you think I was too harsh on her?'

'You lost your temper.'

She waited, wondering if he would deny it, or fly into a rage.

'I thought it was you,' he said. 'When I looked up at the window and saw the figures embracing I thought it was you.'

Angel pressed one hand to her breast. That was quite a revelation, but she was not ready to forgive him just yet.

She said coldly, 'Am I supposed to be flattered that you think I would break my marriage vows?'

He raked his fingers through his hair. 'I did not *think* anything. I was afraid I had lost you.'

The quiet words and the bleak look that accompanied them tore at her heart. It was the closest the Duke had ever come to expressing his feelings and she could only guess what an effort it had been for him.

The clock on the mantelshelf chimed and Jason glanced at it.

'There is no time now, but I need to speak with you. Tonight. After dinner. Can Mrs Watson accompany Rose to the Westberes'?'

'Why, yes, if you think it necessary.'

'I do.' He nodded. 'It is essential we talk. Until dinner, then, madam.'

He gave a little bow and went out, leaving Angel a prey to such conflicting emotions she doubted she would be able to eat anything at all this evening.

In the event, no one from Darvell House attended the soirée. When Mrs Watson brought Nell to the drawing room she announced that Rose was feeling too unwell to go out, or even to join them for dinner.

'The poor child was looking so pale and drawn I sent her straight to bed,' she went on. 'I only hope it is nothing infectious.'

Angel was duly sympathetic, but as they all went in to

dinner she wished that she too might be spared the ordeal of sitting through a long meal. She had no idea what it was the Duke wished to say to her, but she wanted it over.

The atmosphere in the dining room was strained. The Duke said very little, but that was not unusual, and if Mrs Watson noticed that Angel was quieter than usual she made no mention of it, and was happy to encourage Lady Elinor to tell the Duke and Duchess about her day.

The widow had taken her to the Tower to see the wild animals, and it took very little effort on Angel's part to keep Nell chattering away on the subject for most of dinner and afterwards in the drawing room, until Mrs Watson carried her charge off to bed.

If Angel had found the meal difficult, then sitting alone in the drawing room with the Duke was even more uncomfortable. He was clearly distracted, replying mechanically to any subject she proposed. She wished she could put her arms around him and kiss away the frown that darkened his brow, but she lacked the courage. There had never been any words of love between them and she did not think she could bear it if he pushed her away.

She took up her embroidery, deciding that they would sit in silence until he was ready to talk.

Jason watched his duchess ply the needle, her dark head bowed over the tambour frame. Seeing the shadow at the window earlier and thinking it was Angel had thrown him. Only then had he realised just how much she meant to him. How much he would hate to lose her.

Then tell her, you dolt.

But the clock ticked on while he wrestled with his inner demons. It had been so easy with Lavinia. He had declared himself constantly, but her loving smiles, her kisses and caresses, had been nothing but a sham and learning that had broken him. He had started building a wall around his feelings, brick by brick, vowing he would never again leave himself so vulnerable.

And he had made an excellent job of it, he thought, bitterly. That wall was so impregnable now even *he* could not breach it.

Angel began packing away her embroidery.

'It is growing late,' she said, rising. 'I should retire.'

Jason jumped to his feet. 'No, don't go!'

'We have been sitting in silence for nigh on an hour, sir.'

'Yes. I beg your pardon. A little longer, I pray you.'

Silently she inclined her head and sat down again, folding her hands in her lap while Jason paced the room. He reminded her of a caged tiger, like the ones at the Tower that Nell had described earlier.

She prompted him. 'You said you wanted to talk to me.'

'Yes. I meant to do so when I returned from the Strand today, but when I discovered Rose and Babberton—'

'You were enraged,' she said, nodding. 'But they were only taking their leave of one another.'

'Hah! If only I could believe that!'

'You can believe it, Jason. You should. I have no doubt that Mr Babberton's intentions are quite honourable—'

He interrupted her roughly. 'It isn't Babberton's intentions that concern me!' He stopped and raked his hand through his hair. 'It's Rose. What if…?'

He paced again, clearly wrestling with himself.

He stopped and looked at her, and the pain and uncertainty in his eyes made her catch her breath.

'What if she is too much like her mother?'

Angel jerked upright in her chair. 'Why on earth should you think that?'

His chest heaved, and when he spoke his voice was grim.

'After I left Telford today I went to the bank, to look at the Rotherton jewels.' He threw her a quick, diffident glance. 'I thought you might like to wear some of the family pieces. The last time I checked there was a king's ransom in the vaults. Now there is almost nothing.' His lip curled. 'My late wife sold them—and with my blessing, apparently.'

Angel was even more mystified, but he was scowling so blackly she was loath to speak.

At length he went on. 'I was besotted, Angel! In those early years I would have given Lavinia anything her heart desired. I took her to the Strand, introduced her to my bankers and, very foolishly, signed a paper giving her free access to the jewels. Complete freedom to do whatever she wished with them.'

He turned away, walking over to the fire, where he stood, staring down into the flames.

'She chose to sell them all and replace them with paste copies.'

'And she never told you?'

'No.' A sigh shook him. 'What she did with the money I have no idea. Certainly I never saw any sign of it.'

Angel recalled the rumours she had heard. The tales of wild parties. Extravagant gowns. Lovers.

'Oh, Jason, I am so sorry.'

He raised one hand as if to ward off her sympathy.

He went on. 'I came back today to find Lavinia's daughter embracing young Babberton. Proclaiming her love for him just as Lavinia declared hers for me, years ago. If, as I fear, she is like her mother, Babberton will never be rich enough to satisfy her. Damme, he is the son of a neighbour. I have a responsibility for him, too. I cannot let him fall into the hands of a fortune-hunter.'

'Rose is no fortune-hunter, Jason. I would stake my life on it.'

'No? London has gone to her head. Even if she thinks herself in love with Babberton, he is not man enough to keep her in check.' He shook his head. 'I should never have agreed to her coming here. It is not too late to stop the sale of the Kent property. Mrs Watson can take both girls back there, out of the way.'

'Oh, no, pray do not do that! They are enjoying themselves so much, and learning a great deal, too.' Angel went over to him. 'Rose is too honest, too kind, to deceive anyone, Jason. You know that in your heart.'

'I thought the same of Lavinia, once.'

'Jason, I am sure it is not so.'

'You are *sure*?' He turned his head and fixed her with a glacial stare. 'You have spent your life hidden away in the country. What can *you* know of the world?'

Angel could see the hurt in his eyes. He had been tricked by his duplicitous wife and felt ashamed to admit it.

She said gently, 'Not much, perhaps, but—'

'Let be, madam. They are not your children, after all!'

Angel winced, but she raised her head and looked him in the eye.

'True, they are not,' she said coldly. 'But I am well enough acquainted with Rose and Nell to know that I should be *proud* to have them for my daughters. As should you, Your Grace. In fact, I know you will admit it. Once your damned temper has cooled!'

With that she turned in a swish of silken skirts and walked away, praying her legs would support her long enough to get out of the room.

* * *

As the door snapped shut behind Angel, Jason rubbed a hand over his eyes. That was badly done of him. Badly done indeed. He had lashed out at Angel and she did not deserve that. Confound it, she was trying to help him! It was his damnable temper that had prompted him to talk of sending the girls away. He did not mean it. They were his family now. As was Angel.

He stood for a while, thinking of all he should have confessed to her. Not only his first wife's perfidy but his own.

Somehow during his appointment with Telford today the talk had come around to marriage and annulments. A simple enquiry from Jason had elicited the information that these were extremely difficult to obtain and involved almost certain public humiliation for the woman.

Why had he not looked into the matter further before he had subjected Angel to the indignity of sleeping alone for so many weeks? He had demeaned her. It would serve him right if she never forgave him for that.

With sudden decision he strode out of the room and took the stairs two at a time. He stopped at the Duchess's bedchamber and tapped on the panel.

'Angel, may I come in?'

There was no answer. He walked on to his own room. A single lamp was burning but there was no sign of Adams.

He went over to the connecting door and knocked softly.

'Angel, I want to talk to you. Please, let me come in.'

She did not reply. His hand went towards the doorhandle but he drew it back. Even if it was unlocked he would not enter her bedroom uninvited.

He tried again. 'Please, Angel. I want to apologise.'

Silence.

Sick at heart, Jason turned away. He must talk to Angel

tomorrow and hope that it was not too late to put everything right. That she would give him one last chance to be the husband she deserved.

'Your Grace—*Miss Angeline*! We should go in now. You'll catch your death out here.'

Angel was tempted to tell Joan she did not care what happened to her, then berated herself for such foolishness. When she had reached her bedroom she had been too hurt and angry to sleep, and had immediately gone out again to walk in the gardens. Her maid had been scandalised and insisted on coming with her.

'Please, Your Grace, come inside.'

Angel sighed. None of the disasters that Joan had envisaged had happened. No intruders were skulking in the gardens, waiting to molest them, and Angel had not tripped and fallen in the darkness. However, she was grateful for the cashmere shawl the maid had put about her shoulders, and she could not deny that her feet in their thin satin slippers were icy cold. Which was no more than she deserved.

No matter how much she tried to tell herself she had acted for the best, Angel knew her attempts to help Rose and Mr Babberton had failed. And now Jason was going to send the girls back to Kent. She had made everything worse, not better.

Joan had asked no questions about her mistress's heavy sighs. She obviously knew the Duke was in a rage because of Mr Babberton's visit to the house and Miss Rose's subsequent absence from the dinner table, and she had already informed her mistress that everyone in the household knew it too.

'It was inevitable word would get around, ma'am, when you think of it, His Grace storming in like he did, and the second footman being right outside the morning room and hearing every word. It was all that was talked of in the servants' hall this evening, even though Mr Marcuss did his best to stop it. Trouble is, some of the younger maids see Miss Haringey and Mr Babberton as doomed sweethearts, and think the Duke a villain for keeping them apart.'

'But he is not a bad man, Joan! His Grace is trying to do what he thinks is right.'

'Whisht, now, Miss Angeline. *I* know that, and so do most of the servants. They remember the Duke's first duchess, and not with much affection either. I am not one for gossiping, but they all say she led His Grace a merry dance from the start, truth be told, what with her extravagance and wicked ways. And His Grace never allowing a word to be said against her! It's impossible to keep things from servants, as you well know. Not that anyone would dare to speak of it outside these four walls, for it would be instant dismissal if they did, the Duke not being one to pardon such disloyalty.'

No, thought Angel sadly, Jason did not forgive easily.

She shivered and turned to her maid, grasping her hands.

'Was it a mistake, Joan? Was I wrong to marry the Duke?'

If Angel was hoping for a strong denial it was not forthcoming. She felt tears prickling in her eyes. What a silly, naïve fool she had been to think she could ever make him happy.

Joan put a comforting arm about her shoulders and turned her towards the house. 'Come, now, Miss Angeline, it's not like you to be so downhearted. Come inside. 'tis growing late and you know you will feel better after a good night's sleep.'

Angel woke to a grey, overcast dawn and a pressing sense of foreboding which was not lessened when her maid informed her that the Duke had requested his duchess's presence in the morning room before breakfast.

She dressed quickly, but before she left the bedchamber she asked Joan to look in on Rose.

'Mrs Watson is taking Nell to the Ragholmes', and I am very much afraid that if Rose is left to herself she will keep to her room. I hope you can persuade her to come down to breakfast, Joan. It will do her no good to mope.'

'Very well, ma'am. I will do my best, just as soon as I have finished in here.'

'Be kind to her, Joan, the poor child is heartbroken,' said Angel.

She gave a little sigh, straightened her shoulders and went out.

The Duke was already in the morning room when Angel went in. He was standing by the window, his broad shoulders blocking out much of the already poor morning light.

He said, as she shut the door, 'I thought you might not come, after the way I ripped up at you last night. Are you very angry with me?'

'I am, Your Grace.'

'Ah, don't call me that, Angel! I wish you had flown at me last night, told me that I was being quite unreasonable.'

'Would it have done any good?'

'Possibly not. But I need my duchess to remind me that I can be damnably ill-mannered at times.'

'Yes, you can be,' she told him. 'You are often odiously overbearing. High-handed, too.'

'Then I give you leave to tell me whenever you find me being so *odious*, as you put it.'

When she made no reply, he sighed. 'The problem with being a duke is that one is rarely contradicted. One is fêted, fawned upon and allowed to ride roughshod over everyone without ever being corrected.' He bit his lip. 'A duke is also expected to be some sort of superior being. To have no feelings. To show no sorrow or remorse.'

Her anger melted away. She said, remembering the fifteen-year-old Jason, 'And you became a duke far too young.'

'Help me, Angel.' He reached out to her. 'Help me to be a better man. A better husband and father. Tell me when I am being a fool or a tyrant.'

She went to him, saying, as she took his hands, 'And will you promise not to rage at me?'

'I will do my best to curb my temper. And who else is to correct me, if not my duchess?' He shook his head at her. 'I know you did not marry me for love, Angel, but I hope, in time, you could come to care for me.'

'Oh, I do,' she said quickly.

'Truly?' His eyes searched her face. 'As much as you cared for that scoundrel who broke your heart?'

Something between a laugh and a sob escaped her. 'Far, far more than that, Jason. In fact, I have quite forgotten him!'

His look softened. 'You do not know how happy that makes me.' A small sigh of relief escaped him. 'I shall not be sending Rose and Nell away, Angel. That was said in the heat of the moment and I regret it now, very much. But believe me, it was not born of malice. It was inadequacy. I am at a loss to know how to go on as a parent.'

Angel felt a sudden constriction in her chest. Jason was not a man to admit any weakness. She knew it had cost him dear to say that.

'Then we shall learn together,' she said, squeezing his fingers. 'We will make mistakes, I am sure, but I believe, if we both try, we can be a happy family.'

Her spirits sang at the warm look in his eyes. He pulled her closer, holding her hands against his heart, and she held her breath, waiting for him to say the words she longed to hear. Waiting for him to say that he loved her.

'Angel—' He broke off as a knock sounded and the door opened. 'Yes, Marcuss, what is it now?'

The butler did not flinch at his master's impatient tone.

'Her Grace's dresser wishes to have a word with the Duchess, sir.'

'The devil she does!'

Angel shushed him and instructed the butler to send Joan in.

'She would not interrupt us if it was not urgent,' she said, as Marcuss disappeared.

He returned a moment later, with the dresser hurrying in behind him.

'Well?' barked Jason. 'What is it?'

Joan was clearly not to be put off, even by a duke. She said, 'I should like a word my mistress, if I may, Your Grace. Alone.'

Angel went to move away, but Jason held on to her hand. 'You can say whatever it is here, before both of us. And it had better be important!'

Angel tutted. 'Odiously high-handed!' she murmured, before turning back to her dresser. 'Go on, Joan, what is it?'

'It's Miss Haringey, madam,' said Joan, throwing a fulminating glance towards the Duke. 'She has eloped!'

Chapter Fifteen

'Eloped!' Angel's hands flew to her cheeks. 'I do not believe it. Excuse me, sir, I must go and talk to her maid—'

'No.' Jason stopped her. 'We will deal with this together. Bring the girl in here, if you please.'

When the dresser had gone, he turned to Angel.

'Rose is my ward, my responsibility. It is only right that I should be involved in this.' He saw the uncertainty in her eyes and added, 'I shall not lose my temper. I give you my word, but if she has eloped, time will be crucial in finding her. It is best I know everything from the start.'

'I am hoping there is some misunderstanding,' said Angel, clasping and unclasping her hands. 'I cannot believe she would be so lost to all sense of propriety.'

He said grimly, 'Believe me, young people in love are capable of anything.'

They did not have to wait long until the dresser returned, bringing with her Rose's maid.

The girl was shaking as Joan led her forward, saying, 'Now, then, Edith, tell them everything you told me.'

'But I don't *know* anything, and that's the truth!' cried the unfortunate maid, screwing her apron between her hands. 'Miss Rose went out in the early hours and she d-didn't come back.'

'But that's not the whole of it, is it?' put in Joan, folding her arms. 'You must tell them about the letter.'

'Letter?' said Angel. 'She received a letter?'

The maid looked more frightened than ever.

'Y-yes, ma'am. It c-came last evening.'

'Not with the post, then,' muttered Jason. 'Who took it in?'

The girl looked up at him, her eyes wide with fear.

'Well?'

He kept his tone calm, but just the fact of being addressed by a duke was too much for Edith. She threw her apron over her head and burst into tears.

He swallowed an oath of frustration and Angel put a hand on his arm, giving him a warning glance before stepping up to the girl.

'There is no need for this, Edith,' she said firmly. 'No one is going to punish you as long as you tell the truth now. How did Miss Haringey come by the letter? Did you give it to her?'

'Yes, ma'am.' The words were almost lost in a fresh bout of weeping.

'And who gave it to you?'

'The under-footman. He'd been sent to the mews last night, to tell them that we wouldn't be needing the coach after all, and on his way back a man came up with a letter for my mistress.'

'And where is the note now?' asked Angel.

Joan put her hand in her pocket and pulled out a folded paper. 'I have it here, safe.'

Angel took the letter and unfolded it.

Jason looked over her shoulder and scanned it, muttering some passages aloud.

'*"My dearest Rose...cannot leave without speaking to you once more...the Bull and Mouth...will send a carriage for you...waiting at the end of the street at five o'clock to-morrow morning..."* And the rogue has signed it with a K!'

He slammed a fist into his palm.

'Damned scoundrel! So Rose *has* eloped!'

'No, no, look!' exclaimed Angel. 'It says "to bring you to the inn and back again". Do you not see? She intended to come back.'

Joan nodded. 'Aye, and that's what she told her maid. With your permission, Your Grace,' she went on, looking at the weeping servant. 'I will take Edith to her room now. I doubt she can be of any more use to you.'

'Yes, yes, off you go.' Jason waved them away. 'But try if you can to stop her from chattering with the rest of the household.'

Joan nodded. 'I will, Your Grace, never fear.'

Angel said, as the door closed behind them, 'If Rose has not returned, then Mr Babberton must have persuaded her to run off with him.'

'Aye, dashed rogue!' declared Jason. 'I will send out runners to find which way they went.'

He had not gone two steps towards the door when Marcuss came in again.

'Mr Babberton to see you, Your Grace.'

The young man himself strode into the room even before the butler had finished announcing him.

'I beg your pardon for the intrusion,' he said, sketching a quick bow. 'I have just—'

Jason cut him off. 'Where is Miss Haringey?'

'That lady is the reason for my calling here,' replied Mr Babberton, in his measured way. 'I believe she has been abducted.'

'But not by you?' exclaimed Angel.

The young man looked offended. 'No, no, of course not.'

Jason dismissed the butler.

'I think you had best tell us the whole,' he said. 'Quickly, man!'

'Well, Your Grace, I was in the street here earlier, about five o'clock.'

'Wait—what were you doing here at that time in the morning?' demanded Jason.

'I had ordered a hackney to take me to Cheapside, from where I was taking the coach to Surrey. Having a little time to spare, I asked the driver to stop at the corner of Piccadilly and I, er, strolled down here.'

'In the early hours?' exclaimed Angel. 'What on earth did you think to achieve by that?'

'Nothing.' He flushed. 'I just wanted to be near Rose.'

Angel looked bewildered, but Jason understood completely. He remembered how he had felt, standing outside Darvell House yesterday.

He nodded. 'Go on.'

'A post-chaise pulled up at the door and I saw someone come out of the house. She was wrapped in a cloak, but I recognised it as Miss Haringey. She climbed into the waiting carriage, which set off immediately, and at pace.'

'Good God!' exclaimed Jason. 'She has been flirting with some other fellow all this time.'

'No, I will not believe that,' declared Angel.

'Nor I,' said Babberton. 'Rose would not do that. She had no baggage with her, not even a bandbox. The chaise rattled past me but it was too dark to see who was inside, so I ran back to Piccadilly and told my own cab driver to follow. At first it was not difficult, because we took the narrower streets, but it was more difficult after the tollgate at Tottenham Court Road. However, by making enquiries I tracked them as far as Barnet.'

'In a *hackney cab*?' asked Jason.

'Yes, although I had to pay the fellow handsomely to do it, and we were considerably slower than a post-chaise. Only at Barnet he refused to go any further, so I thought it best to come back and tell you what had occurred.'

'Then you did not send this?' Jason thrust the note at him.

Babberton studied it closely and shook his head. 'No.' He handed it back. 'That is not my writing. Also, my coach leaves from Blossoms Inn, not the Bull and Mouth.'

'Rose would not know that,' Angel pointed out.

'And I should never sign a letter in such a familiar manner, even to Miss Haringey.'

Jason looked again at the curly 'K' at the bottom of the paper and his blood chilled.

'Knowsley,' he ground out. 'She has run off with Toby Knowsley. Hell and damnation! He would know the Bull and Mouth. In all likelihood he hired the post chaise from there.'

'And he is your heir,' said Babberton in dismay. 'Could it be she never really cared for me?'

'No, no, I cannot believe that,' Angel told him. 'She would never go off with Mr Knowsley willingly. She does not even like him.'

'Whether she likes him or not is immaterial. She ain't going to marry him,' muttered Jason, ringing the bell. 'I am going after them. They are a few hours ahead, but my curricle will give me a good chance of catching them before nightfall.'

A servant entered and he barked out a series of orders.

When the man had withdrawn Babberton stepped forward. 'I shall come with you, Your Grace.'

'The devil you will!'

'Sir, I insist. You may need me when we catch up with

them, and I am sure I can handle a yard of tin as well as your groom. I will not slow you up, Your Grace.'

Jason saw the determined look in his eyes and nodded. 'Very well. Wait here while I go and change!'

Jason dashed away, and Angel was left alone with Mr Babberton.

'You will have missed your coach to Surrey,' she remarked, to break the silence.

'That is not important. All that matters is finding Miss Haringey and bringing her home safe.' He coughed, and looked slightly embarrassed. 'I took the liberty of bringing in my bags and depositing them in the hall, ma'am. The cab driver was not inclined to wait.'

'No, of course.' She nodded. 'I fear, when the Duke catches up with them, he will challenge Mr Knowsley to a duel.'

The young man's rather cheerful face took on a very black look. 'If he doesn't, then I shall!'

Angel relapsed into silence, realising it was pointless to ask him to keep the Duke out of trouble.

Ten minutes later Jason ran down the stairs to find his curricle at the door and Babberton and his wife waiting for him.

'God speed, Jason,' Angel clutched at his hands. 'Bring Rose home safely.'

'I will. Do not worry.'

He kissed her fingers and smiled down at her, but the anxious look was still in her eyes when he left her.

The hours ticked by. Angel took a solitary breakfast and then wandered disconsolately through the empty rooms. She could not settle to anything, she was far too anxious. She was fearful that Jason would not find Rose and Tobias Knowsley, and even more concerned that he would. The idea of the Duke fighting a duel terrified her. She could not bear the thought of him killing a man or being killed himself.

When the butler came to find her, carrying a folded missive on the silver tray, she snatched it up.

'Oh,' she said, her spirits dipping. 'It is from Lady Ragholme, requesting that Lady Elinor and Mrs Watson might be allowed to remain for dinner.'

At least it meant she need not tell them about Rose until later. She forced a smile to her lips.

'She assures me she will provide outriders to escort them back to town later tonight. I shall pen a reply immediately, Marcuss. Please have a servant ready to carry it to Ragholme Hall.'

The task took only a few minutes, and then she was back to pacing the floor and trying to prevent her imagination from conjuring up the very worst scenarios. The ones in which Jason was lost to her for ever.

The short November day dragged on into darkness.

Angel instructed that dinner should be put back, and settled down in the morning room with her embroidery, plying her needle by the light from a branched candlestick.

Mrs Watson returned with Nell, who was too full of her splendid day out to question Angel's explanation that Rose was at a party of pleasure with her friends.

Once Nell was tucked up in her bed Angel went to find Mrs Watson and tell her what she knew, which seemed pitifully scant, but she refused to allow the widow to sit up with her.

'There is nothing we can do until we have some news,' Angel told her. 'It would be best if you get some rest now. Then you will be fresh to deal with anything that is required in the morning.'

'Very well, Your Grace, I will go to my bed. Although I doubt I shall sleep until I know my darling girl is safe.'

She went off then, and Angel went back to her embroidery, only to be interrupted shortly after by the butler.

'Cook has asked me if you wish him to put dinner back again, Your Grace.'

Angel hesitated, and Marcuss gave a little cough.

'I would suggest another hour, ma'am. It is important that the household thinks we expect the Duke to return shortly.'

She looked up at him. 'Does everyone know what has occurred?'

The butler shook his head. 'No, Your Grace. There was some speculation this morning, of course, but that was confounded when His Grace went off with Mr Babberton.'

'Yes, that is something, I suppose.' She sighed. 'Very well. Another hour, then.'

Bowing, the old retainer withdrew, and Angel was left with her thoughts. She knew Jason would not rest until he had found Rose, but could he bring her home unharmed? And if not, what vengeance might he wreak upon his cousin?

The sound of voices intruded.

Angel threw aside her embroidery and jumped to her feet just as the door opened.

'Jason!' She stared at him, her eyes widening in dismay to see he was alone. 'What…? Where…? Oh, thank goodness!'

The frantic worry faded when she saw Mr Babberton coming into the room, one arm firmly around Rose. He was holding her close against him, but when Rose saw Angel and put out her hands he released her immediately.

'She is unharmed,' he said, as Rose fell into Angel's arms, 'But she is naturally distressed and exhausted.'

'We shall get her upstairs as soon as possible,' said Angel. 'I have already ordered hot bricks to be put in her bed.'

'Not yet!' cried Rose, clinging tighter. 'I could not sleep just yet.'

'Very well, then. You shall sit with me until you are ready.' Angel guided Rose to the sofa. 'But I should very much like to know what happened. Would you mind if we talk of it?'

'N-no.'

They were just sitting down when the door opened again.

'I have ordered refreshments to be brought in,' explained Jason as the butler and a footman put down their trays upon the side table. 'Marcuss says it will be an hour before dinner is ready. I thought some wine and bread and butter in the meantime might not go amiss.'

'And there is a cup of hot chocolate for Miss Haringey,' added the butler, his kindly eyes shadowed with concern. 'If she would care for it?'

Rose did care for it. She declared that the warm drink and a slice of bread was all she required.

Kenelm Babberton immediately fetched them over to her, placing the cup and plate on a table beside her while the Duke poured wine for everyone else.

'How far were you obliged to travel?' asked Angel, when they were all seated.

'To Huntingdon,' said Jason.

'It would have been a lot further if Miss Haringey had not had the presence of mind to pretend that she was a poor traveller,' put in Kenelm, smiling fondly at Rose. 'She insisted she would be violently ill if the postboys did not slow down.'

Rose shuddered. 'It was horrible. Mr Knowsley k-kept calling me L-Lavinia…and saying he w-worshipped me.' She sat up a little straighter, saying angrily, 'He tricked me!'

'By signing himself "K," knowing you would think it was Mr Babberton?' asked Angel.

'No, that, apparently, was mere coincidence, but it worked

in Knowsley's favour,' said the Duke, draining his glass. 'He knew Rose would not consent to an elopement, so he promised to bring her back here.'

'I would n-never have left the house if I had known it was not Kenelm!' exclaimed Rose, sending the young man a look full of apology. 'And I *should* have known. I should have realised that he is too good, too honourable, to suggest a meeting after he had given his word to Papa.'

'You are quite correct, I would not,' replied Mr Babberton, returning her look with an ardent one of his own. 'Even though it was breaking my heart to leave London without you.'

'Yes, well, we can talk more of this tomorrow.' Jason rose abruptly. 'Rose can hardly keep her eyes open. She needs to go to bed.'

'Yes, of course,' said Angel. 'Come along, my dear, I will take you to your room.'

Rose got up meekly and went with her towards the door, but as she passed Kenelm Babberton she stopped. 'I would like to properly express my gratitude to you for rescuing me today,' she murmured. 'Shall I see you in the morning?'

It was the Duke who replied.

'You can hardly avoid it. Babberton is sleeping here tonight.'

Both Rose and Angel stared at him.

'It would be nigh on impossible for him to find anywhere to stay at this time of night,' he said gruffly. 'I have had his bags taken up to one of the guest rooms.'

'Oh, how *kind* you are, Papa!'

Angel observed Jason's look of surprise when Rose threw her arms around him and hugged him. She then gave Kenelm another shy smile before allowing herself to be taken off to bed.

Angel handed Rose over to the care of her maid and went

back to the morning room, where she found Jason alone and sitting on a sofa.

'Babberton is gone off to change his coat before we dine,' he explained, holding out her refilled wine glass. 'Do you mind my being here in all my dirt? I fear if I go upstairs I shall be too tired to come down again.'

'Not at all,' she said, sitting beside him. 'You have had a very wearing day.'

'Damnable.'

One question had been nagging away at her since his return. She said, 'I did not like to ask while Rose was present, but your cousin…?'

'We left him in Huntingdon with his post-chaise, free to go where the devil he wishes.' He hesitated. 'I saw the look on your face when we left. You were worried about what I might do.'

'I was afraid you would fight with him.'

'I was very tempted when we walked into the George and found him in a private parlour, trying to put his arm about Rose. Babberton saved me the trouble. Before I could stop him he pulled Knowsley to his feet and dealt him a crashing blow to the chin. Kenelm was all for calling him out, but I persuaded him against it.'

'You did?'

'Yes. You look astonished.'

'I am. I thought…'

'You thought I would run him through!' He shrugged. 'It didn't take me long to realise the fellow is not in his right mind. He began by talking of Rose's resemblance to her mother and saying he could not help himself. Then he began calling her Lavinia. He took great pleasure in telling me that they had been lovers since shortly after Nell was born, although I know very well he was not the only one.'

His mouth twisted. 'She cast her favours very wide, it seems. Including royalty.'

'Oh, heavens! And that did not make you lose your temper?'

He shook his head. 'I had suspected it already. What I did not know was that she had sold the Darvell jewels to pay Knowsley's gambling debts, as well as her own. The twisted logic being that the money would be his to spend one day.'

'Oh, that was very wrong of them!' exclaimed Angel. 'That makes me so angry. I think now that Mr Knowsley *should* be punished!'

'And so he will be—but not by me. He is already in debt again, and now I have remarried it is unlikely his creditors will consider his claims to be my heir are very strong. He will most likely have to fly the country.' He glanced at her. 'I thought you'd consider that a better solution than my fighting with him.'

'I do,' she told him. 'Not merely because duelling is against the law, Jason, but for your own peace of mind. I know you would regret it if you killed him.' She twisted her hands together for a moment before going on. 'It must have been difficult for you *not* to call him out. Knowing how he and Lavinia deceived you.'

'Do you know, it was not that hard at all? When I saw the fellow gibbering about losing his head over Rose, just because of her resemblance to her mother, all I felt was pity.' He took the glass from her and put it down with his own on the nearest table before pulling her into his arms. 'I was besotted with Lavinia once, Angel, but that was a very long time ago, and for the last few years of our marriage I hated her. I hated myself, too, for being such a fool. I was filled with loathing and regret, but now even that has faded to almost nothing.'

'Oh, has it?' she asked, intently studying his neckcloth.

'Yes. I realise now that what I felt for her was infatuation. Nothing like the deep and abiding love I feel for you, Angel mine.' His fingers gently pushed her chin up and he kissed her. 'It has taken me far too long to tell you that. I have struggled against admitting it, even to myself, but I am saying it now and I will continue to say it every day of my life if you will let me.' His arms tightened. 'Can you ever forgive me for being such a crass fool, my love?'

'Of course I can,' she said softly.

'And…one more thing,' he said, clearly determined there should be no more secrets. 'About the annulment. It is far more complicated than non-consummation and involves a very public investigation, which I would never put you through, Angel. I was quite wrong about it.'

'Now, that I can never forgive!' she exclaimed wrathfully. 'When I think of those weeks…the nights when I longed for you to take me to your bed—'

'You must not think that I did not suffer too,' he said, with feeling. 'Oh, Angel, what can I do to make it up to you? I do love you, you know. Quite desperately!'

'I think it is going to take a very long time,' she murmured, slipping her arms about his neck. 'But those words are a good start. I have been waiting my whole life for you to say them.'

He kissed her face, her eyes, her nose, her cheeks, whispering, 'I love you!' over and over, until she was sighing with happiness. Then, with a growl of triumph, he captured her lips and kissed her long and thoroughly.

Thus it was that Mr Babberton, coming into the room, saw the Duke and Duchess entwined in each other's arms and softly withdrew again.

Epilogue

April sunshine poured down upon Rotherton House, which was filled with family and friends staying for the wedding of Mr Kenelm Babberton and Miss Rose Haringey. The state rooms had been turned into one vast ballroom for the evening celebrations, but now everyone was driving off to the little church in Middlewych for the ceremony itself.

Everyone except the Duke and Duchess of Rotherton.

Angel went in search of Jason and found him in his dressing room, standing before the looking glass and wrestling with his cravat. The floor around him was littered with lengths of discarded muslin, mute witness to his failed attempts.

He met her eyes in the mirror. 'I cannot get the confounded knot right!'

'We have a few minutes yet. The last of the guests have only just left and I have sent Rose on ahead with Mama. They will meet us inside the church.' She hid a smile when another mauled cravat was thrown to the floor. 'Where is Adams? Can he not help?'

'I sent him away. Damme, I have never yet let my valet tie my neckcloth!'

She waited quietly while he arranged a fresh length of muslin about his neck and tied an intricate knot.

'There.' He gave one of the folds a final tweak and looked at himself critically in the glass. 'That will have to do, I suppose.'

She stepped closer and placed one hand on his chest while she inspected his efforts. 'That is very good, but will it stop you kissing me?'

In answer to her teasing, he dragged her into his arms.

'Well, madam,' he said, when he finally raised his head, 'how does it look now?'

'You have probably quite ruined it!' she said crossly, her cheeks burning.

He turned towards the looking glass.

'No,' he said, studying himself critically. 'In fact, I think it looks better. If anyone asks, I shall tell them it is called the Angel's Kiss. What think you?'

'I think you are being nonsensical,' she told him, trying to sound severe, although she knew there was a deep blush of pleasure on her cheeks. 'You have yet to fasten the diamond pin in place.'

'Will you do that for me?'

'Of course.'

Angel picked it up from the dressing table and when she turned back he was holding out one hand, observing its slight tremble.

'I have no idea why I am so nervous today.'

'Hush. Keep your chin up,' she admonished him. 'Your stepdaughter is getting married. It is no wonder you want it to go well. Be easy, my love, it is only a country wedding, like our own.'

He huffed out a sigh. 'I was never this anxious when we were married.'

He was silent as she inserted the pin carefully between the snowy folds of muslin at his throat, then he exclaimed, 'We should have been married in town, with all the pomp that a duchess deserves!'

She chuckled. 'That would have taken a whole year to or-ganise. As it is we have been married for twelve months and thus we can concentrate upon Rose's nuptials.' The pin secure, she placed her hands against his chest again and smiled lovingly up at him. 'Believe me, Jason, I was very happy to be married from Goole Park, with all my family around me.'

'And now, Angel mine?' He covered her hands with his own, his grey eyes searching his face. 'Are you truly happy now?'

'Oh, can you doubt it, my love?' She stretched up to kiss him lightly, then tucked her hand in his. 'Come along, Your Grace. Everyone will be waiting for us. You must do your duty by your stepdaughter.'

'Duty, bah! You know I abhor all this fuss.'

She chuckled. 'You might as well get used to it, my love. Look upon it as practice for when Nell marries. And then, of course, there will be our own children.' She placed one hand on the swell of her belly, where their baby was growing within her. 'I hope this will be the first of many.'

Jason's face softened for a moment, then he said gruffly, 'That is another reason we should not be doing this. You should be resting.'

'Fustian! I am feeling very well.' She threw him a saucy glance from under her lashes. 'When we were in bed this morning you said I was blooming.'

He relented then, as she had known he would.

'And you are. You get more beautiful every day.'

He bent his head and kissed her again.

Angel felt the tug of desire as his lips captured hers, so strong it was a physical ache, and she gave a little sigh of disappointment when he stopped.

'It is my turn to remind you of our duty, madam,' he murmured, his eyes glinting.

He took her arm and escorted out to the waiting carriage.

They bowled through the spring sunshine to the little parish church, where they found the vicar waiting at the door.

'All the guests are inside and seated, Your Grace,' he greeted them. 'If you are ready to join them?'

Jason waved him on. 'Aye, aye, let us go in. Lead the way, sir.'

The vicar went ahead of them and disappeared into the shadowed interior of the church, but Jason held back. Angel glanced up and saw his face was grim, set. The look of a private man steeling himself for another public appearance.

Her fingers moved from his sleeve to his hand. 'Come along, my love. We can do this together.'

The tension eased, he gripped her hand. 'With you beside me, my angel, I can do anything.'

She returned his smile, tucked her hand back into his sleeve, and silently they went together into the church.

* * * * *

Don't miss the stories in this mini series!

A SEASON OF CELEBRATION

Wed In Haste To The Duke
SARAH MALLORY
May 2024

The Kiss That Made Her Countess
LAURA MARTIN
June 2024

MILLS & BOON

More Than A Match
For The Earl

Emily E K Murdoch

MILLS & BOON

USA TODAY bestselling author **Emily E K Murdoch** is read in multiple languages around the world. Enjoy sweet romances as Emily Murdoch and steamy romances as Emily E K Murdoch. Emily's had a varied career to date: from examining medieval manuscripts to designing museum exhibitions to working as a researcher for the BBC to working for the National Trust. Her books range from England in 1050 to Texas in 1848, and she can't wait for you to fall in love with her heroes and heroines!

Look out for more books from Emily E K Murdoch coming soon!

Author Note

This book wouldn't exist without a great number of
people. Anyone missed from the list is entirely my error,
as are any mistakes that you find (please don't look).

Mary and Gordon Murdoch
My wonderful husband
Stephanie Booth
Amy Rose Bennett
Kathryn Le Veque
Awo Ibrahim
Charlotte Ellis
Ishita Gupta
Elsa Sjunneson-Henry
Krista Oliver
Ruth Machanda
The Harlequin typesetting and proofreading teams

DEDICATION

For my bridesmaids. GB, SB, BC and SP.
And to PB, PB, BB and BB.

Chapter One

The room was busy, far busier than Marilla Newell could ever remember in all the three years she had lived at the Wallflower Academy. The heady noises were bouncing off the walls, mingling with each other, worsening the weary headache after such a long day, making it difficult for her to pick out individual voices as she sat quietly in an armchair by the fire.

'Wonderful wedding, charming girl…'

'And who is her family, precisely? I have met neither mother nor father, yet Lady Devereux was telling me…'

'Never been inside the Wallflower Academy, though I have heard plenty about it! I once heard there was a blind woman here…'

The soft satin of the gown Lady Devereux had been so kind to gift her, and Sylvia, too, had small embroidered flowers upon it. They were a different style and shape to those on the bride's dress: Gwen's were forget-me-nots, Sylvia had told her, and these were daisies.

There were differences. Longer petals, a different kind of stitch. As Rilla sat silently in the melee of noise, she allowed her fingers to gently move across them. Daisies. One here… and here. A space of around two inches between them. Very delicate work.

'Is *that* her?'

'No, that's Miss Daphne Smith, nice girl, too quiet for my taste…'

Rilla sighed when the words became clearer as the speakers grew closer, then farther away, hoping that the ache in her feet would soon settle.

It would have been too much to hope that they intended to approach her. She was not the sort of woman, she knew, that any gentlemen bothered to speak to. It had not taken her the full three years at the Wallflower Academy to know that.

Why, Rilla could not recall a single gentleman actually speaking just to her since she had arrived here, which was a great disappointment to her father. What was the point in learning how to attract a gentleman, he mentioned in his latest letter, if she never put her learnings into practice?

Well, the service was over. Gwendoline Knox, newest wallflower to enter the Academy, was married—and to a duke.

Rilla permitted herself a small smile. No one would have predicted that the most recent wallflower to join the Academy would be the next to wed. But then, just because Gwen had been least likely to win a duke, that did not mean that it was impossible.

And she had.

With no father to host the wedding reception, Gwen had graciously accepted the offer to hold it at the Wallflower Academy. Which had its advantages, Rilla thought dispassionately as she sat quietly in her chair, out of the way. And its disadvantages.

Someone approached her, someone who spent far too much time with the carbolic soap and not enough time considering her words.

The smile became wry on Rilla's lips before Miss Pike spoke. It would be the same old topic, of course. The owner of the Wallflower Academy did not appear to have any other.

'Miss Newell,' said Miss Pike sharply. 'It is I.'

Rilla nodded. 'I know, Miss Pike. Please, sit down.'

She was accustomed to uttering the phrase, even though she had no idea whether there was another seat close by that would be convenient. In the murky, shadowy vision she had, it was impossible to tell.

In Rilla's experience, it did not really matter. Either her conversational partner would sit, or they would not. The only difference was the height from which the next words came.

'Miss Newell, I have something of great import to discuss with you.'

Rilla nodded but said nothing. What was there to say? Miss Pike had evidently found a chair, for her voice came from lower and to her left, but nothing Rilla could advance would prevent Miss Pike from her conversation.

It would be the same tired old conversation they had been having for above a year now. It was too much to hope, Rilla thought with a sinking feeling nestling in her stomach, that the woman would actually say something original.

And after such a day, too. Whispers in the church, the half-heard mutters wondering why on earth she was still unmarried, the desperate attempts to continuously plaster a smile on her face…

'I have spoken with your family once more, and they quite agree with me,' came the terse tone of Miss Pike above the hubbub of the wedding reception. 'You would be a marvellous tutor here at the Wallflower Academy. And with the additional help, I could open up the west corridor, welcome even more wallflowers here!'

Rilla nodded, boredom slipping into her soul as she forced herself to remain silent. An ever more frequent habit, now she came to think about it.

It was the same argument over and over, and though the Pike was not rude enough to say it aloud, her meaning was clear.

No one would marry Rilla. No one would offer for her hand. No one wanted a blind wife.

It rankled deep in Rilla's soul that Miss Pike could even think such a thing, but it was so obvious. Why else would she continuously attempt to persuade her to give up her position as a wallflower, and instead become a tutor to others?

'I think that would be a little premature, do not you?' said Rilla quietly. 'I mean, I am still young, not yet thirty. There is still a chance that I could become a wife. Have...have a child.'

She did not need to be able to see to know Miss Pike was scoffing. Rilla could hear it in her shifting movement on the chair, the way she clicked her tongue most offensively.

'Really, Rilla,' said Miss Pike dismissively. 'I am not so sure.'

'But if you were actually attempting to help me wed, to find someone to marry,' said Rilla hotly, trying to keep her voice down as she was unsure who else was around her but was unable to prevent ire from slipping onto her tongue, 'then you would know!'

There was a moment of silence. Rilla tried to hold her tongue.

'You are—'

Someone shouted across the room, blotting out Miss Pike's word. 'I beg your pardon?'

'You are ungrateful, Miss Newell.'

Perhaps she should not have asked. 'I do not ask for special treatment,' said Rilla, trying to keep her voice level. 'Just the same opportunities as the others. You see what Gwen could do, if merely left to her own devices and not prevented from success?'

Well. Gwen had perhaps not entirely been perfect in the odd courtship she and the Duke of Knaresby had entertained.

Not that Rilla was about to reveal that to the Pike.

'Here I am, running the Wallflower Academy, which is solely designed to help ladies such as yourself find husbands,' Miss Pike almost shouted over the hubbub. 'And prices go up every month, and do I ask for more funds from your family?'

A prickle of pain. 'No, Miss—'

'Five miles from London,' the proprietress was saying, though Rilla could barely hear her now. 'And close to Brighton, and as you can imagine it costs a pretty penny to…more than half…a chicken!'

Rilla frowned. A chicken? What on earth was she talking about?

'And another thing—'

The room was becoming rowdier, the noise almost deafening, Miss Pike's words were getting lost in the kerfuffle. A card table had been set up in the Orangery, Sylvia Bryant had told her earlier, and there were real fears from the servants that blows would be had over some of the hands being dealt.

'Have to sort out—'

'Miss Pike?'

Rilla received no reply. It was infuriating, not knowing whether one's conversational partner was merely thinking, hesitating, or had wished her well under the cacophony and departed, thinking that Rilla had heard her goodbye.

Though she had lived her life without sight, Rilla had a vague view of light and dark. It was not enough, however, in the chaos of this room to see whether Miss Pike had walked away.

A hand rested on her shoulder. Rilla did not jump; she was too accustomed to it. It was one of the ways the wallflowers announced their presence.

'It is me. Gwen,' said the bride. Her hand was soft on Rilla's shoulder, and disappeared though the voice continued. 'What were you talking about with Miss Pike?'

Rilla's shoulders sagged. 'She is gone, then? 'tis so noisy in here, I could not hear.'

'I believe she was distracted by Sylvia attempting to run away again.' There was just a hint of mirth in Gwen's words, enough to make Rilla believe Miss Pike had no choice but to dash after the miscreant. Typical Sylvia.

'No.'

'It…it did not appear to be a pleasant conversation between the two of you,' came Gwen's soft voice.

Rilla almost laughed. The woman married a duke not two hours ago, yet was still hesitant to speak her mind. Gwen was part empress, part wallflower. A very strange mix.

'It was not,' she said aloud. 'You may as well know—all the other wallflowers do—though I suppose you are not a wallflower now.'

Rilla heard Gwen laugh.

'Once a wallflower, always a wallflower, I think,' Gwen's voice said, merriment in her tones. 'But you were going to tell me what you and Miss Pike were speaking of. I am sorry it was not pleasant.'

It was not, and it was surprisingly painful for Rilla to admit, but there should be no shame in it. It was not her decision, after all.

'My family and Miss Pike wish for me to give up any idea of marriage,' Rilla said quietly. A hand touched hers—Gwen's, she had to assume. It clasped hers. Somehow, it made it easier to speak. 'They wish for me to settle instead as a tutor here, at the Academy.'

Why did it pain her so much? Not only to say it aloud, but to say it to such a person: a woman she had only met a few months ago, who had already managed to find a match within that time.

And to a duke, too. No wonder Miss Pike was delighted.

'I am sorry,' said Rilla hastily. 'I should not speak of such things on such a wonderful day for you. This wedding reception, it is marvellous.'

'It is altogether too noisy, and has too many people,' Gwen said dryly. 'Over one hundred people, I don't know what Percy— Miss Pike was forced to hire two men to act as additional footmen, you know.'

Well, that explained the noise pounding on Rilla's eardrums, taking away another one of her senses, making it a challenge to navigate the rooms she knew so well.

'Still. You are married now. I hope— I am sure you will be very happy.'

Gwen's hands squeezed hers. 'Thank you, but you do not need to apologize. And I certainly do not agree with Miss Pike.'

'I do not want to be a tutor at the Wallflower Academy,' Rilla said slowly, greater strength entering her voice with every word. 'I have no wish for this to be my life forever.'

The Wallflower Academy was not the worst place to live, to be sure, but to dwell in the monotony of the place for the rest of her life? To be entrapped here through a tutor position?

No. No, Rilla would not permit it.

A gentle squeeze again from Gwen, then she released Rilla's hand. 'You can do whatever you put your mind to, if you ask me. Why, you are the cleverest among us wallflowers, and without your advice and rather sarcastic comments—'

'I did not always intend sarcasm!' protested Rilla.

Gwen laughed. 'I know. And I do wonder sometimes whether...well. Not everyone understands your sense of humour.'

Rilla's stomach churned. Yes, she knew that. Had known it the moment the Earl—

'But I stand by my comment,' continued Gwen happily. 'You can do whatever you put your mind to, Rilla.'

A slow and determined sigh rushed through her lungs as she took a deep breath. 'I know. And I will.'

'Gwen? Gwen, come over here and meet—'

'I'm talking with—'

'—the Marquess of—'

'Oh. Oh, Rilla,' came Gwen's nervous voice with a touch of tension which had not been there before. 'I know you do not like being left alone, but you do not mind if I...'

'Go—meet a marquess,' said Rilla, not unkindly, as her heart sank.

'I'll come straight back,' promised her newly wedded friend. 'It's just, Percy wants to introduce me, and I...well, I'll be back.'

A quick squeeze of the hand, a rush of skirts, and Rilla was almost certain she was alone.

Alone. The word sank into her stomach like a stone. Alone, as she had ever been.

Not that she wished to be introduced in turn to the marquess, whoever he was. No, there was a special sort of awkwardness in standing before a gentleman, knowing that you were being judged, unable to see whether he approved or disapproved of what he saw.

It was intolerable.

Unless he fell head over heels in love with you, a small part of her whispered—the part of her she had tried to ignore for the last three years. And then he would marry you, and—

And then what? Rilla forced aside the thought, even as the longing for love and marriage and companionship and adventure rose in her heart.

That was not her lot in life. Though admittedly, perhaps if she took a leaf out of Sylvia's book and flirted a little...

Fear gripped her at the very thought.

Flirt? Her? She barely knew how. Just being surrounded by all these people that she couldn't see struck discomfort down her spine.

Well, she'd remained downstairs in the drawing room for long enough. Her dues had been paid, she had been perfectly polite, and now Rilla could do what she had wished to do almost the minute she had entered the church.

Retreat to her bedchamber and concoct her next defence against Miss Pike's constant demands that she become a tutor.

Rilla felt the soft heaviness of her skirts shift as she rose and grasped her cane, the reassuring warmth of the wood under her fingers. She had been placed, thanks to some manoeuvring from Sylvia, in the armchair closest to the door to the hall. Six steps—eight, in these formal shoes.

She reached out for the door as she approached it, felt the roughness of the wallpaper, the cooler wood of the door frame. It was open.

Of course it was, Rilla told herself as she carefully stepped through, listening intently for anyone stepping across the marble-floored hall, her cane making a different noise on the different floor. She had not heard the subtle click of the door, had she?

Four steps, and she would need to lean slightly to the right to avoid the plinth upon which, she had been told, sat a planter with a large overgrown something within. Rilla had felt the luscious leaves once, when she had been left alone in the hall waiting for Gwen. Springy, and warm to the touch, like the leaves of the plants in the Orangery.

Another six steps, and she would reach the bottom of the staircase. Almost free. Almost—

'Goodness gracious,' came a male voice as Rilla's cane tapped into something solid, her free hand wandering ahead of her and finding something warm.

She recoiled, drawing her hand back towards her after the sudden contact.

The memory of the touch remained. A strength, a broadness, muscles defined even through a linen shirt and soft wool jacket. A warmth, a presence, something that heated her fingers even through the gloves.

Rilla rocked for a moment on her heels. This was a contact she would not swiftly forget.

'I do beg your pardon,' she said stiffly.

Mortification poured through her chest. Dear God, she would be grateful when the pack of them left and gave her back her Academy.

'I apologize myself. I have never been here before, and I was taking some drinks over to—'

'Ah, one of the footmen the Pike hired,' Rilla said with a nod. 'It is of no matter.'

'One of the—'

'Yes, Gwen mentioned there were a couple of you,' she said, steadying herself now even as her mind whirled with the scent of the man.

Sandalwood, and salt, and lemon. A freshness and a newness that made Rilla tilt forward, just for a moment, to take another breath.

Oh, he smelt delicious.

Heat flushed Rilla's cheeks. She couldn't go around sniffing footmen!

Flirting. Well, it wouldn't hurt, would it, to flirt a little with a footman? He was only at the Wallflower Academy temporarily, after all. And no one would know.

Her whole body was reacting to the man in a way it had never done before. Heat was rising, tendrils of desire curling around her heart, warmth in her chest, an aching need to lean toward him—

Rilla caught herself from falling into his presumably outstretched arms just in time.

Get hold of yourself, woman!

'I suppose you've been traipsing about after these idiots all afternoon,' Rilla said in a low voice.

It was most indecorous to speak so, but then, he was a footman, and a temporary one at that. He'd be gone by the morning, taking his delicious scent with him, more's the pity.

There would be no consequences to this conversation.

'Idiots?' said the man lightly.

Even his voice was delectable. Rilla had never heard anything like it—like honey trickled over a spoon that coated one's lips.

She forced down the thought, and the accompanying warmth that fluttered in her chest.

'The nobility, the guests,' Rilla said softly so that only he could hear her. 'I imagine they've been ordering you about like no one's business.'

Perhaps she ought not to speak in such a manner. Perhaps the footman would be offended. She had no idea.

The noise of the drawing room was echoing around the hall, making it a challenge to concentrate on the hurried and awkward voices before her.

Half of conversation, Daphne had once read in a book and announced in hushed horror to the other wallflowers, was silent. In other words, half was not actually the conversation at all: how people looked, the sparkle in their eyes, the tilt of a head, the warmth in an expression.

All elements Rilla could not see.

She had other senses. The man standing before her had a presence that she could sense despite her lack of sight. He was mere inches from her, and though Rilla wrestled against it, she could not help but lean closer. The man was…attractive. There was no other word for it.

Yet it told her nothing about the man himself.

She was typically so wary of meeting new people. So much of who they were was invisible to her. Their opinion of her, assumed rather than known. The unspoken part of the conversation lost to her.

'You are right, these people have been absolutely outrageous,' said the man in a conspiratorial whisper. 'But don't tell anyone I said that.'

A curl of a smile tilted her lips. It was almost a flirtation! And with a servant!

It should have felt wrong, utterly unconscionable. Somehow the spark of attraction between them overrode any sense of decorum, any typical reticence with the opposite sex.

The last time she had enjoyed such a thing… Well, she could hardly recall.

Miss Pike would be horrified—a flirtation, with a servant?

But this did not matter. He would not matter in a few hours. And so she didn't even introduce herself with her proper title.

'Miss Marilla Newell,' she said lightly.

'Finlay Jellicoe,' the man said beside her in a low, sultry voice. 'And I must say, you are beautiful, Miss Newell.'

A voice, now she came to think about it, that was…warm. Amused, perhaps. A low voice, but coming from a few inches higher than her head. He was tall, then. Whoever he was.

'You flatter me, sir,' Rilla countered, her heart skipping a beat.

'Hard not to flatter a woman so elegant and so refined,' said Mr Jellicoe, his voice quiet, private, as though they were the only two in the world and were not surrounded by a cacophony of unknown voices. 'Beauty will always reveal itself, and I have to say, I am delighted it has revealed itself to me.'

And she giggled.

Giggled! What on earth?

But Rilla felt surprisingly comfortable with Mr Jellicoe; there was no other word for it. There was no tension in her shoulders, and her laugh was natural and light.

Perhaps it was because he was a servant, perhaps because he would be gone. Rilla could not explain it—but he drew something from her that no man ever had.

A longing…to know him better.

The odd thing was, she felt an overwhelming sense that he knew her already. As though this meeting was…fated. Designed.

As though she could be herself with him, as with no other.

The attraction did not hurt, of course, but it was more than that. More than anything she had ever known.

'Is there any chance that you will be retained by Miss Pike? As a footman, I mean,' she heard herself saying.

Which was a ridiculous question to ask. Her, wed a footman? The very idea!

Though a footman that spoke like this and smelt like this and who had a chest that felt like that...

Mr Jellicoe was chuckling gently, and Rilla longed to reach out and feel the movement of his joy. 'I very much doubt it. I, ah, I am not a footman, Miss Newell.'

Rilla stiffened. A half step back was easily taken as a cold chill fluttered through her lungs. 'Not...not a footman?'

'In fact, I am afraid I am one of those idiots being served,' admitted the man. He was still laughing. 'I was actually taking glasses over to my friend, Lord—'

'You rogue,' said Rilla darkly.

'You— I beg your pardon?'

A year ago—perhaps even less—Rilla would have stopped there. She would have demurred, attempted to pass off her rudeness as a jest, and hoped that the conversation would move on.

But she was tired. Tired of always being left out, tired of the Pike's assumptions about her, tired of listening to the wedding vows of other wallflowers as they stepped—or stumbled—up the aisle.

No. No longer.

Rilla was not going to put up with it any longer.

The heat of embarrassment that Rilla always attempted to avoid, and never managed to, seeped into her cheeks.

'I must say, you make a pretty poor wallflower,' said Mr Jellicoe conversationally, as though the whole thing was entertainment for his own amusement. 'Your conversation is magnificent—I'm rather disappointed.'

Rilla's mouth opened, but she was so stunned by the man's ease, she could think of nothing to say.

How dare he just come here and...and speak to her thus!

'Miss Pike tells me you'll be a tutor here before long,' Mr Jellicoe said, utterly oblivious apparently to the fact that she had ceased contributing to the conversation. 'Good for you. I suppose.'

And his nonchalance, his complete inability to understand her obvious chagrin, poured through Rilla's body like the fine brandy the wallflowers had been permitted upon the announcement of Gwen's engagement.

In the mere moments they had spent together, Rilla had felt...well, a kinship, of a sort.

Which was ridiculous, she told herself. How she could have got such an idea she did not know. It was ridiculous, foolish to the extreme.

She was feeling betrayed by a man she hardly knew...but that was rather the point, wasn't it? So swiftly into their encounter, he had presumed to know her, to speak so blandly of her future as though it did not matter...

And she had liked him. Been attracted to him.

It had been a trying day. That was what Rilla told herself later, when she looked back on what she did next.

A long day, and a trying one. She had been pushed beyond all endurance by the whispers in the church, the hushed pity of everyone she passed, the Pike's insistence she would never marry, Gwen's well-meaning but misplaced compassion...

And that was why she finally gave up all attempt at civility.

'You, sir, are a man of the lowest order and I have no wish to speak to you,' Rilla said, glaring in the direction of where the man's voice had last come from, and desperately hoping he had not stepped to the side—or worse, gone entirely. 'I am sick and tired of the boorish behaviour of men like you, and I don't care if you know it!'

And there was no response.

No spluttering. No outraged gasp. No retort that she was wrong, or rude, or disrespectful.

Instead, his voice came low, and soft, and quiet. 'Lowest order? I'll have you know I'm an earl. The Earl of—'

Rilla snorted, relishing the freedom of saying precisely what she wanted. Well, it wasn't as though she would ever encounter this earl again, would she?

'An earl? Of course. I should have guessed by your rudeness,' she said, speaking over the man. 'No manners to even introduce yourself properly. Why am I not surprised!'

'I am surprised,' said the Earl of... Rilla couldn't recall. 'As an earl—'

'I have no wish to hear it,' Rilla said curtly, fire blossoming through her lungs.

She would regret this. She knew she would; she always did when she allowed her frustrations to overcome her tongue. It was a rare occurrence, but when her temper burned, it burned bright.

To think she had believed him a footman! Had allowed herself to relax, to accept his pretty compliments!

An earl! After all she had suffered at the hands of an earl... but Miss Pike did not know that, did she? No, her father had gone to great pains to keep that within the family...

'No wish to hear it?' The earl sounded...not amused, but something else. Intrigued? 'Miss Newell, I admit I am captivated. Tell me...'

'I have no wish to tell you anything,' Rilla said, exhaustion starting to creep into her mind, demanding payment for the debts made earlier that day. 'I wish to go upstairs—alone, sir!'

The last words were spoken as a hand touched hers—a hand that was unexpected, sudden, and unwelcome.

Rilla wrenched her hand away. There was nothing more disorienting, more alarming, than being touched by a stranger when one was not expecting it.

He had probably attempted to help her, Rilla thought darkly, but naturally he didn't know. She'd lived in the Tudor manor that was the Wallflower Academy for over three years. She knew every inch: the wide hallway, the corridors, the drawing room with its sofas and armchairs that the servants and wallflowers knew better than to move, the dining room with Rilla's chair always near one end, two in from the left.

This was her world—her domain. She could, she thought with a wry smile, navigate around it with her eyes shut.

Not that it would make much difference.

'Go away, Earl of wherever you are,' Rilla said dismissively, stepping forward and reaching out for what she knew she would find.

The cool wood of the banister was a relief to her fingertips.

'But—'

'I don't want to hear it,' she said quietly. 'Tell Miss Pike I've retired upstairs. I'm not some entertainment for you, whoever you are. I'm just Rilla.'

Chapter Two

It had been, all things considered, a very long day. And now a woman was shouting at him.

Finlay stood still, as though a strong wind had just passed him and he'd had to lean into it to prevent himself from falling.

Well. That was…different.

Certainly different from Miss Isabelle Carr.

'My lord, I must apologize,' came a voice behind him. 'I had no idea you were speaking with Miss Newell!'

Finlay turned and shrugged languidly, seeing with some relief that he still appeared to have an effect on the ladies.

Miss Pike giggled. 'She is an incorrigible bluestocking that woman, my lord. You must not pay attention to a single word she says.'

Almost against his will, Finlay found his attention drifting to the stairs which Miss Newell had so recently ascended.

Not pay attention to a single word she says?

'Yes, not a single word,' he said softly.

I have no wish to tell you anything. I wish to go upstairs—alone, sir!

A bluestocking. Well, that certainly did not explain why Miss Newell had been so obviously disgruntled to discover that he was an earl. Strange. Finlay had always discovered that it aided people's opinion of him, rather than diminished it.

Most strange.

Finlay blinked. Only then did he realize that the proprietress of the Wallflower Academy was still watching him closely, evidently curious to know what he was thinking.

Not that he was thinking about much. Definitely not.

'Fear not, Miss Pike,' Finlay said, giving a broad smile which made Miss Pike flush. 'I shall not give her a second thought.'

And he truly did not. Well, he did, but it was swiftly followed by a third thought, a fourth thought and a fifth. By the time the following day had dawned and Finlay had suffered through an awkward ride with his betrothed, Miss Isabelle Carr, a monotonous conversation with his mother about the guest list for the wedding, and a dinner which he had agreed to host as a favour to his mother, he had thought about Miss Marilla Newell at least four hundred and thirty-two times.

Which was not, Finlay told himself silently as he nodded along to his friend's words as they entered his own home, technically a second thought.

'That ball was absolute rot,' Lord George Bartlett was saying with a laugh as they entered Staromchor House.

Finlay snorted. 'You always think that when they hand out subpar cigars.'

'And so I should! Outrageous behaviour,' said his friend with another snort as he strode, without invitation, into the drawing room. 'I suppose you have better here?'

It had always been their habit to finish up an evening's entertainment at Staromchor House. Finlay moved almost without thinking to the drinks cabinet, pulling out three cigars and picking up a bottle of brandy.

'A nightcap?'

'Please,' said Bartlett, throwing himself bodily onto a sofa with a groan. 'And a large one. I still have Lady Lindham's conversation ringing in my ears.'

Finlay grinned as he poured a hearty measure into three glasses and then...

'What's wrong, Fin?' came his friend's voice from behind him.

Jaw tight, stomach twisted into a knot of pain, the child-hood nickname helped Finlay to speak calmly. 'Damn. I poured three glasses.'

When he turned around, there was a glittering in Bartlett's eyes that Finlay recognized. 'Damn. I thought of him again tonight, you know.'

'It's hard to go a day without thinking of him,' said Finlay heavily, picking up two of the cigars and popping them in his waistcoat pocket before lifting up two of the three glasses. 'Cecil would have hated that ball.'

'He would have loved hating it,' Bartlett countered with a wry smile, accepting the glass offered to him with a nod of thanks. 'The blackguard.'

The two men fell into silence for a moment, then word-lessly toasted their absent friend before taking a sip of the burning liquid.

'Sit, man,' Bartlett said eventually. 'And tell me how these wedding plans are going.'

Finlay groaned as he dropped into an armchair opposite the sofa, hoping the heavy movement could disguise his disinterest with said wedding plans.

Wedding plans.

It had always been this way. With his father gone for so many years, it had been Finlay's responsibility to uphold the Staromchor title in Society's eyes. That meant dinners, card parties, attending the right balls.

And now it meant ensuring that his wedding would be suit-able for the Jellicoe name.

'The plans are going,' Finlay said, waving a hand. 'My mother and Isabelle are doing most of it.'

'Isabelle,' mused Bartlett. 'It's been weeks since I've seen her.'

Isabelle Carr. Finlay forced a smile back on his face. Since their engagement had been announced, he could not avoid her.

Not that he had wanted to—at least, not at first.

'How did she seem to you?' he asked quietly. 'The last time you saw her, I mean.'

'She…she looked fine.' Bartlett's voice was low, but his eyes did not waver as he spoke. 'It's strange, isn't it? She and him were so similar. When we were young, that time Isabelle cut off her hair, do you remember?'

'I remember I was blamed for it,' Finlay said dryly.

'You couldn't tell them apart from a distance,' his friend continued, a faraway look in his eyes. 'And she's grown, obviously, a woman now. And yet sometimes, in some lights, I can see Cecil in her. It's like…like a part of him is still here.'

Finlay swallowed, hard.

Bravado—that was what Cecil had always called it. Finlay's ability to move through the world with a smile and seemingly no care in the world.

Cecil had always seen right through it.

Pain.

Finlay blinked. There was pain, inexplicable pain, in his hand. He looked down.

His hands were clenched, both of them. One of them appeared to be— Dear God, he wasn't bleeding?

But he was. The pressure of his forefinger pressing deep into his palm had been far fiercer than he had expected, and a small cut, almost like a papercut, was beading blood.

Without altering his expression, Finlay casually wiped his hand on his breeches, thanking fate that his valet had chosen a dark pair for that evening.

He was not going to think of Cecil Carr again. Not tonight.

It had been his own fault for relaxing, Finlay knew. No, the illusion of laughing bravado always had to remain on his face. To admit that he felt any different, to allow himself to feel for a single second the overwhelming pain of—

'And when I last saw her, she looked…different,' said a voice.

Finlay blinked. Bartlett, one of his oldest friends in the world, appeared again before him. 'Different?'

Bartlett nodded. 'Different. I mean, I knew she wouldn't be exactly the same. I hadn't seen her for three years, not since she'd gone to Switzerland.'

'The Trinderhaus Menagerie for Young Ladies,' said Finlay with a grin.

'The Trinderhaus *School* for Young Ladies,' corrected Bartlett with a corresponding grin. 'You teased her something terrible when the Carrs told her she'd be going.'

'She didn't mind overly much,' he said defensively, pulling out the two cigars he had deposited in his pocket. 'Want one?'

His friend nodded, and it took a few minutes to cut and light them. And his mind meandered not to the Trinderhaus School, but to another place where young ladies gathered. To one young lady in particular. One with a sharp tongue and a wit that had intrigued...

When they were both blowing smoke into the room, Bartlett continued as though there had been no interruption.

'I hadn't supposed that finishing school would alter her overly. I mean, it was Isabelle. Spirited, loud, nonsensical...'

'She's changed,' said Finlay quietly.

He had not intended his words to be so harsh. But it was true. The woman who returned had not been the fourth musketeer to their little group. No longer was she the sister who had hung around the three boys something dreadful, the person who had been pretty as a child but nothing to spark desire in a man's chest.

And now...

'She has taken the death of her brother hard, Fin,' said Bartlett softly.

Finlay's stomach lurched. 'We all have.'

And somehow the tether that had kept them all together had been cut. He hadn't realized, not until Cecil's death, just how much they had all relied on him.

'She looks like her,' he found himself saying. 'She looks like Isabelle but all the warmth has gone, the joy. The mischief. She just…sits there, and lets my mother talk.'

'In fairness, no one can stop your mother talking.'

'And this whole arranged marriage…' Finlay's voice trailed away.

He was not going to think about her. Miss Newell. Most definitely not.

When he glanced up at his friend, there was a knowing look in those eyes that told him Bartlett was holding back. Which wasn't like him.

'Come on, out with it, man,' Finlay said easily, or at least as easily as he could manage while his hand stung. 'I won't be offended.'

He had meant the last few words as a quip, but he saw with a sudden dart of the man's eyes that it was apparently a real consideration.

Interesting. What was going on?

'You…you are not in love with Isabelle, are you.'

It was not a question. Bartlett spoke conversationally, as though they discussed whether or not they had fallen in love with their friend's sister all the time.

Finlay's smile held as he said, 'In love? With Isabelle Carr? Of course not.'

It was an admissionn freely made. No shame rushed through Finlay's chest as he made it, though there was a slight tension in his shoulders.

Bartlett was frowning.

'Well, I am happy to say such a thing,' Finlay said, ensuring no trace of defensiveness could be heard in his voice. 'Men of our status are not expected to fall in love, are they? And it's Isabelle, for goodness' sake. We've known her for…forever!'

He and Isabelle had been perfectly clear in their negotiation. A marriage of convenience—that was all this was. Cecil would have…well, maybe not approved. Finlay had nightmares sometimes, that Cecil would not have approved.

But Cecil was not here. Not here to go riding in Hyde Park, or play cards at White's, or—Finlay's stomach lurched—pay off his family's debts. Substantial debts.

The agreement had been made two months ago, and everything was going to plan. Someone needed to marry Isabelle, provide her with a home, protection. Pay off her family's debts—and with no dowry…

He wasn't about to reveal to Bartlett that despite his best efforts, no feelings of warmth had surfaced. None at all.

'Marriage,' Finlay said aloud into the silence, 'for people of our station, it is rarely for love. If love comes at all, that is unusual.'

'You didn't have to offer for her.'

'What, and you were about to?' he scoffed with a grin. 'Come on now—I'm the earl. I've got the income. It made sense for me to offer her my hand.'

'Out of the blue,' his friend pointed out. 'Carr…he died, and then you were gone. I didn't know where you were, couldn't find you…'

Bartlett continued as Finlay took a puff of his cigar and tried not to think about it. That time when he had desperately tried to lose himself in sorrow, certain that he could get out all the emotions and then would feel better.

As he was before. As though nothing had happened.

'And here you are, engaged to her,' said Bartlett with a snort. 'Though I noticed that Knaresby's experience of matrimony has been quite different. You must think him strange.'

Finlay leaned forward. 'No, not at all! My good man, think it through. He found love, which is all to the good. But he would have married without it, would he not?'

They all did, eventually.

And of all women in Society, Isabelle was one he actually

liked. At least, he had before the engagement, but now it was all formality and rules and never being able to actually speak to each other. And the Isabelle Carr he had known, the joyful, smiling sister of his best friend, had disappeared.

A crackle of pain shot up his side. Though he was hardly the same. Not after they had all lost Cecil.

'Before this, I would have ventured to say that Isabelle was one of the most charming women of my acquaintance.'

Finlay shrugged, placing his cigar on an ashtray. He'd lost the taste of it. 'To be sure.'

Most charming. And most changed. And nothing in comparison to—

Don't think about her, he told himself firmly. Miss Newell should not be clouding his thoughts. Should not be distracting him. Should not be tempting him to return to the Wallflower Academy and—

'I worry about you,' Bartlett said, sitting up now and leaning towards him with a serious expression. 'You... We've both lost a dear friend. The three of us, I always thought... I thought we'd grow old together. Be wittering on at White's in fifty years about the youth of today.'

Finlay snorted, mostly to cover up the stinging in his eyes.

'And I don't think you're happy offering matrimony to Isabelle,' continued Bartlett seriously. 'You...dammit Fin, you don't smile anymore.'

He was doing the right thing, wasn't he? Doing what Cecil would have asked him.

There was no way of knowing, but that certainty, though it wavered at times, was the only thing which had kept Finlay together when...when it had first happened.

His jaw tightened. His heart may be unaffected by Isabelle, but he was doing the right thing.

'And she deserves—'

'I know what she deserves, and I know what I'm doing,' said Finlay shortly. 'You don't have to mother us, Bartlett.'

His friend sighed. 'I suppose not.'

Finlay did not reply. He intended to, but at that precise moment, his mind was overcome with the memory— No, the sharp words of a woman worlds apart from Miss Carr.

I'm not some entertainment for you, whoever you are. I'm just Rilla.

His lips lifted in a rueful smile. He was thinking about Miss Newell again. Most inconvenient. What did that make it, four hundred and thirty-four?

By God, he was losing count.

'Besides, what else is a man in my position to do?' Finlay said, ensuring his voice was a mite stronger now. 'I am an earl, I have responsibilities.'

'You should flirt more.'

Finlay laughed. 'With Isabelle?'

'Well, maybe not,' Bartlett said with a shrug. 'If you don't love her…'

'I have respect for her. Great respect. Just because I have not fallen in love with her yet does not mean I shall not do so. In time.'

Perhaps. It did not matter, after all. They had agreed: it was the only way.

'But a flirtation would cheer you up,' his friend said, gesturing around the room as though there were a plethora of ladies just waiting to be flirted with. 'I'm not saying have an assignation.'

'Definitely not,' Finlay said darkly.

'But a flirtation, someone to make you smile, dust off those skills.'

'You think I've forgotten how to charm a woman?'

The very idea! He was known for it, after all. Finlay Jellicoe, the Earl of Staromchor, was one of the most charming men in the *ton*. He had been careful, even in the depths of grief—especially then—to maintain such a reputation.

'I think it's more likely that you'll realize you don't care for Isabelle enough,' Bartlett responded quietly.

Finlay bristled. Not care about her enough? He was marrying her, wasn't he? He was doing his duty—far more than old Bartlett here.

'She won't make you happy.'

'Oh, stuff and nonsense,' Finlay said sharply to the calm face of his friend. 'Don't—'

'You think the marriage will make you happy? Prove it. Flirt with another, and find them dull in comparison,' Bartlett shot back, though with none of Finlay's animosity.

It was difficult not to be a little suspicious. 'You're awfully concerned that I don't marry her—and I made a promise to her. Even if I...well, even if I did meet a woman who I liked better...'

'Now that's an interesting thought,' said Bartlett with a dry laugh as he extinguished his cigar and sipped his brandy. 'I'll throw down a wager for you, Fin.'

'A wager?'

'A wager, a bet, whatever you want to call it,' Bartlett said easily, peering above his glass.

Finlay frowned. 'Look, these wagers of ours, they never end.'

'Oh, it's not going to be as dramatic as all that,' his friend said with a wave of his hand. 'It isn't going to be like last time.'

'It had better not.' Last time had involved a bag of lemons, a dark alley, and a most inconvenient conversation with a peeler. Never again.

'My point is this,' said Bartlett with a grin. 'You need to cheer yourself up, and Isabelle... Well, you have made a commitment to her, and that's admirable. But before you launch yourself into spousal servitude—'

'You really have a way with words, you know that?' Finlay interrupted conversationally.

Bartlett threw a cushion. 'Are you going to let me finish?'

Finlay had caught the cushion. 'Your aim is getting worse.'

The second cushion caught him in the face.

'You think love is inconsequential, immaterial for marriage. I think you are hiding that fact behind your pretence of—'

'The wager, sir,' Finlay teased.

'I wager you'll feel infinitely better for a flirtation,' Bartlett said, a twinkle in his eye. 'I think it'll bring you joy, and won't betray Isabelle in any way, and you'll enter the married state far happier. If I'm wrong, you can…oh, I don't know…choose your punishment.'

Perhaps if Finlay had not been attempting to ignore the throbbing ache in his hand…perhaps if the brandy had not been so potent…perhaps if he had not been looking for an excuse to return to the Wallflower Academy and converse once again with Miss Newell…

She had been so beautiful.

The thought intruded, as it had so often since meeting the wallflower. She had been beautiful. The dark black hair that shimmered almost like starlight. The way her gown had slipped past her curves, allowing one's gaze to meander leisurely. The purse of her lips, full and shell pink, when she argued with him.

Finlay swallowed.

He was being a damned fool, he knew. Tempting flirtation or not, he had made a promise to Isabelle, and regret it he may, but that did not undo it.

He needed to think rationally. Holding Bartlett's gaze, Finlay threw out his hands and shrugged with a laugh which showed the world just how little he cared.

'A wager it is, then,' he said with a laugh. 'A flirtation— what harm can it do? And what do I win, once I win it?'

'Win?' Bartlett grinned. 'You're not going to win.'

Finlay leaned forward. 'When I win?'

His friend examined him for a moment, and a strange emotion flickered over his face. If Finlay had not been concentrating at that very moment, he would have missed it.

'You... I'll buy you and Isabelle a painfully expensive wedding present,' he said quietly. 'With my best wishes.'

Finlay's heart skipped a beat. Wedding present. His wedding, to Isabelle. The woman he had considered more a sister than a woman for most of his life. But he was doing it for—

Agony, bitter agony twisted in his heart. A pressing on his chest. Lungs constricting.

Finlay forced the grief back where it belonged, deep, dark down within his chest. Where it should not be permitted to escape.

It did not matter. He was not going to lose this bet.

Finlay rose from his seat, stepped over to the sofa, took the man's hand, and shook it hard, once, twice, thrice.

'Excellent. We have a wager.'

Chapter Three

Rilla took in a deep breath. It did not help.

'Well, it's only an afternoon tea,' came the happy voice of Sylvia, just to Rilla's left. 'We're hardly being fed to the lions.'

'Speak for yourself,' said Daphne, her tone soft. 'I think I'd rather take the lions.'

Forcing down a smile that Rilla was almost sure her friends would not appreciate, she sat quietly as the two of them chattered away.

'Never heard anything so ridiculous! Go on, wear them.'

'But I can't! They're your only pretty pair of earbobs. You'll have nothing to—'

'How long has it been since he's visited? That's what I thought, you can't remember. Here you go, let me help you.'

A gentle breeze fluttered through the open window beside where Rilla sat. She'd been placed there by Sylvia's gentle hands the moment she'd entered her friend's bedchamber. Rilla did not need to be able to see to know that this kindness was twofold. Firstly, because although she could find a seat with her cane, it was more pleasant to be guided to one without effort. Secondly, because Sylvia's habit of untidiness meant it was quite likely an unknowing foot could easily stumble.

It had only happened…what, five times before?

Rilla brushed her fingertips across the skirt of her gown. It was striped. She hadn't needed Daphne's awkward praise to tell. The contrapoint weave, lines going this way and then that, was more than enough to tell.

Her thumb stroked the weave as a sudden weight beside Rilla told her that one of her friends had sat beside her.

'You know, you don't look the least excited,' Sylvia said from close to her left. 'I thought you'd be jumping at the bit for a change.'

Rilla shrugged. 'It's not so different from any other day, really.'

And any day at the Wallflower Academy was just like any other. Day after day, trickling by like a stream. Unchanging, always the same.

It might all still be new and exciting for Sylvia and Daphne. Try getting excited about an afternoon tea after three years, she wanted to say.

And didn't. What would be the point?

Rilla was perhaps the only wallflower who truly knew what it was to feel alone here.

It had taken her a little while to grow accustomed to the monotony. After all, it was against nature for nothing to change, for the seasons to pass by without much alteration. Other than temperature and a slight difference in scents in the gardens, Rilla could not have known that time was even passing.

Not like at home. The bleats of the newborn lambs, the lowing of the cows as their calves came. The sharpness of the growing barley, the delicate scent of ale as the brewing houses began their work. The rushing of the wind through the wheat, supple then brittle as the changing—

'Rilla,' came Sylvia's voice, with just a tinge of censure. 'You're being most dull, you know.'

Rilla could not help but chuckle. 'I suppose I am right where I belong, then.'

A sudden intake of breath was all the hint she was given. For a moment, just a moment, Rilla's heart skipped a beat.

It was impossible, at times, to guess at the reactions of her fellow wallflowers. Even after a year of friendship, there were nuances she was certain she missed. Oh, they said this and that, but did they truly mean it? Were the expressions on their faces matching those in their hearts?

She could never tell.

Rilla supposed that there were liars even amongst those who were able to organize their features into pleasing shapes. She could not tell from experience. It was impossible to know.

The subtle signs that were her only clues could be so disagreeably similar. A sudden intake of breath from Daphne could mean shock. Or shame. Or embarrassment. Or just her shyness, something that Rilla had discovered swiftly in the hesitations before each of her speeches.

But in Sylvia? The same action could mean something entirely different. The precursor to laughter, a mock shock that sounded precisely the same as the genuine article.

Or something else. Of all her friends, and Rilla had few, Sylvia was the most unpredictable.

'Where you belong?' Sylvia repeated, and Rilla's shoulders relaxed as she heard the teasing tone. 'By God, are you suggesting my bedchamber is the dullest place in the world?'

'Nothing should be happening here, certainly,' Rilla teased back, her heart settling into its old rhythm. 'The Pike will have your head!'

'I... I am sure Rilla did not mean—'

'Well, even if she didn't, I choose to take offence,' came Sylvia's mischievous reply to Daphne's delicate suggestion.

Rilla could not help but smile.

The Wallflower Academy existed to take ladies like Daphne, true wallflowers, ladies who found it impossible to even look at a gentleman without collapsing into fits of nerves, and make them...

Well. Rilla's stomach lurched. Acceptable.

It was an infuriating thought, but there it was.

The trouble was—for the Pike, at least—that as far as Rilla could make out, the Wallflower Academy was packed not with wallflowers, but with troublemakers. Those who did not obey Society's rules, or fit neatly into the boxes it provided.

Daughter. Wife. Mother.

With only six wallflowers currently in residence, Rilla was almost certain that Daphne was the only true wallflower here. And that meant that when the Pike organized these ridiculous events…

Something which had been spoken some minutes ago suddenly crept forward in Rilla's mind. 'Daphne?'

She felt the warmth and pressure of a hand on her shoulder. 'Yes?'

It was a relief to have her friends approach as she preferred. A sudden voice before her was always most discombobulating. 'Did I— Did you say that your father was attending?'

There it was—that hesitation. And because Daphne had left her hand on Rilla's shoulder, she could feel her friend turning slightly. Turning in the direction of Sylvia, who was still seated beside her on the window seat.

Rilla swallowed into the silence. They were doing it again. Well, she supposed they couldn't help it. She almost thought they did not even realize they were doing it.

They were…pausing.

Being born without sight meant Rilla had nothing to explain the strange pauses which littered conversations like sudden gusts of wind across a sunny afternoon. What were they doing? How could a conversation be continued without words? What if one misunderstood what the other was saying—would you ever know?

And then the moment was over.

'Yes, my father… He…he said he would attend the afternoon

tea,' Daphne explained, her throat thick with repressed emotion. 'He said he had a...a lady friend.'

Precisely what the emotion was, Rilla was not sure. The youngest of the wallflowers had never spoken much about her parents, and her father had only visited the girl once in the last six months.

One of the Society afternoon teas that the Pike insisted on hosting, however, was hardly an intimate family affair. But it was something.

'Which means,' came Sylvia's triumphant voice, 'we will finally have something to talk about at one of these tedious affairs. Lord, why do these ladies of Society bother coming other than to gawp at us?'

Rilla's smile was humourless. 'I think that is precisely why they come.'

'Miss Pike hosts them to improve our social skills,' Daphne said quietly as a gong rang downstairs. They were required below.

Sylvia's snort was close to Rilla's ear as she helped her to her feet. 'Social skills, social skills... I have more social skills in my little finger than the Pike does in her entire—'

'You know full well that until we are married, the Pike considers us in desperate need of socializing,' Rilla said quietly, her equilibrium shifting as Sylvia led her around what must be the bed on her right. 'Gwen always said—'

'Gwen had the right idea,' interrupted Sylvia happily.

The air changed; their voices echoed louder, and the carpet changed to a thicker rug. They were on the landing.

'What, marry a duke?' Rilla asked sceptically, slipping her hand into her friend's arm.

She did not need to. If it were not for the afternoon tea, she could make her own way to the drawing room without a fuss, with the cane which was almost a part of her body in her hand.

But with guests milling about, and servants rushing back and forth with pelisses and coats and hats…

No. Much safer this way.

'Marry anyone,' came Sylvia's voice with a tinkling laugh.

Rilla heard the gasp on her other side.

'Sylvia! You wouldn't just marry—'

'To escape this place?'

'It's hardly a prison,' Rilla pointed out.

There was a hearty sniff from Sylvia. 'It's a prison! Don't you want to leave?'

'And do what? Go where?' It was not a pleasant line of conversation. 'I have been offered neither a home nor a husband, so what options do I have? What could be better than here?'

It was a damning thought.

'B-but Sylvia, you wouldn't—'

'Daphne, I'd marry old Matthews if I thought he'd take me away from this place,' came Sylvia's voice as they stepped down the wide, sweeping staircase. 'But don't you be getting any ideas, Matthews.'

'Wouldn't dream of it, Miss Bryant.'

Rilla chuckled. They were on the second-to-last step, and Matthews always kept his position just to the right, by the front door. He never had to announce himself to her as the other servants did. He was always there.

Besides, she could smell his dank, oily boot polish. He was the only footman not to use the same as the others. She could sense him a mile off.

'Now then, the drawing room,' said Sylvia, as though she informed footmen that she would not marry them every day of the week. Which, Rilla had to admit, may well be the case. 'Let's see who today's victims are.'

The victims, if such a term could be used, were surely the wallflowers themselves, though Rilla did not have time to point this out. By the shift in the rug under her feet—softer, more luxurious—she could tell they were now in the drawing room.

In the midst of Society.

The babble of voices suggested that there were perhaps twenty people in there, milling around. Just less than half were the wallflowers and Miss Pike, Rilla presumed, which left ten or twelve of London's Society who had been dragged the half an hour's carriage ride away from London to the Wallflower Academy.

'So,' she said pleasantly, as Sylvia pulled up and halted them. 'Who do we have here?'

It had become their custom since… Now Rilla came to think about it, she could hardly recall when. Attempting to speak to those who came to gawp at the wallflowers was never a very pleasant experience, and so Sylvia and Rilla had grown the habit of standing by the side of the room and carefully cataloguing those who bothered to come all this way out of London.

They were to be treated like they were in a zoo, were they? Well, two could play at that game.

'There are a few peacocks, as always,' Sylvia began.

Rilla smiled despite herself. Peacocks referred to ladies who wore outrageous outfits to ensure they were looked at. There were always a few of those.

'A tiger, but we'll ensure to avoid him.'

A tiger was a gentleman on the prowl, typically one who had got himself into a bit of bother in London and needed a swift marriage to distract from the scandal.

'A pair of sheep following a fox. Male, all of them.'

A trio of men, then. Rilla nodded. A fox was a gentleman who should not be trusted, and two of his followers who thoughtlessly agreed with anything he said were sheep.

Perhaps a year ago she would have replied to Sylvia. Certainly two years ago. But three years at the Wallflower Academy had worn her down, like waves upon a rock, and so much of herself had faded away. Been crushed.

'And my goodness, but he is handsome.'

Rilla nudged her friend. 'No animal this time?'

'You know, I'm not sure what sort of animal this one would be,' breathed Sylvia, her interest palpable. 'Very handsome, though. I wouldn't mind a little conversational practice with him—dragged here by his mother, from what I can see. A demure peacock, almost stylish.'

'You really are terrible, you know?' Rilla said lightly.

Her arm was squeezed. 'You know, I don't recognize the very handsome gentleman, but he rings a sort of bell. Attended Gwen's wedding, maybe?'

Rilla tilted her head on one side. Now that was a tone she did not often hear in Sylvia's voice. Not desire. No, it was curiosity…but something more than that. Something almost startled.

'By Jove, he's coming this way,' Sylvia breathed.

Rilla shifted uncomfortably on her feet. It was disarming, the thought that a stranger was marching towards you, with no sense at all who he was or why he may be doing such a ridiculous thing.

'Not actually towards us, though,' Rilla said quietly. 'There's no reason he—'

'You know, it does almost look as though he is making straight for us, in all honesty.' Sylvia's voice had lowered in volume, surely because the gentleman was coming closer. 'Oh, Daphne! Daphne, it's your father, and who's that with—Daphne, let go of me!'

'Wait,' was all Rilla managed to say.

And then she was gone. Sylvia's exuberance was well known by the wallflowers, which was undoubtedly why Daphne had pulled her away—as a buffer to whatever conversation Daphne did not wish to have. Sylvia did tend to act first and think later; they would both feel guilty, Rilla knew, at abandoning her here.

Because it left her…exposed.

Not exposed, Rilla thought sternly as she ensured her head did not droop with the sudden loss of her companion. She was hardly helpless, and her cane gave her the comfort she needed. Just…alone. That was all.

And besides, she was accustomed to being alone. Alone was what she did best.

A slow smile crept across her face, and Rilla saw no reason to hide it. Yes, perhaps her father was right all along. Perhaps she would be better suited—

'What are you smiling about?' asked a curious, quiet voice.

Rilla's foot hit the wall as she instinctively attempted to put more distance between her and the speaker. Pain throbbed in her ankle and up her shin, but there was no possibility of reaching down and rubbing it. Not when she could precisely tell where the mysterious gentleman who had just spoken was. Too close.

Lord, the idea of accidentally leaning down and headbutting—

'You look very well, Miss Newell,' came the strange voice.

Then the memory slipped into her mind and threw up a name.

'Very well,' he repeated.

Rilla swallowed and ensured that no hint of a grin approached the corners of her lips. She was not amused.

She recognized the scent now. Sandalwood and lemon. She had only encountered one person who smelt like that.

'The earl, isn't it?' she said as airily as possible. 'From the wedding a few days ago.'

'Impressive,' came the reply, confident, calm, collected.

Rilla snorted. 'Not so impressive. I may be blind, but I am hardly a fool. I am more than a match for you. Why, you—'

She bit down on the words just in time to prevent them spilling out. For what could she say? *You have a particular scent that marks you out?*

'Blind,' said the man quietly. Strangely. As though he were not afraid of the word, which was a most strange occurrence indeed. 'You see absolutely nothing, then?'

'I can see right through you,' Rilla muttered before raising her voice. 'Not that it's any business of yours.'

'Of course.' The man sounded…apologetic. And yet unruffled. 'You must forgive my curiosity.'

Rilla often found herself forgiving many things, and in the grand scheme of things, the man's enquiry about her sight was at least spoken with a modicum of respect.

Still. That did not mean she had to suffer his presence. Though her body was hardly suffering—it was leaning. Leaning!

Ridiculous. She was annoyed at this man, she reminded herself sternly. He had made her feel a fool. There she had been, trusting him, flirting with him…

Which admittedly, had been her fault.

Oh, God, she was still leaning!

Rilla straightened up and ensured her voice was cold and distant. 'How odd that you are here again.'

'Oh, not so odd, I assure you,' the earl said, louder now. Too loud. Would not others be turning to look? 'My mother dragged me here as part of her, and I quote, "charitable efforts." She has this ridiculous idea about the unfortunate and the lesser… Well, I saw very little point in putting up a fight.'

Rilla blinked.

Very handsome, though. I wouldn't mind a little conversational practice with him—dragged here by his mother, from what I can see…

Dragged by his mother… Well, that would account for him being here again.

An earl. Here.

Embarrassment bubbled in Rilla's chest, but she did not

permit herself to display the heated emotions firing through her body.

This man, this stranger—he was an outsider. He did not deserve to know what she was thinking. He'd already made her look the fool.

'How are you, Miss Newell?' came the earl's voice gently.

Rilla attempted again to take a step back, forgetting momentarily that her back was almost already up against the wall. It was most alarming. The man had somehow grown closer to her, far closer than was acceptable.

And they were in public, too! What on earth did the man think he was doing?

'Your name is…?' she said stiffly.

The chuckle blew warm breath across her upper arm—a fact she was most definitely not thinking about. Hardly noticing. Not at all. Not in the slightest.

'I told you I was an earl, and I was not lying,' came the cheerful voice. 'I am Finlay Jellicoe, Earl of Staromchor. For my sins.'

'And I suppose they are numerous,' Rilla said tightly.

Really, it was most unfair of Sylvia to abandon her like this. Even if the man was handsome, it was not like Rilla could tell. Or care.

Attractiveness—now that was different. There was a warmth to some people, a strange magnetic quality she could not describe but had felt once or twice. A need to be near. A pull, a tug under her navel that had caused her once to accidentally fall into that gentleman's lap and—

The Earl of Staromchor's chuckle was low, as though they were sharing a secret. Heat flushed across Rilla's cheeks, and she hoped to goodness no one would notice.

The very idea of an earl and Miss Newell, giggling together in a corner!

'I suppose they are,' said the Earl of Staromchor easily. 'But they aren't nearly so numerous as those of my mother. She's accosted a gentleman and appears to be berating him.'

'Berating him?' Rilla said, unable to help herself.

Well. She couldn't be blamed for her curiosity. She had lost Sylvia's eyes…it was only fair that she use this earl's. For the moment. Not that she wanted to.

There came a movement, the slightest of movements. It could have been a wool jacket against her skin, the very tip of her arm. Rilla's lips parted at the sudden sensation, and then it was gone. Like a whisper she had imagined.

'I think that is Lord Norbury,' came Earl of Staromchor's voice. 'He's standing with a wallflower, as far as I can make out. She looks…terrified. My mother isn't that bad.'

Even with the slightest of descriptions, Rilla could not help but identify the wallflower. 'That is Miss Daphne Smith—with her father, I think.'

'Her father,' the Earl of Staromchor mused. 'That would explain, at least in part, my mother's critique.'

'Critique?'

Rilla had not meant to say it. She certainly should not be conversing with this man, this interloper—this earl!—and most definitely not exchanging gossip. Gossip about one of her friends, no less. It was most indelicate.

Unfortunately, her wonder overcame her.

'Yes, it appears Lord Norbury has not been visiting his daughter enough,' said the Earl of Staromchor softly. 'The gossip is all over Town, as you— Oh, I suppose you may not know. I'd heard it myself, but never thought…the differences in name… My mother won't stop talking about him.'

Rilla swallowed. And that was what came of opening her mouth and allowing herself, just for a moment, to be swept up in a conversation.

Daphne's parentage was not something discussed. Not openly. And certainly not with strangers.

'Go away,' she said sharply.

There was a low chuckle just to her left, then it moved to before her. Cutting her off from the rest of the room.

'Here I am, volunteering to come to the Wallflower Academy to aid you in practising your conversation,' the Earl of Staromchor said with a teasing, lilting voice, 'and you wish me to go away?'

'I did not ask for your help, my lord,' Rilla said, pouring as much disdain as she could manage in the last two words.

'Miss Pike did.'

'Miss Pike does not speak for me,' she retorted, though immediately she regretted the sharpness of her words.

She felt heat rise from her stomach and up her chest. It did no good to critique the Pike in public, either. Good grief, she must be tired. She was not usually this…this lax.

'Nevertheless, I am happy to provide the service.'

'I do not need servicing by you,' Rilla snapped. Then the heat in her chest spread across her face. 'I… I mean— You know what I mean!'

'I certainly do. Or at least, I think I do,' came the obviously amused voice of the Earl of Staromchor.

It was an interesting voice. Oh, Rilla did not experience much variety in the way of male voices at the Wallflower Academy. There was Matthews, of course, and John, the other footman. Sometimes Cook, a man with a voice that sounded like fruit cake and spiced currants when he came into the dining room and asked opinions on a new recipe.

But this earl…his voice was different. There was a confidence there, almost no hesitation in his speech. A lilting lightness, a confidence. A warmth, like a summer breeze wafting through a forest, picking up the little scents of growth and life.

It was doing that thing to her stomach again.

It was all Rilla could do not to push past the man and storm to the door. She knew the way; it was but eight or nine steps from here, and other people would simply have to move out of the way, that was what.

But she wouldn't allow this earl to win. She just wouldn't.

'Besides, if anyone needs practice for their conversation, it is you,' she said sharply. 'You are the one who failed to introduce himself when we first met. Allowed me to make a fool of myself with Miss Pike gone. And you…'

You're an earl, she wanted to say. *You're not to be trusted. I know your sort.*

She detected a soft noise, perhaps the shifting from one boot to another.

'You are the one with the exemplary conversation skills, are you?'

Rilla held her head high. At least on this ground, she was stable. 'I don't depend on titles or good looks. I may not be exemplary, but I'm a damned sight better than you.'

She had expected an almost immediate reply. Strange, in a way, she was a tad disappointed to stand in the silence after her bold comment.

It wasn't that she was starved for conversation. Far from it. Sylvia and Daphne were perhaps her closest friends, but there was not a person in the Wallflower Academy that Rilla did not have a passable friendship with.

And that was the trouble, wasn't it? Three years in the same situation, the same place, with the same people. Oh, a few arrived but they left just as swiftly. Look at Gwen, married within months.

'I… You don't… I… I didn't…'

And then Rilla smiled. She had ruffled him. She had ruffled an earl. 'I'm sorry, is this your example of excellent conversation?'

The Earl of Staromchor cleared his throat, and he was close, far closer than she thought possible. 'How did you get here, Miss Newell?'

'Why, through the door after descending the stairs,' Rilla said sweetly, joy twisting around her heart as she imagined how irritated she could make this man.

Well, serve him right. Coming here to help wallflowers practise their conversation, indeed!

'No, I meant—well, before the Wallflower Academy. Where do you come from, who are your people?'

Immediately the joy started to melt away. She was not going to tell him—no. He didn't know her title, he didn't know her father, and it had to stay that way.

If he caught whiff of that scandal…

She had her sisters to think of, Rilla thought sternly, pressing her hands together as though that would prevent her from spilling any secrets. Any details. Or any information whatsoever.

No, this man may jolt her off balance, make it completely impossible to think clearly, and smell absolutely divine…

She was not thinking that an earl smelt divine!

'Your people are, Miss Newell?'

'My people,' Rilla said stiffly, 'are the Newells.'

'And where are they?'

'I don't actually have to tell you, you know,' she said as calmly as she could manage. Where on earth was Sylvia? 'Besides, I have no time for earls.'

'No time for earls? Why the devil not?'

Rilla silently cursed her inability to keep her mouth shut. Just when she had decided that she was not going to reveal any of herself to this stranger—this earl!—she had to go and make a comment like that. It was infuriating.

Most upsettingly, it was herself that she was annoyed at.

'Good day, my lord,' she said curtly.

She made it almost six steps. That brought her within touching distance of the door frame that led back into the hall, and she would have made it, too.

If it wasn't for the most maddening hand on her wrist. A hand whose touch should not have burned, should not have sparked a tingling heat that travelled up her arm.

'Let me help.'

'I know the way,' Rilla said, attempting to step around him.

The trouble was, the Earl of Staromchor had the advantage of her, quite literally. Just as she moved left, she could hear him, feel him mirroring her, stepping in her way. A step to the right and there he was again, her hands outstretched and brushing up against the silk of a waistcoat, the cold metal chain of a pocket watch.

She halted, cheeks burning. What must the rest of the room think!

'All I asked was—'

'Are you here to choose a bride?' Rilla interrupted, hoping to God that her deflection would be sufficient. 'The Duke of Knaresby did, but you know that, since you attended the wedding. So, here to pick a wallflower bride?'

Apparently, it was an excellent deflection. The Earl of Staromchor hesitated just a moment too long before he said, 'I have no need to come to the Wallflower Academy to choose a bride.'

Rilla swallowed, and remembered what Sylvia had said.

And my goodness, but he is handsome.

If this Earl of Staromchor was as pleasing to look at as Sylvia said, then evidently he knew it. Knew that any lady in the *ton* would be pleased to receive his attentions.

All earls were the same. They were interested in what they could get, not what they could give.

'I have no desire to plan a wedding at present,' the Earl of Staromchor continued, his voice low as though they were sharing a private conversation. 'Or, in truth, to be married. In fact—'

'Fascinating as that is,' Rilla said curtly, 'I—'

'Staromchor, come on, we'll be late back to London!'

The woman's voice was loud and rich, sounding like how plums tasted. Rilla turned her head just for a moment to the left where the voice came from, but as she did so, a voice replied.

'Coming, Mother.'

It was the Earl of Staromchor. Footsteps, shifting away.

Rilla swallowed. So. He was gone.

And she was glad, she told herself firmly. No good could ever come out of speaking with an earl.

Chapter Four

Good weather drew Londoners out like bees, and like bees, they swarmed.

The place they swarmed to, Finlay always thought, was Hyde Park, which was as central as one could be to the fashionable part of London. The tall, towering trees shone green light down on everyone who passed beneath them.

And today, that was a great many people.

Safe atop Ceres, the mare he'd brought to Town, Finlay looked out at the crowds of people.

Ladies, as far as the eye could see. Farther. Ladies with tall bonnets that demanded to be seen from a distance, some bearing feathers, some bearing lace. Ladies with gowns that swept along the bone-dry paths, scattering fallen leaves and dust in their path. Ladies wearing blues and greens and yellows, pastels and prints, stripes and even in some cases, spots.

Finlay was not exactly an expert in the world of fashion—quite proudly not so—but even he thought the spots were a bit much.

Though the gentlemen were hardly any better. Some of them were following what he considered to be the Beau Brummell line of things, dark colours, little velvet or lace. Others appeared to be wishing to gather as much attention as the ladies, if not more. They sported gloves lined with fur, top hats that were creeping up to the heavens, canes for those who really wished to make a statement.

And children. Governesses. A few people exercised their dogs, others wandered with their pets in their arms, as though their little feet could not make the ground. Carriages rolled past, trimmed with silk and with golden paint across their wheels. Horses whinnied as they clopped through the place.

Hyde Park was a veritable sea of colour, ever changing, swiftly moving. The streams of people constantly shifted, their colours intermingling then clashing then separating. It was enough to give even the rainbow enthusiast a headache.

Yet despite all those before him, his thoughts did not tend to those he could see, but rather to one of the few ladies who did not appear to be taking the air in Hyde Park today.

Miss Isabelle Carr.

Finlay's stomach twisted painfully at the thought, and not because Ceres had stepped awkwardly across the path to get out of the way of another man who was galloping as though he were late for an appointment.

Isabelle. The shell of the woman she had been before. She had to stop hiding away from the world. It wouldn't— Nothing could bring him back.

She was slipping far from his thoughts. The space in his mind, in his heart, was unfathomably being replaced by a fiery gaze and a delicate figure.

Miss Newell.

He was dragged away from pleasant musings—such as the exact tilt of Miss Newell's head as she castigated him—only by the most important of topics.

Like the Carr debts.

Just that morning when he had stepped downstairs to break his fast, he had been halted from entering the morning room by a dour Turner.

'Turner?' Finlay had asked the butler curiously. 'Don't tell me my mother has given you a wild instruction again. Demands for strawberries?'

'I wish it were that simple,' replied the loyal butler quietly. 'Here.'

From a pocket in his livery, Turner removed a small bundle of letters, tied together with what looked like garden string.

And Finlay's heart had sank.

He had known precisely what they were. He had not needed to take them to the study—the one room that was his own in his mother's townhouse—and break the seals and read them.

'To the sum of fifteen pounds,' Finlay had read aloud, keeping his voice low just in case his mother did what she so often did, and barged into his study to see what he was up to. 'A debt of three pounds, but with interest…six pounds four shillings. Another one, yes…eighteen pounds and thruppence, though as unpaid for several months, rising to…'

It had been all he could do, when Cecil had died so suddenly, to track down the bulk of the debts.

Oh, every gentleman lived right to the edge of his means; that was expected. When Finlay had first met Cecil, up at Cambridge, the two of them had never exceeded their income but often danced right along the edge.

But Cecil and Isabelle's father had been a famous spendthrift, and Cecil's untimely loss came barely a month after their father had died. Finlay's friend was only halfway to understanding how the estate had got into such a mess, and Isabelle was left alone. Penniless.

The trouble was, as Finlay's friend had always said when he had lived, there was always so much more expense when it came to living in London than one expected—and his father had never known when to cut back and economise.

The upkeep of the house, yes—servants, and food. But also clothing. Keeping the horses, stabling the carriage. Keeping it running. And there were dinners to host; one had to host dinners. And parties to attend, and card parties included their own awful debts. Art to buy. Wallpaper to import. Statues to commission.

And then there were all those costs one did not expect. Lawyers and accountants and tradespeople—more tradespeople, Cecil had always said, than could reasonably be expected to even be found in London.

Finlay's smile was pained as Ceres turned a corner in Hyde Park.

Cecil has a way with words.

Had. Had a way with words.

And that was the trouble. For as soon as Finlay was certain that he had paid off the debts of the Carr family, more seemed to turn up. And the worst of it was, Isabelle had no dowry. All had been spent by her father, without her knowledge.

A flash of dark, almost black hair, a laugh.

Finlay's head turned so suddenly he actually cricked his neck. Lifting a hand from his reins to rub at the offending sore spot, he blinked after the woman who had so suddenly caught his attention.

And his stomach settled. It was not Rilla Newell.

Not that he should be thinking of Rilla Newell, he told himself most firmly as he took his reins back in hand and nudged his steed forward. He was engaged—though he'd realized how foolhardy offering a marriage of convenience to Isabelle was about five minutes after the matter had been concluded.

If only words could be taken back...

Though now he came to think of it, Finlay thought ruefully, he hadn't learned. Now there was that ridiculous bet with Bartlett.

And still his mind meandered to Marilla. Miss Newell. Though after such a damning conversation at the Wallflower Academy only a week ago, he supposed he should give up thinking about her altogether.

I don't actually have to tell you, you know. Besides, I have no time for earls.

The trouble was, she intrigued him. Finlay had never encountered a woman with such a visceral reaction to his title.

Well, perhaps a few—but those ladies had smiled, simpered, shot him looks that told him in no uncertain terms that they would be rather pleased to accept his advances.

Meeting with a woman who heard the title and baulked… it was unheard of.

What was even stranger was how the pain in his chest had wavered, no longer pressing on his lungs like…

Finlay blinked. That had only happened when he had been speaking with Miss Rilla Newell.

Now that was worth thinking about.

'…plenty of pleasant ladies to converse with here in Hyde Park,' a man was saying to his companion as they walked past. 'Just don't bother heading towards the Serpentine, the Wall-flower Academy chits are there.'

Finlay swiftly turned in his saddle towards the ornamental lake and his eyes widened.

By Jove.

A line of ladies was meandering with purpose through Hyde Park. At the front was quite clearly Miss Pike, pointing up and around them as they went. The wallflowers followed her in pairs, arm in arm, heads down, evidently not enjoying the public outing.

And at the back…

It was Miss Newell. Finlay blinked, hardly able to believe it.

But a flirtation would cheer you up. I'm not saying have an assignation but a flirtation, someone to make you smile, dust off those skills—

He had an opportunity to charm Miss Newell. Just the thought of it made his body hum, his loins spark with heat.

Because charm he would. True, Finlay had not had much

of a positive start with the wallflower, but all that was about to change. He was well dressed, and they were in public but had been introduced so it was perfectly acceptable, wasn't it, to approach her...

And this time, he was going to turn up the charm so high, she wouldn't know what had hit her.

Metaphorically speaking. Of course.

The main trouble was Miss Pike.

Dismounting from Ceres as nonchalantly as he could manage, Finlay followed the trail of wallflowers as they snaked through the Hyde Park crowds.

'Great architecture to be seen throughout London, but today we are focusing instead on nature,' came Miss Pike's voice from the front of the crocodile. 'Over here, if you look up, you'll see a huge oak tree, one of the finest...'

Miss Newell was right at the back of the line of wallflowers, a cane in one hand and the other tucked in with that of a Black wallflower Finlay could not recall the name of. Cynthia? Simon? No, that couldn't be right.

Following them so close that he was almost surprised that they did not turn to berate him for his ill manners, Finlay considered what his next move should be. The blind wallflower was being led by her companion, and would instantly notice any approach by a strange gentleman.

As would everyone else in Hyde Park.

Perhaps this was a mistake. Perhaps he should just retreat home, admit to George that he didn't care for Isabelle as he should but he had no choice but to go through with the marriage now he had offered it, and...

'Ridiculous idea to leave my cane in the carriage. You know I hate being without it when away from the Wallflower Academy. And to bring me on this nature walk, honestly!' Miss Newell was saying.

Her friend snorted. 'What, you have no other senses?'

'Oh, I can hear the wind through the trees and smell the flowers,' said Miss Newell, breathing in deeply. 'And—goodness. The Earl of Staromchor. Sylvia, why didn't you say?'

Finlay stiffened as the two wallflowers turned their heads. Sylvia, that was her name, looked startled, and Miss Newell…

Miss Newell looked remarkably pleased with herself. As well she might.

'Rilla, I had no idea he was there, but you're right,' said Sylvia, a curious gaze raking over Finlay's features. 'How did you know?'

It was an important question. Finlay would not have described himself as an expert, but by God, he hunted. It should have been easy for him, in the melee of Hyde Park on this sunny Sunday afternoon, to follow the wallflowers with ease without being detected.

And for some reason, pink was blossoming across Miss Newell's cheeks. Most prettily, pairing with the soft, inviting pink of her lips in a way, Finlay was certain, she could not know.

'I… I just knew,' Miss Newell said lamely.

Finlay wasn't convinced, and neither, it appeared, was Sylvia. 'Knew? Poppycock, you must have—I don't know, smelled him or something.'

Sylvia continued chattering away and so she did not, unlike Finlay, spot the sudden dark red that splotched across Miss Newell's face—nor how she turned away from them.

Dear God, was that truly it? She had…smelt him?

Attempting surreptitiously to sniff the lapel of his collar, Finlay was startled by the ladies' sudden movement. They were continuing on with their walk, rejoining the gaggle of wallflowers.

Irritation sparked in his stomach. What, they were just going to walk away from him?

But it appeared Miss Newell had no compunction in brush-

ing off the attentions, however slight, of an earl. By the time
Finlay had caught up with them again, leading Ceres by the
reins, he heard her say, 'No need to talk to him, that's all.'

'No need to—he's an earl!' Sylvia hissed.

'I am, you know,' Finlay said helpfully, casting an eye over
Miss Newell.

She was beautiful. Strange, in a way, that he had not noticed
before. Oh, he'd noticed the pleasing shape of her mouth, the
delicate way her hair swept across in its pins, inviting hands
to—

Dear God. Get a grip of yourself, man!

'Here, you take her,' Sylvia said suddenly, removing Miss
Newell's hand from her own arm and placing it unceremoni-
ously onto Finlay's. She met his eye with a grin, and gave him
such a theatrical wink, he was astonished he wasn't seated at
the Adelphi Theatre. 'I'll distract the Pike with a question about
aqueducts. Miss Pike—'

'Wait!' cried both Finlay and Miss Newell together.

His heart skipped a beat as he glanced at her, now walking
stonily by his side in silence, refusing to turn to him.

Sylvia evidently believed the two of them to be in cahoots,
though to what end, he struggled to imagine. Surely she did
not think…?

Finlay swallowed hard and ensured he kept his head high, ignoring the curious glances that were being shot his way by other
pedestrians in the park. He was walking in public with a woman.
It was perhaps a little unusual, but not entirely scandalous…was it?

This was what he had wanted, wasn't it? The chance to
charm Miss Newell.

To win a wager, Finlay reminded himself. He was engaged
to be married to Miss Carr. Not a love match, certainly not, but
one he was going to see through to the bitter end.

So. Charming. He could be charming. The bet depended
on it.

'May I fetch you a drink, Miss Newell?' Finlay attempted with a laugh. 'I am afraid I am a poor footman, but…'

'Spare me your pleasant nonsense,' came the curt reply.

His laugh died on the wind. Ah. Well, perhaps that was not the best idea. It wasn't as though they had parted on the best terms the last time he had the pleasure of her company.

So. Where to begin?

'Miss Newell, you look radiant today, did you know that?' Finlay said with a wide grin.

Only when the words were out of his mouth did his face fall. *Oh, hell…*

Miss Newell's twisted expression contained no mirth. 'You know, funny you should say that, but no, I can't say I've had much use for my looking glass of late.'

Finlay swallowed. Well, that perhaps wasn't the best opener. But that was of no matter. He had others.

'And what a splendid day it is,' he said cheerfully, waving his free hand about to gesture at…

At what she could not see. Hell on earth, but he was going to have to think harder than that.

Miss Newell's face was a picture of restrained mirth. 'You're not very bright, are you, my lord?'

'I just… I forgot… Well, it is pleasant to be walking with you in Hyde Park, Miss Newell,' Finlay said, pretending to be utterly undone by her wit.

It wasn't particularly hard to pretend, in truth. Not that he would have ever admitted it.

Yet still she kept him at a distance, as she appeared to do with the whole world, as far as Finlay could tell. It wasn't the cane. It was her very demeanour.

Silence. It appeared Miss Newell had no interest in responding to his words, no matter how polite they were.

'And are you enjoying your time in London?' Finlay continued as he steered her gently along the path, which curved to the left.

There was a slight pressure on his arm, and then it returned to the light touch it had been before. A tingling feeling crept up to his shoulder, something warming and unknown, unusual and unfamiliar.

Finlay swallowed. It was a feeling he could dismiss. It meant nothing, obviously.

'Yes,' said Miss Newell dismissively.

He waited for a moment, expecting her to continue, but when she did not he found himself unreasonably lost. Well, how did one make conversation with a woman who evidently had no interest in said conversation whatsoever?

Well, he'd told old Bartlett that he had the charm. Time to butter her up.

'You are clearly a very intelligent woman, Miss Newell,' Finlay said firmly as he followed the wallflowers, wishing to goodness he could sit Miss Newell at a bench where he could accidentally on purpose brush his leg against hers. That always worked. 'In fact, I—'

'I'm not that easily impressed, you know,' Miss Newell interrupted with a blank look that she cast his way. 'I'm not like Sylvia. I don't desire to be admired everywhere I go. Nor am I like Juliet, who accepts compliments so prettily.'

A twisting discomfort was making itself at home in Finlay's stomach, precisely where he did not wish it to be. Though he attempted to distract himself by looking at the plethora of beautiful ladies around them in Hyde Park, he was most bewildered to discover that none of them held the simple elegance that the woman on his arm did.

'I don't want you to be like any of those other ladies,' Finlay said, hardly certain which one Juliet was, and not particularly caring. 'I just—'

'What?' Miss Newell shot back, causing tingles of anticipation, warm and alluring, to shoot up his spine. 'You just what?'

It would be a great deal easier to converse if he were not so damned attracted to her.

She was…unlike anyone else he had ever met. Oh, Finlay had met a great number of people; as a member of Society, it was impossible not to.

And none of them glared like Miss Newell, spoke to him so cuttingly as Miss Newell, made him feel as though speaking to her was a privilege he had not yet earned.

In anyone else, it would be off putting.

But there was a warmth to her, one she evidently could not fully contain. Finlay could no longer ignore the desire she sparked in him, the need to know her better.

To touch—

Steady on there, he told himself firmly. *You're in public. And you don't go around touching young ladies against their will!*

'You're very quiet,' Miss Newell said.

There was a look almost of disappointment on her face.

Warmth crept across Finlay's face. Try as she might to argue the opposite, she wanted to talk to him.

The knowledge buoyed him as nothing else had, and the shot of excitement and joy was unparalleled.

I wager you'll feel infinitely better for a flirtation. I think it'll bring you joy, and won't betray Isabelle in any way, and you'll enter the married state far happier.

Or not at all.

Dammit. He may have to tell Bartlett he was right and lose the bet. What was the penalty for losing, again?

'And it's not like I care,' Miss Newell continued stiffly. 'Your conversation leaves much to be desired at the best of times, when you're not lying about who you are or making a fool of yourself at afternoon tea. But you are preventing me from conversing with Sylvia, and—'

'Look, I'm trying to butter you up here,' said Finlay before he could stop himself, the foolish admission slipping out. 'The least you could do is—'

'Enjoy it?' Miss Newell said, tilting her head towards him. Something blazed in her expression, something he could not fathom. 'And why are you buttering me up, pray? Not exactly the charming opening I thought earls were supposed to have.'

Finlay took a deep breath and attempted to regather himself.

Well. It was exasperating in the extreme, not to be immediately liked. Worse, it was most unpleasant to discover within yourself an expectation of being liked.

If only she could see the amiable tilt of his jaw, his dazzling smile, the way he carried himself. He was even wearing one of his newest waistcoats and jackets, elegant and cut remarkably close to his figure. A figure that, Finlay would previously have boasted, had got more than one woman in a tizzy.

But none of that mattered. Not to Miss Newell, anyway.

Fine. Charm hadn't worked. Time for direct questioning. 'Why don't you like me, Miss Newell?'

Evidently she had not been expecting that. She almost tripped over her own gown, and Finlay reached out and placed a hand on her waist to steady her.

And unsteady himself.

Rapid thoughts of molten desire that were most unsuitable to be thinking and feeling while standing in the middle of Hyde Park rushed through Finlay's body. Unbidden, uncontrolled, all inspired by the merest contact with a woman who pulled herself free of him the moment she had regained her balance.

Finlay almost stepped back, but he managed to keep his presence of mind and retain hold of Miss Newell's arm. For her benefit, he told himself, mind whirling as he attempted to understand what precisely he had just experienced.

'It's not you,' Miss Newell said curtly. 'It's the fact that you're an earl.'

'An earl?' Finlay repeated blankly.

They were standing still now, the train of wallflowers disappearing off along the path. But Finlay didn't care. How could he, when such a beautiful enigma was staring up at him?

Miss Newell's eyes were a startling grey. It was the first time he'd noticed that. No wonder he hadn't realized she could not see the world as it was when they had first met. One could almost be forgiven for not noticing, such was her beauty.

And she hated earls?

'Forget I said anything,' said Miss Newell awkwardly. 'And return me to Sylvia. The Pike will soon notice.'

'I'll return you to Sylvia safe and sound once you've answered me,' Finlay stated far stronger than he intended.

He was not, after all, a cad. They weren't that far behind another pair of wallflowers. He wasn't alone with her. Not really.

What, a small voice muttered in the back of his head, *would Isabelle say about that?*

Miss Newell bit her lip, her head turning, her cane moving as they started again slowly along the path. Was she listening for Sylvia, for the other wallflowers? Was she wondering just how far from them she was?

Evidently she would not risk it. Dropping her head and speaking so quietly that Finlay could hardly hear her, she said softly, 'I'm not actually Miss Newell. Well, I am.'

Finlay blinked. 'Well, that sorts that out.'

There was brief flash of a smile, then it was gone. 'I'm actually the Honourable Miss Marilla Newell and I was… I was once engaged to the Earl of Porthaethwy.'

This time Finlay did let her hand slip from his arm.

Engaged before? Honourable Earl of Porthaethwy?

He blinked, the sunlight of the day suddenly dazzling—or was that her? Miss Newell was a woman far above the station he had assumed for her. What was a woman of that breeding doing in a place like the Wallflower Academy?

'Was once engaged?' Finlay repeated the one part of Miss Newell's statement that gave him the most pause.

Once engaged? A scandal, then?

Miss Newell shrugged, though there was evidently more pain in that expression than she knew she was revealing. 'He broke off the arranged marriage the day he met me. I was sent to the Wallflower Academy the following week. There. Now, will you return me to my friends?'

But Finlay could think of nothing but the outrage that was curdling around his heart.

Broke off the arranged marriage? The cad, the lout, the—

'The very idea!' he said hotly, words breaking out against his will. 'I don't see what— I mean, why should he care about… about…?'

Finlay swallowed.

Rilla was glaring just past his ear. 'He didn't care that I was blind. He knew that—everyone knew that. I was born that way. No, he broke it off for quite a different reason. Only earls know how to end a match.'

And he understood that, didn't he?

It was that annoying voice again, and this time, Finlay swallowed hard and was unable to ignore it.

Because it wasn't entirely wrong. There had been moments, hadn't there—more frequently with every day that passed— that he considered breaking off his arranged marriage with Isabelle?

Not because there was anything wrong with her, no, but because…

Well, he didn't have a good reason. Something in him just rebelled at the idea of wedding a childhood friend. Particularly when she was so…so altered. So lost.

'Are you going to return me to Sylvia or abandon me here?' Miss Newell said darkly, cutting through Finlay's thoughts.

'Though you are an earl, I wouldn't be surprised if you chose the latter.'

And that did it. Finlay pulled himself together, puffed out his chest, smoothed back his hair…then realized that every single one of those motions was lost on the woman before him.

Blast.

'I shall return you to Miss Pike now,' Finlay said quietly, deflating. 'And I hope I shall soon—'

'Oh, no,' said Miss Newell firmly, reaching out and deliberately placing her hand on his arm without a hesitation. 'No, Your Lordship. I wouldn't bother to hope.'

Chapter Five

'And she will be here any moment!' declared Miss Pike, a froth of excitement in her tone. 'A duchess visiting the Wallflower Academy is hardly a run-of-the-mill event, and some of you—yes, you, Daphne—are dreadfully unprepared. So please, for goodness' sake, be on your best— Sylvia Bryant, put that footman down!'

Hurried footsteps grew louder then fainter as the Pike traversed the drawing room, moving from the polished floorboards to the rug then out to the hall. Muffled laughter. A muttering in a low voice, embarrassed, contrite.

Rilla smiled.

Well, as there was no telling what mischief Sylvia would get into next, she had ceased attempting to predict it around four weeks after the woman's arrival.

After all, had she not orchestrated a most unpleasant encounter with *that earl*?

Try as she might, she could not conceive why the blackguard had sought her again.

It was irritating. He was irritating. And much against her wishes, the true vexation was that he had not appeared the last five days at the Wallflower Academy.

And why would he? Rilla asked herself darkly.

Besides, she didn't want him to. The delectable-smelling man, the one whose presence raised her hackles and made it impossible to concentrate, why would she want him here?

Dragging herself away from remembrances of strong hands on her arm and the sense of danger, of being separated from the other wallflowers, Rilla returned to the conversation in the room.

And immediately regretted it.

'Duchess here,' Daphne's voice whispered, sotto voce and filled with terror. 'Why she would want to come here—'

'No need for that, now!' Sylvia's voice was half mirth, half frustration. A sudden weight dropped onto the sofa beside Rilla. 'I don't see what was so bad about—'

'I think you know precisely what the problem was here,' came the Pike's stern yet steady tone. 'Leave the poor footmen alone, you know they can't— Ah, here she is. Now, let me go and greet our honoured guest.'

Rilla's nerves prickled as chatter rose up once more about the arrival of a duchess.

A duchess.

What on earth was she coming here for? She certainly couldn't be meeting with a friend, and they were just too far out of London for this to be a coincidence. Besides, the Pike had been informed in advance. That meant planning.

Another one of the nobility coming here to peer at us to see what a wallflower looks like, Rilla thought darkly. *And they wonder why the London Tower menagerie is so popular...*

New footsteps. Light, measured, definitely coming from the hall.

Rilla's spine stiffened, her stomach tightening into a knot. Could she avoid notice? It was always a challenge, being the one who could see naught but a vague sense of light and dark. Avoiding unwelcome conversation was just that much more difficult.

And there was no time now to retire to her room. That would require crossing the hall, and there was no possibility she could avoid—

'Her Grace,' intoned Matthews's voice from about ten feet from Rilla, 'the Duchess of—'

Her heart sank.

And then it rose.

'Gwen,' Rilla breathed.

She was nudged none too gently in the side.

'Now how on earth,' muttered Sylvia as the footman droned on, 'did you know that?'

There was only one person in the world, Rilla was certain, who still scrubbed the back of their neck with carbolic soap out of habit, but also now wore the delicate rose scent her husband had presented her on their wedding day.

It was a jarring medley, and it was altogether Gwen.

'Gwendolyn Devereux, wife of the Duke of Knaresby.'

'Yes, yes, we don't need any of that nonsense,' came the ruffled voice of Gwen. 'I only came to see Rilla and Sylvia. We don't need all this.'

'But Your Grace!' The Pike was obviously rattled, though Rilla could hardly comprehend why. She'd managed to get a duchess to cross the threshold, hadn't she? 'Visiting all the wallflowers, it would do a great deal for their reputations, elevate them.'

'I'm here, and you are fortunate I came at all,' shot back the determined voice of the duchess.

That was Gwen. She may have been sent to the Wallflower Academy, but she was no shrinking violet.

'Yes, move a chair here.'

A scraping noise jarred Rilla's nerves and a hint of worry fluttered around her mind. It was always so much more difficult to navigate a space like the drawing room once something had been moved.

'Don't you worry, Rilla, I'll ask him to put it back,' came Gwen's voice, closer now, and lower. She was seated on the chair opposite her. 'I know you like sitting in the sunshine there.'

Despite herself, Rilla smiled. 'Thank you.'

It was a kindness not everyone offered, and as chatter erupted around the drawing room, she surmised most of the wallflowers had returned to their conversations, embroidery, and reading.

Still. That did not mean they could speak freely.

'The Pike's gone,' came Sylvia's carefree tone with a laugh. 'Lord, Gwen, when she was banging on about a duchess, I never conceived that it could be you.'

'I sometimes get surprised myself when I'm announced into a room.' Gwen's words spoke of shyness and surprise, but Rilla was not fooled. She could hear the pride, the delight, the joy.

Did anyone else hear it? Was she perhaps the only one who could tell, who was concentrating on the slight shake in the vowels, the hesitation of the consonants?

Sylvia snorted. 'Don't be daft, you love it!'

'I certainly do not.'

Rilla allowed the words to wash over and around her. It was like bathing in a pool of warm light. Or at least, what she presumed it would feel like.

She was so…so lonely.

Perhaps it was only when surrounded by chattering ladies, like now, that she noticed it. Alone with her thoughts, never truly sharing them, never wanting to share them. Lost in a sea of wallflowers.

Though she had hardly noticed it before, she had missed her friend. Gwen had been a part of the Wallflower Academy for a mere matter of months, but Rilla could not deny that she had grown to truly like the woman.

The woman who was now, apparently, the toast of the *ton*.

'So kind, so affectionate,' Gwen was saying in that lilting, carefree tone. 'And he is just…'

Wonderful, by all accounts. Try as she might, Rilla could not entirely attend to the words of her friend. No, she was altogether distracted by a thought which, once made, could not be unmade.

Gwen had made love to her husband.

Heat sparked in her cheeks, but Rilla could not dislodge the revelation from her head. What was it, to be touched by a gentleman? To have him love you, to connect to that most intimate place? To bear oneself and never worry again that you would be alone?

Shifting awkwardly in her seat, she tried not to consider it. It was not as though she would ever be blessed with such knowledge.

One night, one encounter would surely be enough to satiate her appetite. One—

'But you've hardly spoken, Rilla.'

Rilla allowed herself to nod. 'I suppose not. I suppose I have nothing new to offer because…'

Because she could not see.

Those were the words Rilla did not say aloud, but they hung in the air, heavy in their unspokenness. All three of them knew what it was she had not said. She had never feared being open with them, her friends.

The way people spoke to her, or did not speak to her. The way they presumed she was helpless, useless, ignorant! The assumption that no one would wish to marry her.

Why were they treated as prospective brides, and she treated like a dried-up old spinster of a teacher? The very idea of staying here at the Wallflower Academy, helping others to marry when no one wished to wed her…

How she longed to find someone who knew her, truly knew her…and loved her.

Rilla had hinted at as much when she had spoken briefly to

Gwen at her wedding, but this was the first time she had admitted to so much in front of Sylvia.

The sudden intake of breath to her right proved her expectation correct.

'But she can't do that!'

'She can do whatever she likes, she's the Pike,' Rilla opined wryly.

She was nudged in the shoulder.

'Don't be ridiculous,' Sylvia said, and the merriment and teasing had left her voice now. 'You can't actually be considering—she can't force you to leave!'

Rilla sighed, reached into her corset—an excellent place for keeping things, it was a misery that true pockets were not the province of the lady—and pulled out the letter that had arrived that morning. The paper was expensive; she could feel the delicacy of the grain. 'Here. You can read it. I don't mind. Sylvia already has.'

The hand that took the paper approached as a waft of rose water confirmed it was Gwen who had taken it.

'Keep it,' said Rilla with as airy a manner as possible. 'I know it by heart.'

It had surprised people, when she had first arrived at the Wallflower Academy. Her ability to memorize things once spoken to her was astonishing, apparently.

Rilla could not think why. How else was she supposed to enjoy things? She was hardly going to always find someone to read her letters to her, over and over again.

Under the genteel chatter around the drawing room about the right thread for this next portion of embroidery, and where someone's missing book was, and just how precisely Sylvia thought she was going to get away with her next adventure, Rilla heard the unfolding of the paper.

Her fingertips unconsciously moved to the seat of the sofa. The velvet underneath was soft, comforting, warm, a balm compared to the words shortly read aloud by the newest member of the aristocracy.

"'My dear Marilla,'" Gwen began to read softly. 'Oh, it's from your father.'

She must have glanced to the end, or perhaps there was a difference in the handwriting between men and women. Rilla did not know.

'Yes. My papa.'

"'My dear Marilla,'" Gwen repeated. "'Thank you for your last letter. Do consider speaking to Miss Pike about opportunities to better yourself.'"

'Better yourself?' Sylvia's voice dripped in resentment. 'I hate that he wrote that. I thought you were rather splendid already.'

Rilla reached out, lifting a hand, and her friend knew to take it and squeeze it. A lump came to her throat and though she had intended to say something witty and amusing, nothing came.

Sylvia squeezed her hand back and held on to hers, dropping their clasped fingers onto the sofa.

She must have nodded at Gwen, or indicated somehow to keep going, for the duchess continued.

"'I will admit, my child, that it would be a relief to us if you did consider leaving the Wallflower Academy and taking up a position somewhere that indicated that you had resolved not to marry.'"

'Not to marry?' Gwen's voice was startled as she repeated the words, but then she continued reading. "'Your two younger sisters—'"

'I don't want to hear this again,' Sylvia cut in. 'It was bad enough reading it the first time.'

'Keep going, Gwen,' Rilla said, her heart contracting painfully. 'Or I can recite it, if you wish? "Your two younger sisters are unable to attend Society events, not with an elder sister out and unmarried. If you wish them to ever find suitors of their own, then you will need to take a step of kindness and move out of their way. You know the estate is entailed, and you know I have to marry off as many of you as I can. And if you are so fortunate as to meet an earl again, do us all a favour and steer clear. Yours faithfully, your ever-loving Papa.'''

Silence fell after this pronouncement. At least, silence between the three of them. Daphne and Juliet appeared to be bickering good-naturedly over a skein of red thread in another corner.

Sylvia's hand squeezed hers. 'It's outrageous.'

'It's certainly not a letter I'd wish to receive,' said Gwen quietly. 'Though I must admit, marriage to Percy has put paid to the unpleasant missives my mother was sending.'

'Another benefit of winning a duke, I suppose?' Sylvia quipped.

Rilla sensed Gwen's smile, imagined the tilt of her head which had once been described to her, the flush upon her cheeks.

Whether she was correct or not, of course, was quite another matter.

'Oh, I cannot imagine not being Percy's wife,' Gwen said, happiness radiating from every syllable. 'Being loved, being adored in the way that he loves me—one reads about such things, but you never expect it to happen to you. Why, the other day…'

Rilla did not attempt to reach out for the return of her letter. She did not need the paper back to have the awkward words of her father ringing through her mind.

And it was hardly her place to interrupt the happy words of a newly wedded wife.

Envy was an unpleasant emotion. It prickled and stung as it meandered through the chest and into the heart, poisoning everything as it went.

It was not as if two people could not be happy at one time,

or that Gwen's happiness marked or prevented her own. It was simply that Rilla could not help but feel sad. There was something unpleasant about the idea that she herself would never—

'And have you met Rilla's earl?' Sylvia's voice said, cutting through her thoughts.

Rilla opened her mouth immediately. 'He is not my—'

'He approached you right in this room,' said Sylvia, with a triumphant air that was most disconcerting. 'And at Hyde Park—the cheek of the man! He must admire you greatly to do such a thing.'

'An earl?' Gwen's voice was all curiosity. 'Who is your earl, Rilla?'

'He is not my—'

'Well, he's certainly not mine,' chortled Sylvia. 'I think you've made quite an impression there.'

Nausea blossomed up in Rilla's chest.

I think you've made quite an impression there. Her father's words echoed through time. *And His Lordship wishes to end the engagement. What in God's name did you do?*

'Rilla? Rilla, are you quite well?'

Try as she might, Rilla could not force down the sickening feeling sweeping over her chest. Her fingers gripped Sylvia's tightly, a mooring stilling her in a storm.

'Rilla? Should we send for a doctor? She's awfully pale, and she's not responding...'

'I am quite well,' lied Rilla, hoping she had injected sufficient warmth into her voice. 'Quite well.'

End the engagement. Well, the Earl of Porthaethwy was perfectly entitled to walk away, since they had not yet wed. It was just a betrothal. Just the sum of her hopes and dreams. Just an insult to herself and her family when he walked away, right there, at the altar. Just—

'Oh, bother, there's my coachman,' Gwen declared. Rilla

heard a trace of anger in her voice. 'And I had hoped to tell you— Blast. I'll have to go.'

'Go?'

'Do not ever marry a man without meeting his mother. That's all I'll say, Sylvia,' Gwen said in a dark tone as her voice shifted. She had stood up. 'I'm expected back for dinner, and I'll need to change and—'

Rilla allowed her friends' chatter to wash over her. The moment had passed. Their attention was no longer fixed on her.

Which was all to the good, she attempted to tell herself a few hours later, as she was putting the final touches to her toilette before one of the Pike's official dinners. Attention on her was never good.

Especially when offered by arrogant earls who thought they could merely walk up to a woman and have her swoon into his arms…

Look, I'm trying to butter you up here. The least you could do is—

Enjoy it?

'Another Wallflower Academy dinner,' Rilla said with a sigh as she gently lifted a long string of jade beads over her head, arranging them over the bodice of her gown. 'Another chance for the wallflowers to impress. Or, as the case may be…'

It was a good idea in the main, she supposed. The Pike had instituted six official dinners with members of the *ton* during the Season, hosting them at the Academy itself.

All in the attempt to marry off her charges.

Rilla did not wait for Sylvia this time. She knew the way well enough, and Matthews, judging by the scent of boot polish, was holding his usual station at the bottom of the staircase. The chatter in the drawing room was loud, but Rilla did not bother to approach.

Why should she? There would be naught but awkward conversation, loud chatter masking the sound of her footsteps, and the chance that some fool had moved a chair.

That was the last thing she needed—to fall flat on her face. No, the dining room was safer.

Only twice did Rilla wonder, as she stepped across the hall and made her way to the dining room, whether Finlay was in the room filled with all the noise.

Only twice. Which was impressive, Rilla decided as she opened the door and stepped forward, hands reaching for the chair at the end of the table. The warm wood met her fingertips. Because she had thought about Finlay almost constantly while dressing for dinner.

One, two, three...

Rilla counted the chairs as she moved down the left-hand side of the table. Ten—a large dinner then, at least twenty-two.

Pulling out the chair right at the end of the table, so as to keep out of the way as best as possible, she sat and waited for the gong.

It was not long. The sonorous noise echoed around the house and the door opened. Footsteps, many and heavy, laughter and hands clapping on backs, mutterings and noise...it was overwhelming.

Rilla was relieved she had chosen to seat herself before the racket assaulted her ears. It was so much harder to concentrate on navigating, on finding her way around—

'Miss Newell,' said a voice that was far too familiar. 'We meet again.'

Rilla's stomach dropped out of her chest, through the chair, and into the floor. 'Sylvia.'

The word had slipped from her mouth before she could stop it.

The Earl of Staromchor cleared his throat. 'N-no, it's not— it's Finlay.'

Trying her best not to panic, sheer irritation driving her forward, Rilla snapped, 'Where is Sylvia?'

'Don't get your bloomers all knotted up,' came a clear voice across the hubbub, causing gasps from some and mutters of, 'My word!' from others. 'I'm coming!'

Rilla suppressed a smile. Well, no matter what else happened in the world, there was always Sylvia. Always the same.

'Get out of my— I live here, you know. If you don't move—'

'What on earth is she doing?' breathed the gentleman now seated beside her.

Rilla stiffened, a cold wash of terror flowing over her again.

Had he not taken the hint? Had he truly seated himself beside her?

'Sylvia is my…my…'

The words were impossible to say as shame poured into her chest.

All she had to do was squash down all feeling, she told herself sternly. Force away all hints of desire, pretend she didn't want to converse with him…

But it was no use. The man intrigued her, most annoyingly, though she would be mistress of herself. She would focus on the dinner, and not the dinner guest.

Oh, how she hated these dinners. She had asked the Pike again and again if she could be excused from them, yet the woman had not accepted her more than reasonable request. And so she had made a bargain—an agreement, with Sylvia.

A Sylvia who was panting as she sat on Rilla's other side. 'Honestly, the state of some of these men. I would hardly call them gentlemen!'

'Neither would I,' Rilla said pointedly to Finlay—to the Earl of Staromchor, she corrected herself—before turning back to Sylvia. 'You…you will assist me?'

'Always,' came Sylvia's prompt response without any hint of embarrassment.

Some of the tension that had crept into Rilla's shoulders melted away. There was no one she could depend on quite like Sylvia.

And besides, she could feed herself, and dress herself, and walk confidently with a cane; she was no child! It was, however, helpful if someone arranged the food on her plate in a set way, so she could easily find it, and then place the cutlery in her hands. Sylvia had sat beside her for every meal at the Wallflower Academy for just such a purpose.

'I actually wished to speak to you privately,' came Finlay's voice on her right.

Rilla ensured that her expression remained perfectly still. 'And yet you cannot.'

'But I—'

'We are at dinner,' she pointed out coldly, hoping the man would take the hint.

Honestly, were all earls this dim-witted?

'Privacy is impossible.'

Thank goodness.

In the quiet of her own mind, Rilla knew how deeply she was tempted. There was something about this man. Not merely his persistence, which made no sense before one even started.

No, it was something else. When she had first spoken to him, believing he was nothing more than a footman...

Well, it had been like talking to Matthews. And yet nothing like talking to Matthews. There had been warmth, and ease, and comfort.

And now she would have to forget all that, push it away most decidedly, and concentrate on what was before her.

What was before her?

'Some sort of meat and vegetables,' said Sylvia's voice, as though she had heard the silent question. 'Smells good, if you ask me.'

'Chicken,' said Rilla nonchalantly. 'Seasoned with dill, sprigs of rosemary from the garden to garnish. Honey-roasted parsnips, burnt slightly, I believe, along with winter peas and what I believe are boiled potatoes. Yes, definitely boiled.'

Well, it was hardly difficult. They all had noses, didn't they?

She reached out for the napkin she knew would be just to the left of her plate.

It was not there.

'Allow me,' came a quiet voice she was attempting to ignore.

Rilla's fingers splayed out in a futile attempt to stop the inevitable. Finlay merely moved around her. The sudden sensation of her napkin on her lap was intrusive, but so much more was the sense that he had leaned forward, invading her personal space...

Bringing a scent of sandalwood and lemons. A warmth, his breathing fluttering on her skin. The sense that if she just leaned forward, just an inch, she would touch—

'I just wish to talk with you,' came Finlay's soft voice. He must have leaned back, for the sound was not as loud as she had expected. 'There is no crime in that, Miss Newell.'

Rilla snorted. *No crime, indeed.*

'I have no interest in talking to an earl.'

'If I could take off the title to please you, I would,' came the sardonic reply. 'But as that isn't possible, do you think you could remove your prejudice?'

It was most difficult to glare at someone you could not see, but Rilla attempted it nonetheless.

The whole dining room was filled with chatter now—mostly the gentlemen to each other, as far as she could hear. The wallflowers of the Academy were not known for their comfort in the presence of so many people.

Hoping to goodness her words would be hidden under the noise, Rilla said darkly, 'I don't want to talk to you, my lord.'

'Finlay.'

'My lord,' Rilla repeated, gripping her hands tightly together in her lap. 'And I'm hungry. Sylvia?'

Feeling exposed as she always did when it came to meal-

times, but a thousand times more now that she had such a brig-
and to her right, she parted her lips.

And waited.

'She's talking to the gentleman on her left,' came Finlay's
voice. 'M-may I?'

The hesitation in his voice sounded genuine, but Rilla's
stomach lurched. How could one tell? How could any gentleman be trusted when she could not look into their eyes and
know, for certain, their intentions?

Her stomach growled.

Oh, this was ridiculous. It was only food, wasn't it?

'You may cut up the chicken,' Rilla said stiffly. 'And…and
then place the fork in my hand.'

There was a noise on her plate. Then the scraping noise on
the crockery ended, and Rilla waited.

The arrival of the fork in her hand was gentle. Then came
the brush of a thumb over her palm, and a rush of heat poured
up her arm.

Don't think about it.

She speared a piece of chicken and lifted the fork to her
mouth, chewed, and swallowed her mouthful in silence, relieved yet slightly surprised that the earl had not spoken. Her
heart thundered, her stomach churned—because of the chicken,
Rilla tried to convince herself—and she forced her breathing
to remain regular.

'More?' His voice was soft, intimate, his breath warm on
her neck.

He must be leaning close to her, Rilla thought as her head
spun. Oh, God, but it was so sensual. So intimate.

'Y-yes, please,' she breathed.

This time she waited expectantly as he cut more chicken
and returned the fork to her. Waited for his fingers brushing
against hers. Her breath caught in her throat. And then his fingers returned, lingering this time, sliding against hers.

Rilla knew she shouldn't be enjoying this, shouldn't be permitting a man, any man, to do this.

And in public!

So why did this feel so…so…?

Good grief.

She wasn't starting to…to trust him, was she?

'I've never gained so much enjoyment,' came Finlay's quiet voice, 'from food. Not ever before.'

Rilla hastily swallowed as her fingers tightened around her fork. 'If you think I'm going to let you—'

'Don't you enjoy this?'

Damn and blast, the man was incorrigible.

'If you don't want to be thrown out by the—by Miss Pike,' she amended swiftly, 'I would recommend stopping.'

'You don't like it when we touch?'

Heat blossomed in her chest and Rilla knew it was too much to hope that the colour, whatever it was, had not reached her décolletage. The man was…was flirting with her.

Flirting! With her!

'If you can't behave, I shall have to ask Sylvia to—'

'I can behave,' came Finlay's quiet voice, and Rilla felt the loss of his presence as he moved back, a sense of emptiness around her. 'I can behave.'

Very much doubting that, yet unable to stop herself, Rilla sighed. 'Then…then you may help me.'

'And…?'

'Don't talk to me,' Rilla said darkly, wondering what on earth she thought she was doing. 'Consider it a compromise.'

Chapter Six

I can behave.

Then...then you may feed me.

And...?

Don't talk to me. Consider it a compromise.

Finlay jerked away as the half dream, half memory faded into immediately obscurity.

Damn. It had been remarkably pleasant, too.

'And that is why the modiste absolutely has to be a French-woman,' said the Dowager Countess of Staromchor sternly, the carriage rocking the three of them side to side. 'In truth, Miss Carr, I do not see how you can advocate any other.'

Finlay blinked blearily at his mother, seated directly opposite him in the Staromchor carriage, and then his gaze slid to the woman beside her.

Miss Isabelle Carr.

She was not flushing at his mother's rudeness, nor stammering her objection to the woman's demands.

No, she was just looking out of the window as the carriage rattled down the Brighton streets. No expression tinged her face, nothing at all. It was curiously empty.

'Miss Carr?' Finlay's mother said sharply.

Finlay winced as Isabelle turned to his mother with a blank, almost confused expression.

'I beg your pardon,' she said quietly. 'Did you say something?'

He had known it would be a bad idea from the very start.

Of course he had; it had been his mother's. The dowager countess had been absolutely certain that all he and Isabelle needed to spark more romance between them—her words— was time together. Time to enjoy each other's company. Time to fall in love.

Poppycock.

She had insisted, however, and Finlay was hardly in a position to deny her. It appeared that Isabelle had been unable to argue with his mother, either. That, or she simply did not care.

And so a trip to Brighton was decided. A week there, no more. A chance to take the waters, enjoy the sights, see Prinny if they were lucky, and attend the Assembly Rooms. Brighton was a place, his mother had assured both of them, that no one would suspect the engagement. It was easier to keep it quiet, she had said. There had been enough gossip about the Carr family, in the dowager countess's acidic tone, to last a lifetime. So, Brighton it was.

Which was where they were headed now.

'Hard to believe the wedding isn't that far away.' His mother beamed with a knowing look. 'And once your happiness is all tidily sorted, I can see to my own.'

Finlay rolled his eyes at that. As though his mother did not prioritize her own happiness already. Why, from the bills that had arrived from the modiste last week, and that dinner she'd thrown—

'Don't you roll your eyes at me, young man.'

He smiled weakly. 'My apologies, Mother.'

His mother sniffed. 'I should think so. Here I am, a widow.'

Finlay groaned this time, though with a wry smile. It wasn't as though he hadn't heard it all before, after all.

'Losing your father so long ago, and here I am, without the continuation of the line,' the dowager countess continued with a glint of steel in her eye. 'Something you are, at least, going to finally correct in the near future.'

It took all Finlay's self-control not to look at Isabelle, which unfortunately meant that he had little left over to prevent his cheeks from reddening.

Well, really! Talking about such a thing before Isabelle!

'You look troubled, Miss Carr,' said the dowager countess with a raised eyebrow. 'Why, I would almost say that there was something on your mind. Pray, tell.'

Finlay looked again at the woman he would be marrying in just a few short months. Not that the *ton* knew that yet.

His mother was right. Isabelle did look distracted. At least, she did not appear to be attending to those she was seated with in the carriage.

Cheeks flushing, the younger woman reached into her reticule, pulled out what appeared to be two letters, seals broken, and offered them to Finlay with a trembling hand.

He couldn't help but notice the tremble. Dear God, what had happened to her? The Isabelle Carr he had known before she had disappeared off to that godforsaken finishing school had once trounced him so hard in chess, she had crowed all day and been sent to her bedchamber for unsportsmanlike behaviour.

Isabelle had argued that as she was not a sportsman, it did not matter. Then she had climbed out of her window down the wisteria and made faces at him, Cecil, and Bartlett through the dining room windows.

Where was that woman now?

'I… I am afraid… Well, I did not expect any more, but…'

Isabelle pressed the letters into Finlay's hand as he wished to goodness she would just call him Fin, as she'd used to.

The letters were cold against his fingers. He did not need to look to see what they were.

More debts.

'Oh, dear, how frightfully uncomfortable for us all,' said his mother, quite unnecessarily. She whipped out her fan and fluttered it, as though that would make the unpleasant sight of bills disappear. 'Dearie me.'

Finlay quickly pocketed them. 'Thank you, Miss Carr,' he said formally, as was required of him. 'I will pay them the moment we return to London.'

Isabelle did not reply. She had already turned away, hands clasped together in her lap, gaze directed out the window.

It was not as though she could see much. The autumnal evenings had drawn in faster than Finlay had expected and night had fallen early that afternoon. Grey clouds had gathered on the horizon, and though the expected downpour had not yet occurred, he would be surprised if they returned to their lodgings in the dry.

But between now and then...

'Ah, here we are,' announced the dowager countess, all hints of debts and money forgotten. 'The Assembly Rooms. I have heard the food is much improved since we were last here—not that it could be much worse! Indeed, as I told Lady...'

Finlay allowed his mother to witter on as he stepped from the carriage and offered a hand to Isabelle. She took it, descended without meeting his eye, then waited silently on the pavement for the dowager countess to descend.

For a moment, he was tempted to say something.

Do you miss him?

Do you wonder why? Why him? Why us?

Do you ever think...?

'I see they haven't lit the place any better,' sniffed the dowager countess.

Finlay jumped. Evidently he had helped his mother from their carriage without noticing.

'Not nearly enough candles,' his mother continued, striding forward without waiting for either of her two younger charges. 'I shall have to speak to someone about that.'

Finlay had never liked Brighton, and he was reminded of why as he entered the Assembly Rooms with Isabelle on his arm.

The place was crowded. Once again more people had been

admitted than was proper, and they were all paying the price for it. Not a single person appeared comfortable in the crush, and the multitude of candles and smoke from the many cigars heated the room up something terrible.

And worst of all, there was no one of his close acquaintance to be seen. It was to be expected. They were not, after all, in London. And yes, it was mollifying in part to see so many pretty young ladies immediately turning to him and smiling, beaming at his handsome features, the expensive cut of his coat, the way he was immediately at home in any room.

But for some reason, the typical pleasure Finlay gained from being so admired...it felt lacking. Not that there was an absence of it, but it lacked the potency of the past.

Don't talk to me. Consider it a compromise.

An unbidden smile crept across his face as warmth flickered through his chest. A teasing remark from Rilla was suddenly far more pleasurable than the sycophantic expressions of a dozen women. Which did not make sense.

Fawning was already occurring ahead of him. Evidently someone had realized that a dowager countess had entered the place, for there were two gentlemen already offering his mother food, drinks, and likely as not the chance to redesign the decor of the place.

Finlay glanced at Isabelle. Her eyes were downcast. Her lips were pressed together, not pursed in an attitude of judgement or thought. They were merely closed, with no expectation that they would open.

When had it suddenly become so difficult to speak to the woman? If he had met Isabelle now, he would have described her as dull.

Dull? The woman who had, at the age of seventeen, smeared her father's telescope with ink and paid off all the servants not to tell him for three whole days!

Dull? The child who had learned to swim by pushing Cecil into a river and been forced to rescue him!

Dull? The woman who, when she had written to her brother upon first arriving at the Trinderhaus School for Young Ladies, had described her companions with such boldness that he had almost split his waistcoat laughing!

Where was that Isabelle?

Finlay's gaze flickered over the woman who would in a short time be his wife, and he felt nothing. What on earth was he doing? This was madness: he'd had doubts about the suitability of this match the instant he'd offered it. Did it really help Isabelle to be tied to a man who could not love her?

Surely there was a way to… Well, end the engagement. Only a few people knew about it, so the scandal would not be overtly disastrous. Did…did she wish to end it?

'Isabelle,' he said awkwardly.

'George,' Isabelle breathed.

Finlay frowned. 'What do you— Oh, thank God.'

Shoulders relaxing the instant he saw a familiar face, he steered them towards a table covered in canapés and slapped the arm of the man with his back to them.

'What the devil are you doing here?'

Lord Bartlett turned, mouth full, and sprayed pastry all down his front. 'Isabelle!'

Chuckling as his friend reddened, trying to put down the canapés he was holding and brush the pastry from his front at the same time, Finlay felt a surge of relief. Well, at least there was one person here he could speak to. And, if he were careful…

'Didn't expect you to be here, Staromchor,' Bartlett was saying, his tone easier now he was no longer covered in flakes of pastry. 'Isabelle—Miss Carr, I mean…'

'I did not know you were in Brighton,' Isabelle said in a rush, voice low and eyes downcast.

And Finlay saw his opportunity.

Well, it wasn't as though they didn't know each other. They had grown up together; they all had! And it would give him a chance not to speak awkwardly to his betrothed for five minutes together. That was a risk he had to take.

'Bartlett, you wouldn't mind taking care of Isabelle for me for a few minutes, would you?' Finlay said, speaking over the two of them.

Both Bartlett and Isabelle were staring.

'Taking care of her?' Bartlett said.

'A few minutes?' repeated Isabelle.

'Excellent,' said Finlay firmly, lifting her hand from his arm and placing it on Bartlett's. 'I just need to— I have to…'

His voice trailed away as he stepped from them, hoping Bartlett would forgive him for abandoning Isabelle in his lap.

There was just a small twinge of guilt as Finlay helped himself to a glass of wine, downed it, then gave it back to the footman who had offered it.

Cecil would not have approved.

It was a painful thought, and one he could not ignore. He had attempted to do what was right by Isabelle, and he was certain Cecil would have approved of that. The marriage, that was.

The abandoning Isabelle because Finlay just didn't know what to do with a woman so changed…

Probably Cecil would not have approved of that part.

He had attempted to be honourable. He was doing the best he could. What else could Finlay do—just watch his best friend's sister fall into penury?

No. No, he had taken steps against that. These thoughts that pained him, that reminded him Isabelle was hurting just as much as he was, that eventually the name of Cecil would have to be mentioned between them, that if he entered into a marriage like this he would be lonely for the rest of his life…

Finlay would certainly have done something about those

thoughts, rattling through his mind like a barouche without any concern for its passengers, except for—

Except for a flash of something in the corner of his eye.

It was just a movement. A moment. If he hadn't spent so much time in the carriage thinking about Marilla, perhaps the genteel movement of a woman ten feet away would not have caught his interest.

But he had been thinking of her, and so Finlay did look around when he saw a woman who looked remarkably like her. The same dark black hair, the same figure, the same bearing. So similar, in fact, that a twinge of guilt crept into his heart as he looked over.

Isabelle deserved better than that—better than him. If he didn't get his act together…

Finlay blinked.

It wasn't a woman who looked like Marilla.

It was Marilla.

'I said,' came an irate voice with the force of a gale, 'are you going to ask Miss Carr to dance?'

Finlay blinked for a second time. This time his view of Marilla—*Marilla! What on earth was she doing here?*—was blocked by a woman of more advanced years and significantly advanced irritation.

'Mother,' he said weakly.

'I have been attempting to speak with you for nigh on five minutes,' said the Dowager Countess of Staromchor with a glare.

An exaggeration, Finlay was sure. Certainly he could not have been so lost in his thoughts that he had… Well, perhaps it was five minutes. It couldn't have been!

'And you're not listening again,' intoned his mother darkly. 'What are you thinking about?'

Finlay swallowed, and knew he could not tell the truth. And so, unusually for him, he told a lie. 'Cecil.'

His mother's face immediately softened. 'You dwell too much on the past, my dear.'

'It is hard not to,' he said honestly.

'And yet you have the future to look forward to, a future with a good woman,' his mother pointed out. 'Honestly, Staromchor, anyone else would hope that you had romance on your mind!'

She fluttered her fan suggestively and waggled her eyebrows over its ribbon.

Finlay's stomach lurched. It wasn't possible, surely, that his mother had guessed… But then, he had acted in a most outrageous way at the latest Wallflower Academy dinner. It had occurred over a week ago, and he had half expected the scandal sheets to mention the disgraceful way that he had been seen feeding Marilla.

It wasn't his stomach that lurched this time, but something a little further down.

Flirt. That was what Bartlett had said. Was there anything more flirtatious than that?

And the man was right. He did feel better for it.

'I must say, I am delighted Isabelle is starting to finally worm her way into your heart,' Finlay's mother said with an approving nod.

Finlay's jaw dropped. Then he cleared his throat and closed his mouth swiftly, as though he had always intended to do that.

His heart—Isabelle?

How could his mother be so wrong?

'And while on the subject of your betrothed,' the dowager countess said with a beady eye, 'I think you have been remiss.'

Finlay frowned. 'Remiss?'

Had he not done everything in his power to sort out the tangled mess Cecil had left? Had not every debt been paid? Had he not offered marriage, the one thing left in his power, to the woman who would otherwise be left alone in the world with no one to—

'You have barely spoken to her since we arrived, you know,' his mother said sternly. 'You palmed her off to that Bartlett boy!'

'That Bartlett boy' had a moustache, was over six feet tall, and had punched a man clean out in the boxing ring last Tuesday.

Finlay said none of this. 'Bartlett knows Isabelle just as well as I.'

'But he is not engaged to be married to her,' his mother pointed out sharply. 'You are.'

He was. And Finlay was going to do precisely what was required of him, as soon as he stopped staring past his mother's shoulder at Miss Newell.

Miss Newell, who was alone. How was that possible? Where was Sylvia, the Pike, others from the Wallflower Academy?

'Outrageous that you aren't dancing with Miss Carr,' the dowager countess was saying, half to him, half it seemed to herself. 'What people will say, I don't know.'

'I don't care what people will say,' Finlay said before he could stop himself.

It was now his mother who was in the corner of his eye; all his attention was taken up with the radiant Miss Newell. A Miss Newell who was wearing a gown of elegant blue silk, a foil to her hair and her colouring, one hand clutching that cane of hers.

'Society will talk,' his mother was saying. 'It's the look of the thing that we have to worry about. If it looks—'

'I don't care how things will look,' Finlay said, ignoring his mother's outrage and incoherent splutters. 'It would be abominably rude of me not to greet an acquaintance.'

His heart almost skipped a beat as he waited for his mother to respond.

The dowager countess was biting her lip. 'I suppose that's true.'

'I wish to speak to Miss Newell.' And before he could

change his mind, before any hesitancy could enter his chest, he pushed past his mother and approached…

Marilla.

She was standing on her own at the side of the Assembly Rooms. Evidently her companions, whoever she had come with, had been asked to dance. Marilla Newell, however, was clasping a dance card utterly unmarked with pencil, her gaze downcast.

Finlay cleared his throat and, fighting the urge to put his hand on her arm, said quietly, 'It is I, Miss Newell. Finlay Jellicoe. Earl of… It's Finlay.'

Why, precisely, he did not wish to speak about his title, he could not fathom. Well. Marilla—Miss Newell—had given him plenty of reasons to cease speaking of such a thing. Her broken engagement, a topic which he dearly wished to speak on, had to play some part of that.

But to despise him so utterly merely because he shared a peerage with a cad?

'Staromchor?' Rilla's eyes widened, her cheeks flushing most prettily.

And she had no idea, Finlay realized with a strange lurch in his chest. No idea how tantalizing she looked to him in that moment. No idea how close he was…

Although apparently she did. Miss Newell took a step back, thankfully missing a footman who was transporting a silver tray of empty glasses, and frowned.

'What…what are you doing here?' she breathed.

Finlay tried to smile, then remembered she could not see the expression, and shrugged.

Damn and blast, but he was a fool.

'It's the Assembly Rooms,' he said feebly. 'In Brighton. Much of the *ton* is here.'

'But this is Brighton,' Miss Newell said, most unnecessarily. Her voice caught.

Did he make her breathless?

'It is indeed,' Finlay said, his smile finally natural. 'I might ask you what you are doing here, far from the safety of the Wallflower Academy.'

Miss Newell scoffed. 'I need no such safety. I am hardly about to be ravished by a passing gentleman.'

Fighting all his instincts to tell her that she was indeed most ravishing, and he would be more than happy to offer his services, Finlay instead accidentally bit his tongue.

God in heaven—he was supposed to be flirting with her!

Say something, man!

'And what are you doing here?' Miss Newell asked, bearing the conversational burden. 'Not in the Assembly Rooms, I mean. In Brighton.'

Finlay hesitated. There was so much he could tell her. So much. About Cecil, and his death, and how much it hurt. About Isabelle, and the Carr family debts, and how he was trying to do the right thing but it was a millstone around his neck and every moment he thought about it the rope grew tighter.

About how changed Isabelle was, and their marriage of convenience, and Bartlett's words a few weeks ago about a flirtation and joy and a last hurrah before succumbing to the drudgery of the married state.

About how his mother had dragged him here, and there was nothing he could do but allow himself to be swept away by the storm of the decisions he had made. Decisions he had made before he had ever met Miss Marilla Newell.

'S-Staromchor?' Miss Newell's sightless eyes flickered over him, around him, her voice uncertain. 'You…you are still there, aren't you?'

There was a flinty sharpness in the depths of that voice. Here was a woman, Finlay was starting to see, who assumed the worst of people. Did she really think he would just walk away without declaring the conversation at an end?

Or was this merely another method of hers to keep people away?

'I am still here,' he said softly.

Something like a shadow of a smile flickered across Miss Newell's face. 'I thought so.'

'How could you tell?'

'The world is different when you are close.'

Heat evidently blossomed over her cheeks and was mirrored by the heat in his own. Finlay could never have hoped for such a sign of her regard, but—

'I should not have said that.'

'I am glad you did,' returned Finlay, his heart skipping a painful beat. 'And I wish you would call me Finlay.'

He did not have to listen for the shock; he could see it on her face and in the way her breasts rose with the sudden intake of breath. Every part of his notice seemed attuned to Miss Newell.

'Why on earth would you wish that?' she said softly.

Finlay grinned, wishing to goodness she could see him. This whole conversation would be so much easier if he could reply with a mere sparkle in his eyes, a look of wicked mischief.

As it was, he was forced to say aloud, 'Because…because I wish to call you Marilla.'

It was an intimate request—but then, when a man had fed a woman by hand, in public, such things ceased to be so wicked. At least, in his mind.

Evidently not in Miss Newell's. 'And why on earth would I give an earl permission to do that?'

'You know, the least you could do is attempt to see past my title,' Finlay said with just a hint of irritation.

It wasn't until Miss Newell raised a sardonic eyebrow that he realized his error.

'Ah. Erm…figure of speech,' he mumbled.

Damn and blast it, he would have to go and say something

like that! Attempt to see past his title? He had to say that…to a blind woman?

'I know what you meant,' Miss Newell said softly, and there appeared to be real understanding in her voice. 'Lord knows, you aren't the first to fall foul of a slip of the tongue.'

And a roar of anger, unbidden and uncontained and most unexpected, rose in Finlay's throat.

'Who the devil has done that?'

'Oh, most people,' Miss Newell said, seemingly misunderstanding his ire. 'Do not concern yourself, my lord. I do not take offence, not any longer. I am more than a match for them.'

Yet there was a tired lilt to her voice that suggested something else. Some other kind of injury.

'You don't have to push people away all the time.'

'Yes, I do,' she said firmly, a renewed strength in her voice. 'I always do, and I always will. Besides, I like being alone.'

Finlay had not intended to speak the obvious truth, but there it was. 'No, you don't.'

A flicker—just for a moment, it looked like she was about to say something. But she could not deny it, even if the flush in her cheeks suggested she did not appreciate him stating it.

Finlay swallowed. 'I still wish to call you Marilla.'

The words had slipped from his mouth before he could stop them, but Finlay saw to his surprise that Miss Newell did not shy away from his tenderness.

Her lips curled into a smile. 'I suppose you do. But the people I like call me Rilla.'

Oh, hell. What did that mean?

'So,' said Finlay, desperately attempting to calculate precisely what the best approach here was. It would be so much easier if there weren't so much noise in this place, the music and the chatter rising to such a pitch that his ears seemed full. 'So…'

It appeared for a moment that she was not going to put him out of his misery. Then she dipped her gaze to her hands.

'You may call me Marilla, I suppose,' she said airily, as though she had bestowed a great gift. 'I am still not sure about you, Finlay Jellicoe.'

A barb of boiling-hot steel pierced his heart as Finlay grinned like a dolt. Hearing his name on her lips—it was almost as potent as being given permission to speak her name.

Almost.

'Marilla,' he breathed, wishing he were closer to her. 'Marilla…'

'But you must wish to return to your party,' Marilla said, the stiffness which had momentarily melted away now returning to ice over her expression. She turned to look towards the dancers, her face impassive. 'Do not let me detain you.'

Finlay closed the gap between the two of them. Perhaps it was not very politic. Perhaps others would stare, and gossip would arise, and Isabelle would see and break off the engagement.

He stepped back. 'I have no wish to return to my party.'

Marilla raised an eyebrow. 'You…you do not?'

Finlay shook his head, muttered a curse under his breath that was thankfully lost in the thrum of applause and warm laughter as a dance ended and the assembly applauded both dancers and musicians, and knew what he was about to say was a dreadful mistake.

A mistake he wanted to make.

'I would rather spend time with you, Marilla,' Finlay said softly. 'I find that lately, I would always rather spend time with you.'

Chapter Seven

But really, this was a most ridiculous idea. Of all the people who could be chosen for such an idiotic, unthinking, preposterous—

'I know I can rely on you,' said the Pike sternly as a wall of noise hit Rilla in the face.

It was almost unbearable. Like losing another sense. The barrage of noise was heavy like iron, a painful medley of sharp and soft. Sharp like the clack of heels on marble, the slam of a door, the clink of a glass hitting stone, shattering. Soft like the rush of fabrics, the gentle laughter, the susurration of a thousand voices murmuring.

Rilla staggered slightly, putting out her hand to she knew not where, the other grasping her cane. Damned cane. All it did was remind her of her difference.

Oh, God, she had known this would be a mistake. She should have put her foot down, refused point-blank to come. One would think, after all, that her almost complete lack of sight would protect her from such nonsense.

How on earth would she navigate such a situation?

'I've got you,' came Sylvia's quiet voice.

There came a hand on her arm, a steadying sensation, the world righting itself…but the noise was still incredible.

Where had the Pike brought them, a cattle market?

'The Assembly Rooms at Brighton are most impressive,' the Pike's voice continued, as though she had neither noticed nor cared just how unsettled Rilla had become. 'You can see, Miss Smith— Miss Smith, are you attending?'

From the fractious tone of the woman, Rilla presumed Daphne was not.

'I am sorry, Miss Pike.'

'I did not choose the three of you to attend me on this trip to Brighton merely for my own benefit,' snapped the curt voice of the Wallflower Academy proprietress. 'You three have been my charges the longest, and it is time you put what you have learned in my lessons to good use—in public!'

'And yet here I am, and I can't think of a single thing I've learned in that damned lesson of hers,' Sylvia muttered in Rilla's ear.

Rilla attempted to nod. They were no longer moving, which was a great relief, but it was still highly disconcerting.

She did not like leaving the Wallflower Academy. Not because its environs were particularly pleasing. No, it was that once Rilla had grown accustomed to the layout of a place, it was highly unsettling to be dropped somewhere entirely unfamiliar. The corridors of the Wallflower Academy were well known to her, her seat in the drawing room, her place at the pianoforte, her knitting bag. Even the gardens held no surprises for her.

It was all hers, and everything right where she expected it to be.

But this...venturing out to Brighton, of all places, a carriage ride away and with none of the certainty she relied upon...

Rilla's jaw tightened.

To be reduced to a dependent.

Sylvia's hand had remained on her arm. 'Let's find a quiet place near the wall, shall we?'

Rilla attempted to show her gratitude through her lack of complaining, though wasn't sure whether her friend understood the great effort.

Miss Pike chattered on with every step. 'And as chaperone,

I am expecting you, Miss Newell, to provide a careful examination of—'

'Miss Pike,' Rilla said, her tongue loosening as she and Sylvia came to a stop. Yes, she could feel the sense of a wall behind her. Good. That would reduce the approaches that strangers could make. 'What on earth did you think you were doing, bringing me here?'

There was a hesitation, a momentary silence. She presumed the proprietress of the Wallflower Academy was looking, bewildered, at the two other wallflowers.

Rilla had once asked Sylvia to explain what bewildered looked like. Oh, she knew how it felt. That strange dizziness in one's mind, the sense the world was shifting, an inability to understand what on earth had happened.

But what did it look like?

'Why, I brought you to act as chaperone for Miss Bryant and Miss—'

'And how precisely do you expect me to do that,' Rilla interrupted, as sweetly as she could manage. 'Considering I cannot see?'

It was perhaps a tad harsh. Lord knew, Miss Pike had never treated her poorly due to her lack of sight. But still, Rilla had had enough. Wrenched from the one place she felt comfortable, suffering motion sickness all the way along the coastal road, then forced out of their snug lodgings to attend a gathering in which she could not participate?

No. Not without protest.

'Ah,' came the voice of the Pike.

Rilla heard what appeared to be a snort. It came from Sylvia's general direction.

'I suppose it will be difficult for you to—'

'Miss?' said a new voice. A low one, a dark one—a man's voice. 'Though we have not had the pleasure of being introduced, would you do me the honour of dancing with me? Mr Jones is the name.'

Rilla forced down a smile. Well, it was equal odds which of her friends the man had approached. Both Daphne and Sylvia, apparently, were very pretty. Refined. Elegant.

The response of the Pike, on the other hand…

'Not properly introduced!' she was saying, in full flow. 'No, no, I am sorry, young man, this simply won't do. Come on, we'll find the master of ceremonies. You too, Sylvia.'

'But—'

'But me no buts,' uttered the woman grimly. 'Miss Newell, you stay there. You…you just stay there.'

Footsteps sounded, hurried and accompanied by the continued muttering of the Pike, and started to drift away. And then they were gone, and Rilla was left alone.

Letting out a large sigh, she supposed it wasn't the end of the world. She had no difficulty in standing for long periods of time, and all she had to do was wait for the Pike's feet to tire and they would all return to their temporary lodgings.

In fact, it was pleasant to be left alone with her thoughts for five minutes. After that carriage ride and Sylvia's incessant chatter—

And then he was there. Before her. Finlay.

Words slipped from her mouth without much intervention from her mind, and before she knew it, Rilla had blurted out, 'But this is Brighton.'

If only her voice could remain steady and that she was not alone.

Oh, but that isn't true, is it? whispered a voice just in the back of her mind. *You haven't been able to stop thinking about him, have you? Why, in the carriage ride here when Sylvia was enumerating the multiple ways the Wallflower Academy had injured her, you allowed yourself to imagine—*

Their conversation meandered and Rilla found herself struggling to pay attention sufficiently to speak. Words that she was most certainly not going to say continuously threatened to burst from her lips.

I've never gained so much enjoyment from food. Not ever before.

If you think I'm going to let you—
Didn't you enjoy it?

What did he want from her?

None of that was appropriate to say. Admitting such a thing to anyone was shameful indeed, but to disclose to the very object of her desire that she was so conscious of him, so warmed by his presence? For that was what this was, wasn't it? Rilla had never felt anything like it before, and she had run the gamut of emotions in the past.

Fear, anger, joy, bitterness, regret…she had known them all.

But not desire. Not this delight that he was here, Finlay, in Brighton. Not this wish she could step closer to him, feel his skin against hers.

And then she was giving him the opportunity to leave, and he did not take it, and Rilla could not understand why he was being so…so odd. So attentive. So—

'I would rather spend time with you, Marilla.'

Rilla's lips parted.

How could he say such a thing, with calm, and equanimity, and a sense he was telling the absolute complete truth?

'Besides, I want to dance.'

A cold chill rushed across her collarbone. 'I am not stopping you.'

'No, but I'll need your hand,' returned Finlay with alacrity.

This time Rilla really did laugh. 'You are jesting.'

'Not in the slightest.'

'But…' He had to be jesting. Rilla could not see the man,

but honestly, he was being ridiculous! 'I… I don't know how,' she said quietly.

Admitting such a thing was an unpleasant experience. Rilla knew well the limitations the world placed upon her, and it was galling to admit that there was something she could not do.

Dancing was all very well at the Wallflower Academy ball-room, with the Pike shouting out instructions and no one likely to get in her way. That was different.

But here? In public? In the Brighton Assembly Rooms?

'My cane… I cannot possibly…'

'I'll give it to a serving woman. Here…'

It was pulled gently from her hands, her one anchor to time and space, and then she was at sea, utterly lost, ready to be buffeted back and forth in the noise and the clamour.

A hand rested on her arm, then came a tug. Rilla stepped forward, unable to resist the pull.

'Finlay…'

'You know, I do like it when you call me Finlay,' came the low, guttural voice of the man who appeared to be pulling her through a crowd of people. Rilla could feel fabrics brush up against her arms, just past her gloves. 'Though you should probably call me "my lord" now that we are in the line.'

And he was gone and Rilla panicked, flaring dread rising as she stood somewhere in the middle, she presumed, of a room filled with people.

'One step forward, curtsey,' Finlay said quietly.

It was not an order. Not quite.

True, there was a certainty in his speech that brooked no opposition. Here was a man who spoke and was accustomed to being obeyed.

And it wasn't as though she had much choice.

Rilla did not have to think. Her feet obeyed, her knees bending as she curtseyed towards a gentleman she could not see in a rush of other skirts either side of her.

'And back,' came his command.

A shiver of something hot and delicious rushed through Rilla's back. People did not order her about! She had her own thoughts, her own determination, her own—

And wasn't it wicked, being told what to do by such a man as this?

The music continued and for a moment she froze, unsure what to do, conscious of the many eyes now following her.

'Step left, right hand up,' came the now expected instructions. 'And back…'

It was a slow dance, for which Rilla was thankful. A fast dance would have made it impossible for Finlay to give her moment-by-moment directions, but her ear was so attuned to his voice now, she could make out even the slightest hint through the din of the dance.

And what a dance. Each time Finlay's hand touched hers, every time his presence thrummed beside her, Rilla could not deny the sensual attraction that flowed through her.

He was…

And she was…

In danger.

That was the thought that rose to the top of her whirling mind as Finlay promenaded her, slowly, down the set.

Feeling like this was not safe. Feeling like this about anyone was…was a weakness. It was a chance for them to hurt her, to disappoint her. To reduce her to something she was not.

Caring for this earl was only going to bring her pain, and she most certainly should not permit it.

When the dance ended, therefore, Rilla told herself sternly that her heart was thundering in her chest due to the efforts of the dance, and no other reason.

'Some fresh air?' Finlay's hand had taken hers again, placing it on his arm as her cane was pushed into her other palm.

She did not pull away.

Because I require someone to navigate for me, Rilla thought sternly.

For no other reason.

The Brighton Assembly Rooms surely had a balcony. That was her first thought after Finlay had woven their way through the hubbub of people—no sign of the Pike, thank goodness—and opened a door to reveal fresh air.

But when Rilla was guided down steps instead of onto a terrace into the night air, she started to realize they were not stepping outside, but leaving.

Leaving the Assembly Rooms. Alone.

The sharp scent of salt and the crunch of pebbles under her feet revealed a very different story.

'You…you have taken me to the beach!'

'Well, when in Rome. Brighton,' Finlay amended, and she could hear the laughter in his voice. 'Here, sit on my coat.'

It was most disorientating, lowering oneself not to a chair or sofa but to the crunch of pebbles. But there was something intoxicating about the sea breeze tugging at her curls, the smell of the sea and driftwood piercing in her nostrils, the gentle lapping of the sea not too far away.

And the warm presence of Finlay beside her.

'Now, tell me,' he said jovially, as though he frequently escorted wallflowers out of public places to interrogate them on beaches. 'What's next for Miss Marilla Newell?'

Rilla was nonplussed. Well, it was hardly an exciting question. 'The Pike will probably tire in an hour or two, and…'

'I don't mean tonight,' came his quiet voice.

'Oh,' she said, a mite unbalanced. 'Well. We do not intend to stay long in Brighton, and Sylvia—'

'No, I don't mean— I mean the future. Your future,' said Finlay. His voice was gentle, encouraging. 'You cannot intend to stay at the Wallflower Academy forever. Not a woman of your beauty and wit.'

Beauty and wit.

When was the last time someone had described her thus? Rilla could not recall. She could not recall it ever happening.

And perhaps it was the unseasonably warm breeze, or the lull of the tide, or the fact that her heart was still fluttering from the dance. Perhaps it was the rebellious nature of leaving the dance, the scandalous nature of being alone with an earl.

Whatever it was loosened her tongue. Rilla found herself saying, 'Well, whatever I intend to do, I can't... I won't go back home.'

A subtle sound was accompanied by a movement. Finlay appeared to be leaning back on his hands. 'And why is that?'

Rilla wet her lips.

How was it possible to feel so safe with a gentleman, and yet so in danger?

'I... I do not believe they would welcome my return. My sisters—one is married, and I have two younger who are un-married—are awaiting my marriage or admission into spin-sterhood, and then they can enter into Society.'

'I do not see why.'

'You know how it is The elder must marry before the younger enters Society. And in truth, I do not think my parents ever fully recovered from the scandal of my broken engage-ment,' Rilla said, more harshly than she had intended. 'With no brothers and an entailed estate, something has to be done and I am not the daughter to do it. A Newell wedding would blot all that out. My sister Nina's two babies have already done some of the work, bless her.'

The words had flowed before she could stop them, and she was not surprised at the silence from the gentleman beside her.

Yes, sometimes you just had to speak, and that speech would drive away the only man who had bothered to pay more than five minutes of attention to you. What had she been thinking? There was no reason for—

'That is…that is outrageous!' Finlay spluttered, voice breaking with seemingly suppressed emotion. 'Your broken— I am most certain it was not your fault, so why should you be punished for some brute's…? Damn. Oh, damn. Oh, fiddlesticks.'

Rilla was laughing now.

How could she not be?

'You do not have to fear. Sylvia swears like a sailor. There are few curses I have not heard.'

The almost inaudible chuckle made her heart skip a beat. 'I do apologize. It's just… Well, you are the most interesting woman I have met in…in a long time. And beautiful. The idea of not wishing to— I mean, any man who has eyes in his… damn.'

She did not even have the wherewithal to be offended.

What was Finlay trying to say? Was he…? No. He couldn't be.

'You are trying to seduce me.'

'Can you be seduced?'

'No,' said Rilla, perhaps a mite harsher than she had intended. 'So I wouldn't bother if I were you.'

'But half of the fun is the flirtation,' came Finlay's teasing voice. 'More than half, if the flirtation is of any calibre.'

Despite herself a slow smile crept over her face. 'And you believe you offer flirtation of a high calibre?'

It was a foolish thing to say. What did she know? How could she compare Finlay Jellicoe's flirting to any other man's?

No man had ever bothered.

There was a shifting movement beside her. Even if she had not felt the pebbles move, she would have known Finlay had moved to be closer to her. His scent was stronger, and she could feel the warmth of his chest as his shoulder touched hers.

And even without those two senses, she would have known. How, Rilla could not explain, but she would.

There was something about Finlay that made it impossible not to know when he was close.

'I only offer flirtation of the highest calibre.' His voice was warm, soft, smooth, enticing. It was a voice a woman could grow painfully accustomed to. 'And you may attempt to deny it, Marilla Newell, but you like me.'

She did like him, and she would deny it, if pushed.

This man—any man—was not supposed to charm her so utterly, so quickly. She was not supposed to think about that dance as shivers of heat shot through her body. She should not want to feel his hands on hers once more. To know his touch.

Well, there was only one way to nip that in the bud. Some good old Rilla Newell sarcasm.

'I knew you would be attracted to me,' she said airily, as though she said such things all the time. 'But you do not have to make it so obvious, my lord.'

Rilla expected a laugh. She expected a denial. At the very least, she expected him to rise, brush off the dirt from his breeches, then coldly suggest he return her to the Assembly Rooms.

What she did not expect was for a warm hand to graze her cheek, a thumb to part her lips, and a low voice to say, 'I'm going to kiss you now. Unless you want me to stop.'

Rilla wet her lips, mouth dry, and before she could speak, Finlay Jellicoe, Earl of Staromchor, was kissing her.

And oh, what a kiss. With searing heat and delicate power, his tongue teased her lips apart and lavished pleasure on her mouth such as Rilla could never have imagined.

Every part of her body had come alive. She could sense herself on the beach, kissing Finlay, in a way she had never known herself to feel. The temptation to lean back, pull him against her, feel the crush of his chest, the weight of him—

And then it was over.

Rilla blinked, her eyes dry.

Had she just...? Had he just...?

'Well,' she said with a long, low breath. 'As long as you don't fall in love with me, Your Lordship, I suppose I shall chalk that up to high spirits.'

It was a foolish thing to say. The moment she had said it, Rilla cringed.

She cringed even harder when the man seated beside her chuckled, a low rumble in his chest making her think of heat and the way he seemed to know precisely how she wanted to be kissed.

'I wouldn't worry about that,' came Finlay's low voice. 'I have no intention of falling in love with anyone.'

Chapter Eight

~~~

It was not a long walk from the Brighton Assembly Rooms to his lodgings, but after kissing Marilla Newell senseless on the beach, Finlay decided not to take a carriage back. The cool of the evening was required.

His thoughts meandered back to those stolen kisses, causing him to almost slip off the pavement as his footsteps came too close to the edge.

'Watch it!'

Finlay turned, slightly stunned, to see a barouche driver shake a fist in his general direction. He merely grinned.

How could he do anything else? He had shared what was perhaps the most incredible evening with a woman, one he could never have predicted. Just a few short weeks ago, Marilla was nothing to him. He had not even known that she had existed.

Dear God, a world without Miss Marilla Newell. How had he managed to stand it?

It had been a wrench to leave her, but as Miss Pike had started to look for her wayward charge, there had been no choice. Not after being informed by a strangely morose Bartlett that Isabelle and his mother had called the carriage to return to their lodgings an hour ago.

Finlay knew precisely what would happen if he stayed. He would offer to escort the Wallflower Academy party to their lodgings, and before he knew it he would start to declare nonsense about love and affection and marriage.

And he couldn't do that, could he?

Finlay's wandering feet should have taken him straight to the rooms his mother had taken. It was but a five-minute walk.

But in the gloom of the evening, with partygoers dressed in their finery, pie sellers yelling their wares, and a great deal of noise and excitement on every street, Finlay found calm in the midst of them.

And in that calm he knew he had to ask himself one question.

What was he going to do about Marilla?

Finlay passed the building which held his mother and Isabelle but did not turn aside. He could not go up now. He needed to think—and he could not help but feel that the presence of his mother would hardly help matters.

Instead he continued on, passing a lamp lighter, two gentlemen clearly already deep in their cups, and a woman who was attempting to solicit their interest.

I knew you would be attracted to me. But you do not have to make it so obvious, my lord.

Finlay's manhood stiffened at the mere memory of what they had shared together, what he had wanted to share with her. All his thoughts, his feelings, his emotions.

His heart.

For all that this had started out as a bet, a jest between himself and Bartlett, Finlay knew it could go so much further than that.

No, this was getting out of hand. Try as he might to convince himself that his heart was not getting entangled, he could no longer pretend it was something else. That meant he had to act; he had to speak to Isabelle.

Guilt crushed his chest but Finlay could see no other alternative. He had to break off his engagement with Miss Carr, break it to his mother that he had made another choice, and break all Society's expectations by courting Marilla.

Oh, it would hardly be an enjoyable conversation. There

was nothing more that he wanted to avoid, now he came to think about it.

Isabelle would be alone, unprotected, unguarded.

But she will have no debts, Finlay tried to console himself as he stepped across the road and walked around a corner.

Almost all the Carr debts had been paid, had they not? He had done that for her. True, it would be a challenge to find a husband without a dowry, yes, but there were no outstanding arrears to drag her down.

'You did that, at least,' Finlay muttered.

'You talking to me, fine sir?' said a newspaper seller, gazing up at him.

Finlay blinked. 'What? Oh, no. No, my apologies.'

'Least you could do is buy a paper,' sniffed the young man.

Now that he came to look properly, he was nothing more than a child, really. Finlay stuffed a hand in his pockets, pulled out a sixpence, and gave it to him. Then he kept on walking.

'Oi! Oi, doncha want ya paper?'

Finlay ignored him. His mind was already whirling with too many thoughts, too much information. Too many decisions.

And the thing was, there wasn't anyone he could go to for advice.

He knew what his mother would say. He had made an offer to Miss Carr, and he should honour it. A gentleman should have nothing less expected of him—and an earl? His word was law. His word was supposed to be trustworthy.

He couldn't go to Bartlett. Oh, how Bartlett would crow over him, Finlay knew, if he made the mistake of going to his closest friend. After all their talk about a flirtation, Bartlett would find it most amusing that Finlay had managed to lose his heart—and to a wallflower, of all people.

Finlay's stomach lurched.

The trouble was, the one person whose opinion truly mattered to him was…was Cecil.

Brushing away an errant tear that Finlay was not going to permit to fall, he could not deny that it was Cecil's advice he craved. A rush of guilt poured through him every time he considered breaking off his engagement with the man's sister—but then, Cecil had never asked him to offer a marriage of convenience to Isabelle, had he?

Finlay had done so because he had thought it right, but had Isabelle expected such a thing?

He tried desperately to remember her reaction when he had first, awkwardly and stiffly, proposed the match.

Had she appeared in any way excited? Joyful? Relieved, even?

No. No, there had just been a sort of stoic acceptance.

Relief sparked in his chest, removing some of the twisting doubts around his heart. Well, Finlay had to speak to her, break it off. Why, for all he knew, she would be delighted to be free. She hardly cared for him, as far as he could tell.

And she was a pretty sort of woman, he supposed. There would surely be someone else willing to marry her.

Finlay's shoulders lightened immediately as the load bearing down on them melted away.

He was going to marry Marilla.

Well, first he had a little work to do on that front, he supposed. Marilla may welcome his kisses, but marriage—that was quite another thing entirely.

Granted she was a member of the Wallflower Academy. Surely she would accept the hand of any passable man to get out of that place?

And to be sure, he had the slight inconvenience of a fiancée. That was nothing that a quiet and delicate conversation couldn't solve.

And then, Finlay thought as his heart rose, he could start the charm offensive. Show Marilla that earls were not all blackguards—that this earl, at the very least, was not.

The fluttering in his chest was growing, paired now with the warmth he had felt on the beach.

Yes, it was sudden. But when one knew, one knew. That was all there was to it.

All he had to do was break off an engagement a few weeks before the wedding, try to calm his mother from her hysterics— he knew she would have them—then propose to Marilla and convince her to marry an earl.

Finlay sighed as he approached the front door that led to his lodgings. Simple.

Shutting the door behind him and leaning against it heavily, Finlay congratulated himself on his decision. After all, it wasn't as though he had to do anything about it now. He could relax this evening, perhaps have a long bath to soothe his aching muscles, and then tomorrow—

'Ah, Your Lordship,' said Turner politely, stepping into the hall. 'I thought I heard you enter.'

Finlay stifled a smile. It was Turner's pride that he always was there to welcome the Earl of Staromchor back at all hours. It had become a form of competitiveness with the most senior footman, and once again, the older man had triumphed.

'I have placed your guest in the drawing room, and your mother is entertaining her,' said Turner, his frown still lining his forehead.

Finlay's heart skipped a beat.

Guest? Her?

Surely it was not possible. Why on earth his mother would invite Rilla he had no idea. He had never mentioned—

'Miss Carr, I believe, has rung for some supper,' said his butler delicately. 'Apparently the fare at the Brighton Assembly Rooms tonight was insufficient.'

The slight slump of his shoulders was, Finlay hoped, covered by the debonair shrug that he swiftly forced. Oh, of course.

Technically, he supposed, Isabelle was their guest. Foolish of him. 'Oh. Oh, I suppose so?'

'Shall I announce you?'

'Thank you, but I am almost certain my mother and my betrothed know who I am,' said Finlay, frustration seeping out. 'That will be all, Turner.'

Whether or not his servant appreciated the abrupt dismissal, he was not sure. Finlay did not look up when his butler marched away, and dropped his head in his hands when he was certain he was alone.

Oh, God. He had to face her—though perhaps this was for the best. The conversation had to be had, and it was far better to do so in private with his mother in attendance so that she could accept the change in their plans.

Now all he had to do was find the right words.

But as Finlay approached the drawing room, it appeared there were already plenty of words already being spoken in the elegantly apportioned room. The door to the corridor was ajar, and just as Finlay reached out for the door handle, some of those words caught his ears.

And he froze.

'I care deeply about his happiness, of course, but I cannot help but feel—'

'You will make him very happy, I am sure.'

Finlay hesitated, guilt searing through his heart.

It was his mother and Isabelle, talking in quiet voices. Their voices were full of restraint, somehow, as though they were talking around a particular topic for fear of disturbing it.

For fear of what it could reveal.

'His happiness is… It is the most important thing to me,' Isabelle was saying, her voice warm and full of affection. 'There is not a single day that does not go by when I do not think of him.'

Finlay's mouth fell open.

He had never heard Isabelle speak in such a manner. There

was more than warmth and affection in those tones—there was love.

And he knew damned well it was love, because that was how he knew he sounded whenever he thought of Marilla.

Surely...surely he had not been so blind? Surely Isabelle Carr had not fallen in love with him?

'You do not speak with him about it, I suppose?'

That was his mother. Finlay leaned closer to the door, careful not to push it open any farther, desperate to hear more.

'Speak to him about…?'

'About how you feel,' came the dowager countess's voice. It was serious—far more serious than Finlay could recall her ever being.

Well, this was a serious business, he thought darkly. This marriage of convenience was about to become something entirely different.

'Oh, I could never speak to him about the depths of my feelings.' Isabelle's voice almost sounded apologetic. 'Besides, I do not think it would be appropriate. He does not expect it. He would not… I do not think he would wish it.'

And the guilt Finlay had been pushing aside as much as he could all evening, from the moment he had decided to take Marilla to the beach, roared through him like a dam had broken.

How had he been so—well, there was no other way to say it—so blind? All this time, he had been operating under the assumption that Isabelle was as nonchalant about their engagement as he was. She had never shown much interest in him, hardly spoken to him since Cecil had died, had never suggested she felt any joy in becoming his wife…

And now he was to learn that this was merely because of the depths of her feelings?

'Love is a strange thing,' the dowager countess was saying. Even through the door, Finlay could hear the power of her words. His mother was someone who always knew her own mind. 'A person may think they are in love, but in fact all they have is admiration and affection borne from childhood.'

Finlay swallowed. Had Isabelle ever shown any preference for him when they were children? He could not recall…but then, he had hardly been thinking of such a thing, had he?

'Oh, but this is far more than mere preference.' Isabelle's voice was direct, determined; she was absolutely sure of herself. Finlay could not recall ever hearing her speak so—not since she had returned from the Trinderhaus School for Young Ladies. 'I love him, my lady. Everything he says is music to my ears, everything he does is the best thing a man has ever done!'

Finlay's eyes widened. *Oh, hell.*

'Whenever I am with him, I can think of nothing but the pleasure I gain from being in his presence,' continued Isabelle, her voice warming with every word. 'Whenever I am not with him, I am overcome by longing, by counting down the days, the very hours until I can be with him again.'

Hell's bells.

'I do not believe I have ever met a man who has so perfectly attuned himself to my needs, my wishes,' said Isabelle tenderly. 'The kindness he has shown me—'

'He is a very kind man,' the dowager countess agreed lightly. 'I suppose.'

Finlay almost snorted, but managed to stop himself in time. Well, that was hardly high praise from a mother, but as it was his mother, it was rather more than he had expected. She never was one for over-the-top declarations of affection.

Very kind, indeed.

'He is the very pinnacle of manhood,' Isabelle said, her voice lowering. 'I love him, my lady. He is the only person I could ever conceive of marrying. Being his wife—'

'Your wedding is in a few weeks.'

'Y-yes. Yes, I know.'

Finlay allowed a long, slow breath to escape from his lungs

as the two women continued chatting. He did not listen to the words, not any longer. He did not need to.

Well. Isabelle Carr was deeply in love. It could not be denied— he did not need to see her to sense the depth of her feeling.

How she had managed to keep such powerful affections so hidden, he did not know…but then, Finlay was starting to realize that there was a great deal about the feminine psyche that had passed him by.

Perhaps Bartlett knew about all this?

'I am not sure what to do.'

Finlay tried to slow his breathing as Isabelle's words cut through his mind.

'Do? I do not believe there is anything to do. You are getting married.'

'And marriage is a very important thing, yes,' came Isabelle's soft voice. 'I would not wish to—'

'You love him,' said the dowager countess sharply.

Finlay's heart rose to his throat. His fingers were clutching the door handle so tightly that even in the shadowy darkness of the corridor, he could see the whites of his bone pressing through the skin.

'I love him,' came Isabelle's voice, and it was bolder now, sharper. More like the Isabelle he had known.

Was she still in there somewhere?

He heard his mother sigh. 'Well, in that case, there is nothing for it.'

Finlay straightened up, resolve stiffening in his chest.

Yes, there was nothing for it; his mother was completely right. How precisely he had managed to entrap himself like this, in a cage, he did not know, but the point was that he had.

Isabelle Carr loved him.

It was not a love he had wanted. He had not demanded it, nor attempted to gain it. He had not courted or wooed; he had believed the whole thing to be a marriage of convenience that benefited her, yes, but did not touch her heart.

Well, now he knew he was wrong.

Finlay had only tried to do what was right, to care for Cecil's sister. Now he would have to do what was right, even if it kept him from the woman he…he felt something for. What it was, he would not yet name.

Not yet.

Whatever it was, it was hotter and far more tempting than the staid loyalty he felt for Isabelle. But he had to put that aside.

He stepped into the room.

'Finlay!' exclaimed Isabelle, cheeks suddenly splotched with red.

'There you are,' said the dowager countess, a frown on her face but a similar concern in her eyes.

Finlay attempted not to notice. He really should not have been eavesdropping, and he was hardly going to admit he had done so.

Still. There was one way to put Isabelle's mind to rest, and he was going to do that right now. Even if every word would have to be dragged from him. Even if Marilla's face swam in his mind, her laughter, her joy. Even if she was a woman he was now divided from forever.

The two ladies were seated on a sofa together near the fire. The drawing room had, until this moment, been one of his favourite rooms in these lodgings. The place was decorated in the French style—not too French, because Napoleon had made it far too unfashionable thanks to his ridiculous antics. But the paints were that delicate blue that the French so preferred, and the chandelier was designed to the French taste. The paintings on the walls, however, were distinctly British, the pianoforte in the corner Italian.

It had been a room where Finlay had spent a great deal of time. They always came here, whenever it was time to indulge his mother with a trip to Brighton. He had always been happy here. There had never been anything to connect it with sadness.

Now it would always hold the memories of this moment. This disaster. This decision.

'Miss Carr,' Finlay said formally. 'I wish you to know I am completely committed to this marriage. Our marriage.'

Isabelle was blinking furiously.

Dear God, was she blinking away tears of joy? Finlay thought wretchedly.

'That…that is… Well, I—'

'And I want you to be sure of this,' Finlay continued, hating every word but knowing she needed this reassurance. Lord knew he had hardly given her much over the last few weeks. 'There is nothing, nothing that will prevent our marriage from going ahead.'

'Staromchor,' his mother said quietly. 'I would wish to have a small word in your ear.'

Finlay glanced at his mother, almost irritated she was interrupting this very important conversation.

After all that she had just heard from Isabelle, did his mother not understand that this was crucial? That the poor woman evidently needed to be reassured, that she wanted to hear some sort of warmth from him?

The Dowager Countess of Staromchor was frowning. 'Staromchor. I really must speak with you about—'

'This is not the time, Mother,' Finlay snapped, turning away and back to Isabelle.

His future bride, for that was how he must consider her, was a beetroot red. 'Actually, my lord, I—'

'Look, I know you have expected more from me, and I suppose most of that is my own fault,' Finlay said in a rush, forcing the words out now in the hope that if he said them quickly enough, they would not be so painful. 'I have been an inattentive fiancé, I am afraid, but that changes from this moment on.'

Isabelle blinked, evidently confused. 'It…it does?'

'This marriage is important, and it will go ahead,' Finlay said firmly, as though there were nothing he wished for more in all the world. 'You deserve a wedding, Isabelle, and…and affection. I will do my best to give it to you.'

Even if I cannot match the depths of feeling you so clearly have for me, Finlay thought wretchedly. *Good grief, what did a man do when his wife was head over heels in love with him, and he was just…nonplussed?*

Well, he would have to learn. In a month or so, he would have a wife, and he would have to make it work.

Isabelle was still stammering. 'I… Well, I—'

'You can be assured of that,' said Finlay stiffly, walking over to her and bowing low.

Would it be too much to kiss her cheek? Yes, probably.

'You will be my wife, and I will be your husband, and we… we…'

He saw Isabelle swallow hard as she looked at her hands.

'We will live,' she said softly to her fingers, 'happily ever after.'

Nausea rose in Finlay's chest as the enormity of what he had done began to overwhelm him.

He was going to marry Isabelle Carr. He could no longer see Marilla, not in that way. Not as a woman who entranced and inspired him.

And he was instead to be wed to a woman whose insipidity had somehow come from nowhere, despite the fact that she apparently loved him.

'Happily,' Finlay said, his mouth dry. 'Happily ever after.'

Chapter Nine

It was a feeble protest that Rilla had put up. So feeble, in fact, that she had been slightly concerned that the Pike would suspect something.

As it was…

'I knew you would finally come around to my line of thinking,' Miss Pike declared importantly, rustling in the carriage as though she were a leaf in the wind. 'And Miss Smith is grateful, I am sure, for the companionship!'

If she knew Daphne, Rilla thought darkly, and she did, the woman was about as miserable as it was possible to be. She was a true wallflower, one who would have escaped this evening's entertainment if she could.

'So kind of the dowager countess to invite you, Miss Smith, to her card party this evening,' trilled the Pike as the carriage slowed to a jolting stop.

Rilla's wry smile must have gone unnoticed by the proprietess, for there was no reprimand. To the contrary, the Pike was unusually gracious to her, helping her down from the carriage without so much as a complaint that it delayed them from entering wherever it was they were, and placing her cane carefully in her hands.

'Now, this is a big night for Miss Smith,' the Pike hissed in Rilla's ear, as though Daphne was not standing right beside them. 'Heaven knows why she was invited.'

'I do believe she can hear you, Miss Pike,' said Rilla in a calm voice.

Her cane tapped on the ground experimentally. It was most irritating, having to depend on such a thing. The Wallflower Academy grounds were so well known to her now, she did not need a cane. She barely needed an arm to traverse the gardens, or even make her way to the stables. Not that she had much cause to.

A warm and slightly shaking hand took hers and then placed it on an arm. Daphne.

Guilt seared through Rilla as the three ladies moved up a small flight of steps. She was just as ignorant as Miss Pike as to why Daphne—Daphne Smith, of all people!—had been invited to such a thing.

Still, she could hardly complain. The Pike had demanded that Rilla act as chaperone, a ridiculous request yet again, but this time she was hardly going to argue.

She was going to see Finlay again.

Pushing aside the thought as best she could, Rilla submitted to having her pelisse taken off her by an unseen footman, her heart hammering.

The last time she had been with him, he had been kissing her furiously.

What on earth would he say when—

'Ah, Miss Smith, Miss Pike— Oh.'

Heat rushed to Rilla's cheeks. She had presumed she would have at least a few moments at the dowager countess's card party to collect herself before being thrust into the presence of the man she—

Of the man who had kissed her, Rilla attempted to tell herself. Nothing more.

Well. A little more.

Parts of her were unfurling like leaves which had closed during the cold of wintery night, desperate to feel the sun again.

The parts of her which had been subdued by the long sojourn in the Wallflower Academy were awake again.

She was ready to open her heart.

But the expected joy was not accompanied with the heat that was suffusing her lungs, drying out every breath, making it impossible to talk.

Because when Finlay had spoken there was such…such coldness.

'Oh, my lord, such a wonderful evening, I know we shall have a pleasant time,' Miss Pike was trilling in her best fawning voice. 'And to think, Miss Smith has caught your mother's eye! I did speak to her once about her acting as a sort of guide, or sponsor, you know. Almack's is such a wonderful place to find suitors, and I wondered…'

'My mother is in the room to the left,' came the short reply from Finlay. 'Please, Miss Pike, Miss Smith. Do go on in.'

Something settled a little in Rilla's stomach, making it less likely that her luncheon would be making an appearance.

Of course, he had to be stiff and sullen before the Pike. The last thing they wanted was for her to think that they…

They what?

Rilla had been unable to untangle precisely what it was that she felt for the man, and had most studiously avoided interrogating it. What good would that do?

Still. It was pleasing to be here, to be around him. The moment the Pike and Daphne were gone, they could—

'What are you doing here?' Finlay said, voice tinged with shock.

Rilla took a step back, her cane tapping on the ground instinctively to ensure she did not fall down an unsuspecting step.

Even with the cane, her head reeled.

What the—

'I don't know what you—'

'My mother's invitation was for Miss Smith, with Miss Pike as her companion.' Finlay's voice was distant.

Discomfort prickled against her temples. 'Miss Pike said—'

'Trust Miss Pike to take it upon herself to invite another. And you, of all people.'

Of course, came the sinking thought that nestled painfully in her heart, weighing it down like a lump of lead. Of course.

What had Rilla been thinking? She should have known that nothing would be different. That he wouldn't be different. That an earl couldn't be trusted.

All expectations of warmth and connection, of perhaps a repeat of the florid kiss he had poured down on her—all was forgotten.

She had to leave.

'Where do you think you're going?'

'Out,' Rilla snapped, unable to bear it. She had turned to what she recalled was the direction of the door. 'My pelisse, if you please.'

'You cannot think to—'

'Why stay? I am clearly unwanted, though that is hardly a new sensation and so I do not know why it bothers me so,' Rilla said, the words spilling out before she could stop them. 'My pelisse, please.'

Footsteps. The rustle of silk.

And yet no pelisse was placed in her hands or around her shoulders. To the contrary, Finlay spoke in a low voice, and not to her.

'Give it to me, and return to the door, please.'

Irritation sparked in the edges of Rilla's eyes. Trust an earl to order people about and just assume they would follow. What had she been thinking?

'This is why I shouldn't have trusted an earl,' she said in a low voice as presumably the footman returned to the door-way. She'd just have to hope he would follow the precept of most servants and pretend he could not hear a single thing. 'Just when I thought—'

'Thought what?'

Rilla struggled to articulate what was more a sensation than a thought, a feeling not a meaning.

She thought that there had been something between them. Something different. Something that meant her first kiss was going to mean something, go somewhere, though where precisely, she did not know.

Oh, she felt so foolish. How could she have come here, to his mother's house, and expected a welcome!

No, women like her were for kissing on a beach out of sight of the world. Not for actually acknowledging in public.

'You cannot out-argue me, you know,' came the irksome tease.

Her temper once again flared. 'I think you will find I am more than a match for any earl!'

'I will not deny it. Any earl would be lucky to—'

'Forget I said anything. Forget I came.' Rilla moved forward, pelisse or no. The very thought of staying here was unbearable.

'Rilla, wait!'

A hand on her arm. She jerked away violently. 'I told you. I hate it when—'

'And I suppose I should have just let you fall down the stairs and break your neck?' Finlay snapped, pulling her roughly back so that her arm burned. 'You might just have to accept that sometimes people are actually trying to help you!'

'And you might just have to accept that sometimes people don't want your help!' Rilla had attempted to keep her voice down, cognizant that other guests could arrive at any moment. And that blasted footman was still there. Oh, well, at least it would be something to protect her reputation.

Though she was not entirely sure, Rilla thought Finlay swore quietly under his breath.

'You are making this impossible.'

She had to laugh at that. 'I am? You are the untrustworthy one. The last time I saw you, it was kisses and—'

'Keep your voice down!'

But Rilla was fired up now, heat burning through her veins, shame and embarrassment coursing through her. To think she had let this man kiss her! Kiss her, and on a beach, in the dark!

And now he did not even want her here?

'Why is my presence here so odious to you?' she demanded, trying to keep her voice low. 'Why?'

There was a moment of silence. The silence grew longer and longer, and eventually what broke it was Finlay clearing his throat.

'I… I cannot say.'

Rilla snorted. 'What a surprise.'

'I don't like keeping secrets.'

'And I don't like being one!' she retorted, her cheeks burning at the merest hint of a suggestion. 'I mean, it's not like I am… I am not your… I won't be…'

'You do not have to sound so mortified,' came Finlay's quiet voice. 'Nothing happened.'

And just when she did not want them, tears promised to burn in the corners of her eyes.

Nothing happened. Oh, no, to an earl, she supposed nothing had happened. Just a fervent kiss on a beach. Just a sharing of herself in a way she had never done before. Just a connection formed that was heightened by the secrecy, and the smell of the sea, and the knowledge that such an assignation was forbidden.

Just Finlay, a man she had thought…

'I should have known,' Rilla said, her voice thick as she attempted to control her emotions. 'It's always the same. You know, I comforted myself when I was a child, and the maids were teasing me behind my family's back—they denied it when confronted, of course, and were permitted to stay—I comforted myself by telling myself that things would be better when I was older. Better!'

There was an odd sort of noise from Finlay. A sort of—could a grimace make a noise?

'You were teased by…by your family's maids?'

'Oh, yes, the maids, a footman. Once our housekeeper changed all the furniture in our drawing room so that I couldn't navigate by myself. I got a black eye, in the end,' Rilla said, the words pouring from her like water, righteous anger launching them forward. 'A village boy almost drowned me in a pond. Once, our vicar pulled me up to the front of church to demonstrate how the blind would no longer exist in heaven.'

'The bounder!'

'And that's nothing compared to what I endured when I was sent to school!' Now tears were threatening to pour down her face, but Rilla did everything she could to hold them back.

And she was well practised at such an art. Her life had required her to be.

'And yet again, and again, I told myself that when I was a woman, I would at least be respected,' Rilla continued, her fingers gripping the top of her cane as though it were the only thing rooting her to the earth. 'And I was engaged to the Earl of Porthaethwy.'

'I was going to ask you about that.'

'But of course, God forbid that I be happy,' she shot back at him, speaking over the quiet question with a rapid hiss of her own. 'I've never felt wanted, or safe, never known who to trust, and you are the perfect example, Finlay Jellicoe, of why—'

'Rilla…'

'Don't call me that,' Rilla said sharply. 'You haven't earned the right.'

Her words hung in the air, weighty with meaning and caught in the web of tension between them.

It wasn't supposed to be like this. A kiss like that, on the beach, was meant to be the beginning of something. Not the end of something.

Were her desires, her dreams, truly so odious to anyone she encountered? Once again Rilla forced back the tears, holding herself upright and ensuring her head did not drop.

There was no shame in wishing to be married—unless one was a wallflower, she supposed. And it wasn't as though a kiss was just a kiss, to some gentlemen at least. She had not expected, nor demanded, promises of happily-ever-after.

Even if her heart had longed for them.

'I'll call your carriage,' came Finlay's quiet words when the silence was eventually broken.

And the last remnant of hope—that he would fight for her, that he would try to convince her—died in Rilla's heart.

'Thank you,' she said stiffly. 'I'll wait in it.'

'And I will visit you at the Wallflower Academy to...to apologize properly.'

'I won't hold my breath,' Rilla said darkly, as the harsh fabric of a footman's livery brushed against her arm. She was being guided now, and not by Finlay. 'Do not bother to lower yourself, my lord, by coming to the Wallflower Academy unless you are certain—absolutely certain—that you can bear to be seen with me.'

A part of her hoped that Finlay would accompany her out to the carriage. A part of her hoped he would help her into it, and then be overcome with remorse and longing, and enter the carriage after her, and—

But they were foolish hopes. Hopes that were proved wrong.

And as Rilla waited for what felt like hours in the Wallflower Academy carriage, waiting for Miss Pike and Daphne to be finished at the card party, she told herself the same thing again and again.

You are not a match for an earl.

Chapter Ten

The Tudor manor rose beautiful and golden in the afternoon sun. With winter drawing ever closer, the sun was low enough to cast glints of sparkling gold on the windowpanes in the three-storey building.

And as Finlay rode along the drive and glanced at the formal gardens to his left, he saw two women. One he immediately ignored. The other was Marilla Newell.

And that was when he almost fell off his horse.

'Oh, damn!'

The rest of his curse was silenced by the unsettled neighing of Ceres, his horse. The two women turned, both staring curiously in the direction of the man who evidently couldn't control his own steed.

Finlay swallowed the embarrassment.

At least she hadn't seen him make a complete prat of himself, he told himself as he dismounted—shakily—and straightened his riding coat.

'I think your earl has fallen off his horse,' came the murmured whisper of the woman holding on to Marilla's arm.

Oh, for the love—

'I didn't fall,' Finlay called over the ten-yard gap between them. 'I… I dismounted.'

'He's not my earl,' he heard Marilla mutter into her friend's ear.

It wasn't Sylvia. This was a different wallflower: Miss

Smith, if he remembered. Not that he had much interest in her. It was the woman she was guiding around the formal knot garden he wished to see, though he could not have hoped to orchestrate such a perfect meeting as this.

Well. Discounting almost falling from Ceres, that was.

If only he could separate them, Finlay found himself musing as he stepped forward, hands hanging by his sides.

Were hands supposed to hang by your sides? What on earth did hands do, anyway? What had he ever done with his hands before? Had he ever had damned hands in his whole—

'My lord,' gushed the wallflower, dipping in a low curtsey that far exceeded what his rank demanded.

Finlay did not look at her. He looked at Marilla.

She was radiant. A delicate blue gown with a cream spencer jacket matched the bonnet which partially hid her dark rich curls. There was a frown on her forehead, a pained one that should have told him immediately he was not about to be welcomed.

And he did not care.

Staying away from Marilla Newell had proved impossible. So putting aside his guilt, and telling himself most firmly that there was no law against an engaged man talking to another woman, here he was.

Like a fool.

Finlay swallowed. The last time they had been together, he had refused to give any explanation as to his rudeness and aloofness, and she had revealed…well, some rather awful things about her past, and just how deeply he had hurt her.

Could hurt her again.

And yet…

'Would you be so good as to leave us to talk, Miss Smith?' Finlay asked with one of his most charming grins.

Miss Smith. Well, it was an innocent enough name for the illegitimate daughter of Lord Norbury, he supposed. His mother hadn't been able to stop wittering about the man all week. Apparently he—

Miss Smith immediately stammered, in a rush of red cheeks and downcast eyes, 'Oh, b-but that wouldn't do at all, m-my lord, I c-couldn't possibly.'

'Do you want to ruin my reputation?' came the expected hiss of Marilla.

'Just for a few moments, thank you, Miss Smith,' said Finlay smartly, as though the very idea of opposition was preposterous.

Miss Smith had dropped Marilla's arm in apparent shock. 'Oh, that won't be—'

'Excellent,' said Finlay brightly, taking the abandoned arm of Marilla just as swiftly as Miss Smith released it. 'My, there appears to be a very pleasant walk about this knot garden, Miss Newell. Will you favour me with your company?'

Miss Smith had already walked a great distance by the time he had finished his pronouncement, and was not surprised when Marilla instantly wrenched her arm from his.

'No one is impressed by your posturing,' she said tartly, turning away.

There was no real malice in her words. At least, Finlay did not think there was. He was still learning the contours of Marilla's moods, the changes so instant he could barely keep up.

But he wanted to. By God, he wanted to.

'It's not posturing,' Finlay said as he watched her. 'And you were the one who announced me with my title, I didn't— How are you doing that?'

He hadn't intended to actually ask the question, but it was impossible not to.

It was a miracle. Despite the complexity of the garden, the multiple low hedges weaving around in intricate knots, Marilla was walking around them seemingly without a care in the world.

How was she not falling over?

Marilla glanced back over her shoulder. 'Doing what?'

'That!' Finlay knew he should have explained himself better, but he could barely articulate it. Stepping forward, he tried to take her arm. 'Let me help.'

'It may surprise you to learn that I don't need your help,' said Marilla tartly. 'And I don't appreciate people just touching me whenever they feel like it. If I want help, I'll ask!'

Her voice rang clear and sharp across the garden. A pair of ravens squawked unhappily and rose from a nearby oak tree.

Finlay bit his lip.

Well, when she put it like that...

'I am sorry.'

Marilla turned her ear to him as though attempting to take in every facet of every syllable. 'I beg your pardon?'

'I apologize. I shouldn't have touched you. I just—' He caught himself just in time. 'There is no excuse. I am sorry.'

She stared at him, those delectable lips parted in shock.

'And while I'm at it, I suppose I have a few more apologies to offer,' Finlay said quickly, before she could send him away. 'I—'

'If you are going to apologize for that kiss,' Marilla said in a warning tone.

His shoulders slumped, though he was momentarily heartened by a flashing thought.

She wants to be kissed again.

'No,' said Finlay quietly. 'No, I am afraid it is far more serious than that. It's... Well, I should not have been so abrupt with you. At my mother's card party.'

'No, you should not.'

There was a hardness to her words which concealed her true thoughts. Her face, too, was difficult to read.

Finlay swallowed. 'I cannot pretend to share all, Marilla—

Miss Newell, apologies. I am not a perfect man, and I make no claim to be. I would, however, like…like to be a friend to you.'

More than a friend. But he had committed to Isabelle Carr, so a friend was all Marilla could be.

Perhaps the tension and the regret seeped into his voice as Finlay added, 'Lord knows why you would forgive me. I'm not sure I would forgive me. I… My mother has expectations of me.'

Expectations that I will marry a completely different woman.

And quite unexpectedly, a slow smile spread across Marilla's face.

'Well. That's the first time I've heard an earl admit to being unforgiveable. And you are… Well, you are not the only one whose parents have expectations. You are forgiven. This time.'

Continuing to pick her way through the complex knot garden, she did not forbid him from joining her. That was the rationale Finlay offered himself, at least, for moving to walk by her side.

They continued in silence for a few minutes, until Finlay said, 'I still don't know how you're doing it.'

'Doing what?'

'Walking. I mean, without your cane,' he explained. 'Navigating sight unseen.'

Marilla said softly, 'I know this garden well. I helped plant it when I first arrived, three years ago.'

Three years?

Finlay had not realized that the woman—that any wallflower—had been here quite so long. 'And so…so you know it off by heart?'

'Do you learn the corridors of your home "off by heart"?' she chided him gently. 'Just because I cannot see, that does not mean that I cannot recall where I walk. And I walk here often. I like it here.'

Finlay looked about them.

It was a pretty enough garden. Most of the flowers were over by now, and a few weeds were starting to break through the soil at the borders. Precisely why it was so beloved to Marilla, he could not fathom.

'The feel of the box, the scent of the bay and the lavender,' Marilla said, answering his unasked question. Her hand trailed into the border, brushing her fingertips on the plants. '*Buxus sempervirens. Laurus nobilis. Lavandula.* They are beautiful.'

'You are very clever.'

'I have a great deal of time on my hands,' she returned with a laugh. 'And I like learning. It is why the Pike—excuse me, Miss Pike—believes I should be a governess or teacher. Believes no one will ever care enough for me to…to offer for my hand.'

And that was when Finlay knew he was in danger.

In danger of caring, of admiring this woman too much. In danger of allowing the desire he felt for her, the attraction that such a bold and intelligent woman sparked in him, overwhelm him.

In danger of wishing to be here more often, to be beside her more often, to be a part of her life.

'You are very quiet.'

Finlay's gaze jerked up, and he saw a curious expression on Marilla's face. Wasn't that interesting—that a woman who had never seen a curious face could still offer one?

'I was just admiring your knowledge of Latin,' he lied.

Well, there was absolutely no possibility he could reveal the truth.

'A true bluestocking, if ever I saw one,' he continued.

'You say that as though it were an affront,' Marilla said lightly, turning a corner as they crunched onto a gravel path and leading him into what was evidently the rose garden. The bushes had been cut back hard, though a few petals still rested on the cold soil.

'I do not know many ladies who would relish being described as a bluestocking,' Finlay pointed out.

'But I am not a bluestocking. Not really,' she shot back. 'What, because a woman is not traditionally beautiful and she has a passing understanding of books, she must be a bluestocking?'

Marilla laughed. It was a light laugh, a teasing one, one that rang through the air like music.

Finlay's stomach lurched.

'Don't you project your feelings of inadequacy onto me, Finlay Jellicoe,' Marilla said, nudging him in a way that made Finlay's heart skip a beat.

Swallowing hard and telling himself he had absolutely no desire to kiss her again, no, not at all, Finlay said, 'Look, Marilla…'

'No,' she said softly.

Finlay halted. She had come to a stop beside a climbing rose by the wall, her fingers outstretched, brushing up against the prickly stem as though to see what efforts the gardener had made.

And there was an inscrutable expression on her face.

'What do you mean, no?' Finlay said quietly. 'When I asked— I mean, at Brighton, you said I could call you Marilla.'

Don't think about that kiss don't think about that kiss don't think about—

'I said that my friends called me Rilla,' she said without turning to him. 'I think it…it is time for you to call me Rilla, don't you?'

Finlay swallowed hard. 'And you should call me Finlay.'

'And you'd like that.' Rilla's voice was soft, and they were the only two people in the entire world. 'It would bring you happiness, and that…that is something in short supply in your life, isn't it, Finlay?'

His jaw fell open.

Dear God, how could she possibly spot that? He hadn't told her about Isabelle—not that he was sure how he would explain that—and she was blind. She couldn't see him, couldn't know how often his face fell into melancholy or know how frequently he only appeared to be attending to what was going on around him.

So how the devil did she know?

'I can sense a great sadness in you,' Rilla said, turning around and once again answering his unasked question. 'I can't explain the perception, but I do have it. Even if you do not speak sadly, even if you have no wish to tell me about it—you are not obliged to. But you are sad, aren't you?'

Finlay hesitated. He could tell her. He could attempt to explain about Isabelle, about how the girl he had known had transformed into a stranger, a woman he did not understand.

Finlay had realized that morning, in horrendous clarity, just what his life was going to be.

His married life.

Isabelle, there but not there. And himself. And he was trapped; he couldn't get out. He had made a commitment to her, a promise to care for her. How would he, in all honour, escape it? Escape her?

And now he was here, standing in a dead rose garden, being told by a blind woman who he was starting to truly care about that he was sad.

Finlay brushed away the tear that fell. Thank God no one was here to see it.

'You cannot see me,' he said aloud, awkwardly. 'You cannot possibly know if I am happy or sad.'

'That's where you are wrong,' Rilla said softly. She had turned from the rose now to face him, and took a step forward as she spoke. 'Do not misunderstand me. Those who are blind are not magically able to "read" a room. And yes, I cannot see you. I have only a vague sense of light and dark, and it's not something that has ever changed. But I don't need to see to know.'

'How, then?' Finlay asked quietly.

After all, he'd done his damnedest to keep his gloom away from Society's prying eyes. Grieving Cecil…it was best done in private.

But it appeared there was no private when it came to Miss Marilla Newell.

There was a sad sort of expression on her face as she tilted her head. 'I have learned to pay attention to the unspoken words, as well as the spoken ones.'

A lump formed in Finlay's throat. Somewhere, a robin started to sing.

'Besides, there is so much more to communication than mere speech,' Rilla continued. 'Tone of voice, inflection, hesitancy. The way people move—I cannot see it, but with you…you are a very physical being.'

Finlay was not the only one to flush a dark red.

'You know what I mean,' Rilla said into the silence. 'You… Well, you know what I intended by that.'

He did. It was just a little startling that she could be so perceptive, so understanding of him after just a few encounters. Even if each one had felt intense, and deep, and far more meaningful than anything he had ever shared with anyone else.

Finlay brushed his hair from his eyes as though that could bring him some sort of equilibrium, but it did not. And that was when he found himself opening his mouth and saying something he had not said to anyone.

'My friend died.'

Rilla stepped forward, but then halted, as though she were not sure if her presence would be welcome.

Oh, how he wished she had continued, that her hands had been outstretched and he could have taken them, grounded himself with her touch.

For he was exposed now. Naked, as though he had peeled off all his clothes and bared himself for the world to see.

'What was their name?'

The lump in Finlay's throat made it almost impossible to speak, but he finally managed to say, 'Cecil. Cecil Carr. Well, I suppose he was Lord Carr, but I always knew him as Cecil.'

Speaking his name… Finlay had expected it to be painful. He rarely permitted himself to do such a thing, after all. His heart could only take so much.

Yet speaking it here, in the quiet and the gentleness of the rose garden, with only Rilla as his audience…

The lump in his throat lessened.

'I am sorry for your loss,' Rilla said softly. 'Losing a friend…that is awful.'

Finlay found himself nodding. 'Yes. Yes, sometimes…sometimes I wake in the night. It's dark, and I'm alone, and it's cold, and I wonder why I have woken. Nothing seems to have happened, no noise to startle me, and—'

The words ceased, almost immediately.

There was a pain in his chest, a tightening around his heart he knew all too well. This was the grief, this was the agony that prevented a single syllable being uttered.

He had been a fool to think he could speak of Cecil.

'And then,' Rilla said softly.

She was closer now, just a few feet from him. Almost close enough to touch.

And though he did not feel her contact, Finlay was heartened by her closeness. The sense of peace she brought him was unlike anything he had ever known.

The hand squeezing his heart relented. It began to beat again. His lungs relaxed.

'And then I remember. He is gone, and to a place where I cannot bring him back,' Finlay said quietly, his voice taut. 'And I think, how could I have forgotten? Forgotten Cecil, my closest, my very best friend, how could I forget that he is gone?'

It did not require an observant person like Rilla to hear the self-loathing in his voice. Finlay knew every word was dripping with it.

What sort of a person was he—what sort of a man forgot such a thing?

'I believe it is natural,' Rilla said softly. 'In our dreams, we wish—we long for the things we have lost. The people we have had to say goodbye to.'

Finlay's dark laugh filled the small garden. 'Say goodbye— I didn't have time to say goodbye. I didn't even tell him…there was never any need to tell him how much his friendship meant.' He cleared his throat. 'An accident. A hunting accident, one the fool was too tired to go on but too polite to decline the invitation and… I should have been with him.'

He could have saved him. If he had been there—

'Being there wouldn't be enough,' came Rilla's soft words.

Finlay flinched, the strange sensation of hearing her speak what he had just been thinking hotly jarring in his chest. 'You speak as though you know.'

There was silence, but only for a moment.

'My mother,' Rilla said, in a dry, matter-of-fact tone which quickly cracked as she continued to speak. 'I was with her, and yet you think you would know what to do, you think you can save them, but when it happens…'

Finlay stepped closer to her, needing to feel her presence. It soothed, just as much as it burned. 'My father died when I was small, but so long ago that to be honest, I barely remember him. I have my mother, of course.'

'Who is formidable.'

It was difficult to disagree. Finlay breathed out a laugh, the stinging in his eyes ignored as best he could. 'She means well, and so do I, and so we've got on rather well over the years. But she doesn't understand me like…like Cecil did.'

Rilla brushed the top of a lavender bush with her fingertips, and the scent burst into the chilly air. 'My mother was my champion. Losing her—it was more than losing a parent. Like losing my sight, all over again.'

'Yes, that's exactly it. Like losing a sense, one you could not realize was precious until it was gone.' Finlay tried to take the bitterness from his voice, but it was difficult—though perhaps it was the only thing preventing him from weeping.

There was silence between them, but it was not painful. In fact, now Finlay came to think about it, the tension and unbearable pressure on his chest were fading. Melting.

Bearable, once more.

'I don't know how you do it,' he said with a breathy laugh, desperate to close the gap between them but knowing that if he did so, the warring tears would finally win. 'Speaking with you, it's like…it's like speaking to myself. I haven't…haven't been able to talk about this, with anyone. Not like this.'

Rilla's smile was rueful. 'Loss speaks to loss without the need for manners.'

Finlay snorted. 'I suppose so—another thing I've lost with Cecil's death. There's something special about a friend like that, and not knowing it was coming, no way to tell Cecil how important he was, had always been. We were meant to…'

Oh, God, he was going to cry. And the tears came, just a few, and they were silent and so he hoped to God that Rilla would not notice.

The hearty sniff he was forced to take, however, could not be ignored.

'We were meant to grow old together, reading newspapers and complaining about the youth of today,' Finlay said, trying to laugh but there wasn't enough air in his lungs. 'Talking politics and moaning about the cold of the winters. And now he's just…gone. Just like that? How is that possible?'

He had not expected an answer. There was no answer, as far as he could tell. There never would be a rational explanation for Cecil Carr not existing and the world continuing on without him.

When the answer came, it was as soft and as silent as the tears running down his face.

Rilla took his hand.

How she had done it, he did not know. Finlay did not care. The comfort of her skin against his, the warmth, the knowledge that she was standing with him just letting him feel, letting him say all the things he had not said to anyone else…

They stood there together for a few minutes. Or an age. Finlay wasn't sure. It did not matter. Every second was precious.

Eventually he squeezed her hand, and Rilla squeezed back. When he tried to speak, it was on a breathy laugh as though he could sweep all the true emotion away. 'H-how did you know that I needed comfort?'

'I didn't know,' Rilla admitted softly, her voice thrumming with a warmth he had never heard in her before. 'I just guessed.'

Finlay's chuckle lightened, ever so slightly. 'I suppose I should not presume on your powers of deduction too heavily.'

'No, you shouldn't. I was wrong about something.'

'Which was?' he asked.

Rilla did not speak immediately. She appeared to be considering whether or not to speak. When she did, it was hesitant, unsure. Finlay would almost guess she was…ashamed?

'I thought… Well, you have always sounded very carefree. I admit, I did not think you had such depths to your character.'

Finlay shook his head wryly, then recalled she would not sense such a motion. 'If you don't care, then it can't hurt.'

Rilla's laugh was dark, and it pained him right to his core. 'Perhaps we are not so unlike after all.'

'What do you mean?'

She had already stepped away. 'Nothing.'

'Do not give me that. I know you better than that,' Finlay shot after her.

He had not intended his words to be so aggressive, and now that they had been spoken, he regretted them.

Rilla had halted, however, and she did not continue to move away. 'Yes. Yes, you do, don't you?'

Finlay swallowed.

'And yet we are so different,' she continued, a dark humour in her tones. 'I am a wallflower here only because no one bothers to take much of an interest in me. I have no choices, no power, no options for my future.'

'I know all about no choice and no power,' Finlay said without thinking.

It had been a foolish thing to say, but his marriage had been on his mind and the words had slipped out before he could stop them.

Rilla frowned. 'What on earth would an earl know about a lack of power?'

Finlay hesitated. He was dancing along a dangerous line here now. The flirtation had been wonderful—Bartlett had been right—but they were verging on something else here, weren't they?

More than a kiss stolen on a beach. More than a walk together, fingers slipping by each other, hearts skipping beats.

He had shared with her now, and she had with him. He knew her better than any lady in the *ton*, and somehow all the other ladies of the *ton* were dull in comparison.

He needed to tell her about Isabelle.

The thought was sharp and unpleasant, but he could not deny its veracity. This had gone on too long now. Rilla deserved to know—and Isabelle deserved to have his full attention. They may not care about each other in that way, but she was to be his wife.

And yet he couldn't. How could he utter Isabelle's name when Rilla had returned to him, her fingers reaching out for him, splaying across his chest?

Finlay's heart skipped a painful beat. 'Rilla...'

'Finlay…'

'There you are, Miss Newell, I— Oh, goodness! My lord!'

Finlay did three things in very rapid motion.

Firstly, he released Rilla's hand, though it cost him a great deal to sever the tie to comfort which he had only just found.

Secondly, he raised his other hand swiftly to brush the remaining tears from his eyes. There could be no evidence that Finlay Jellicoe, Earl of Staromchor, had done anything so pedestrian as crying.

And thirdly, he turned with a charming smile that he knew always worked and bowed low. 'Miss Pike.'

When he straightened, it was to see the proprietress of the Wallflower Academy looking aghast.

'Miss Newell—and my lord—speaking privately in the rose garden? It's outrageous!'

'Miss Pike,' Rilla began stiffly. 'It's only—'

What precisely it was 'only', Finlay was never to discover. He was too fascinated by the way all Rilla's warmth, her softness, her comfort had disappeared. The chill had fallen and she was now as reserved and as aloof as she had been when he had first revealed his true identity.

Lowest order? I'll have you know I'm an earl. The Earl of—

An earl? Of course. I should have guessed by your rudeness.

How did she do that?

'And here I am, attempting to make good matches for all my wallflowers, and—'

'There is nothing to be concerned about. We have only—'

'I was looking for you, Miss Pike,' Finlay interrupted hastily. 'And then I was walking with Miss Smith and Miss Newell, and now I am delighted to find you.'

The two women halted their words immediately.

Yes, the mention of Miss Smith had immediately cooled the proprietress's concern; he could see that.

Miss Pike blinked. 'Me?'

'You,' he said warmly, stepping towards her and ensuring that he added a brilliance to the smile and a glitter to his eye.

That was it, be the roguishly charming man that everyone in the *ton* knew him to be…

'Oh, my lord,' said Miss Pike, a pink flush covering her cheeks.

'I was hoping to gain your permission to take a pair of your wallflowers riding,' Finlay said smoothly, as though nothing would make him happier. He ignored the snort of ridicule behind him. No matter how sensitive Rilla was proving herself to be, there was always an undercurrent of mischief. 'Three days hence—perhaps the Misses Newell and Bryant?'

Chapter Eleven

Nothing else smelt like the local village church. Nothing.

'In the name of the Father, and of the Son…'

Rilla breathed in deeply, finding comfort and solace in the dependability of the little church that sat just outside the Wallflower Academy.

Beeswax candles. Heavy starch in the vicar's vestments. The hardness of the pews, lightly scratched along the seats. The cool of the stones beneath her feet. Snowdrops. It must be the Wallflower Academy's turn to provide flowers, for the place was heady with their scent, and they were the current favourite of their proprietress.

In a world in which Miss Pike attempted to change her fate, and in which gentlemen bared their souls to her without her quite knowing what she had done to receive such intimacies, the building was another one of her anchors.

'Amen.'

Rilla swallowed, attempting to follow the church service rather than get carried away by the memories of two days ago.

But it was a challenge. Finlay had—they had never spoken like…

It was more than she could ever have imagined.

H-how did you know that I needed comfort?

I didn't know. I just guessed.

'The reading today is taken from…'

Rilla heard the rustle of pages as fifty or so of the congregation rustled through the Bibles provided on each pew. She heard the genteel cough of someone just behind her, the shifting of someone who was evidently uncomfortable.

It was just another Sunday morning. One which would surely pass just as all the others had.

Except that she had a man on her mind, and Miss Pike was seated next to her and determined to—

Well. Irritate her.

'I suppose your father has written to you,' breathed the woman on her left.

Rilla did not permit a single inch of her face to alter. What on earth was the woman thinking—and after her etiquette lesson only yesterday! 'We are in church, Miss Pike.'

'It's very important. The moment I read it this morning I knew I had to speak to you about it. I merely wondered—'

'Then Moses said to the people, "Commemorate this day, the day you came out of Egypt…"'

'If you had heard—'

'"The land he swore to your ancestors to give you, a land flowing with milk and honey—you are to observe this ceremony in this month—"'

'The news!'

Try as she might, Rilla could not bring herself to grace the woman with a glare. She had worked on her glare for many years, her sisters assisting her at times, and Sylvia had aided her in perfecting the raised eyebrow.

The trouble was, none of those attitudes seemed particularly appropriate for church.

Even if the vicar was, apparently, almost as short-sighted as she was blind.

'Miss Newell,' murmured Miss Pike, nudging her with her elbow as though that would incentivise her to respond. There was tension in her tone that Rilla had never heard before. 'Have you heard from your father?'

Rilla sighed heavily. She would much prefer to indulge in memories of Finlay nudging her, Finlay taking her arm, Finlay revealing his heart to her in such a manner…that of a friend.

No, not quite a friend. Sylvia and Daphne were perhaps her closest friends at the Wallflower Academy, and neither of them had ever wept on her shoulder.

But it was not as though Finlay had said anything about… affection.

'Miss Newell!'

'I heard from my father two weeks ago,' Rilla murmured under her breath, not bothering to turn her head to the side. The woman had to learn.

No, Finlay had said little of affection—nothing about it, in fact. His attention had been fixed, quite rightly, on the friend he had lost.

Besides, earls could not be trusted.

The little voice at the back of her mind which had sought to keep her safe, protected, isolated all these years finally managed to break through the chattering in her head about charming young earls.

He was an earl. Finlay was of that class of gentlemen who thought not only was the world beneath him, but it was supposed to do his bidding. He was part and parcel of the whole nobility, a part of Society that looked down on mere gentry like herself.

'And he mentioned the end of next month?'

And yes, Finlay appeared different from many of the gentlemen of that set she had encountered, Rilla had to accept. He had a…a depth to him no other man had ever revealed to her. And yet…

'You know, then, about the change of circumstances coming?'

Yet it was all too easy to deceive her.

It had been Rilla's greatest fear, ever since that awful encounter with that boy, years ago. She had known the village pond was closer than that, yet he had still called her forward.

And she had believed him. He had said they were friends. Did not friends trust each other?

The subsequent soak had been terrifying. Pond weed inhaled, water clogging her lungs... If her father had not been there...

Rilla blinked. 'End of next month? Change of circumstances?'

Now that Miss Pike's words had finally caught up with her mind, she had probably spoken too loudly. There was an awkward cough from Sylvia beside her, and Rilla heard with a twist in her stomach that the vicar's sermon had momentarily halted.

'That...that is to say... Where was I? Ah, yes. That is to say, when we examine this passage closely...'

'I was not aware of a change of circumstances,' Rilla said quietly, now desperate for the previously loquacious Pike to speak up. 'Miss Pike?'

'I had presumed your father had informed you.'

Now the older woman's voice sounded unsure, unsteady. Most unlike the woman Rilla had known for the last three years.

Oh, how she wished they were no longer in church. It would be easy, then—or relatively easy—to encourage Miss Pike to reveal what awkwardness was to hand, and then Rilla could acclimatize to it. She always did. Always adapted, always found a way through.

Though it was all too easy to deceive her, Rilla had ceased to be so trusting a long time ago. The worry at the back of her mind that she was being taken advantage of never truly disappeared, but there was little she could accuse the Pike of.

Arguing in favour of her becoming a tutor, yes.

But actual cruelty?

No, the woman didn't have a cruel bone in her body. It wouldn't even occur to the Pike to—

'I refer, most unwillingly, to the fact that your father will cease to pay for your place here at the Wallflower Academy at the end of next month,' Miss Pike said in a soft rush.

Rilla was suddenly very aware of her body. Of her buttocks sitting on the pew, her spine against the back rest, her fingers clasped together in her hands, her lungs tight and painful. Her lips parted in shock. Her breath became ragged.

Cease to pay for your place here.

The idea that she would have to one day leave the Wallflower Academy…

It was home. In a way, it was more home than home had ever been. Oh, her father meant well—she was almost sure of it—but with her mother gone and the estate entailed, Rilla had learnt from a young age not to consider Newell Place as her true home.

No, it was here. The Wallflower Academy. It was the place where she had been permitted freedom, the first friends she had made, her escape from—

And now they were going to make her leave?

'And as we can see from the verses that follow, we notice that…'

'I… Cease to pay?' Rilla breathed.

Miss Pike shuffled awkwardly beside her as she whispered, 'I cannot just keep people forever, Miss Newell, you know that. Your father has paid for my help for three years, and you have never…'

Ah, this old tune.

Rilla allowed it to wash over her. She knew this speech, had heard it many times. It was the standard Miss Pike 'I've done everything I can to help you get wed, and you've done nothing' speech. Sylvia was often treated to a variation. Daphne, too.

But though the repetitive phrases may have comforted her

in the past, perhaps even made her smile, Rilla could not do so now.

What was she to do? Where was she to go?

Surely not back home, back to her father. His latest letter had been most clear. He had no wish for her to return; her sisters needed a chance to enter Society without the mark of her past hanging over them. And besides, Nina was still living close by.

So where did that leave her? Where…where could she go?

'And as you are welcome at home—'

'I am not welcome at home,' Rilla said through gritted teeth. Not after they'd all taken Nina's side.

Another elbow in her ribs from Sylvia. She was being too loud again, but she couldn't help it.

She had nowhere to go.

What was to become of her?

'Sort something out,' Miss Pike finished in a low murmur.

Just then the vicar said, 'Hymn number forty-two.'

The congregation rose and Rilla rose with it, moving on instinct instead of any rational thought.

Her mind was buzzing, attempting to take in what she had just been told—and the infuriating thing was, she noticed as the organ started up and voices rose in song, that she couldn't stop thinking about Finlay.

You are clever.

Here she was, about to lose her home, her sense of place and purpose…and her mind instead decided to meander down the trail that led not to solutions, but to an earl who could not be trusted?

An earl who kissed her like the devil on a beach in Brighton, and then simply did not mention it again, as though it had never happened?

The rest of the church service was a blur. Rilla was certain that it had happened; it would have been most strange if it had not. But if she had been asked about it later, there was not a single detail she could have provided.

When the processional music struck up and the congregation bowed their heads as the vicar and the sexton passed by, Rilla found her heart was thundering along with the heavy bass of the organ.

What was she to do?

'Are you coming, Rilla?'

Sylvia's voice cut through her panic and she jerked her head. Somehow the music had ended. The chatter of the end of church had begun.

Her friend's voice was light and airy. She had evidently not heard the shocking revelation from the Pike, Rilla realized, and so was ignorant of the coming disaster. And she would keep it that way.

There was no need for more people to worry.

'I... I will, presently,' said Rilla quietly. 'Don't worry, I can find my own way home.'

The final word she uttered stuck momentarily in her throat. Home? Where was home? If the place her family lived was not home, and the Wallflower Academy could no longer be home in five weeks, then what on earth was she supposed to call home?

But Sylvia either did not notice or did not care. She was gone, her scent of lavender disappearing as the noise of the church started to dissipate.

Eventually there was just one set of footsteps.

'Miss Newell?' came the voice of Miss Pike.

She sounded nervous. It was strange, to hear her so uncertain, and Rilla almost grinned.

Well, it was good to see that Miss Pike had a heart after all.

'I am quite well,' Rilla said softly from her seat on the pew. 'I just wish for a little reflection time in the quiet of the church. That is all.'

There was silence, no answering response from the Pike, but no footsteps to suggest she had departed. Evidently she was unsure quite whether she should leave her here.

Rilla forced down a snort. It was not appropriate in church, and most of all, the Pike would scold her for it—and she wasn't in the mood for being scolded.

'Nothing is going to happen to me here,' Rilla pointed out dryly. 'This is a church, Miss Pike. I will be alone for a short while, then I will return to the Academy.'

'Yes, well...the reverend is coming to luncheon to instruct the wallflowers, but...but I suppose you have a great deal to think about.'

Rilla's throat tightened. 'I do.'

Only then did the footsteps depart, growing fainter as Miss Pike reached the door. And then there was silence.

Shoulders sagging, Rilla allowed herself to feel the weight of what she had so recently been told.

No more money for the Wallflower Academy—and no warm invitation to return home. So where would that leave her?

She was gifted with nothing more than a few minutes of solitude before footsteps appeared again. A prickle of irritation curled around Rilla's heart. Could she not be trusted to sit quietly in a church? Was the Pike truly about to interrupt her, when all she wished was for silence?

'I want to be alone,' Rilla said harshly as the footsteps grew closer.

They suddenly stopped. And then came a scent of lemon.

'F-Finlay?' she breathed.

It was a foolish thing to say. It could not be him. Why the Earl of Staromchor would have left his own church to drive or ride out of London to see her, she did not know. There was no logical reason.

'I have to work out how you do that,' came the light, cheerful voice of Finlay Jellicoe. 'Budge up, there.'

Hardly able to think as her mind whirled, Rilla obeyed, shifting along the pew what she believed was a sufficient amount. A person sat beside her. A person who smelled of sandalwood, and lemon, and whose warmth was moving powerfully through her.

His arm was pressed against hers. His leg—

Rilla swallowed.

His leg was pressed against hers, their hips connected in a way that even through several layers of clothing, a burning heat spread through her.

There was surely no need for him to sit that close to her... was there?

'What are you doing here?' Rilla asked sharply.

She had not intended the words to become an interrogation, but fear and worry were tinging her blood with every thrum of her pulse, and the anxiety poured into her words.

Besides, what could this man possibly want from this strange friendship? What did he want with her?

Oh, he had kissed her—but they had never spoken of it. Sometimes Rilla wondered whether she had dreamt the entire thing. It would not be the first time she had wished to kiss an earl.

'I came to see the church. My mother asked me to...well, look at churches. No reason why,' came the nonsensical reply.

Rilla snorted. 'You do know that makes no sense, don't you? What does your mother need a church for?'

'What are you doing here?' Finlay returned, seemingly without concern that she had been so rude.

'This is my parish church,' she snapped in return, heat blooming in her chest, rising in temperature quite beyond her control.

And she knew she was being unreasonable, but right now, the whole world was. Why should she be sent away from home, abandoned by her family? Why should she be turned out of the Wallflower Academy—had she not helped countless wallflowers find husbands? Did not Gwen owe some of her happiness to her? And Mary before her? And Sarah before her? And when Elizabeth—

'There's no law against stepping into a church, Rilla,' Finlay said sedately, evidently unruffled by her hostile tone. 'In fact, I rather think they encourage it.'

'I wanted to be alone,' Rilla said hotly, unable to stop herself.

'Then be alone with me,' came the gentle reply.

Rilla had to swallow the retort that he was being ridiculous, for two reasons.

Firstly, because her temper was about to get the better of her, and that was never a pleasant occurrence at the best of times.

And secondly because…because he was right.

She had never noticed that before. But Finlay spoke the truth—she could be alone with him, and quite happily. The heat seeping from his body into hers wasn't fuelling her bitterness; it was calming her, washing away the anxiety and leaving calm in its wake.

His presence soothed her.

'You…you are not offended? By the way I speak to you, I mean,' Rilla said awkwardly.

The chuckle beside her rustled up her arm and into her side. 'I suppose other people placate you, accept whatever you deal out to them, just because you can't see.'

Rilla blanched, but unfortunately had little in the way of retort because it was true. It had always been true. The awkwardness people felt around her as a child had swiftly led to her being treated differently, and one aspect of that was the delicacy with which she was treated.

In some cases it was welcome. A little more grace, a little more patience—who would refuse that?

But Rilla knew, even if she had never admitted it before,

that it also led to people accepting rudeness from her that they would never accept from someone like Sylvia or Daphne.

And Finlay had noticed.

'I don't pity you, you know.'

Rilla started, still staring towards the front of the church. 'You don't?'

'Not because you cannot see, I mean,' came Finlay's soft voice. 'Though I do pity you in a way.'

Already the tension was returning to her shoulders. 'And why, precisely, would you?'

'You have fewer options than me,' Finlay said softly. Despite that, the low pluck of his voice seemed to reverberate in the empty church. 'I...well, I don't have every choice set ahead of me, but I certainly have more choices than you. Your future... what does it contain? You never told me, the other day.'

Rilla swallowed back the hated tears.

She would not cry. She would not.

'You don't have to talk to me about it. But I'd like you to.'

And it was the gentleness that prompted her to speak. She had never met a man, or anyone, who spoke with such gentleness. Such understanding.

'I... I do not have much longer at the Wallflower Academy.'

For some reason, the man sitting beside her stiffened. 'What do you mean?'

'Oh, never fear, no man is about to sweep me off my feet and propose marriage,' Rilla said, forcing herself to laugh. As long as she was the one doing the laughing, then it didn't matter if others laughed, too. 'No, it's... Well...'

It wasn't a lack of money, and even that would be shameful enough to admit. It wasn't a lack of space—the Wallflower Academy was busy at the moment, to be sure, but there was plenty of space in the old Tudor manor for her.

It was a lack of care, she supposed, though wild horses would not get her to admit to such a thing about her father.

Rilla sighed, her head dropping. 'I think if I had just married the Earl of Porthaethwy, none of this would be a problem. My father wouldn't—none of my family would be ashamed. There would be no scandal—'

'It wasn't as much a scandal as you think,' came the interjection of Finlay's voice. 'I mean to say, I had never heard of it.'

'I am not sure whether to be pleased or mortified that my life has had such little impact,' Rilla said dryly.

They sat for a moment in silence, and she could not help but notice just how comfortable it was.

He made her comfortable.

And then Finlay made her distinctively uncomfortable by shifting in his seat and asking in a low voice, 'What happened between you and the Earl of Porthaethwy?'

Rilla trotted out the tried and tested formula instinctively. 'There was naught but a misunderstanding.'

'Which was?'

No one had ever asked her that. A misunderstanding was usually sufficient to ward off even the most nosey of gossips.

But this wasn't a gossip. This was Finlay. A man who absolutely should not matter to her, and by God, he mattered.

'I… He wouldn't accept my explanation, my apology, when…' Rilla swallowed. Old wounds never healed, not entirely. The scars still rested on her heart, and tugging at the injury threatened to cause an ache she was not sure she could accept.

But if she were to tell anyone, it would be him.

Sighing heavily, she tried to keep her voice light. 'It was my own fault. I can admit that now, though it was a most challenging thing to accept when I was younger. But I know now that the blame was my own.'

'Blame?'

'I was not always the paragon of virtue that you see before you,' said Rilla, trying to keep her tone light. 'I was…arrogant,

I suppose. I revelled in the idea that I would be a countess—an earl, did you know, an earl wished to marry me? And the Earl of Porthaethwy, he was coming a week before the wedding. His Lordship arrived, for the first time. A house party before the wedding, to meet me, to meet the whole family. The match had been arranged when we were young, and…'

Her voice trailed away. How could she admit this? How could she reveal just how foolish she had—

Her gasp echoed around the church.

Finlay had taken her hand. No request, no hesitation—he had just reached out and taken it in his. His warm fingers entwined with hers and he pulled her hand into his lap, holding it there as a secure anchor against the storm that was railing in her chest.

Rilla swallowed. And could somehow continue. 'Nina and I were in the drawing room. My sister, my next-youngest sister. This was two…no, maybe three days since Lord Porthaethwy had arrived. She asked me what I thought of him, and I… I was young, you must recall, and I did not know what I was about. Anyway, I… I spoke cuttingly of the man.'

'Ah,' came Finlay's voice. 'I have a sense where this is going.'

'I thought to impress, I suppose. I was almost giddy with excitement. I was getting married, and I was to be a countess, and at that age those sorts of things mattered,' said Rilla bitterly. 'I spoke in a way— Oh, how I blush to even think of it now. It is hateful indeed to look back upon the person you once were, and realize that you were unformed, unfinished.'

'What did you say to him?' came Finlay's curious voice.

Her chest tightened painfully. 'None of your business.'

'It's just, to break off an engagement…'

'I was not… Well, not the person I aim to be now,' Rilla said, heat burning her cheeks. 'It was nothing serious, of course, but he was a proud man, and I injured that pride. The damage was done.'

'Naught but a misunderstanding, I'm sure.'

Rilla laughed ruefully. The pew was cold under her free hand as she clutched it tightly. 'I think perhaps more accurately I should say that the Earl of Porthaethwy did not wish to be understanding. I had offended—nay, mortified him. He would not accept my apology, nor that of my father.'

Strange. She had not permitted herself to think of those days for such a long time now, it was as though the colour had been taken out of the memories she held. They were so distant now, yet they were a part of her. Had made her who she was.

'And so he left me at the altar.'

'He—'

'Yes,' said Rilla as lightly as though she barely cared. She would not permit the man to continue to injure her. 'Yes, he waited until the moment that would hurt me, hurt my family the most. There I was, having just swept up the aisle on my father's arm...'

'The brute!'

'He was hurt.' That was what she had told herself then. 'He wished to punish me, I suppose, and earls can do whatever they like in Society. Why not shame the entire Newell family by thrusting aside my hand when it was offered, declaring to the whole church that he had no wish to align himself to a woman with a sharp tongue and an even sharper heart?'

Finlay was spluttering so dramatically his words were almost entirely incomprehensible. 'I— The cheek— If I had— Your father must—'

'It was an arranged marriage,' she said as lightly as she could. 'He never would have chosen me, not of his own free will. And the whole thing, it should not matter, I should not care.'

'I think we're past the point of "should." You obviously cared, in a way. You must have been mortified.'

Mortification did not adequately cover it.

'And I never spoke to the Earl of Porthaethwy again,' Rilla

continued, pushing past his astonishment. She could not dwell on this story much longer. 'I attempted to apologize, but it did not matter. I had injured, insulted, and I was not to be forgiven. He married my sister Nina in the end. My father was insistent that the connection still be made, and after all, he had four daughters.'

She could well imagine the look of astonishment on Finlay's face.

'I am sorry—he merely exchanged one sister for another?'

'What did the substitution for one over the other matter? I did not attend the wedding.'

'And your sister?'

'We have not spoken since. I suppose she feels a duty, a responsibility to honour her husband, and I suppose, rightly so,' Rilla said, attempting to keep her voice level. 'I know I have not visited. No invitations have been forthcoming.'

Some things broken never mended. And it was her fault. Her pride, her arrogance, her determination to be adored, admired. To finally be the fortunate Newell sister.

It was her fault, all her fault—and by the time she'd concocted a way to make it right, it was too late. Too much time, too much silence, too much distance for too long. Too much pain, too many tears. Too many nightmares of standing there, the scent of the church candles, the shocked gasps echoing…

Finlay's hand squeezed hers. 'I am sorry.'

'Don't be,' Rilla said briskly.

'Just take my kindness, will you, and don't brush it away?' Finlay's voice was level, and there was concern, and what could be considered affection if one were seeking it. 'You don't have to always push people away, Rilla.'

Rilla blinked back tears.

Perhaps she did not—but she certainly should have done when it came to Finlay Jellicoe, Earl of Staromchor.

Because here she was, falling in love with him.

Oh, it was a disaster. After guarding her heart so well, for so long, she had managed to allow him in—and he was an earl, too.

Try as she might, Rilla could not deny the intensely emotional tie between the two of them. That connection, the soft and gentle comfort that they shared, belied the undercurrent of attraction.

And it was the thought of attraction that led Rilla to pull her hand away and rise abruptly.

'I should return to the Wallflower Academy,' she said firmly. 'The reverend is having luncheon with us.'

'Yes, I should return, too,' Finlay said. The rustle of his greatcoat suggested he too had risen. 'Would you like a hand?'

It was the first time he had offered, and Rilla knew it would be churlish to push him aside. Besides, she wanted the contact. Desperately.

His arm was steady as he led her out of the pew and into the aisle.

'I hope you still intend to come riding with me tomorrow.'

'With you and Sylvia,' Rilla corrected, heat flushing through her chest.

But she wouldn't. Her, riding? It was the most ridiculous thing she had ever heard.

'I greatly wish to take you riding,' came Finlay's soft voice. 'Will you not give me the chance to show you?'

Give him a chance.

Had she not been giving him chances every moment she was with him? Did he not know how much she had already compromised for him? Was he unaware that she had undermined her resolve to stay away from earls, her determination never to open herself to a man like that again?

Rilla swallowed. 'I suppose I can walk with you to the stables.'

'Good,' said Finlay, his voice low and warm. It vibrated through her, promising possibilities that were simply not possible.

Their footsteps echoed on the stone-flagged church aisle.

'I suppose it is a good thing we did not meet at the altar,' Rilla attempted to jest. 'It's something neither of us will be doing anytime soon.'

The silence from Finlay suggested, much to her horror, that she had gone too far. But as he stepped towards the church door, his hand over hers on his arm, she could have sworn that he had spoken softly. So softly she could barely hear the words.

'I wouldn't bet on that.'

Chapter Twelve

'Ah, there you are,' said the disapproving voice of Miss Pike. 'We were beginning to believe you had forgotten.'

Forgotten?

Finlay could not comprehend doing such a thing. Forgetting would mean that Rilla was out of his thoughts for more than a minute, which was not something he had managed to achieve since he had deposited her on the doorstep of the Wallflower Academy yesterday.

'I was momentarily delayed in London,' Finlay said smoothly as he stepped into the Wallflower Academy hallway and bowed low to Miss Pike. 'I regret it most sincerely.'

Which was true, though perhaps not in the manner the proprietress of the Wallflower Academy believed.

Yes, he was sorry for the accidental rudeness. But he was more sorry that he had missed even a moment of Rilla's company.

She was standing just behind Miss Pike and was wearing the most splendid riding habit that he had ever seen. It was dark green, and swept down to the floor with elegant brass buttons in the military style along the shoulders and cuffs. She wore a jockey bonnet of last year's style upon her head, and there was a glare in her expression.

Finlay swallowed, his mouth dry. He should have expected it. There were times when he forgot that Rilla was also the

Honourable Miss Newell. Her family must have some wealth, with a title like that. It was entirely appropriate for her to be well dressed.

And entirely inappropriate for him to be staring with his mouth open.

Closing his jaw with a snap and hoping to goodness only Sylvia, similarly attired and clearly stifling a giggle, had noticed, Finlay cleared his throat.

'And what a lovely day you have for your ride, too,' Miss Pike was saying, though whether to himself or to the two wallflowers, Finlay was not sure. 'I trust you will be able to assist Miss Newell in any way necessary.'

'Miss Newell has no intention of riding whatsoever,' said Rilla sharply, pushing past the older woman and striding confidently towards the Academy door. 'But I'll indulge this nonsense and accompany you to the stables. Come, Sylvia.'

Disappointment twisted in Finlay's chest. Well, it wasn't as though he could have expected anything different. Rilla had never made any declarations of her feelings. Of course, neither had he. But surely she had noticed? Surely she had guessed, after he had kissed her on the beach in Brighton, that he felt something for her.

'And how is Miss Carr, my lord?' asked Miss Pike sweetly from behind him.

Finlay whirled around, his tails flapping in the sudden breeze he had created. Sylvia had departed, racing after the swiftly disappearing back of Rilla. They were alone.

He tried to smile. 'Miss Carr?'

'Your betrothed, Miss Carr,' said Miss Pike, a slight frown puckering her forehead. 'How many other Miss Carrs do you know?'

Cursing himself for not considering this, Finlay attempted to gather his thoughts. Right. He should have expected the announcement to have been read by all. 'She…she is well, thank you.'

What else was he supposed to say?

'I must say, I think it very gracious of you to take time away from your betrothed to help some of our wallflowers practise their conversation and riding,' Miss Pike was saying lightly, as though this occurred every day. 'Marilla and Sylvia will chaperone each other, naturally, and as you are already engaged, there can be no thought of impropriety.'

Finlay's smile weakened. 'Yes. Yes, I quite agree. Now, if you will excuse me, Miss Pike…'

The Wallflower Academy stables were just to the left of the house. Finlay had stabled one of his own steeds there once, when he had come to that dinner.

That dinner when he had fed Rilla. Oh, that sensuous delight, nothing could compare to—

Well. He supposed that something could.

He would have to tell Rilla, of course. There was nothing else for it, not now Miss Pike knew about the engagement. The engagement he had thought was not public knowledge.

Swallowing hard and thanking his stars—and his valet—that his riding breeches were a little loose at the front, Finlay stepped into the stable yard.

Rilla was standing in the middle of it. She had her arms crossed. Rilla's moods were changeable, and passion ran deep in all of them. What had irritated her?

Apprehension and anticipation warred in Finlay's chest as he moved forward. Oh, but one more afternoon surely would not hurt. He would tell her tomorrow. Four and twenty hours, what difference would it make?

'I said you were being ridiculous, and this proves it,' Rilla was saying smartly to Sylvia. 'You cannot think he would believe—'

'Ah, there you are, my lord,' Sylvia said, interrupting her friend. To Finlay's surprise, she gave him a huge theatrical wink he was certain he would have seen from fifty feet. 'I find to my sadness that I have a stone in my shoe.'

Finlay blinked. 'A…a stone.'

Rilla snorted. 'Sylvia, the man wasn't born yesterday.'

'And as such, I will have to spend a great deal of time sitting here, on a mounting block, attending to my boots,' said Sylvia proudly, sticking out her leather boot from her long skirts. 'I fear it will take me most of the afternoon to—'

'Sylvia,' growled Rilla.

Finlay looked bemusedly back and forth between the two women. Evidently there was a scheme afoot.

'So I think the two of you should start on riding without me,' Sylvia said, winking again most ostentatiously. 'I'll catch up when I can, my lord, but it would be a true shame if Rilla were to miss out on a ride merely because I was improperly shod.'

Finlay grinned. It was an excellent excuse—he would have to remember to thank Miss Sylvia Bryant at a later date. For the present, however…

'Miss Pike will be furious,' Rilla said sharply as Finlay stepped to her side.

'Miss Pike believes you are being chaperoned,' he pointed out. 'May I take your hand?'

The beautiful woman shook her black curls back, but evidently did not have the heart to decline. 'You…you may.'

Heat shot through Finlay's body, as it always did when it came into contact with Rilla. Oh, these were the warning signs he should heed, and yet he did not seem able. All he wanted to do was be with her—touch her. Be touched by her.

Finlay almost tripped over a perfectly flat cobble as he led Rilla to his horse Ceres.

'And what precisely are we going to do together?' Rilla asked sarcastically as Sylvia disappeared off into the stables. 'You must know that I cannot ride. Me, sitting alone on a horse, guiding the reins? Preposterous—and in truth, I don't think you will be able to teach me.'

His heart stirred as the delightful idea of an afternoon spent with Rilla, alone—with a ready-made excuse—filled his chest.

This was far better than he could have hoped. Pushing aside the discomfort of keeping his secret from Rilla could be done for a little while longer. His feelings for Rilla, after all, were far stronger.

'That indeed would be a great challenge, and I agree that I would not be up to such a task,' he said seriously, ignoring her sarcasm and looking through it to the pain and the embarrassment beneath. 'But I do not intend to.'

There it was—the flicker of uncertainty, the nervousness Rilla was feeling momentarily expressed on her face.

And Finlay's chest ached. What must it be, to never quite know who to trust? To always be wondering when the next embarrassment would come? When someone would take advantage of your lack of sight, never knowing if one was about to be tricked?

His temper burned against her sister, the earl, the pair of them—but that was not something he could do anything about, not today.

Today, he was about to do something quite different.

They halted before Ceres.

Rilla frowned. 'So…so if we are not going riding, why am I wearing this ridiculous get-up?'

'I don't think you look ridiculous,' said Finlay without thinking. 'I think you look beautiful.'

No amount of silence could prevent him from noticing the flush on Rilla's cheeks—nor could he avoid the fact that it suited her complexion well.

So did the slow smile that tilted her lips. 'You…you do?'

'I do,' Finlay said softly, his own cheeks burning now at the intimacy of their words, matched only by the soft, private tone of their conversation.

'I… I don't know what you mean, then,' Rilla said, the sarcasm and protective anger melting away. 'What will we be doing this afternoon?'

'We'll be riding,' Finlay said promptly.

'But you said— Finlay Jellicoe, put me down!'

And he did…though perhaps not precisely where Rilla was expecting.

'Hold on here, and here,' he said, guiding her hands to the reins.

Though surprising her was a delightful achievement in itself, Finlay congratulated himself for his brilliant idea, too. It wasn't just the execution which had to be just right; it was the inspiration itself.

And seeing Rilla in that dark green riding habit, astride his mare with her head held high and an imperious look on her face?

Finlay's manhood stirred.

That was inspiration.

'You have to be jesting,' Rilla said faintly. 'You cannot—'

'You wish me to take you down?' Finlay asked seriously.

For he would, if she asked. He was no cad, would not force Rilla to do things she had no wish to merely because he could exert his will on her.

And besides, there would be a benefit to lifting her down. The movement had offered closeness and a tantalizing opportunity— which he did not capitalize on—to kiss her again. Rilla in his arms had been something he had thought about far too often. He would not be averse to doing it again.

Rilla hesitated, and Finlay grinned. There was a woman who was bold, and brilliant, and who held herself back just as often as others held her back. 'I just do not comprehend what you could possibly think is going to help. I cannot see, Finlay!'

It took a great deal for Rilla to say that, he knew. And that was why he did not explain, but merely acted on the next part of his plan.

'Finlay!'

Finlay had mounted Ceres in one easy stride. He'd been mounting horses without a block since he had come of age, even before then, and it was not exactly hard.

It was most definitely not a hardship to mount just behind Rilla, pulling her into his arms and taking the reins from her, breathing in the scent of her body, feeling the warmth of her in his chest, her head resting against his neck.

'Finlay Jellicoe!' Rilla said, her breath warm against his cheek. 'This is most scandalous!'

'Perhaps so,' said Finlay, nudging Ceres forward and speaking calmly as they left the stable yard and started to trot gently along the path towards the greater park. 'Do you want to be taken back to the Wallflower Academy?'

He knew the answer; he did not need to hear it. He could feel it in the soft languidness of her body, the comfort she was drawing from him, that they were drawing from each other.

Oh, there was nothing like this. Nothing like being with the woman you—

Finlay swallowed as he slowed his steed to a walk now that they were out of sight of the Wallflower Academy.

That had been a close one. He had almost thought there, for a moment, about love.

It was not a feeling he was going to permit himself to even think about. Not in the slightest. Not even consider. He could not love Miss Marilla Newell. He certainly did not love Miss Isabelle Carr, but that did not mean that he could go around offering his heart to others.

He was going to be married in less than three weeks.

Finlay swallowed hard, pushing all thoughts of Isabelle out of his mind. Surely it was not a betrayal if he had never promised love and affection to begin with. No one could expect anything else from him. He had done everything that had been expected—more, perhaps.

Somewhere deep inside Isabelle Carr was the woman she had once been.

Perhaps, Finlay tried to convince himself, *after they were married...*

The revulsion that stirred at the mere thought was not a good sign.

'You are very quiet,' said Rilla softly.

Finlay tried not to shrug. 'I suppose I am.'

It was not as though he could share his thoughts with her. Why he had kept the truth of Miss Isabelle Carr—the very existence of Miss Isabelle Carr—from Rilla, he did not know.

Well. He had a vague guess.

Bringing those two worlds together, those two women together, even in conversation, would mean having to face up to the fact that he wanted one but could only have the other.

That he was going to be miserable with one, and miserable without the other.

That one of them he respected, and the other he...

Finlay cleared his throat as he nudged Ceres along a left-hand fork in the path. Perhaps...well. Men had mistresses all the time, didn't they? He was in fact unusual in his circle of friends, *not* having one. He had considered it an offence to Isabelle once their engagement had been decided upon, but even before then, Finlay had never wished to engage in such a thing without...well, without his emotions involved.

But now that they were...

'You know, I feel like I can tell you anything,' he said before he could stop himself.

Rilla was silent for a moment. Then she asked, 'Where did that come from?'

'I, uh...'

'You say nothing at all, and then you say you can tell me anything?' She turned slightly in his arms. 'Do you have something to tell me, Finlay?'

His stomach lurched.

Only that I'm lying. That I'm keeping from you information that you would almost certainly want. That I'm being torn in two directions, between who I should be and who I am.

Finlay swallowed. 'No. No, nothing.'

Hell's bells, man, this can't continue.

Trying not to think about the delicate woman curled into his chest, exclaiming with delight at the strange sensation that riding provided, Finlay prodded at his conscience.

Would he, in turn, be content if Isabelle took a lover?

After a moment of introspection, he believed that he would. Well, their marriage had begun as one of convenience only, had it not? Though now he'd overheard her declarations of love, perhaps it was unlikely that Isabelle would wish to look elsewhere…

'And this is riding?'

Finlay's focus snapped back to the woman in his arms. 'I beg your pardon?'

'Well, is this…it?' Rilla said, a slight tension in her voice.

It was a bizarre question. After all, the rolling hills, the frost-tipped branches of the forest of their left, the way the sunlight glittered…

And then Finlay felt very foolish indeed.

When was he going to learn that so much of his experience was different to Rilla's? That he could not simply amaze and dazzle her with new sights, as though that would make her care for him?

Not that he was attempting to do that. Obviously.

Finlay fought the instinct to press a kiss into her hair and instead said softly, 'We are riding along a path covered with leaves. Most of them have decayed, with the winter approaching, but there are toadstools and mushrooms pushing up through the foliage, striving to reach the sun.'

Rilla's breathing changed. Unless he had been acutely attuned to it, he would not have noticed.

He took that as encouragement to continue. 'On our left is the forest—or woodland, I suppose. I never knew the difference. Trees stand tall against the sky, their branches bare. I can see the remnants of nests, the evidence of a summer well lived. There are several ravens, or crows, sitting in one tree and they examine us as we pass.'

'A family?' Rilla breathed.

Finlay chuckled, his chest pressing against her back. 'Perhaps. And on our right are the fields, soaring out into the distance, kissing the horizon. The hedgerows are brimming with berries, and birds flicker in and out, guzzling themselves full for the winter ahead. There'll be squirrels in there, I suppose, and mice perhaps. I can't see.'

'Neither can I.'

He stiffened for a moment, then softened as Rilla's laughter rippled through his chest.

'Tell me more,' she said, a giggle in her voice.

More? How could he possibly think about the countryside around them when Rilla was in his arms?

'There are clouds in the sky,' he said, his Town upbringing starting to betray him. 'Erm…big clouds. Fluffy clouds.'

Rilla snorted. 'Snow clouds.'

'Now how could you possibly know?'

'Can you not smell it?' She took in a deep lungful of air, while Finlay did his absolute best not to notice the most tantalizing swell of her breasts. 'That's snow on the air. I could smell it a mile off.'

'It's not going to snow.'

'Have it your way,' Rilla said with a grin, nestling into him. 'But I'll be proved right, you'll see.'

'You are not too uncomfortable?' Finlay said aloud, concern twisting in his chest. 'I do apologize, I have barely asked.'

'It is a most strange sensation, I will admit,' said Rilla, a laugh lilting in the air. 'I imagine it is like being at sea. The undulation, not knowing what is going to happen…it's a loss of control.'

'Not something you enjoy, then,' said Finlay ruefully.

She had never told him that she needed to be in control, but it was obvious, was it not? Anyone who spent more than five minutes in the same room with Rilla would surely know that.

Rilla shrugged. The movement tightened her in his arms and Finlay revelled in it. 'I thought I would not, in truth—though I admit, I did not think you would actually get me on a horse.'

'And I am sorry for not asking your permission,' Finlay said, regret pouring into the joy, tainting it. 'I know how much you dislike being touched without your permission.'

'You…you remember that?'

Rilla's voice sounded surprised, which was a surprise in itself to Finlay.

'Of course I remember that,' he said, startled. 'I remember everything you say.'

They continued to ride in silence for a few minutes. Finlay was not certain if the silence was awkward for Rilla, but in himself he felt nothing but contentment and satisfaction.

After all his hopes and planning for such an afternoon, he could not have conceived of such a pleasant day. Rilla in his arms, Rilla happy—what else could he want?

'I love to hear you describe what's around me. What's around us.'

The sudden lurch in his chest was most definitely not something he should pay attention to, Finlay told himself. Nor the rising affection, the warmth in his chest, the way he wanted to nuzzle and kiss that delicate neck…

'There's not much else to tell,' Finlay said aloud, partly to redirect himself from his most distracting thoughts. 'Though there's you, I suppose.'

Rilla snorted. 'I know what I look like.'

'Do you?' he could not help but ask. She was warm in his arms. They had never felt empty before, but now he knew he would be bereft once she had left him. 'Do you know how you shine, Rilla?'

She turned at that, her gaze flickering over him as though attempting to discern whether he was chiding her. 'I don't know what you mean.'

'I think you do,' Finlay said softly, trying not to think of that spectacular kiss they had shared. 'I think you know what I think about you. What…what I feel for you.'

Whether it was him who moved first, or Rilla, he was not sure. All Finlay knew was that the woman he cared about deeply had turned in his arms, lifting up her lips to him in a silent plea for his attention, and he had given it most willingly.

Oh, God, it was a challenge to stay on the horse. Rilla's lips had parted almost instantly, inviting him in, and Finlay's grip around her tightened as every part of him longed to pour himself into her.

He made do with his tongue, desperately tasting the sweetness of her mouth, the delicacy of her affection, and tried not to moan too loudly.

But Finlay could barely stand it. Rilla had somehow woven her fingers in his hair, and he had never felt so close, so intimate with a woman before.

This was it; she was it. He adored her. He—

I wager you'll feel infinitely better for a flirtation. I think it'll bring you joy, and won't betray Isabelle in any way, and you'll enter the married state far happier. If I'm wrong, you can…oh, I don't know…choose your punishment.

The memory of Bartlett's words caused Finlay to break the kiss, to lean back, panting, to look at the woman with whom he had intended to enjoy nothing more than a flirtation.

The pang in his chest suggested otherwise.

No, this had gone much further than he had intended. This had gone beyond mere appreciation, beyond respect and admiration, beyond like.

Despite having no intention to create an entanglement before his wedding to another, Finlay had fallen completely in love with Rilla Newell.

Soft flakes of snow started to fall from the sky.

Chapter Thirteen

By the time Finlay whispered in her ear that they were about to enter the stable yard, Rilla knew two things.

Firstly, she knew that Finlay had never mentioned matrimony. He had probably never even considered it—the thought would never have passed through his mind. He was an earl, a man who would marry a beautiful heiress without any hint of stain upon her character.

It was surely no coincidence that Finlay had never spoken of his marital prospects.

Her own reputation was not so marred as it could be, but the fact that she had been sent to the Wallflower Academy and never visited by her family would surely cause eyebrows to rise. And that would be before anyone discovered her shameful history with the Earl of Porthaethwy.

No, Finlay would not marry her. The idea would never occur to him; Rilla was certain. Earls with egos like that did not marry women like her.

Secondly, she knew that when Finlay kissed her, every inch of her came alive in a way that she was certain would never be sparked again.

He knew her, truly knew her, and he desired her. That much was undeniable. Rilla did not care how carefully constructed the man's persona was in Society—he may be charming and light-hearted in company, and more serious and grieving in private, but no man could pretend that sort of desire.

Which made her just like…just like any other woman.

And so with these two facts in her mind, Rilla came to a most astonishing conclusion as Ceres's shod shoes clattered on the cobbles of the stable yard: seducing Finlay Jellicoe, Earl of Staromchor, would be her best opportunity in her life to know what it was to make love.

Rilla knew she could not just suggest such a thing bluntly and without careful consideration. The trouble was, her time was running out. In a few short weeks, her sojourn at the Wallflower Academy would be over, and she would be seeking her fortune elsewhere.

Perhaps, Rilla could not help but think ruefully as the horse was brought to a stop and she lost the sensation of Finlay sitting behind her, she would end up as a governess after all, just as Miss Pike had wished.

But how precisely she made her way in the world after the Wallflower Academy was immaterial. She had this time, this moment now, to create a memory she would never forget.

And besides. She wanted him. A dull, throbbing ache between her legs told her that there was more pleasure to come, if that could be believed. More joy, more sensuality, more decadence— more of Finlay.

She wanted that.

So when Finlay said softly, 'May I help you down?' and Rilla offered her hands out into the unknown, she knew what she must do. What she had to do, if she wanted to continue without adding a regret to the list she bore in her heart.

Finlay's hands were warm, and strong, and gentle. He lifted her down carefully, almost reverently, and as her boots touched the cobbled stones beneath her, Rilla found her lungs were tight and breathless.

Oh, Lord, she was a walking cliché. He made her breathless!

Despite having her full balance now, Finlay's hands did not leave her sides. When Rilla took a step forward, pressing her breasts against him and feeling the rapid rise and fall of his chest, she knew he was just as breathless as she was.

'Is…is there anyone else here?' Rilla asked, her mouth dry.

After all, it would never do for the conversation she intended to have with the man to be overheard. Miss Pike would be the least of her problems.

She felt the brush of air as Finlay turned one way, then the other.

'Strangely, no,' he said quietly, hands still around her waist. 'I think I can see— Yes, they are all inside the servants' hall. An early dinner, perhaps? It appears that we are alone.'

Alone.

Well, thought Rilla, steeling herself for what was about to be a very bold declaration, *there is no time like the present.*

'I like you, Finlay,' she blurted out.

And immediately cast her face down.

She liked him?

Was that truly what she had managed to say, after carefully constructing a logical argument for why they should make love at the swiftest opportunity?

That she *liked* him?

Rilla felt, as well as heard, his chuckle.

'Goodness, I thought you hated earls.'

'I do not generally hold them in particularly high regard, no,' she said as heat suffused her cheeks. 'In my experience, earls are insufferably proud, indeterminately arrogant, and unable to listen to a woman for five minutes together.'

Finlay's second chuckle was deeper. 'And yet you like me?'

I don't like you, Rilla wanted to say. *I… I think—*

'My dislike of earls in general has been tempered somewhat, yes, by…by getting to know you better,' she said aloud, forcing down the declaration of affection she knew would not be returned. 'And I… I trust you.'

Why it was so difficult to admit to such a thing, she did not know—but Rilla knew it mattered.

Trusting Finlay, not only to respect her but to treat her kindly, learning to expect kindness from a man whose position and station in life suggested she would receive naught but pain...

'I am grateful for your trust.' Finlay's voice was low, his breath warm, and she could feel his fingers momentarily tighten on her waist. Then they relaxed—though they did not release her. 'Earning your trust is something I think very... very precious.'

Here they were, Rilla thought. Right on the precipice of what they wanted to say, and yet neither of them willing to be the first to admit it.

They wanted each other.

Desire was not the domain of a respectable young woman. Oh, she knew the basics—the physical mechanics of lovemaking. It had been rather a surprise to learn that that was what happened, but since meeting Finlay, Rilla had come to understand that the stirrings within her whenever he touched her were the first steps on a journey she wished to take...with him.

And now, here, standing in Finlay's arms, knowing him to be a man of passion and caring, desire and understanding, grief and love, as well as joy and jesting...

He was far more than she had presumed.

Rilla took a deep breath. And if she didn't speak now, she would always wonder, *What if...?*

'Finlay,' she said firmly.

'Rilla,' he returned with a gentle chuckle.

Deploying the intense glare Sylvia had helped her to perfect, Rilla said, 'I am attempting to be serious here.'

'I wouldn't dare stop you,' Finlay said quietly. 'Though that doesn't mean that I have to be serious in turn.'

Rilla raised a hand and splayed it against his chest—and

gasped. She had meant it as a censure, but all thoughts of that had melted the instant she had felt his heart.

Thump-thump-thump-thump…

It was racing. In fact, Finlay's pulse seemed to be just as frantic, perhaps more so, as her own.

'Rilla?'

She swallowed. Perhaps she was not about to request something that would be denied, then. Perhaps he wanted this just as much, or perhaps even more, than she did. But she knew what she wanted. Just one encounter, she was certain, would be enough. Wouldn't it?

Well, she would never know if she never asked. 'Would you make love to me?'

Shame soared through her chest at the inelegant—and painfully direct—question. What had possessed her to speak so frankly? Dear God, he would think her a harlot, a strumpet, a woman utterly devoid of—

'I beg your pardon?' came a strained voice from Finlay.

Rilla twisted in his arms, attempting to get away. She would find the wall of the Tudor manor and from there she could make her way around to the front door—and then never leave it again.

How on earth could she be so—

But Finlay had tightened his grip, making it impossible to escape. 'Rilla!'

'Forget I said anything,' she said hastily, her words almost tripping over themselves as she struggled to free herself. 'And let me go, damn you!'

And then she was released.

The sudden space around her, the sudden lack of Finlay, took her quite by surprise. Rilla almost stumbled, her head spinning.

'But just so you know, before you march off,' said the Earl of Staromchor quietly. 'Yes.'

Rilla froze after a single step.

Yes?

He couldn't mean— Surely he did not mean…?

Turning slowly on the spot to where Finlay's voice had last been, Rilla breathed, 'Yes?'

'Yes,' said Finlay matter-of-factly, as though they were discussing something no more important than the expected change in the weather. 'Yes, I… I would very much like to make love to you. Now, in fact. Damn, Rilla, I have done for quite some time.'

Heat was stirring across Rilla's décolletage, but it was not shame, or guilt, or embarrassment, but—eagerness.

For quite some time?

'I know you have no wish to marry. That is, a marriage between us would be impossible,' Rilla said, straightening herself and attempting to approach this as a simple conversation.

Simple conversation? Had anything ever been less simple?

'That is not what I am asking for,' she said, her voice stronger. 'I just… Before I leave the Wallflower Academy, I need to know…know what it is to be loved.'

A hand took hers, and Rilla could tell it was Finlay. Her body was attuned to him in a way she could never have predicted.

'Leave the Wallflower Academy?'

Rilla hesitated—but this was not the time for that conversation. She would tell him tomorrow. What harm would it do, keeping a little truth from him?

'One day,' she said, a little awkwardly. 'I ask this of you, Finlay as…as a favour.'

'I cannot offer marriage to you today,' said Finlay softly. 'And I would still very much like to…to make love to you.'

Make love. Was this what Gwen had experienced, rushed Rilla's wild thoughts? Was she finally about to experience something that she had longed for?

How long they stood there in silence, hands clasped, luxuriating in the knowledge that they were going to enjoy one of life's most delicate pleasures, Rilla did not know. A minute? An hour? She could have remained there all day, she was certain, and as long as she had the certainty of Finlay's presence, she could have endured anything.

As it was, the very worst she had to endure was the uncertainty of what happened next.

Well, it wasn't as though she proposed lovemaking frequently. What did one do, once two people had agreed that they would quite like to take all their clothes off and…?

'Is there a side door?'

Rilla blinked. 'I beg your pardon?'

'A side door,' Finlay repeated. His voice was low, molten, teasing tendrils of desire across her skin. 'I don't think Miss Pike would appreciate seeing me ascend the staircase and enter your bedchamber, do you?'

A jolt of shock rocked Rilla's body. 'But you can't mean now?'

'Why not now?' His voice was urgent, his fingers tightening around hers. 'I don't want to wait for you, Rilla. I want you now, right now. I need you right now.'

And he was kissing her, and his other hand was tangled in her hair, and pins were cascading to the cobbles but Rilla did not care.

How could she when he was kissing her like that, his lips pressing hard hot desire into her, his tongue causing ripples of pleasure that thrummed through her body and settled in that aching spot between her legs?

When he finally released her, Rilla was once again breathless, but far more decisive. 'There's a side door just here. Wait, where is the entrance to the stables?'

Finlay took her hand, made a point with her finger, and moved it. 'There.'

Getting her bearings, a miracle considering how her head was spinning, Rilla took a step forward. 'This way.'

The side door by the stables was unlocked, as it always was before night fell. And Rilla would have known that, unequivocally, if they had managed to reach it.

Unfortunately their need for each other swiftly scuppered their plan to enter the house. The side door was at least, as far as Rilla could make out, ten yards from them.

Not that it mattered. Not with Finlay's arms around her, his lips trailing kisses down her neck.

'We...we shouldn't.'

'No one is here—they are at dinner. I told you,' Finlay said, his voice somehow raw and eager at the same time. 'And I want you, Rilla.'

How was any woman supposed to defend herself against such unashamed desire? How could woman prevent herself from succumbing to such words, spoken in such a tone, by such a man?

'Here, then,' Rilla found herself saying, pulling him in the opposite direction.

'Where are we—'

'You'll see,' she said breathlessly, stepping forward confidently.

Riding may have been a diversion previously unavailable to her in the past, but Rilla had spent a great deal of time around the stables as she waited for the other wallflowers to mount and dismount their horses. She knew the cobbles well, knew that when she reached the stable door, they would become slabs of stone rather than the small, uneven cobbles that typified the stable yard itself.

And so when she reached out in confidence, she was rewarded. The door to the stables opened to her, and with Finlay's hand in hers, she pulled him through.

'You will have to tell me,' Rilla said, her breath short and her cheeks burning as she spoke so directly, 'which of the stalls is empty.'

Finlay's breath caught in his throat. That was the only indication that he had responded at all to her words.

When he finally spoke, it was with an incredulous—and impressed—tone. 'You cannot mean to—'

'You want to wait until we creep down a corridor, pause for the servants' corridor to be empty, go up three flights of stairs, ensure there are no wallflowers on the bedchamber corridor, hope we are not seen, then—'

Rilla's mouth was hushed by a passionate kiss. It spoke of eagerness, and surprise, and delight in her equal hunger.

And when Finlay finally released her, his breathing was quick and his hands warm. 'Dear God, you are magnificent.'

'I don't know about that,' said Rilla, trying to force away the shyness she felt.

She wanted this. She wanted him. There would be no time, no space in her mind for regrets.

'The stall at the end is empty,' said Finlay, his voice low. 'This way.'

Rilla allowed herself to be led along the corridor that ran between the four stalls on either side. The sound of creaking hinges rippled into the air, and she stepped forward with Finlay's hand on the small of her back.

Well, perhaps slightly lower than the small of her back.

Her lungs tight and her heart thundering, Rilla heard the squeak of the hinges as the door to the stall closed. Then she felt the warmth of Finlay's breath on her face. He was standing right opposite her.

What was his expression? Not for the first time, Rilla wished she had that additional insight into the people around her—but this time, there was no painful tinge to her wish.

Finlay Jellicoe had never hidden himself. Not since those ridiculous footman antics at their first meeting, anyway. He would tell her, show her, reveal in his movements and the shortness of his breath precisely what he was thinking.

And he was probably thinking, Rilla thought ruefully, what on earth they should do next. After all, it was not typical to make love to a wallflower in a stable.

'May I take off your jockey bonnet?'

'Yes.'

His hands were gentle. As the jockey bonnet came down, so did the final pins that had been barely containing her curls. Both pins and curls fell down her shoulders, and the appreciative sound she heard told Rilla that the effect must be pleasant.

'May I take off your riding habit?'

Rilla's chest tightened, just for a moment. 'Y-yes.'

'We can stop at any time,' Finlay's voice said, soft yet unshaking. 'Any moment you wish to—'

'I want you,' Rilla said.

Did he know just what she meant by that? Of course not—how could he? She barely knew what she meant by it, by all these feelings and emotions rushing through her, making it impossible to decipher just what she felt for Finlay.

Except love.

As her riding habit slipped from her shoulders, Rilla shivered. 'What about you?'

'What about me?'

She smiled. 'I cannot help but notice that you are still wearing all your clothes.'

'So are you. Mostly. Something I would like to rectify immediately,' came the seductive murmur of Finlay as he pressed a kiss into the base of Rilla's throat.

Unable to help herself, Rilla's head tipped back as she welcomed the intimacy. How did he make her melt under every kiss? He had a way with him that she could never have imagined—and would never forget.

'But I understand,' Finlay added. 'Here.'

Rilla frowned as her fingers were clasped in his own and brought forward. Then her brow unfurled.

'Undress me,' he whispered.

He had guided her hands to his coat—somehow his riding frock coat had obviously been cast aside—and his own hands had dropped to his sides.

She was in complete control.

'Kiss me,' Rilla breathed as her nervous hands undid the first button of his waistcoat.

There was strength under these clothes; she could feel it, and she could sense the strength of restraint as Finlay kissed her. His chest tensed as each button was undone, and Rilla tried to concentrate as his meandering lips teased that delicate spot beneath her ear, her neck, the curve of her collarbone and the swell of her décolletage.

'You're not making this easy,' she gasped, her fingers slipping on a button as his lips danced across the top of her breasts.

'Good,' growled Finlay, his hands cupping her buttocks with a groan. 'Neither are you.'

The idea that anyone, let alone an earl, would find her so enticing was unfathomable to Rilla, but she did not have the concentration to consider that. Not now she had finally managed to undo all the buttons before her.

Well. Not all the buttons. Tempting as it had been to allow her fingers to drift down to his breeches, she was not brave enough for that. Not yet.

'Take them off,' she breathed.

Finlay's hands left her body, just for a moment, as coat, waistcoat, and shirt fell to the stall floor. Rilla had sensed the straw beneath it, knew it would be soft when he…when Finlay…

Rilla swallowed. 'Now me.'

Turning on the spot and hoping to goodness they would not be discovered, she pulled her hair to one side to reveal to Finlay the ties at the back of her gown.

This undressing was not nearly so laboured. In a few quick heartbeats, Finlay had pulled loose all the ties keeping her gown upon her person. It pooled swiftly to her feet, leaving her in naught but—

'Dear God.' Finlay's breath blossomed out onto her now bare shoulder.

Rilla turned hurriedly, fear flooding through her chest. 'If you have changed your mind...'

'Changed my— I'm only regretting not suggesting this to you weeks ago,' Finlay said, his voice thick with desire.

Heat burned her cheeks as her secret place throbbed. 'You only met me weeks ago.'

'Exactly,' Finlay said darkly. 'May I lay you down? I've moved some blankets—you'll be quite comfortable.'

It was an entirely new exercise of trust, allowing Finlay to slowly guide her to the blankets that he had placed on the straw. With any other man she would have felt exposed, in danger—at every moment fearing that this had been a trick merely to make her ridiculous, or destroy her reputation completely.

But this was Finlay. She could trust Finlay.

She was not alone on the straw and the blanket for long. Heat seared along her skin as Finlay joined her, the rough, wiry hair of his thighs brushing up against hers.

Rilla gasped.

This was really happening. The pleasure of his presence, his touch, was about to take on a new meaning.

Fingertips trailed seductively along her hip. 'I... I don't want to hurt you.'

Rilla reached out without hesitation. Her hand cupped a cheek. 'Then don't.'

The answering kiss was slow, and passionate, and seemed to pour all the words neither of them could say between them. Rilla clutched at him, needing to know he was there, needing to know just how greatly he desired her.

And he showed her. As Finlay tilted her head back and worshipped her mouth, his hands were not idle.

Rilla whimpered as his thumb brushed across her secret place. 'Oh, Finlay—'

She was unable to say any more. Not merely because the kiss deepened, taking all breath away—but because Finlay had gently slipped his thumb into her slick folds, causing a spark of unimaginable pleasure through her body.

Oh, God—this was lovemaking?

How did anyone stop?

Finlay did not. As his tongue ravaged her mouth, teasing pleasure she had never known from it, his thumb and finger were stroking a rhythm in her secret core that was throwing fuel on the fiery ache that needed...needed—

Unable to help herself, Rilla tilted her head back. 'Oh, God, Finlay...'

The explosion was exquisite. Her whole body rippled with ecstasy, her limbs quivering at the pleasure which tightened her core and made every part of her glow with fiery heat.

His unrelenting fingers finally slowed. Rilla's panting breaths seemed to echo around the stall.

'That was...'

'I know.' Finlay's voice was thick with emotion, the words breathed not spoken into her ear. 'I've never seen anything more beautiful, Rilla. You're...you're so beautiful.'

Rilla blinked, as though that would steady her whirling mind. To think that such delicious sensuality was mere inches away from any pair, just under their clothes...

How would she ever be in Finlay's presence again without wanting this?

'God, I want you,' he groaned, sinking a kiss into her neck that fluttered longing once more through Rilla's chest. 'You can't know— But if you don't want—'

'I want you,' Rilla said quietly, knowing with a new sense of certainty that whatever followed was precisely what she wanted. What she needed. 'Take me, Finlay. Take whatever you need to.'

Her breath hitched as Finlay's lips brushed over one of her nipples, then tightened as his tongue laved, swirling around the delicate skin.

The ache was back.

'Take me,' Rilla breathed, and there was a pleading note there that she had not intended but could not, would not deny. 'Please.'

He did not appear to need convincing. Finlay's presence shifted, moving from her side to above her. The delicate nudge at her knees was enough. Rilla parted them, welcoming him in. Welcoming the intrusion, yet knowing it was precisely what she wanted.

There was a shift in the straw on either side of her head. Finlay was…leaning on it, perhaps?

'You can stop me at any point,' Finlay said hurriedly, pausing between words to snatch kisses from her willing lips. 'Rilla, you have to know—'

'I know,' she panted, the ache between her thighs desperate now for whatever satisfaction he could give her.

'You have to know how I feel about you.'

'I know,' Rilla said, blinking up into the vague darkness above her.

And there was a pause, and then Finlay was crushing his mouth on hers.

It was the perfect kiss. Rushed, a little raw, but perfect because of that, not despite it. It was a kiss that said they were equals in desire, equals in need—equals in all the ways that mattered.

And it was during that kiss that he—

'Finlay!' Rilla moaned in surprise as something thick and long pushed into her most intimate spot.

Her body knew what to do, far more than her mind. Swelling, shifting, welcoming him in, the stretch was uncomfortable but only for a moment. Rilla gasped, the ripples of pleasure now startlingly familiar.

Oh, this was—

Finlay blew out a sudden breath. 'God, Rilla, you feel so good.'

Good? A much too insufficient word.

'You feel perfect,' she managed, hands fisting into the straw as her back unconsciously arched, drawing him deeper. 'You are perfect, Finlay, perfect for me, perfect for— Oh, God!'

Rilla had not intended to cry out, but the gentle shift Finlay made, out and then spearing into her once more, was too much.

Pleasure roared through her, a fire she could never have predicted but now wished to light all over her body.

Burn.

'Rilla,' Finlay moaned, pulling out almost completely then thrusting back into her with a groan that suggested he was experiencing at least part of the sublime sensuality that she was. 'Yes, yes, yes…'

What words were spoken between them after that, Rilla could not recall. Words and kisses and moans intermingled as Finlay's gentle rhythm became harsher, harder, until she was floating on waves of pleasure that suddenly launched into ecstasy and it was no longer possible to hold it in.

'Finlay!' she sobbed.

The peak of her climax muffled all sound, removed all sense of place, and it was only thanks to her hands, which had somewhere released the straw and instead clutched his shoulders, that she knew Finlay was there.

With her. Beside her, within her through all this.

And then she heard him. 'Rilla, God, yes,' came the muffled grunt as he thrust, shuddering, into her.

The sudden pressure was quickly understood. Rilla felt the pressure of his shoulders on hers, the rough hair of his chest upon her breasts, his arms sinking around her as Finlay collapsed into her arms.

She held him. Held the man who had shown her so much. Held the man she loved.

And was complete. Complete and truly happy for perhaps the first time in her life.

Chapter Fourteen

Happiness was not something Rilla was particularly accustomed to. She had learned not to grow attached to it, and so now that it was here, it was rather a shock.

Sylvia and Daphne had both noticed the following morning and made sure to inform her in their own very different ways.

'You…you seem less morose,' Daphne said hesitantly as they all sat in the drawing room attending to their needlework.

Well. The other wallflowers attended to their needlework. Miss Pike had recently given them a lesson on the correct way to sit while embroidering, to best show off one's natural assets and to entice a gentleman to approach and ask what they were working on.

It sounded like hogwash to Rilla, but then it did not matter much to her. It wasn't as though she could do needlework.

'Less morose?' Rilla repeated sardonically.

It was Sylvia's laugh that filled the room. 'Less miserable, more like! You've been wandering around with a smile on your face all evening. What has got into you?'

And Rilla had flushed, for her friend could not know precisely how her words had been most suggestive.

I cannot help but notice that you are still wearing all your clothes.

So are you. Mostly. Something I would like to rectify immediately.

'Into me?' she said, trying not to laugh. 'I don't know what you mean.'

'It's that earl, if you ask me,' Sylvia said conversationally. 'Oh, would you like a glass of water, Rilla?'

'No. No, I'm fine,' Rilla said, her eyes watering as she attempted to slow her coughing fit. 'Perfectly fine. How is your father?'

It was a low blow, but desperate times called for something truly desperate. Besides, the gossip was all over the Academy: he had been seen, in Almack's, dancing with a woman. And not in a genteel, aloof manner, either.

'I haven't seen the Earl of Staromchor for a while,' said Daphne softly, her gentle voice even quieter. She must be concentrating. Rilla knew Daphne was always quieter when she was concentrating.

'But wasn't that him today?' came Sylvia's disinterested voice. 'I thought it looked like him, in the grounds, just ten minutes ago.'

Rilla stood up immediately. Then she wished she hadn't.

Sylvia's chortling laugh filled her ears as Rilla made her way to the hall. 'I knew it! You tell me all about it when you get back, Rilla. I want to know how you plan to seduce him!'

Little did her friend know, of course, that she had already most decidedly seduced the man, Rilla thought with a grin as she reached for a shawl hanging up in the hall and made her way to the front door.

And if Finlay was here, then his only reason could be that he wished to see her. Why else would he come all this way?

He had not been able to make any promises to her when he had left after their amorous encounter in the stables. And she had not expected him to.

I know you have no wish to marry. That is, a marriage between us would be impossible.

Still, it would have been nice to know when she would be seeing him again.

The cold air hit Rilla hard in the chest as she stepped out into the afternoon air. Goodness, but winter was here.

'Finlay?' she said quietly.

'I'm here,' came the expected answering voice.

Turning, Rilla beamed in the direction of the man she adored. Though the future was uncertain, her connection with Finlay was not one that could be denied. Her prospects aside, she had found what she wanted. True affection, true respect. What could be better?

'I was attempting to consider how I would find you,' came Finlay's voice, which was warm yet stilted.

Because they were in full view of the Wallflower Academy, Rilla surmised. Well, she could hardly blame him. They had done their best to keep their assignation to themselves. It would hardly be possible to keep such a thing under wraps if they were seen together.

'Rilla, I—'

'Why don't we—'

They both halted, and after a brief laugh, Rilla indicated her head to the left. 'A walk would do us both good, I think. Give us the opportunity to…to talk. In private.'

And more, she thought with a flicker of a smile.

Oh, she would hope for more, even if their encounter in the stables was perhaps to be the only time they managed to make love. Though Gwen had managed it with her duke. How precisely she had managed to smuggle the man into her bedchamber, Rilla did not know—had never thought to ask her. And it wasn't as though she could write to the Duchess of Knaresby and ask such a scandalous thing…

'Yes. Yes, a walk.' Perhaps it was her imagination, but Finlay sounded distracted. 'Good. Fine. Yes. May…may I take your arm?'

Rilla beamed, her heart skipping a beat as he once again asked her permission. Oh, it was so delightful when he did that.

'Yes.'

Their footsteps swiftly moved in time, mirroring her heartbeat as they walked around the front of the house and around the side by the kitchen gardens.

Step-step, thump-thump...

This was what she wanted. To be in step with a man she loved. To have him by her side, at all times. To know that if she needed him, he would be right there.

How had she managed to find such a man after all this time? After such a disappointment? After believing that all earls, nay all men, were unworthy of her trust?

'Rilla,' said Finlay in a slightly strangled voice.

Rilla tilted her head towards him. 'Yes?'

There was silence. No, not quite silence. Now she was concentrating, she noticed that his breathing was a little laboured. As though he had run here, which he most certainly had not. Perhaps he was nervous?

Nervous? What did the Earl of Staromchor have to be nervous about?

'Rilla, I... I need to tell you something.'

Rilla's shoulders relaxed. Oh, if that was all, then there was no concern there. This was the great declaration, wasn't it? When Finlay finally admitted that he loved her. Then she could happily tell him that his affection was reciprocated, and then...

Well, what happened after that was a tad vague. But it would not matter. They loved each other. They could overcome anything.

'I had hoped to tell you this in private, but—'

'We are near the gardening sheds, aren't we?' Rilla said, interrupting him.

Finlay stopped and she halted with him. 'How on earth could you tell?'

'I can smell the onions, and there's wild garlic that grows

just outside the potting shed,' said Rilla with a wry laugh. 'Really, it's not that difficult.'

She had expected Finlay to laugh, to admit that once again he had underestimated her. As so many people did.

Instead, Finlay grunted, 'Excellent. Let's go behind here.'

Rilla almost tripped as he pulled her forward hastily, but managed to stay upright as he tugged her around to the left. Then for some inexplicable reason, he released her hand.

Allowing her fingers to move in the space around her, she grazed her palm gently against the wood wall of the potting shed. Fine, that would give her a point to navigate by.

'Finlay,' she said softly.

He sighed heavily, then his forehead was pressed against hers. 'Rilla.'

They stood there in silence and Rilla breathed him in. Not just his scent, though the fragrance was delectable. No, Finlay himself. He was everything to her now. So much of her life she had lived without being understood, and though he had made more than his fair share of blunders, he had adapted.

He had wanted to know how to improve. To know her.

And now they had shared the most precious, the most wonderful thing.

'I have…have something to tell you,' Finlay breathed.

'And I will listen,' Rilla said softly. 'You know you can always talk to me, Finlay.'

It was the wrong thing to say. At least, that was how it appeared. The earl groaned, and suddenly crushed his lips against hers in a potent kiss that pushed Rilla against the shed wall.

It was intoxicating, being pinned against the rough wood with nothing but the softness of Finlay on her lips and the hard wall of his chest before her. Rilla splayed her fingers against his coat and felt the woollen scarf wrapped around his neck.

But she couldn't think about that. She was far more interested in the searing kiss pressing against her mouth, the tease of Finlay's tongue as it slipped along her lips, parting them, the decadent pleasure that poured through her body as he began to ravish her mouth.

Rilla moaned, and that only seemed to spur him on. Finlay's hands were on her shoulders but they slipped to her waist, pulling her closer and making it impossible to escape him.

As though she would want to.

'Rilla, I—'

'I know,' Rilla said in a ragged voice as Finlay started trailing kisses down her neck, her breasts heaving with every arduous breath. 'I know.'

Precisely what he had intended to say she did not know. But she knew what he wanted, was sure that this pressure, this aching need that was throbbing through her was undoubtedly mirrored in him.

And that was why, when Finlay released her and stepped back, Rilla reached out with a whimper of need.

'Finlay?'

'I shouldn't do this. I hadn't intended to. I meant to do something quite different,' came Finlay's voice, rough and coarse.

Rilla's heart skipped a beat. 'What are you— Finlay!'

There was no other option than to cry his name as she felt his hands somehow on her knees. Was he— Surely Finlay could not be kneeling before her?

'Finlay?' she repeated, her voice now a whisper in the hope they would not be overheard.

Being discovered like this, with a man kneeling before her... Surely he was not going to propose?

Rilla swallowed hard, but all thoughts of proposals disappeared the instant another sensation rushed over her knees. This time it was not the warm and steady touch of a gentleman who knew precisely how to please.

No, it was the movement of her skirts.

Then and only then did she get an inkling of what Finlay was about to do.

'Finlay,' Rilla said for a third time. This time her voice quavered with unadulterated lust.

She had guessed right. Kneeling before her, and probably getting damp knees in the process, for it had rained most heavily that morning, Finlay was lifting up her skirts and…

And kissing up her thigh.

Rilla tried to breathe steadily as she leaned against the shed, depending on it for stability as her whole body quaked with mounting pleasure.

Surely he couldn't—he wouldn't? Gentlemen did not do such a thing, did they?

They most certainly did. Before Rilla could even think about telling Finlay to stop—and she definitely did not want him to—his lips had reached between her legs.

And licked.

Shivers claimed her body, making it almost impossible to stand, but the solid potting shed behind her and Finlay's grip on her hips kept her steady.

Though neither of those forces could steady her mind. Whirling, twisting with astonishment at the sparks of pleasure formed with every nibble, lick, suck of Finlay's mouth, Rilla clutched at his shoulders in an attempt to remain upright.

'Oh, Finlay,' she whimpered, the pleasure overwhelming.

It was decadent, it was outrageous, it was scandalous. If they were to be found…

And somehow, the suggestion that they could be discovered at any moment only heightened Rilla's enjoyment. Which was indecent. And delicious.

Finlay's tongue darted inside her and Rilla moaned, the aching heat growing at such a fast pace she could hardly keep up.

'Yes…'

The whisper was not precisely a request, but Finlay seemed to understand what she meant by it.

The intrusion, the welcome intimacy, deepened as his tongue delved into her wet folds, and Rilla's head tilted back against the rough wood of the potting shed as her pleasure built…

'Finlay,' she choked out as her climax rolled over her.

It was short, sharp, sudden. More than she could have imagined, and yet in many ways entirely different from the roll in the hay which they had enjoyed previously. Rilla's body washed with pleasure, the ecstasy hot and burning, exacerbated and fed by the strange sensation of Finlay kneeling between her feet, his head under her skirts.

Just when she thought it was over, Finlay's tongue swirled around the nub of her pleasure and he pushed her higher, thrusting her over a peak she had never reached, and Rilla cried out just as jackdaws squawked and took to the air.

And then she was blinking as the man she loved withdrew from her body, still holding her tight.

It was a wonder, really, she was able to stand at all.

Finlay chuckled as he brought his arm around her waist. 'Steady on there.'

'You think that I can remain steady after…' Rilla swallowed.

It had been difficult enough to keep her voice down as he brought her to such pinnacles of pleasure, but her mouth was still dry and her heart still frantic.

This man—she loved him. And surely he must love her, even if the words themselves had not been uttered between them.

Love was not something one said. It was what one did, and Finlay had proved, several times now that he was a man she could trust. An earl she could trust, far more than she could have believed possible.

And as for the future…

Well, the future would come whether she wanted it to or not, Rilla reasoned as she steadied herself on her feet and slipped her hand into Finlay's arm, feeling the roughness of his coat against her fingers.

What the future would hold, she did not know. The one thing she did know was that Finlay would be in it.

What else could she possibly want?

'I had not intended to ravish you so utterly,' Finlay said in a low voice as they started to walk slowly towards the Wallflower Academy.

Rilla laughed, joy bursting in her chest. 'Oh, I wouldn't say that was utterly.'

Flirting with Finlay was as natural as breathing. So too did it seem natural that his chuckle radiated through her side, making her feel his laughter as well as hear it.

'Well, we are close to the stables.'

'Finlay!'

'Perhaps I can show you just how utterly I adore you.'

Flickers of delight were cascading down Rilla's spine and heat blossomed on her cheeks at the inappropriate suggestion.

'We were fortunate not to get caught the first time,' she reminded him, squeezing his arm.

Finlay sighed dramatically. 'I suppose so.'

'And Miss Pike has decided to ban us from the stables,' Rilla added, recalling the awkward conversation over breakfast.

There was a snort from beside her. 'Dear God, there is no possibility she suspects, is there?'

Heaven forbid.

'No, no,' Rilla said hastily, their feet moving from the grass to the gravelled path. It crunched under their feet as she continued, 'No, this is because of Sylvia.'

Another snort. 'I should have guessed.'

'She is perhaps not the wallflower the Pike envisioned for her Academy,' said Rilla with a grin.

'What has she got up to this time?'

'From what she will admit to me, I believe Sylvia was attempting to steal a horse,' said Rilla in a confidential tone.

She was rewarded by another chuckle from Finlay. 'She didn't!'

'It won't be the first time she's tried to run away from the Wallflower Academy,' said Rilla darkly, though a smile still lingered on her face.

How could it not, when she was with the man she loved?

'Sylvia and her schemes… I tried to talk her out of the last one, but apparently—'

'So it is thanks to Sylvia's antics, then, that we will have to find a new location for…conversation?' came Finlay's low, seductive voice.

A thrill rushed through Rilla as she thought of all the joy and pleasure they had to look forward to in their future. Days and days of it. Precisely what she was going to do when the month was up and her place at the Wallflower Academy was gone, she did not know…but surely Finlay would not allow her to be destitute?

And an idea, a wonderful idea, one she had barely allowed herself to consider but now sparked in her mind as bright as the sun, soared into her consciousness.

Well—they loved each other, did they not? Those words had not been exchanged but they did not need to be. Rilla knew how she felt about him, knew how Finlay felt about her.

He could not marry her—surely he would have offered for her hand if he thought her position appropriate for that of countess— but perhaps that was not necessary.

Rilla swallowed hard. Could she do it? Did she love him enough to become Finlay's mistress?

'Finlay,' she said softly, hardly sure how precisely she was supposed to broach such a topic, but knowing she must.

After all, she had been the one to proposition him to make love to her, had she not? And that had worked out splendidly. More than splendidly. Far better than she could have imagined.

'Rilla,' he said quietly.

A shimmer of need washed over her but Rilla pushed it aside. She needed to concentrate to ask this question.

'Finlay, would you…would you ever consider—'

'Ah, I thought it was you, Miss Newell! And—my goodness. My lord. What an honour!'

And Rilla's heart sank.

Of course.

There was no possibility she could have this conversation without being interrupted. And of all people to interrupt her...

The scent of carbolic soap wafted through the air as footsteps approached them. 'I have just been to the village, my lord, picking up a few things for my wallflowers. I trust you have had a pleasant walk? Where is Miss Bryant? I presume she accompanied you? This is more than a little unsettling, my lord. You hardly need to be schooled in the rules of the *ton*.'

Rilla tried not to permit heat to flood her cheeks, certain her embarrassment would be obvious, but there was nothing she could do to stop it.

Pleasant walk? Yes, some parts of it had been most pleasant indeed...

'You have some beautiful gardens and grounds here, Miss Pike,' Finlay was saying politely. 'I look forward to seeing them in the summer, when the flowers are out.'

'Oh, just a few borders of my own design,' came the immodest voice of Miss Pike. Rilla stifled a smile. 'Gardening is, after all, one of life's most simple pleasures. I typically find...'

Rilla ceased paying attention.

Well, she had heeded the Pike's lectures on the benefits of gardening quite enough times over the years. The woman was hardly going to say something new and surprising after such a long—

'And I do apologize, my lord, I have been most remiss! I have not enquired as to your mother's health. She must be run ragged, preparing for your wedding.'

And all sound disappeared.

It was most disconcerting. Oh, there were sounds, noises in the far reaches of her hearing, but they appeared deadened, as though underwater or a long way off.

I have not enquired as to your mother's health. She must be run ragged, preparing for your wedding.

The words each individually made sense, but as Rilla attempted to weave them together to make sense of them, a dizziness rocked her head and she almost stumbled, leaning heavily on Finlay's arm.

Finlay was saying awkwardly, 'Ah, yes…erm…th-thank you, Miss Pike, for your kind—'

'I had no idea that the wedding was so soon,' prattled on Miss Pike as Rilla attempted to gain her balance. 'Just a few weeks! You yourself must be very busy with the final preparations.'

She must be run ragged, preparing for your wedding.

'Yes, yes, very busy,' came Finlay's voice.

But Finlay was a long way off. Though Rilla still had her arm linked into his, the man was suddenly distant. Unknown to her. A stranger.

Who was this man, then, who purported to be Finlay Jellicoe, Earl of Staromchor?

She had been so certain that she had known him, had understood him. Had cleverly deduced that he was a man to be trusted, a man to whom she could give herself without regret. And now here she was, being forced to listen to the man, whoever he was, talk about his…his wedding?

'I suppose my invitation has been lost in the post…they are getting careless,' the Pike was saying in that delicate tone of self-importance that was all her own. 'Well, I must be off. I have wallflowers waiting for these. Good day, my lord. Come, Miss Newell.'

Whatever 'these' were, Rilla could not tell. She presumed that the proprietress of the Wallflower Academy had showed Finlay something and had not seen fit to bother to explain it to her.

Not that it mattered. Nothing mattered, not anymore. She stepped forward, forgetting for a moment that she was trapped by her hand in his arm. There was nothing in the world that mattered, because the man she had trusted, the man she had been certain she knew—

'Rilla,' said Finlay hastily in a low, urgent tone. 'Rilla—'

'I don't want to hear it,' Rilla said, half in a daze.

She slipped her hand from his arm. It took two attempts as the brigand attempted to clasp her fingers the first time she tried to move away from him, but then she managed it and her hands were on the wall of the Tudor manor.

It earthed her, grounded her, as nothing else had.

So. Everything that she thought she knew about Finlay, as it turned out, was a lie. Once again she had thought herself in love, thought that she could be happy. Once again she had permitted an earl to matter to her, to creep into her heart and have weight with her emotions, and once again she had been disappointed.

She must be run ragged, preparing for your wedding.

Rilla swallowed hard, desperately hoping that the tears threatening to spill would not fall—would not give him the satisfaction of seeing just how hurt she was.

Finlay was to be married. Had been engaged to be married, to another woman, the entire time.

Oh, she had been such a fool.

But no longer. Rilla straightened herself up, ignoring whatever it was that Finlay was saying in a rush of words that made it almost impossible to decipher, and said coldly, 'Stay away from me, Earl.'

Chapter Fifteen

'I do apologize, my lord, I have been most remiss! I have not enquired as to your mother's health. She must be run ragged, preparing for your wedding.'

And that was when Finlay knew he was the absolute worst human being who had ever lived.

Rilla had stiffened in his arms, and though he had turned immediately to her, desperate to show her how remorseful he was, he could not speak.

There were no words.

He had betrayed her, completely and utterly—and the worst of it was that Rilla could not see the contrition on his face. No, she had to stand there in silence and suffer listening to Miss Pike.

'I had no idea that the wedding was so soon,' prattled on Miss Pike, preventing him from saying anything. 'Just a few weeks! You yourself must be very busy with the final preparations.'

'Yes, yes, very busy,' Finlay found himself saying.

Rilla had said nothing, done nothing, merely stood there. Her expression was cold, stiff, as it always was when Rilla was seeking to distance herself from what was happening around her.

And he had done that. Him, and his lies, his deception, his inability to admit the truth: that he was engaged to be married to a woman who was devoted to him.

It pained him as nothing had ever hurt before, but what could he say when Miss Pike was still standing there?

'I suppose my invitation has been lost in the post... They are getting careless,' Miss Pike was saying with a sharp glance in his direction. 'Well, I must be off. I have wallflowers waiting for these. Good day, my lord. Come, Miss Newell.'

She waved the basket under her arm which was full of brown paper parcels, and turned on her heels before walking off.

The instant he judged her to be out of earshot, Finlay brought his mouth close to her ear. 'Rilla. Rilla—'

'I don't want to hear it,' Rilla said dully.

That was when she tried to pull free of him. Finlay attempted to hold on to her, desperate not to lose the connection they had, that they shared—emblematic of the closeness he was terrified to lose.

But he could not, would not hold her against his will. He was not that sort of man. He would not demand a woman's intimacy when she so clearly wished to revoke it.

It was as though he had been punched in the gut as Rilla took a step back from him, clinging to the wall of the Wall-flower Academy as though it was the only dependable thing in the world.

Nausea rose in Finlay's chest. What had he done?

She must be run ragged, preparing for your wedding.

If only Miss Pike had not been foolish enough to mention the wedding.

But no, Finlay could not blame her, much as he might wish to. It had been his choice to keep such a thing secret, his decision not to inform Rilla of his betrothal.

He had been the one to accept her offer of lovemaking. Dear God, he had been the one to lick her to ecstasy just minutes ago.

And despite his best intentions, which had been to come to the Wallflower Academy and finally admit to Rilla that he had a prior commitment and could no longer enjoy her company as he would wish…

Despite all that, it was Miss Pike who had revealed the truth. *Hell.*

Finlay's gaze raked over Rilla's face and saw the devastation he felt. Christ, she was trying not to cry; he could see the tension in her temples as her eyes sparkled.

He was the lowest of the low. He had to explain.

'I know I should have told you from the start and I had intended to but I was in too deep before I realized what I was about and it grew harder and harder to—'

The words tumbled from his mouth, almost nonsensical in their speed, and evidently Rilla was not interested.

She had straightened up, back against the wall, as she said, 'Stay away from me, Earl.'

Mortification rushed through Finlay's chest.

Oh, it was not bad enough that he had completely destroyed all faith and trust between them. It wasn't enough that he had lied, and had now been caught out in said lie in a most shameful way.

No, it was worse than that. He had manged to confirm to Rilla just what she had believed when they had first met: that earls were not to be trusted.

'I should have told you earlier.'

'You should have,' said Rilla quietly, her voice distant, as though they were discussing the weather. 'And yet you did not.'

Finlay swallowed. This would have been a much easier conversation if he could have arrived with his engagement broken completely, Isabelle Carr nothing more to him than an acquaintance he used to know as a child.

Oh, hell. How had he managed to create this situation? One bad decision after another, but each one made because he had thought it was the best thing at the time. The best thing for Isabelle.

How had he managed to get this so wrong, hurt so many people?

'Who is she?'

Finlay winced. The ice in Rilla's tone was surely merely a front, something designed to keep her true feelings at bay, but after all they had shared it was excruciating to hear all warmth gone.

Less than an hour ago, they had been happy. But that time was over.

'Her name, please, my lord,' said Rilla, as though she were merely enquiring about a pair of kid gloves.

Finlay took a deep breath. 'Isabelle. Isabelle Carr.'

'Carr?' Rilla nodded slowly. 'Ah, I see. Cecil's sister. You must care for her very much.'

'It's not like that.'

'Then why are you marrying her?' Rilla said, cutting him off.

Finlay attempted to gather his thoughts, flying about him with no consideration for his exhausted mind.

Why was he marrying her?

A fortnight ago he would have said it was nothing more than a marriage of convenience. Something required as a man of honour, not because he had ruined Isabelle's, but because she had precious little else to sustain her.

And now...

Now there was guilt. Oh, there was guilt. He should never have listened at the drawing room door, but he could not forget what he had heard.

His happiness is... It is the most important thing to me. There is not a single day that does not go by when I do not think of him.

She loved him, depended on the marriage going ahead. The true affection had been so potent that he had not needed to see her speak to believe her words. And he could not cause that woman any more grief. She had already suffered enough.

'It… She…' Finlay pulled a hand through his hair, desperately attempting to marshal his ideas. 'It was a marriage of convenience.'

'Was?'

'I offered her marriage when her brother—when Cecil died,' Finlay said, rattling on hastily in the hope it would be less painful that way.

The wind blew between them, a chill in the air. It would snow soon.

'Why would you do that?' Rilla's voice was calm, as though attempting to discover why a friend had chosen a particular hue for a painting.

If only he had time to think—if only his frantically beating heart would give him solace, rather than course panic through his veins with every squeeze!

'I— It's hard to explain.'

'You said it was a marriage of convenience.' Rilla's hands were clasped before her. 'Was. What is it now? Are you in love with her?'

'No,' Finlay said immediately. Of that, he was sure.

'And yet you will marry her.'

'I— It's not as simple as…' His voice trailed off as he attempted to think.

It was his own fault. If he had just been open about Isabelle's existence at the beginning…

Finlay's shoulders sagged. But he had so swiftly been caught up in Rilla's presence that all thoughts of Isabelle were entirely forgotten.

He swallowed hard. 'She loves me.'

'Ah, there it is,' said Rilla darkly, in a sardonic tone that cut straight into Finlay's chest. 'Of course she does! What woman would not fall in love with the charming earl?'

'It isn't like that,' Finlay snapped.

'Isn't it? You are engaged to be married, you absolute cur, and you knew that I had once—that I had almost married. Was it not enough to make me the laughingstock of the whole Wall-flower Academy? How can I ever trust—'

Rilla's voice broke off as she raised a hand to her mouth, forcing down a sob that broke Finlay's heart.

He had done this.

Rilla was right; he had known her history with the Earl of Porthaethwy and he had ploughed on regardless. He had wooed her, flirted with her, charmed her, and he had known at every turn that nothing could happen between them.

Nothing that would last, at any rate.

'I wanted to end the engagement,' he said, his voice cracking.

Rilla snorted. 'But you have not.'

Finlay closed his eyes, desperately forcing the tears away. 'No—not yet! I intended to last night, but she was out, and... I will. I will, I promise.'

Oh, God, he sounded like such a scoundrel saying that.

But Rilla had not heard Isabelle talking so passionately about her affection. She had lost her brother—they had both lost Cecil, but Isabelle was the one alone in the world.

What, was he to deny her any happiness whatsoever?

But there could only be one happy woman: Rilla or Isabelle. Finlay knew he had been forced to choose between them.

And there was only a wrong choice.

'I... I made you no other promises,' Finlay said, grasping on to that fact like a lifeboat in a storm. 'I never intended for you to care.'

'You have broken no vow, either,' Rilla retorted. 'Do you feel proud of yourself?'

Finlay's jaw tightened. 'No.'

'Oh, God, I said to you before that I was more than a match for an earl, and yet here you are, proving me wrong!'

'No, Rilla, I—'

'I am worth far more,' she said imperiously, holding her head high. 'I am certainly worth more than this.'

How could she say that? How could they even be having this conversation here, right in front of the Wallflower Academy, where anyone could see them?

Oh, God. Where anyone could see them.

Finlay turned away from Rilla for a moment and saw precisely what he had hoped not to see. There, in the large bay window that jutted out from the morning room, and therefore where there was an excellent view of the front of the house, was...

A troop of women. He recognized Sylvia and Daphne, but there were also half a dozen other ladies, all goggling. Hell. There must be an afternoon tea or something. Of course there was.

Finlay swore under his breath.

'There is no need for language like that!'

'No, it's just—'

'And I did not demand any promises,' Rilla said, countering his earlier point.

'Rilla, there are people watching.' Finlay tried to take her arm to pull her away from the window and the gawping gazes of the wallflowers, but she continued on, her voice catching as words spilled out.

'But I presumed that friends—lovers—had an unspoken expectation of honesty. More fool me.'

Finlay's jaw was tightening again, causing a throb of pain to stretch to his temple. This was all going wrong, but he had to admit, even if it were only to himself, that there was no possibility of it going right. He had made this decision. Now he was having to face the consequences.

'You should have been honest with me,' Rilla said quietly. 'You should have said... That poor woman, and here I am... I would have wanted to know if there was no future for us, of any kind.'

That sparked indignation in Finlay's chest. 'I did. You said that you knew we could not wed!'

'But I hadn't thought about marriage, not really,' she said fiercely, and Rilla actually took a step towards him, her body seeming to thrum with certainty. 'I hadn't expected *that*! When I thought about our future, I thought... I hoped...'

Finlay's stomach lurched.

Was it possible? Could it be that Rilla had considered becoming his mistress?

They could have been together in a small way. He could have found his joy and happiness with her while Isabelle...

The thought of his future bride poured cold water over that idea.

He was no rake. He could not take one woman to the altar, knowing that she was desperately in love with him, then betray her with another woman.

His stomach twisted painfully. Though hadn't he done just that? Self-loathing and regret mingled with pain in his chest. How had this gone so wrong?

Finlay took in a deep breath and rubbed his chin, his jaw tight. 'I know you probably think very little of me in this moment. I may not love her, but I have to respect her. Respect her feelings.'

'Like you respected mine?'

He hung his head, shifting on his feet. 'You...you're right. I lied to myself, Rilla. I made myself believe this whole damned situation wouldn't hurt anyone. And I've hurt you, and I'm so sorry, you're the one I would least like to hurt, Rilla, I—'

'Don't call me that,' she said sharply.

Pain flared in his chest, but it was quickly subsumed by despair. 'I was weak, Rilla, I was a fool, but you have to believe me, no one can loathe me more than I loathe myself! You've never made a mistake? Rilla—'

'I told you before, my friends call me Rilla,' she said, and now she was crying, tears gently falling down her cheeks, and Finlay's heart twisted in agony. 'You may call me Miss Newell, for the purposes of this conversation.'

A flicker of hope. 'This conversation? And after?'

'Oh, there won't be an after,' Rilla said with a sniff. 'You think I wish to speak to you again after this?'

Finlay turned away for a moment in an attempt to gather his thoughts. If only there was a way to prove his affections... but what was the point? He would be Isabelle's groom in ten days. Ten days—that was all—and he would be parted from Rilla forever.

Though he wasn't sure they could be much more parted than this.

She was closing herself off from him, distancing him from her true self, and there was nothing he could do but watch it happen. Hate it happen. Hate that he could do nothing about it.

'I... I hoped—'

'When you said that you were not getting married anytime soon, that was a lie,' Rilla said, speaking over him as a cloud shadowed the sky. 'Your friendship, our connection, whatever... whatever this is, it was all based on a lie. Did you think you could lie to my face because I can't see?'

Revulsion poured through Finlay's chest. 'No.'

'Yet you did so anyway,' Rilla said with a nonchalant shrug that cut to his very soul. 'I wasn't important enough to tell the truth to just a wallflower, no prospects, no family—'

'I love you!' Finlay blurted out.

He had imagined a completely different moment when he would tell her this. When they were in each other's arms, perhaps. When they had just finished kissing. Maybe when he had just finished feeding her strawberries, Rilla's lips stained with the juices and his own lips hungry for hers.

He had certainly hoped for a different response.

Rilla snorted. 'Don't be ridiculous.'

'I am not being—'

'A man in love doesn't hurt the person he purports to love,' Rilla said, and there was pain in her voice, which Finlay hated to hear. 'A man in love—a gentleman!—does not lie about his marital prospects!'

'I never lied. I just never—'

'Told the truth?' she said, finishing the sentence for him.

Finlay turned away for a moment, trying to collect himself, but when he turned back to her she was still standing there, still Rilla, still perfect.

'I should have known,' Rilla said softly. 'Never trust an earl.'

And the fire that flared in his chest had nothing to do with Isabelle, or his upcoming marriage, and had everything to do with Rilla's words.

'I'm not saying that I am a paragon of virtue,' he said quietly. 'But blame me for my actions, not my title. You were just as guilty of treating me poorly when we first met.'

'You made me think you were a footman!' Rilla interjected hotly.

'I thought we had moved past our assumptions about each other, but clearly I was wrong!' Finlay said bitterly before he could stop himself.

Regret soared through his heart immediately.

What did he think he was doing, speaking to a woman like that? Speaking to Rilla like that—to anyone like that?

Finlay's head hung low.

Dear God, he was just as bad as she thought he was. Perhaps worse.

But there was still something he could do, if he could just kiss her, show her...

'Rilla...'

'Rilla!'

Finlay stepped back hastily as he glanced over his shoulder to see Miss Smith, her blond hair now paired with scarlet cheeks, staring at the two of them.

'What are you doing to her?' she said, a mite accusingly.

'Nothing,' snapped Finlay, knowing he should be more patient, knowing the poor woman had no idea what was truly happening, but unable to restrain his ire. 'I'm not doing anything.'

'That is precisely right. His Lordship is doing nothing,' said Rilla with a sardonic smile. 'Go on in, Daphne. I will join you presently.'

The wallflower did not seem particularly convinced, but she did not appear to have the force of character to disagree. She turned slowly, fixing her eyes for the longest moment in a stare, then trotted up the steps to the Wallflower Academy.

Only when the door closed did Finlay take a deep breath. Now to show not tell Rilla precisely how he felt.

'And on that note, I will bid you good day,' Rilla said darkly.

She had managed to take three steps before Finlay grabbed her arm. 'Let me help.'

'I have had quite enough of your help, thank you,' she snapped, wrenching her arm away. 'Don't touch me!'

'But I can help you up the steps,' Finlay persisted, walking alongside her.

He was bound to her in honour, even if he could not be bound to her in any other way. Did she not know that? Could she not see that he adored her? Had she not listened when he had said that he loved her?

'Oh, I know this path,' Rilla said with a laugh that held no mirth. 'I know this path well. It is one I have walked for many years—alone.'

Finlay swallowed, wishing he could console her, wishing things could be different.

'At this rate, I will be walking alone for many years to come,' Rilla said as they reached the steps up to the Wallflower Academy. 'But you know what, Finlay?'

Her voice had modulated, calmed. Hope, pathetic and small, rose. 'What?'

'I would rather walk it alone than with you,' Rilla said sweetly before she turned, walked up the steps, and slammed the door behind her, leaving Finlay standing before the Wallflower Academy entirely alone.

Chapter Sixteen

Staying in one's room for three days and requesting meals to be sent up to you was the sort of thing that great ladies did, Rilla reflected as the haze of light she could just perceive moved slowly across her bedchamber.

Still. That did not prevent her from doing it.

After all, it was not as though there was anything downstairs that she wanted. Company was abhorrent to her. The well-meaning questions flying about the place were anathema to her, and Rilla had already suffered the curiosity of those who had spotted herself and...and the Earl of Staromchor arguing.

A tear crept from her eye, sliding down her face and onto the bedlinens. Rilla did not bother to contain it. What was the point? There was no one here to see it, no one to judge her for making such a foolish choice as to trust an earl.

Not that she didn't judge herself.

I should have known. Never trust an earl.

A second tear followed the first one. She had fallen in love with Finlay Jellicoe, Earl of Staromchor, and try as she might she could not just cease loving him because it was inconvenient. Because he was marrying another woman. Because they were to be separated for the rest of their lives.

Rilla swallowed. What she had expected from him, she did not know. It was all so clouded now, clouded with the confusion of pain and their argument.

A man in love doesn't hurt the person he purports to love. A man in love—a gentleman!—does not lie about his marital prospects!

I never lied. I just never—

Told the truth?

And now all she could think about was Finlay and the woman he would marry. Was she beautiful? Did she sing well, play the pianoforte, embroider cushions and dance elegantly while listening to Finlay's words?

The knot in her stomach twisted most painfully.

Because it did not matter, did it? Finlay had made a commitment to that woman, and in all honour he certainly should continue with it.

Even if it hurt.

The pain of losing him was exquisite. Rilla had known hardship, known pain, known the separation between people you loved…or thought you loved. She had known betrayal. She was hardly new to expecting the worst in people.

Yet he had somehow wormed his way into her heart and now she was crippled by the affection within it that she could no longer give. It was a physical ache in her chest, as if a heavy weight had been placed there, and no one but Finlay could remove it.

But she couldn't just stay up here moping. Rilla knew, better than anyone else at the Wallflower Academy, just what was at stake if she did not find herself a situation.

I refer, most unwillingly, to the fact that your father will cease to pay for your place here at the Wallflower Academy at the end of next month.

Taking a deep breath and propping herself up against some pillows, Rilla tried not to think about the Pike's latest recommendation.

'A perfectly good school not ten miles away,' the woman had shouted through the keyhole only last night. 'They are looking for a well-bred, elegant woman to take charge of literature and history, and I thought—'

'They won't want a woman like me,' Rilla had shot back at the proprietress through the door.

Which had been a mistake. It had only encouraged Miss Pike to rattle on about how she was the daughter of a baron and an honourable and there was nothing anyone could dislike about her.

As if she did not know what Rilla meant.

The trouble was, the idea had kept Rilla up all night. It was a good situation, two hundred pounds a year, and bed and board included; it would certainly afford her a comfortable life. She may even be able to put a little aside for the future. For when she would be no longer useful, and therefore have nowhere else to go…

Rilla had finally arisen that morning with a headache and no clear direction. If only he hadn't—

Pushing thoughts of Finlay aside was getting harder and harder. Intrusive, warm thoughts about how comforting it was to find herself in his arms, how strong he was, how she had sunk into his embraces and kisses…

Sighing heavily, Rilla turned onto her other side. Today was the last day she would permit herself to lie about the place, she promised herself.

Tomorrow she would rise and tell the Pike that—

A timid knock on the door made Rilla jerk her head in that direction.

'Go away.'

The knock was repeated, louder this time. Rilla sighed and fell back onto the bed. The Pike had been sending wallflowers almost hourly since she had flown upstairs after the argument with Finlay.

She did not want to see anyone.

But that did not appear to matter. The Pike was determined that Rilla entertain, God forbid, and that was the direction her requests—demands—tended.

Come and converse with the wallflowers.

Come and sit with the wallflowers.

Come, tell the wallflowers the pitfalls of losing one's heart to an earl...

Another knock, this time even harder.

'I said, go away!' Rilla said sharply.

'I knew you would say that,' came the wretched voice of Daphne Smith. 'I told the Pike you wouldn't want to see me. No one ever does.'

A shard of guilt slid into her heart.

Oh, very clever, she thought darkly. *Well done, Miss Pike. You knew I could not be angry at someone like Daphne Smith.*

'Come in,' she said wearily aloud. 'The door is unlocked.'

Rilla never locked her door now, not after the key was once jostled from the latch and it took her over an hour to find it. The sense of being trapped, of being unable to escape, had been formidable.

The click of the door opening, then the snick of it closing again, sounded around the little bedchamber. Rilla pulled herself into a proper sitting position on the bed and looked defiantly in the door's direction, not bothering to wipe away her tears.

She could sense the hesitation of her friend. One of her two friends, really—being a wallflower at the Wallflower Academy naturally led some to a competitiveness that Rilla simply did not care for.

But Daphne was not like that. She was a true wallflower, a woman who hated being the centre of attention for more than five minutes.

Even when it was just the two of them, she was hesitant.

'I suppose the Pike wants me to come downstairs,' said Rilla into the silence. 'Please, sit.'

The creak of the wicker chair in the corner suggested that Daphne had accepted her invitation. Her assumption was confirmed when her friend spoke, the words coming now from the corner rather than the door.

'We are all very worried about you.'

Rilla snorted. 'I doubt that.'

It was perhaps a tad cruel, but it was also the truth. The Pike would be worried, certainly, but about what on earth to do with her when the money ran out, not about Rilla herself.

'I am very worried,' came the tentative voice of Daphne. 'Worried for you. No one should feel alone.'

And some of the bitterness and resentment against everyone in the world melted away.

'Thank you,' Rilla said awkwardly. 'You... Well, you did not have to trouble yourself.'

'I am happy to do it,' said Daphne softly. 'I never had a sister, and I thought— Well, when I was sent to the Wallflower Academy, I hoped...'

The trailing off of her words was in some way worse than her actually saying them.

A twist of discomfort surged in Rilla's chest. She and Sylvia had always been close, and Gwen had joined them for a time. Daphne was always on the outside looking in. She was a naturally shy woman who could not compete with the rambunctious Sylvia or the dry-witted Rilla.

It was not a pleasant thought, to believe she had left out someone who had so desperately craved friendship.

'I would like to be a friend to you,' she said awkwardly.

There was a slight chuckle from the corner. 'I don't want your pity, Rilla.'

'I did not mean it like that.'

'I know, and it speaks well of you that you would wish to... well, make amends is not quite the right phrase, but I do not know what is,' came Daphne's quiet voice. 'And I would like to be a friend to you. I would like to help, if I could. If you wished to talk to me about...about him.'

Him.

The entire Wallflower Academy had apparently watched her argument with Finlay with open mouths, from what Sylvia had said through the door yesterday. It showed great restraint on Daphne's part, Rilla thought, that she did not say his name.

'There's not much to say,' she said swiftly.

Not much that she was willing to say, anyway.

Rilla's fingers tightened around the bedlinen, the comfortingly familiar weave of the fabric grounding her.

'I suppose not,' came Daphne's soft reply. 'And I have no wish to force you.'

And it was precisely because Rilla knew that Daphne would never consider forcing her to spill her secrets that she felt as though she might.

After all, thoughts had been whirling around her mind for days and she had gained no relief from them. It was frustrating to the extreme to think that she may never fully understand why Finlay had done what he had done. She might never get the answers she sought, never again feel the brush of his fingers along her arm…

Rilla swallowed. 'It's…complicated.'

There it was again, another chuckle from the wallflower. 'I presumed that.'

Laughing despite herself, Rilla sighed. Opening up to anyone wasn't exactly the sort of thing she typically did. It was always easier to hold herself at a distance, to allow the cold and stiff expression on her face to keep others away.

Once bitten, twice shy.

But it was more than that. Rilla had never noticed it before, but the three years she had been at the Wallflower Academy had reduced her somehow. She had squashed herself, forced down her instincts, her personality, made it almost impossible not to succumb to the fear of…

Fear of what?

Rilla could not articulate it. Fear of what had happened, happening again.

But now the very worst had happened. She had fallen in

love, truly, for the first time, and that love had been betrayed. Nothing could be worse than that, could it?

'I trusted him,' Rilla found herself saying, her voice breaking.

She sensed a creak of the willow chair, a footstep, and then a depression on the bed near her feet.

'Tell me about it,' said Daphne softly.

And she did.

The words came slowly at first. It had been many years since Rilla had been open, truly open, with anyone. Besides, it was shameful, to reveal just how easily she had been taken in.

I know you have no wish to marry. That is, a marriage between us would be impossible…

The only parts of the story she neglected to mention were…

Well. Daphne did not need to know about that particular moment in the stables, did she? Or the proposition that came before it. Or the moment of intimacy by the potting shed near the kitchen garden.

Rilla swallowed.

No. Definitely not.

Daphne was an excellent listener. Rilla supposed it was due to the fact that the wallflower was often excluded from conversations—a thought that made her cringe with shame.

And before she knew it, she was nearing the end of her tale.

'And Miss Pike enquired about his wedding,' Rilla said miserably, her chest tight just thinking about it. Her hands had moved to her lap, clasping and unclasping. 'His wedding. And it was—oh, Daphne, it was so humiliating! To know I had given my…had given my heart to him, and he had known all the while that he was betrothed to another…'

That was when her voice faded into nothing.

Rilla swallowed hard, but there was no force left in her tongue.

What else was there to say? She had been taken in, and cruelly, but there was no brother to defend her and her father would surely not disgrace the family name again by intervening.

Miss Pike would merely censure her for getting entangled with an engaged man, Rilla thought darkly, and Sylvia—

Well. Sylvia would probably bodily attack the man, which wouldn't help, either.

What she needed, Rilla thought darkly, was for Finlay to wake up one moment and realize he had changed his mind. That he could not, would not go through with the wedding. That he would—

Carr? Ah, I see. Cecil's sister. You must care for her very much.

Her stomach lurched.

What, would she take a man like Finlay away from a woman who had, by the sound of it, already gone through so much?

'I am sorry,' came Daphne's soft voice.

Rilla laughed ruefully. 'As am I.'

'It seems a most unfortunate situation.'

'Most unfortunate, yes,' she replied sardonically. 'An earl who took advantage of me—which should not have surprised me—who is going to go and marry a woman he…he doesn't even love.'

Which was another reason why the whole blasted situation was such a disaster, Rilla wanted to say, but couldn't bring herself to.

Finlay was going to be miserable.

There was no doubt in her mind: he did not love this Miss Carr. He was only marrying her for some strange sense of duty. Did they both have to be miserable?

'I wish there was an answer,' came Daphne's gentle voice. 'I suppose in times like this, there is no one solution, no way to make everyone happy.'

Rilla blinked away tears. Daphne was surprisingly astute. 'N-no. No, there isn't.'

Finlay could only wed one woman and he had made his decision. It was one he may regret, in time. She regretted it already.

Could he not see—did he not understand how happy they could be?

'Unless…' Daphne said slowly. And then she said nothing.

Impatience flared in Rilla's chest. 'Unless what?'

'Well, it was just a passing… I would not like to presume… but—'

'Really, I must insist that you— Ah, Miss Smith. Miss Newell, I see you are feeling better,' uttered the voice of Miss Pike, coinciding with the snap of the door being thrust open. 'Excellent.'

Rilla sighed.

The Pike meant well. She knew it, all the wallflowers knew it. But the woman had no sense of timing.

What had Daphne been about to say?

'Now, I have not wished to press you while you were…unwell,' said Miss Pike sternly, stepping towards the bed and halting somewhere nearby. 'But as I can see that you are now entirely better—'

'Miss Pike,' Daphne said softly, but she was entirely ignored.

'I have come here to request your decision,' Miss Pike continued firmly. 'I believe you have had sufficient time, and time is, as it were, not your friend in this matter.'

Rilla winced. Yes, the proprietress of the Wallflower Academy certainly had a way with words. Not that Rilla could deny anything the woman had said. Time was certainly not her friend in this matter, and a decision was needed.

There was not much of a choice. Teaching, or penury on the streets?

'Well, you will be delighted to hear I have made a decision,' Rilla said stiffly. 'I will accept a post anywhere away from here. Where he can't— Where I won't have to meet—'

'You will?' came the delighted tone of Miss Pike.

'You will?' repeated Daphne, evidently confused. 'What post?'

'If you had wished to teach here, I would have welcomed that, naturally,' the Pike continued, once again ignoring the shy wallflower. 'And I am confident you will make an excellent teacher at—what was it called? I can't remember, I've got it written down somewhere. Arrangements will have to be made. You can take the Wallflower Academy carriage most of the way…'

Rilla allowed the words to wash over her as a dull sensation settled in her chest.

So, it was decided.

She would be leaving the Wallflower Academy and not to be married, as her father and the Pike had so desperately hoped—but to be a teacher. To accept that she required wages now to live.

'I'm sure some of the reports of the fractious nature of the pupils are completely fabricated.'

Rilla's shoulders tensed. But she couldn't fight any longer. She had no one on her side, supporting her cause. Her father had no interest, and Finlay…

She blinked back her tears furiously. Finlay had made his choice. He would be marrying Miss Isabelle Carr, and she was certain they would find a way to be happy together.

Could she have been happy with him?

Some moments, Rilla could not understand him. A man who had everything, a title, a position in Society, a fiancée—why had he dallied with her?

And then she recalled the openness in the garden, the closeness they had shared, the knowledge, knowledge she had felt in her bones, that she was the only one he cared about.

Oh, it was all such a confusion.

'So you can be gone within a week,' the Pike finished with a falsely bright tone. 'Won't that be nice?'

A wave of nausea flooded through Rilla at the thought.

Leaving the Wallflower Academy was an inevitability—she knew that—but leaving its comforting, familiar halls would be a wrench.

'Very nice,' she said aloud.

'Yes. Well. Right,' said Miss Pike, perhaps a little rattled by Rilla's lack of fighting spirit. 'I'll leave you two alone, then.'

Footsteps sounded, and a flutter of carbolic soap wafted through the room before the door snapped smartly behind her. The departing footsteps grew fainter on the other side of the wall, and then there was silence.

Silence, that was, until Daphne cleared her throat.

Rilla jumped. Goodness, she had almost forgot that the wallflower was still there.

'Why did you not argue with her?' Daphne asked. 'I… Well, I do not mean to presume, but I did not think you wished to be a teacher. I have heard you and the Pike argue about it before.'

'What choice do I have?' Rilla said dully.

A woman without choices—most women, now she came to think about it. Choices were made by a father, brother, husband, someone else. Or there were no choices at all.

'But—'

'Daphne, I have no choice,' Rilla said sharply. 'Finlay, the Earl of Staromchor, is wedding someone else. I don't have a home to go back to, my father won't welcome me at home, and with no money to pay for my place here at the Wallflower Academy… I have nowhere else to go.'

Chapter Seventeen

Finlay pushed open the door, ignored the bell, ignored the astonished gasps from the customers about the place, and did what no gentleman had ever done before.

He marched past the modiste's assistant and into the fitting area.

'My lord!'

'Sir, please, you cannot go back there, it is for the ladies—'

But Finlay did not care.

He had taken three days to think it through. Three days, he had reasoned, was enough time to truly sit with the decision he wished to make. Time to consider if it was truly what he wished to do. Whether it was something he could live with.

And no matter how much time passed, his resolution remained: he had to marry Rilla Newell.

The instant he had come to the decision, he had to enact it—and this was the first step. To be sure, when Turner had said that his mother and Miss Carr were out, he had presumed they were at Hatchard's, or a bakery, or Twinings tea shop.

Still. Once he'd made the decision, nothing was going to hold Finlay back. Not even—

'Really, sir!' Another modiste's assistant, an apron over her gown and a wide-eyed expression of horror on her face, attempted to bat him away. 'This area is for ladies. There is a young Miss here for the final fitting of her wedding—'

'I know,' said Finlay sharply. 'She is my betrothed.'

Or at least, she was for the moment. A moment that would not last very long.

Ignoring the startled expression on his mother's face, Finlay marched past the two sofas and an armchair which were evidently there for the friends and family of whoever it was being fitted, and approached a screen.

'Isabelle?'

There was a startled yelp, a genteel curse, and Madame Penelope's head appeared around the side of the screen.

'You have made me prick my thumb,' she said darkly. 'I hope you have a good reason for barging in here, my lord.'

'I quite agree with you, Madame,' came the dour voice of the Dowager Countess of Staromchor behind him. 'I do not understand, Staromchor, why you suddenly have lost all sense of decorum. Really! A modiste's!'

Finlay ignored them both.

Well, he ignored them both as much as he could. It was impossible to prevent his ears from pinking. Especially as now he looked around him, he could see... Ah.

His mouth went dry.

Well, it was a lady's domain, he supposed.

The chintz everywhere was not his style, nor were the delicate shades of pink and leafy green that Madame Penelope had chosen to decorate the place with.

It looked more like a boudoir than a shop.

And it was even more like a boudoir, Finlay realized with growing apprehension in his lungs, because on display just to his right were a number of garments that were designed ... well, to be underclothes.

His face was now burning.

Hell's bells, but he hadn't expected this.

What man knew anything about the attiring rooms of a modiste's?

Finlay turned to his mother, who raised an eyebrow.

'I hope you are satisfied,' she said calmly, looking up from a pamphlet with a variety of different styles of gowns printed on its pages. 'I suppose this will be the talk of the Town, you forcing your way into a modiste's and risking seeing Miss Carr's wedding gown, too.'

It was the mention of the wedding gown that stiffened Finlay's resolve.

He had to finally speak his mind about this wedding. It had gone on for too long. He was starting to think, in truth, that he should never have made the offer to Isabelle in the first place.

The instinct had been a good one, Finlay knew, but it was not one which he could surely be expected to hold for the rest of his life.

I did not demand any promises... But I presumed that friends—lovers—had an unspoken expectation of honesty. More fool me.

His shoulders snapped back and he held his head high. No, mortified Madame Penelope and irate mother aside, he had to speak his mind.

He had not expected to do so in front of so many people, of course...

Finlay looked around and spotted no less than three assistants, one holding a plethora of ribbons, another merely blinking in astonishment.

Right. First things first.

'I wish to speak to Isabelle—to Miss Carr,' he amended hastily, in a voice he hoped was both commanding and charming. 'Alone, if you don't mind.'

The three assistants scampered away, but his mother rose and drew herself up in a most impressive manner.

'I do mind,' she said sharply. 'I cannot just permit you to be alone with Miss Carr. That would be scandalous. The very idea, a gentleman and a lady together, alone—and unmarried!'

Try as he might, Finlay was unable to put aside all thoughts of Rilla. Of the time they had spent together alone, of the things they had enjoyed while alone…

Perhaps his mother was right.

'My lord?'

The voice was gentle, and nervous, and it came from behind the screen.

Finlay's stomach twisted in a painful knot but he could not turn back now. He had to act. He had to have this…this show-down, for want of a better word.

He had hoped to speak with Isabelle at her lodgings, but the housekeeper had said she was getting her wedding gown fitted and—

Well. He had rather lost his head. The idea of Isabelle, a woman painfully in love with him, having her wedding gown fitted before he could speak to her…it could not be borne.

Which had led him, circuitously, to this awkward conversation.

Madame Penelope disappeared for a moment behind the screen again, and when she emerged she was not alone.

Isabelle Carr stood there, gazing with a curious look.

Finlay's heart skipped a beat.

Not because affection had suddenly welled in him—quite the opposite. A part of him, and he had not realized it had even existed until this moment, had wondered whether he would eventually fall in love with her. Whether the Isabelle he had once known would resurface, once they were married, and they could enjoy a sort of companionable respect in their marriage.

But seeing her like this, dressed in her finery, the elegant blue silk gown delicately fitted around her bust, her hair taste-fully shaped upon her head…

It was nothing. She was nothing compared to the sight of Rilla, straw in her hair and her unseeing gaze trusting.

Finlay swallowed.

There was no easy way to do this. Best to just get it over with.

'I can't marry you,' he blurted out.

The silence that followed this pronouncement was absolutely excruciating.

At least, Finlay had thought so. It was only then that he realized that the scream of astonishment from his mother was perhaps worse.

'Not…not marry her?'

'Ah, I think I hear a customer calling,' murmured the modiste quietly. She stepped past Isabelle, past Finlay, and out into the shop proper.

At least, he presumed that was where she went. Finlay had not taken his eyes from the woman who, until a minute ago, had been his betrothed.

Isabelle's eyes were wide and her lips had parted in silent shock. Evidently his statement had made it impossible for her to speak.

Wretched guilt tore at Finlay's heart. This was his fault, all his fault. If he had not been so charming, so polite—if he had not attempted to make Isabelle comfortable in the marital decision they had taken, she would not have fallen in love with him.

And now he would have to stand here and watch her crumble.

'I know I should have said something sooner,' Finlay said awkwardly, taking a step forward and ignoring the impassioned speech from the dowager countess behind him.

'The scandal sheets! The whole of the *ton* will be filled with the news that my son has abandoned his bride.'

'I offered you marriage out of convenience. We both agreed to that—to provide you with a home,' Finlay said stoically, not taking his eyes from Isabelle. 'And though I fully intended until just a day ago—'

'Disgrace upon our name! No one will ever touch us again. We'll be forced to—'

'Once I realized that I could not marry you, I knew I had to tell you instantly,' continued Finlay doggedly.

Oh, Lord, only his mother could make this situation about herself.

'And I am sorry…truly sorry, Isabelle.'

'Why?' breathed the young woman, her face pale. 'Why won't you marry me?'

Finlay winced. But this was the decision he had chosen, and he could not back away from it now just because it was uncomfortable. 'Because…'

'I shall lose my voucher at Almack's and then what will I do? Oh, the shame of it all!'

Finlay squared his shoulders and ensured that he looked Isabelle directly in the eye as he said the words he knew would cut the deepest. 'Because I am in love with someone else.'

That cut his mother's tirade short. 'And I… Wh-what?'

He did not look around. He could console—or attempt to console—his mother later. He would have all the time in the world to do that, and to acclimatize her to Rilla, if she decided to take umbrage at the fact that he had chosen his own bride.

Oh, please God, let Rilla accept him.

Yes, the dowager countess could be calmed another time, but Isabelle?

Finlay did not look away from the young woman. A young woman who had lost her only family and had no one else to turn to. Who would now have nothing to live on, no one to protect her…

'Isabelle,' he said, taking a step forward. 'I will still help you—'

His words were cut short by such a bizarre occurrence, all words fled from his mind.

Isabelle raised both hands to her face, covered her eyes, and…laughed.

It wasn't a snort of panic or the beginnings of tears—at least, he did not think it was. No, her shoulders were shaking from the fit of giggles she appeared to be experiencing.

Finlay swallowed awkwardly. She was having a most strange reaction to the news, but then perhaps this was just her way of attempting to understand what was happening to her. It was hardly an everyday occurrence, a broken engagement mere days before the wedding itself.

Right, now, what had he decided? Oh, yes.

Finlay stepped forward, awkwardly patting the arm of the now hysterically giggling woman. 'Please do not concern yourself. I have thought long and hard about it, and I will give you a thousand pounds.'

'Finlay Jellicoe!'

'A thousand pounds,' continued Finlay, throwing a dark look at his mother over his shoulder. 'That should be more than sufficient for your needs for the rest of the Season, at least I think so, and I am sure that by that time you will most definitely have found another man to marry you.'

Which would be a relief from his shoulders, he thought woefully, hating that he had placed her in such a terrible position.

First the loss of Cecil, and now the loss of him. Would it be any wonder if Isabelle decided to leave the marriage mart and take a Grand Tour on the Continent?

Perhaps an Italian prince or a French count would take pity on her. Perhaps she would become someone else's problem.

Finlay instantly felt guilty for such a thought, but he could not blame himself. He had taken the weight of responsibility of caring for Isabelle Carr without considering just how heavily it would press upon him.

Now he had just informed her that the safety and security of marriage had been, at least from him, removed.

No wonder she was so hysterical.

'Please, Isabelle,' Finlay said in a low voice, patting her self-consciously on the arm again. 'Do not distress yourself.'

'The woman can be distressed if she—'

'I know you are deeply in love with me,' he said, hoping to goodness that she did not mind him revealing that he knew of her feelings. 'But your affections... I am sure they will fade with time, and it will be as though you never cared for me in that way. I hope... I trust that we will be able to return to being good friends. As we once were.'

As I thought we would be forever. You and me and Cecil and Bartlett. God, what had happened to us?

At his words, Isabelle dropped her hands from her face, and Finlay was astonished to see that she was...smiling?

Perhaps she was in shock. Perhaps after losing Cecil, she had no other way of accepting difficulty than through laughter. It was odd, to be sure, but—

'My dear Finlay,' said Isabelle with a broad grin. 'Please do not concern yourself.'

One may as well tell paint not to dry. 'But—'

'I am in love with someone else.'

This time it was Finlay's turn for his lips to part in astonishment.

I am in love with someone else.

It wasn't possible—no. He must have misheard.

Finlay cleared his throat as tingles of anticipation washed over his body. 'I do apologize. I do not think I heard you.'

'I am in love with someone else,' repeated Isabelle, soft pink tinging her cheeks. 'Someone who wants to marry me.'

It could not be happening.

Finlay did not understand—he had heard her most clearly, had he not? Isabelle had been effusive in her regard, passionate in her affection, far more than he could have imagined.

Oh, I could never speak to him about the depths of my feelings. Besides, I do not think it would be appropriate. He does not expect it. He would not... I do not think he would wish it.

I love him, my lady. Everything he says is music to my ears, everything he does is the best thing a man has ever done!

He could not have misheard, nor misunderstood, all that. 'But…but…'

'And why you believe that I am in love with you, I really do not know,' continued Isabelle blithely, a small line appearing between her brows as she frowned. 'I do not believe I have ever given you cause to believe that from my behaviour.'

Finlay's mouth dropped. 'But I heard you!'

It was probably not the politest thing he could say, and he was not surprised when his mother behind him snapped, 'I beg your pardon?'

'I heard you, the two of you, talking,' Finlay said, a shade discomforted at having to reveal that he had been eavesdropping. 'I assure you, I did not intend to—'

'And you heard what?' asked Isabelle.

Hell's bells, why did it feel so awkward to repeat this?

'Well, a lot of talking about…about being in love with me. How deeply you felt, how you adored me.'

Whenever I am with him, I can think of nothing but the pleasure I gain from being in his presence.

It had been strange to hear, but it was far more mortifying to repeat. Finlay hardly knew where to look, but as his gaze eventually returned to Isabelle, she…she was laughing again.

Laughing, at him?

'Look, I know this has all been very difficult for you,' he said a little stiffly. 'But—'

'Oh, Finlay, you dear sweet man,' said Isabelle, shaking her head with a laugh. 'You presumed that I was speaking of you, then?'

A flicker of uncertainty awoke in his chest. 'Well…well yes, obviously. Who else could you be speaking of?'

And the pink tinges in her cheeks darkened as Isabelle held his gaze. 'Why, George of course.'

George. George? They did not know anyone called George. Finlay blinked. 'Who the devil is George?'

'Lord George Bartlett,' Isabelle said, her eyes shining. Bartlett.

Bartlett? What the hell was going on?

And then the memory of their conversation that late night resurfaced in Finlay's mind. Bartlett had been concerned, had he not, very concerned about Isabelle's well-being? They had discussed her in depth and the man had been worried about her.

Far more worried than he himself had been, now Finlay came to think about it.

Bartlett and Isabelle?

'And I have been feeling so guilt-ridden, all these weeks,' Isabelle was saying as Finlay forced himself to pay attention. 'I have been spending every moment with him that I could, and yet my remorse about lying to you, about keeping this hidden—'

'Why on earth did you not say something?' Finlay said, a slow smile starting to creep across his face. 'Do you mean to tell me that the blackguard is in love with you?'

Isabelle's expression was warm. 'He tells me so.'

'Then why—'

'I did not know of his feelings before…well, before you offered me marriage,' Isabelle confessed, hugging herself as the evident regret of her actions rose. 'I thought— Well, I had no other choice.'

'Charming,' muttered Finlay, his smile broadening.

Isabelle shoved him hard on the shoulder, and there she was, the Isabelle he had known, the one who had pushed him about when they were younger and had thought nothing of cutting off her own hair so that she could play pirates with them.

The three of them. The three boys: Cecil, himself…and Bartlett.

'When a woman has few options, she takes the option presented to her,' Isabelle said with a snort. 'Even if it was you.'

'Outrageous!'

'And before I knew what was happening, George and I... Well, there it was. You had paid off so many of my debts.'

'I had not bought you,' Finlay said sharply.

Isabelle nodded. 'I know that, but you must admit, it put me in rather a delicate situation.'

He supposed it did. That was the trouble with money; it always ruined perfectly good friendships.

Still, it did not explain why Bartlett was so damned silent about the whole thing. 'And Bartlett never thought to say anything?'

'Neither of us wanted to offend you, and though George was certain you were not in love with me—'

Dear God, it was so obvious, Finlay thought with rising disbelief.

Had not Bartlett asked closely about his feelings for Isabelle? Had he not been most interested to discover whether Finlay had fallen in love with her?

'But I wasn't sure, and just when I was attempting to tell your mother that I was in love with another—'

'Mother!' Finlay turned around, nettled. 'You knew?'

The Dowager Countess of Staromchor shrugged. 'I knew she cared for another, but that is by the by.'

'Mother!'

'You think every marriage is made between two people who love each other? Come now, Staromchor, I raised you to be smarter than that,' said his mother in a cutting tone, seated still on the sofa and with the pamphlet open in her lap. 'Hardly anyone marries for love. I knew you would be a good husband to Isabelle, so what did it matter if she had feelings for another? Those feelings would fade.'

'They will not,' Isabelle said sharply, and Finlay grinned as the rambunctious tomboy he had known sparked back to life once more. 'I happen to believe that if love can be found, then it should be grasped as tightly as one can. How often does love arrive? Should we not seize it when it does?'

Finlay swallowed.

I love you!

She was right. Both of them. He should have offered Rilla his heart the moment he had realized it belonged to her. And now…

There was still a chance it was too late, even with the complication of Isabelle removed from him.

It was removed, wasn't it?

'Just to be clear, then,' Finlay said hurriedly, and Isabelle's attention moved back to him. 'Our engagement is at an end, and you are…happy?'

'Ridiculously so.' His previously betrothed beamed. 'No offence meant, you understand. But I wish to marry the man I love.'

There was a loud sob that filled the modiste.

Finlay blinked. He had not made such a sound, and neither had Isabelle. Which could only mean…

The two of them turned around slowly, Finlay hardly able to believe his eyes, as he saw his mother sobbing on the sofa.

'Mother?' he said weakly.

'I… I am in love with someone, too!' declared his mother, tears rolling down her cheeks. 'And I declined him b-because… a small scandal, but that was twenty years ago. I want to marry him, but I said no, I do not know why!'

'Mother?' Finlay repeated again, hardly able to keep up with all this change.

'Right, I had better go,' said Isabelle smartly, starting to pull her gown off.

Finlay snapped a hand over his eyes, now utterly bewildered. 'Where are you going?'

'Why, to find George and make him marry me, of course,' Isabelle said lightly. There was the sound of fabric pooling to the floor, and Finlay wished to God she had stepped behind the screen. They weren't seven years old anymore. 'And what about you, Fin?'

It was the childhood name they had all used, and its utterance here, at Madame Penelope's after his engagement was put to an end, was a moment of realization for Finlay.

He dropped his hand and grinned at the troublemaking Carr that he and Bartlett—he and George, heaven forbid—still had in their lives. 'Good luck.'

'You, too,' said Isabelle, pulling up a sprigged muslin gown and hastily doing up the ties.

'Me?'

She snorted and laughed as she marched out of the modiste's. 'Did you not say you were in love with someone else?'

And a moment of clarity dropped into Finlay's mind as he realized what he had to do next. 'Rilla.'

'And now he might not marry me! Why did I decline...? My fear of scandal... What was I thinking?'

After, that was, he had comforted his mother.

Good grief.

Chapter Eighteen

'Here we are, then,' said a gruff voice Rilla knew well, and strangely thought she would miss. 'The Markhall School for Girls.'

Rilla had felt the carriage slow five minutes ago, the surface of the road shifting from the rough country lane to the slightly smoother gravel path.

They had arrived, then.

'C'mon,' the driver snapped gruffly.

Rilla bit back her tongue and forced down all the explanations that she had already made to the unfeeling and unpleasant man. Her fingers curled around the unopened letter she could not see. She was depending on the driver to guide her in and out of the carriage; this was all new to her, and she did not know where she was going.

A heavily gloved hand grabbed her own.

Trying not to cry out with the discomfort of someone suddenly touching her, Rilla allowed herself to be tugged forward in the carriage, moving in a haze of uncertainty and distrust.

'Step,' snapped the tired voice.

She had tried to be patient. She would certainly not like to be a carriage driver, spending hours and hours out in the elements, freezing in the winter and baking in the summer sun. The wind was surely a cruel whip across one's face, and one's fingers and toes were doubtless ice in this weather.

But that was no call for rudeness.

'Oh,' Rilla muttered as her foot caught on the first step. Then she had her bearings and was able to descend from the carriage with relative decorum.

The instant her booted feet crunched on the gravel she gained her equilibrium, she snatched her hand away from the driver.

'Thank you,' she said ungraciously.

It did not appear that he had noticed. His footsteps, heavier than hers and faster, had moved around to the side of the carriage, and soon they had returned. The hearty thud of her trunk being dropped beside her was unmistakable.

'Nice place,' the carriage driver grunted.

Trying her best not to be sarcastic, Rilla shrugged. 'It makes no difference in the end.'

And it didn't. Whether or not the Markhall School for Girls was pleasing to look at was neither here nor there.

Even if she could see, Rilla could not help but think darkly, the place was not going to be improved by fine stonework.

No, she was here to do a job. The students of the Markhall School for Girls were the important factors to secure her future happiness, and she would not know that for some time.

She would simply have to hope, to trust, that they were not as odious as she feared.

'Y'want yer bonnet?'

Suppressing the desire to point out that if she'd had any warning that she was about to be dragged out of the carriage, she would certainly have picked up her bonnet, Rilla said instead, 'Yes, if you please.'

Her courtesy was not returned. The bonnet was thrust into her hands, the surprise at the sudden movement meaning that she almost dropped it.

Then the door snapped shut behind her, and there was a creak of wood and leather.

'Good luck, Miss,' grunted the man.

Rilla turned immediately, real panic flaring now in her chest. 'But Miss Pike instructed you to—'

'I reckon as you can find your own way in,' the driver said curtly, jerking the reins and causing one of the horses to neigh in indignation. 'Night is drawing in and I want to be on my way afore dark. Good luck, as I say, Miss.'

'But—'

Whatever words of remonstrance she had intended to utter would have made little difference, Rilla was sure, even if the man had heard them. As it was, he had urged the horses on and the rattle of the carriage made her attempts at speech completely moot.

Only when the sound of the carriage had entirely died away did Rilla swallow and allow the emotions flooding through her veins to appear on her face.

Oh, damn.

Her cane was still in the carriage.

She'd accidentally left it in the carriage when she arrived... and now it was rattling on its way back to the Wallflower Academy.

Ah, well. She would have to learn quickly, that was all.

Rilla had known, from the moment that the Pike had suggested that she go and become a teacher for a school, that leaving the Wallflower Academy would be a deprivation.

None of them could truly understand. It was like having her right arm cut off, the familiar sensations of the Wallflower Academy removed from her.

This gravel was different. It crunched at a different pitch when Rilla took a hesitant step to where she believed her trunk had been deposited. It took her three attempts to kneel and find the blasted thing, and in the end, it was only when her toe clipped the corner that she was absolutely sure.

Straightening up and holding the handle of the trunk in her

hand, Rilla rammed her bonnet on her head and turned her face up to what she presumed was the school.

And then she swallowed.

How had she managed to learn the routes and routines of the Wallflower Academy? It had all seemed so long ago now, she could barely recall. It was as familiar to her as her own limbs.

Well, she had to start somewhere.

With a sinking heart that was partly to do with her practical predicament, and partly to do with the unopened letter clutched in her hand, Rilla took a step forward. Hating that she had to do this, she put out a hand.

Then she halted.

Rilla turned, back to the direction the dratted carriage had gone, and swore under her breath.

It took five minutes of careful exploratory stepping for Rilla to find the portico, then another minute to navigate the six steps whilst holding on to her seemingly increasingly heavy trunk.

By the time she had deposited it on the stone before the front door, Rilla's shoulders ached and her temples were starting to throb.

It had been a long journey, and now…now the difficult part was about to begin.

She did not irritate herself by seeking a doorbell. Instead, Rilla rapped hard on the door with her fist.

It would have been far louder with a cane, she could not help but think, *but there it was.*

The door did not open for several minutes. When it did, a voice far sharper than Miss Pike's snapped, 'Yes?'

Rilla curtsied, hating that she had no idea if this woman was a maid or the headmistress. 'Miss Marilla Newell, at your service.'

'Miss Marilla— Dear God, you're the teacher?'

Still no real clue as to the voice's owner, Rilla thought darkly, though it was not a good sign, whoever it was.

'Yes,' she said aloud.

The owner of the voice sniffed. 'I should have informed your previous headmistress…teachers are supposed to come around the back.'

Like a servant, Rilla thought with an ever-sinking heart. That was indication enough that this place was not going to be the haven of learning and new home she could grow comfortable in as she had hoped.

Still, she was far away from everything and everyone that she knew. If there was ever a time and a place for a fresh start, it was the Markhall School for Girls.

No Sylvia, no Daphne, no Miss Pike, and no…no Finlay Jellicoe, Earl of Staromchor.

Which was all to the good. Of course. There was no reason that she would want to see them, especially not the latter. No reason at—

'Well, don't just stand there—come in,' sighed the voice. 'I am Miss Hennessy. You may call me ma'am.'

Rilla nodded, apprehension flowing through her veins. 'Shall I just leave my trunk—'

'You can bring in your trunk. Our teachers don't have airs and graces,' said Miss Hennessy curtly. 'Honestly, what did they teach you in your last position?'

It was only then that Rilla realized just what a false reference Miss Pike had provided.

Dear Lord, had the woman intimated that Rilla had already been a teacher?

What on earth was she supposed to say?

'It was…a very different establishment,' Rilla said demurely, leaning to pick up her trunk as her shoulder protested.

Miss Hennessy sniffed. 'So I see. Come on.'

Her footsteps on what sounded like hardwood floors immediately began to move away, and Rilla hastened to follow her.

If only there had not been such a large step into the building.

Careering forward and only just managing to prevent herself from smashing her nose onto the floor by whirling her arms like a windmill, Rilla's heart was thundering painfully by the time she righted herself.

'No time for fun and games,' came the distant voice of Miss Hennessy. 'Honestly, were you always larking about at your old place? We don't have much time for that here.'

Rilla swallowed her irritation as she turned vaguely in what she presumed was a hall. 'Miss Hennessy, I do not know what the Pike—what Miss Pike—told you about me in her letter to you, but—'

'Not much, scarce enough to place you with a subject.' Miss Hennessy appeared to be moving away, though where precisely, Rilla could not tell. 'Keep up, will you?'

'The reason I mention this,' Rilla continued doggedly, putting her trunk down and deciding once and for all that she was not going to cart it about like a servant, 'is because Miss Pike appears to have neglected to tell you—'

'I am sure there are many things your precious Pike hasn't—'

'To tell you that I am blind,' Rilla said, with the patience of a saint.

Miss Hennessy's voice immediately disappeared.

And there it is, Rilla thought dully as the silence elongated most painfully.

There was always the awkward silence after a statement of that nature. Next would be the frantic apologies, then the questions about precisely how it happened, and what she could see, and whether she had seen a doctor...

'I beg your pardon, I'm sure,' said Miss Hennessy, her voice growing in volume as her footsteps echoed towards her. 'Why on earth didn't you say?'

'I... I presumed you knew,' returned Rilla, slightly dazed.

Where was the apology? Where were the questions? Where were the recommendations of different eye drops, poultices, and for some reason, liquors that different people had recommended her over the years?

'Honestly, why would you presume that? I am glad you told me, though,' said Miss Hennessy briskly. 'It makes things a good deal clearer. Do you want my arm?'

Rilla's mouth fell open.

It was…refreshing.

Miss Hennessy would never gain many friends, not with that acidic nature and sharpness of tongue—but it was far pleasanter to be subjected to that than the pity she'd expected.

Despite herself, a wry smile crept over Rilla's face. 'That would be most welcome, thank you.'

It was not the softest of touches when Miss Hennessy pulled her arm into her own, but at this point, Rilla did not care. Perhaps this place, though strange and unfriendly at first, could become a kind of home.

Exhausted from her journey, Rilla did not attempt to memorize the path from the hall to whatever place it was that Miss Hennessy was taking her. Left, right, up a flight of stairs then down a few steps, the place appeared to be a maze.

'Here we are,' came Miss Hennessy's voice, accompanied by the click of an opening door. 'Your schoolroom.'

Rilla's stomach lurched as she was guided into a place that was far lighter than the corridor before it.

Her schoolroom.

Well, the Pike had been attempting to convince her to become a tutor at the Wallflower Academy for…how long now? Eight months? Longer?

Perhaps she should have known from the very beginning that she would end up here, Rilla thought darkly.

In a schoolroom, in an unwelcoming school, in the middle of nowhere.

'Most people don't want to teach here,' came the sharp voice of Miss Hennessy as she released Rilla.

Rilla raised an eyebrow. 'Oh?'

It was as non-committal an answer as she could manage, without giving offence or leading to further questions.

Miss Hennessy's sniff occurred from several feet away now. 'Yes, we are too far from London to be of interest to most.'

The words slipped out before Rilla could stop them. 'I have no wish to be near London.'

'Really,' came Miss Hennessy's wry response, no question within the word. 'I thought as much.'

Heat burned Rilla's cheeks, but there was nothing she could do about it. She was not about to bare her heart to anyone at the Markhall School for Girls, much less Miss Hennessy, who had still not clarified whether she was housekeeper, fellow teacher, or headmistress.

No, the sorrows that plagued her heart were hers alone, and she would bear them as best she could.

Even if it meant pain beyond what she had ever known.

'I suppose it was a great wrench,' came Miss Hennessy's next words. 'Leaving your previous position.'

A far greater wrench than Rilla had expected. Until the very moment of departure, she had considered the Wallflower Academy to be what it was for so many: a strange sort of prison, attempting to mould the women termed wallflowers into something that the *ton* preferred.

Only when she had left it did she realize just what a sanctuary it was from the world.

And now it was gone—or more accurately, she had gone, and now her very independence had been similarly taken from her.

'Is that a letter?'

Rilla's hand tightened around the paper. 'Yes, it is.'

'But how do you…?'

The question was left delicately on the air, as though that would make it less distasteful. In truth, Rilla could hardly blame her. It was a question borne of curiosity, not malice, and it was not a difficult one to answer.

'I cannot read,' Rilla said airily. 'I usually have a friend read my letters to me and then I memorize them. It is easier that way.'

She really should have asked Sylvia or Daphne to read it for her before she left. Rilla's finger stroked along the soft grain of the letter. There hadn't been time.

Lying to herself, now, was she?

She hadn't wanted to see them. Hadn't wanted to hear the disappointment and the disgrace in their voices. Would they treat her differently? Had they forgotten her already?

'And who will read your letters now?' came the voice of Miss Hennessy.

Rilla swallowed. Well, there was no time like the present for trying to make new friends. Goodness knew, none of them here could be as shy as Daphne nor as wild as Sylvia.

'If you would do me the honour?' she said formally, holding out the letter.

Miss Hennessy did not reply in words, but perhaps that was unnecessary. Her eager steps forward and the way she half took, half wrenched the letter from Rilla's hand suggested her nosiness was perhaps on par with Sylvia's after all.

Rilla was silent as she heard the breaking of the seal and the unfolding of the page. It had been good paper, a high quality; her fingertips had told her that much. Her father had perhaps wanted to wish her good fortune on the start of her new endeavour. It would have been more pleasant if he had visited, but—

'"My dear Rilla…"' said Miss Hennessy aloud. 'Rilla?'

Her stomach lurched painfully. 'It is what my family and some close friends call me.'

I told you before, my friends call me Rilla.

It was impossible to tell whether Miss Hennessy approved of this. With a sniff, she returned to the letter.

'"My dear Rilla, I am so sorry that I was not able to see you before you left the Wallflower Academy. It had been my intention, but as you can imagine, I have had a few important things to take care of before then."'

Rilla forced her expression to remain still.

Of course her father would put almost everything before her. Why was she surprised?

"'Having discovered that you will be leaving before I can return, I hope you will do me the honour of receiving me at the Markhall School for Girls, and we can continue our very important discussion then,'" Miss Hennessy read.

A frown puckered at Rilla's forehead. Important discussion? It had been a good many years now since she and her father had had a discussion of any description. What on earth did he mean?

"'Your very faithful Finlay.'"

Rilla staggered, the weight of the name Miss Hennessy had just read unsettling her to such an extreme that her knees buckled. 'Wh-what did you say?'

"'We can continue our very—'"

'After that,' Rilla snapped.

She was undoubtedly offending Miss Hennessy, the only person at the Markhall School for Girls she knew, but that did not matter. Not with those words ringing in her ears—words she could not have heard.

"'Your very faithful Finlay,'" repeated Miss Hennessy in a bemused voice. 'Who is that—a brother?'

There had never been anyone less like a brother in her entire life.

Despite the fact that her head was ringing and her knees felt as though they were about to collapse at any moment, Rilla managed to say, 'No, a…a friend. Thank you, Miss Hennessy, I will have my letter back now.'

The accompanying sniff was unwelcome, but expected. 'Well, I'll leave you to get accustomed to your schoolroom. Just ring the bell by the blackboard, and I'll send someone to show you up to your room. Good evening, Miss Newell.'

'Miss Hennessy,' Rilla said in a hoarse voice.

The door snicked shut behind her, and Rilla staggered back until her fingers found a wall. Then she leaned against it and closed her eyes.

He was being cruel.

All that talk about continuing their discussion—there was nothing more to discuss! Finlay was not truly in love with her, and though he was not in love with Isabelle Carr, he was about to marry her.

What else was there to say?

'He is not coming back,' Rilla said into the silence of the room. 'And you would be a fool to wish for it.'

A fool to wish for greater heartache. A fool to hope for something that simply could not be.

The door to the corridor clicked open.

Rilla straightened as best she could. Well, she did not want Miss Hennessy to think she could be so easily exhausted. Her place here was only secure if she could teach all day, after all.

'I am quite well,' she said firmly in the direction of the door. 'In fact, I do not believe I have ever been better.'

'Excellent,' said the voice of Finlay Jellicoe, Earl of Staromchor. 'I am delighted to hear it.'

Chapter Nineteen

Finlay had to put the past behind him and attempt to make those things right. He had already given Bartlett and Isabelle their wedding present—an impressive gold clock—and had managed to calm his mother sufficiently, though he had still not gained a clue as to who this gentleman was that she was supposed to have fallen in love with.

Now it was time to tend to his own affairs.

Swallowing hard, wishing to goodness he had a speech prepared and certain that merely seeing Rilla would thrust it out of his mind anyway, Finlay opened the door.

When he stepped into the room, his breath was quite literally taken away.

There she was. Rilla. The woman he loved.

He had never seen her quite so downcast. Her travelling pelisse was stained with mud at least three inches deep, and her bonnet was askew, as were her dark midnight curls. There was a look of pain in her expression that even her straightening up against the wall she had been leaning against could not distract from.

And then Rilla spoke.

'I am quite well,' she said, turning to him and evidently presuming he was someone else. 'In fact, I do not believe I have ever been better.'

And Finlay's heart stirred as it had never stirred before.

She was so brave. Here she was, to all intents and purposes alone, with a new life ahead of her—one Rilla had not chosen.

And still she was determined to face it head-on.

It was all he could do to keep his voice steady. 'Excellent. I am delighted to hear it.'

Finlay was gifted a brief moment of satisfaction. There was nothing quite like the woman you loved gawping at you, utterly confused, her jaw dropping and her fingers tightening on—

Was that his letter? Was the fact that Rilla was still hold-ing it a good sign?

No, it could not be that simple. Within a heartbeat, Rilla's expression had transformed into one that was stiff, polite, and worst of all, aloof. He knew she only put on that appearance when she wanted to be distant from the person with whom she was conversing.

So, he had a great deal of ground to cover. There was a chance, perhaps, that she would not forgive him at all.

Though the thought of being separated from Rilla forever was bitter bile on his tongue, Finlay had to accept it was a pos-sibility. There was nothing he could do here, save tell the truth.

And apologize. Dear God, she deserved an apology.

'Rilla, you have to let me explain,' Finlay said hurriedly, launching into a declaration that his mind managed to drag up from the depths of his imagination. 'I know you probably don't want to hear it.'

'You're right,' came Rilla's curt reply. 'I don't.'

Finlay only hesitated for a moment, then forced himself to take a step closer. If he could only tell her everything he had done since he had last seen her, then surely she would under-stand.

She may still not wish to have anything to do with him, but she would at least understand.

'I'm afraid I'm going to tell you anyway,' said Finlay, cring-ing at the inelegance of his behaviour. Most unsuitable for an earl. 'The moment you left me standing outside the Wallflower Academy—'

'Which you rightly deserved.'

'Which I deserved,' Finlay accepted, trying not to allow himself to get drawn into a debate.

He could see what was happening. All Rilla wanted to do was protect herself, prevent herself from ever feeling hurt again.

And he knew why. Finlay had hurt her. He had hurt himself, too, but that had been different; he had been in possession of all the facts. It had been Rilla who had been thunderstruck by the revelation that he had been engaged to another.

Now he had to make it right, push through Rilla's defences one last time, make her see his bruised and battered heart, and...

Wait for her to make her decision.

'I wanted to tell you everything, but I had to—'

'What are you doing here?'

'I'm trying to tell you,' Finlay said, his voice rising in volume. 'If you would just let me—'

'Are you the new footman?'

Finlay whirled around. There stood a woman who could only be a teacher at the Markhall School for Girls. She was wearing a very masculine-styled gown with a sort of fitted waistcoat around the bodice, and her spectacles were topped by a pair of frowning brows.

'F-footman?' he spluttered.

Then a noise caught his ear—a noise he had not expected, but nonetheless lifted his spirits magnificently.

Rilla was laughing.

Finlay turned to her, delight soaring through his chest as he watched the woman he adored giggle with unrepressed laughter.

'I do not see what is so amusing,' sniffed the woman who had stepped into Rilla's new schoolroom. 'I only asked—'

'Miss Hennessy, this is the Earl of Staromchor,' said Rilla with a grin, managing to stifle her laughter long enough to speak. 'I apologize for laughing, but the misunderstanding—'

'Oh!' Miss Hennessy went scarlet.

Finlay waved a hand and cast her a charming smile. 'Please, do not concern yourself. It happens all the time.'

Rilla snorted with laughter behind him.

'Well, I— Right, so… Your Lordship is an acquaintance of Miss Newell?' spluttered the teacher.

Finlay swallowed.

An acquaintance?

Oh, they had shared so much more than mere acquaintance-ship…but at the same time, he could hardly describe Rilla as a friend. Not in this moment. Not when he was uncertain whether or not she would even permit him to attempt to explain…

'Something like that.' Rilla's dry voice held no hints as to whether she would let him continue, but her next sentence did. 'Please excuse us, Miss Hennessy. I believe the earl has some-thing important to tell me. If you would be so good…'

It was delicately done, and Finlay had to remind himself once again that Rilla, far from being an abandoned wallflower in the Wallflower Academy, was the Honourable Miss Newell.

Dear God, there was so much of her he still had to learn. So much more of Rilla to discover.

If she would let him…

Miss Hennessy was all awkward apologies, curtsies, and kowtowing. By the time she had shut the door with as genteel a click as she could manage, nerves had once again seized Finlay's heart.

He turned back to Rilla, who was now staring with a bold-ness typical of the woman he cared so deeply for.

For a moment, silence hung between them.

Then their mutual laughter echoed in the otherwise empty room.

'A footman,' Finlay said dryly. 'I must just give off that sense.'

'I think it more likely that anyone in my presence immediately becomes more servile,' Rilla said dryly.

Finlay winced, but only for a moment. Rilla was a woman, he knew, who could quite happily laugh at herself. If she were saying such things, it was because she felt comfortable doing so.

'Look,' he said quietly.

The laughter left Rilla's lips, but her openness appeared to remain.

Finlay took a deep breath.

Well, here goes—everything.

'It is true that the initial flirtation I enjoyed with you was never meant to mean more,' he said quietly, then hurried on, 'but I promise it was not nearly so bad as you probably think.'

A sardonic eyebrow rose. 'You have no idea how bad I think it was.'

'Oh, I can probably guess,' Finlay said darkly.

After all, had he not heard some of the lewd things the members of White's had suggested about innocent and largely unprotected ladies of the *ton*? There was a reason he had moved clubs.

'Was that all I was?' cut in Rilla, her voice once again harsh. 'A bit of fun?'

'Not in the slightest. Well, yes,' Finlay said, stepping forward and wishing to goodness the woman before him could see how contrite his expression was.

Her frown deepened. 'Well? Which is it?'

'Both, I suppose,' he said awkwardly, twisting his fingers before him as his heartrate started to quicken again. 'It *was* fun, talking to you. I had never experienced so much joy in the presence of a stranger.'

It was difficult to admit such a thing, but far more difficult to see the complete distrust on Rilla's face. 'I find that hard to believe.'

'I am telling you nothing but the truth,' Finlay said simply. 'Bartlett's encouragement to flirt with someone before I was chained to Isabelle...it was the perfect excuse. I already wished to know you better.'

That was clearly not something she had expected to hear.

Rilla's expression softened, just a mite. 'You...you did?'

'I did,' said Finlay, taking another step forward. A great expanse still separated them from each other, an expanse he did not believe he could yet cross. But perhaps, with enough time, enough trust...

'And our conversations swiftly became so much more than that—more to me, at any rate.'

'You think they did not mean anything to me?' Rilla's whisper was full of heartbreak.

Finlay swallowed, crushing the instinct to pull her into his arms and kiss away all the misunderstanding, the mistrust.

He would not do that to her. Rilla would not be touched by anyone, including him, without her permission.

'Our conversations, our time together... I have never felt so...so seen,' Finlay said, conscious of his poor choice of words. 'Dammit, I cannot explain.'

'I know what you mean. At least, I think I do,' said Rilla quietly.

Her hands had left the wall, as though it was no longer required to sustain her. Was that a good sign? Finlay's head was spinning so rapidly, the room almost swaying before him, he could not really tell.

He swallowed. 'Our connection has meant so much to me that I have... I have broken off my engagement.'

His heart rose to his mouth as he waited for Rilla's response.

It did not come. She merely stood there, still as a statue, as though she had not heard his words at all.

Finlay cleared his throat. Rilla said nothing. He shifted from one foot to the other, certain she would be able to hear the movement. Still she was silent.

When he could endure the silence no longer, Finlay said, 'It was really only a marriage of convenience, as I told you. Yes, I paid off her family debts, and I felt a debt of honour, but… but that is nothing compared to you.'

He had presumed such words would inspire a response, but still Rilla remained taciturn.

And though his instinct was to speak, to fill the silence, Finlay forced herself to remain quiet. This was all new information for Rilla, information she surely could not have been expecting. The very least he could do was give her the chance to absorb it.

When he truly felt as though he would burst with the unsaid words rolling about his chest, Rilla said quietly, 'Will… will Miss Carr…will she be able to live? Without the money and protection, I mean, of your name?'

'If anything, I believe I was holding her back,' Finlay said wryly, a spark of mirth in his lungs. 'She had already fallen in love with someone else. Their engagement will be announced tomorrow.'

'But…but you said…you said she was in love with you!'

'No need to sound so surprised,' Finlay said, a dart of pain searing his heart. 'I had thought, but I was mistaken. It appears that another man, a better man in my estimation, captured her heart months ago. It was only our arranged marriage that was preventing them from being together and now…now that is at an end.'

And his heart leaped as Rilla did something he could not have imagined when he first entered the room.

She took a step towards him.

'This…this bet. Was it to bed me?'

'No!' Finlay was horrified at the insinuation, that she could believe such a thing of him.

Dear God, had he proved himself to be the rake he had never thought he was?

'Absolutely not!'

'Because I can imagine two gentlemen, an earl and a…?'

Finlay winced. 'A viscount.'

'An earl and a viscount, from my experience, would have few qualms in—'

'Bartlett—Lord Bartlett—is not like that,' Finlay said firmly. 'In truth, I cannot think of anyone less likely to do such a thing, or even think such a thing. No, it was…it was to charm you. To flirt, to enjoy a woman's company.'

Rilla breathed a wry laugh. 'And we have done so much more than that.'

'And I want more,' said Finlay, his mouth dry as he tentatively approached the crux of the conversation. The centre, the part that mattered the most. 'So much more.'

He took a step towards her, making sure his footstep was heavy. She did not blanch or move away.

Finlay's heart skipped a beat.

He was going to do it.

'Rilla— Marilla, I suppose I should say—'

'You're not going to…are you?' Rilla peered in his direction with flushed cheeks.

And that was when he knew. Finlay could not have known beforehand, not in advance of turning up at the Markhall School for Girls and hoping to goodness that whoever opened the door would let him in.

But in this moment, he knew.

She loved him. She wanted him, had been devastated not just because of the lies, but because Isabelle Carr's existence would make it impossible for them to be together.

And the affection he felt for her stirred so powerfully, it

was almost as though it was pouring out from him, invisible perhaps to the naked eye but perfectly evident to Rilla Newell.

'Goodness, I love you,' Finlay said simply.

Rilla's pink cheeks turned red, but she took a step towards him. 'And I love you.'

The simplicity of it all—that was what he loved. The fact that loving each other did not have to be difficult or complicated. Life might make it so, but at the very centre of who they were was love. Love for each other. Love for what mattered.

Finlay grinned as he caught Rilla's hands in his own, and she did not pull away. 'When we are married—'

Rilla snorted. 'I never had the impression you were particularly fond of the married state!'

'I did not want my life chosen for me, dictated by honour and forced down a particular path,' Finlay quipped, warmth spreading from the connection of their fingertips. 'And it's not. This is my choice—you are my choice. And yes, it may perhaps shock the *ton*.'

'Oh, good,' said Rilla darkly. 'Another scandal.'

'But as long as I have you, I don't care,' Finlay finished seriously. 'Rilla, you said before that you were more than a match for an earl.'

'Oh, don't repeat what I—'

'And you were right. You're more than a mere match—you... you are everything,' he said, taut emotions finally pouring out of him. 'My better half, my best friend—the one woman in the world who makes me laugh and makes me think, usually at the same time. More than a match? You're more suitable a match for me than anyone I've ever met.'

The woman he loved tilted her head as she laughed. 'You were never going to take no for an answer, were you?'

'I would always take no from you, if you do not wish it,' he said quietly. It was important she knew that. 'Even as my wife, you will never get dictated to, Rilla.'

Her twisting smile aroused his manhood. 'And what would you have done, then, if I had rejected you?'

Finlay stared. Then he pulled Rilla into his embrace and she stepped willingly into his arms. 'You know, it did not even cross my mind.'

Their kiss, when it came, had been awaited forever—and as Rilla melted into his passionate affection, Finlay was certain he would never see the world the same again.

Epilogue

Her hands were shaking as they carefully smoothed her gown, but there was a smile on Rilla's face that had been there from the very moment she had awoken.

It was, after all, her wedding day.

'Such an exquisite gown,' Daphne said softly just behind her. 'You look wonderful, Rilla.'

Rilla's smile did not shift as she shrugged. 'I suppose so.'

What she looked like did not matter, not really. Not when she was going to become the wife of the best man she had ever met.

'And the service! Oh, it will be beautiful,' continued Daphne in her soft, shy voice. 'I have stuffed not one, but two handkerchiefs up my sleeve, just to be sure.'

And it was indeed most pleasant.

Finlay had surprised her with some careful planning that had brought such joy, Rilla had been unable to express it as they had left the church. Only when the wedding party had entered the Wallflower Academy and stepped through to the ballroom, where the wedding reception was being hosted, had Rilla managed to find time to thank her husband.

'You were so thoughtful,' she said between two hasty kisses.

Finlay had laughed. 'Well, I thought you deserved to have a little beauty in your day, Lady Staromchor. Your special day.'

'It is special because I am marrying you,' Rilla pointed out, splaying her hand on her husband's chest and being rewarded by the *thud-thud-thud* of his heart.

Lady Staromchor—she was the Countess of Staromchor. Now, that was a strange thought.

'You're the reason this day is just perfect.'

But his decisions had not hurt. Instead of going for the traditional roses, he had told her as they had walked from the church to the Tudor manor of the Wallflower Academy, he had instead instructed the florist to select those with the headiest scents.

Oh, the church had smelled divine.

'Isabelle helped,' Finlay said, his voice quavering as he said his previously betrothed's name. 'Which was to her credit, I must say.'

Rilla's stomach lurched, but only slightly.

It was perhaps fate that the two of them should find each other after both exiting an engagement—although of course, for very different reasons.

From the little Rilla knew of Miss Isabelle Carr from the single meeting they had shared, she seemed a very pleasant kind of person. It was natural, surely, for there to be awkwardness between them. They had, after all, both been engaged to the same man.

'I hope she will be happy,' Rilla said aloud.

'Oh, she will be.' Finlay's voice was confident, with none of the wavering that had accompanied it when he had been asked by his mother days ago whether he preferred the cream linens or the champagne for their wedding reception. 'Bartlett will take good care of her. Far better care than I could—that is certain.'

Rilla was not sure about that, but then she was hardly going to argue.

'And…and Nina? Your other sisters, your father? You have spoken to them to your satisfaction? I had no wish to intrude when I saw you together…' Her new husband spoke quietly so that, in the hustle and bustle of the ballroom, only she could hear him.

Trying her best not to disturb the pins Sylvia had dug into her midnight curls, Rilla nodded. 'And they were most gracious in their congratulations, too. I think… I hope that this is the beginning of a renewal. Of an understanding between us that has been lost for many years.'

It had been an awkward conversation. Rilla had almost been surprised that her family had bothered to come—but then, an earl was an earl. She had finally done what they had wanted, but she had done it on her terms, and to an earl who was far superior to the one they had initially chosen.

And Nina had listened to her apology.

Rilla let out the breath she had not known she had been holding. A new beginning.

'Oh, dear, it looks like one of the hired footmen is lost,' Finlay's voice said wearily.

Trying to stifle a grin, Rilla said, 'Well, you had better go and assist him, my love. After all, you were a footman the first time we met.'

His hasty kiss was followed by a snort of laughter, one that grew quieter as Finlay stepped away, leaving Rilla to stand alone.

But this time, she did not mind.

Finlay may not be standing right beside her, but she was still strengthened by his love, his adoration. Knowing that he cared about her so, that she had nothing to prove to anyone, to the world, was enough to keep her head as high as her spirits.

'I have an announcement to make!'

Rilla knew that voice, and tried not to groan as silence filled the ballroom of the Wallflower Academy.

The Dowager Countess of Staromchor. Finlay's mother. Her new mother-in-law.

She was a difficult woman to be around, to be sure, but as

she now had a lifetime of being her daughter-in-law, Rilla supposed she would have to attempt to get used to her, if she could.

If she could.

'I have an announcement,' repeated the dowager countess. There was another sound, something that sounded like tinkling glass. Was she tapping on a champagne glass?

A hand slipped around hers, and Rilla squeezed it immediately. She knew that hand.

'What on earth is my mother doing?' Finlay breathed into her ear.

Rilla ensured to keep her expression steady. 'I have absolutely no idea. I thought you would.'

'There is no announcement as far as I know,' he said softly as curious chatter rose up around the room. 'Isabelle and Bartlett have eloped.'

'Eloped?' Rilla repeated, perhaps a tad louder than she ought.

She did not need to see to feel the stares pressing against her skin. Well, she could not help it—anyone would have responded loudly to a remark like that.

Besides, it was her wedding. Her wedding, to Finlay—a man she loved, and who she had never believed could love her in the same way she loved him. It was understandable that people would be looking at her.

Staring at her, no doubt.

Finlay's chuckle was light. 'I should have known they wouldn't be able to wait for the preparations of a wedding. They had kept their affection hidden for so long, they simply could not prevent themselves from heading in a carriage to Gretna Green.'

A slight tinge of envy crept through Rilla's heart. 'What an excellent idea. We should have done such a thing.'

Her new husband nudged her shoulder. 'Don't be daft—and miss whatever spectacle my mother is going to make of herself?'

Rilla groaned, but kept it as quiet as she could as her new mother-in-law cleared her throat loudly.

'This is a splendid day for the Staromchor family,' the dowager countess said in that grand voice she had. 'But I could not let this moment of happiness go by without revealing…without saying… Well, I am to be married!'

Somewhere in the ballroom, someone dropped a glass. It smashed, the sound a mixture between tinkling and shimmering, and Rilla's mouth fell open.

The Dowager Countess of Staromchor…was engaged to be married?

'What the—' breathed Finlay.

He was not the only one. A great deal of consternation appeared to be fluttering through the ballroom, from what Rilla could sense.

'Mother!' Finlay hissed. The dowager countess must be close to them, then. It was hard to tell, since the woman always spoke so loudly. 'What are you saying?'

'I am saying, dear boy, that there is no reason why Lord Norbury and I—'

'Father!' gasped Daphne from just behind them.

Rilla could hardly breathe.

Finlay's mother—and Daphne's father?

She turned, eager to assist her friend in what must be a mortifying and astonishing situation, but without the knowledge of precisely where she was there was no chance of finding Daphne. There was almost a stampede of well-wishers marching on the dowager countess, pushing past Rilla, jostling her, making it almost impossible to stay upright.

Panic welled in her chest and she instinctively cried, 'Finlay—'

He was by her side in an instant. 'I have you.'

His steady, comforting hand was already on her waist and Rilla reached out for him, love blossoming once more in her chest. 'Did you have any idea—your mother and Daphne's father?'

'Not a clue,' Finlay said darkly. 'I suppose I was too wrapped up in my own complicated romance that I became blind to my mother's.'

Rilla snorted.

'Ah— I mean...'

'I know what you meant,' Rilla said hastily. 'Of all people in the world, I know to trust your intentions. Can you see Daphne? Is she quite well?'

'She...' Finlay's voice trailed off.

Concern gripped her stomach. 'Well, is she?'

'She has left the room,' her husband murmured in her ear, lowering his voice. 'Looking quite distressed, I think. Sylvia has gone after her.'

Rilla relaxed. It wasn't as though she could do much for her friend, and Sylvia was far better at comforting people than she was. The young woman would soon have Daphne laughing again.

It was a shock, to be sure. It would also make Daphne her... her step-sister-in-law?

All thoughts of attempting to calculate just how the Staromchor family would now be formed were scattered, however, as Finlay pressed a kiss to her temple.

'You look radiant.'

'You know, I feel radiant,' confessed Rilla with a shy smile.

'And that is the most important thing,' Finlay said, his voice full of pride.

Pride in her.

She could hardly believe it. There was such joy in her heart it was overflowing, spilling out whenever she spoke to anyone, making it impossible for dour worry to overcrowd her heart.

She was loved. She loved a man who was good, and noble, and who felt things so deeply. Finlay was a man not made for her, but who had made himself what she wanted, what she needed.

A life full of richness and meaning was ahead of her, a life Rilla could never have imagined, let alone presumed to claim.

She would be leaving the Wallflower Academy after all, but she now had a home, a heart quite given over to her, to fill her life.

'Miss Pike appears most disconcerted,' Finlay said, narrating the room's surroundings as he knew she appreciated. 'A few guests have accosted Lord Norbury, who looks pleased yet red-faced. My mother is adoring all the attention, as you would expect, and I—'

'Yes, how are you?' Rilla said, a teasing lilt in her voice.

Another kiss was brushed against her temple. 'You know full well that I would much rather take my wife home and ravish her than stand about with all these people.'

Rilla shivered. She was quite aware of her husband's mind, in truth, but she knew what was expected of them, even if neither of them wished it.

They would remain here, at the wedding reception, for another hour at least. Then, and only then, would they be permitted to depart.

Depart, and start the beginning of a happy life together.

'Ah, I see Miss Pike wishes to distract people,' came Finlay's laughing voice. 'She's about to instruct the musicians to— Yes, there they go.'

Music expanded just to Rilla's left. She had attempted to convince the dowager countess and Miss Pike that a dance at their wedding reception was most unnecessary, but they had both discounted her objections. The dowager countess said she wished to dance, and Miss Pike said it would be a wonderful opportunity for her wallflowers to gain practice.

'After all, the gentlemen your future husband will be inviting to his wedding will doubtlessly wish to dance with my wallflowers,' Miss Pike had said only the previous day. 'Will they not?'

Whether Rilla herself would dance apparently had not occurred to either of the women. In truth, it had not occurred to her.

But she smiled broadly as Finlay squeezed her hand and said, 'My darling wife. Will you give me the honour of this dance?'

This dance, and the next, and the next, she wanted to say. *All the dances of my life, for the rest of my life. And all the days, and all the nights, all the griefs and all the joys. The moments I never thought I could share with another. And all the rest.*

'Yes,' Rilla breathed. 'With all my heart.'

And as they stepped forward, her arm in Finlay's, Rilla did not care whether anyone was watching. The whole wedding celebration party could have melted into thin air and it would not have mattered.

What mattered was the man beside her. The man who would be by her side for the rest of her life.

Being safe, being loved, being adored in his arms was the only way she knew how to live—and as Finlay placed her in the set and whispered, 'I love you,' Rilla knew nothing could compare to this. Nothing.

Except, perhaps, the next dance. And the next. And the next…

* * * * *

HISTORICAL

Your romantic escape to the past.

Available Next Month

The Kiss That Made Her Countess Laura Martin
A Cinderella To Redeem The Earl Ann Lethbridge

Lady Beaumont's Daring Proposition Eva Shepherd
A Deal With The Rebellious Marquess Bronwyn Scott

Keep reading for an excerpt of a new title
from the Historical series,
MISS ISOBEL AND THE PRINCE by Catherine Tinley

Prologue

Scotland,
1796

It was time to leave. Again.

Maria knew it but had been refusing to think about it. Tomorrow she and her three darlings must uproot themselves from this, their home. The only home her daughters had ever known. A place they had felt safe. Until now.

Briefly, she wondered if she should tell milady the truth, then dismissed the notion. It was a story too fantastical to be believed, too risky to be told. Especially now.

Instead, they would leave their haven, their sanctuary, departing before the guests began to arrive. As she had done many times before, she bemoaned the twist of fate that had seen milady—now simply her dear friend Margaret—seek company for the first time in years. Without letting Maria know—and why should she, when she was mistress of the house?—she had invited a group of former friends to visit. Renton Ashbourne. Thaxby. Kelgrove. All had accepted, and all were even now on their way. Milady Margaret had expected Maria to be pleased, that much was clear, and had looked decidedly crestfallen at Maria's response.

'But, Maria, you have been encouraging me to move

on, to accept that my dear husband is gone, to focus on my son, and the future. This is a momentous decision for me—to engage again with the people we knew in London.' She frowned. 'I have had little contact with the *ton* since his death, as you know.' She lifted her chin. 'And now I am ready to try again. I could not face going there.' A visible shudder ran through her. 'But inviting them here, for a quiet house party, that I can do—at least, I *think* I can.'

'Of course you can! For you are so strong. We both are!'

'I have learned from you, Maria. Each time I felt my life was worthless I would see you, also widowed, also young, but with no home, no family. Your determination to see your girls safe and well has been my inspiration!'

Safe and well.

A shiver of fear ran down her spine. Those who loved her, those who hated her, those who were indifferent to her... all would be here for Margaret's party, but she would not.

Margaret had been predictably horrified on hearing that Maria and her girls were leaving.

'But why? And where will you go?'

'I am not sure. Somewhere quiet, out of the way. It is better so. Besides, I have relied on your good heart and hospitality for long enough. Five years and more! You are healed enough now from the loss of your husband to start to engage in society again. You no longer need me.'

'But I do! I need your friendship! Are we not friends, Maria?'

At this, Maria had clasped her hand. 'Of course we are! And I promise to write to you. It is just...' She swallowed. 'Margaret, you have never pried into my circumstances. I will always be grateful for everything you have done for me—'

'Oh, stuff and nonsense! What was I supposed to do—

send you outside to give birth in the stable? And you were so shocked to have *three* babies, not one.' She gave a rueful smile. 'My son was a sturdy toddler by then, but I knew enough to help you in those early weeks, along with Nurse.' Her eyes grew distant. 'And then, by the time you were well and managing, you and I were fast friends.' She eyed Maria intently. 'I must confess to a certain curiosity, though. You seemed…frightened. Of someone or something.'

Maria nodded. 'I could not tell you. I still cannot. But know this—I did nothing wrong. Nothing! Those who wished me harm did so for their own reasons.'

Margaret spread her hands. 'I do not doubt it. And I do not mean to pry. But I ask you to reconsider. Stay with me—with us. This has been your home for five long years. Your girls and my son are best friends—as we are. Stay.'

'I wish I could.' There was a catch in Maria's voice. 'But I must think of my safety. And my daughters' safety.'

Margaret gasped. 'Someone would threaten your children?'

'I know not. But I cannot take that chance.'

Margaret was thoughtful, frowning. 'My house guests. You fear one of them?'

Maria eyed her steadily.

'I am so sorry, Maria! Who? Which one?'

But Maria shook her head. 'I have no proof. Of *anything*. So I dare not accuse. I must simply survive in safety and keep my daughters safe. So please, tell no one about me, if you can. And if you must, you may mention me as a friend—the widowed Mrs Lennox and her three children. No one needs to know they are triplets, and no one needs to know my first name.'

'Very well, but I cannot understand it!'

In the end Maria prevailed, as she had to. Tears were

shed on both parts, then Maria, sorrowfully, packed up their modest belongings. Clothing. The books and music sheets gifted to them at Christmastide, and for their fifth birthday earlier this year. Maria's respectable savings—for dear Margaret had insisted on paying her these past years, as her companion, and for helping with young Xander's education. Opening her strongbox, Maria counted the coin within, feeling reassured there would be enough to keep them for many months, until she found a suitable situation.

Other treasures were there, too. Earrings from her grandmother. His last letter to her. And the other thing. The treasure. Carefully she unfolded the velvet cloth, blinking as the jewels within caught the light. So beautiful! So distinctive!

So dangerous, for the piece would be easily recognised by anyone who knew about it. Even now. Wrapping it up again, her brow furrowed, she set it to one side, along with the letter. The earrings, though, those she would take with her. A legacy for her daughters, and a reminder that once, she had had a grandmother who loved her.

NEW RELEASE

BESTSELLING AUTHOR

DELORES FOSSEN

Even a real-life hero needs a little healing sometimes…

After being injured during a routine test, Air Force pilot
Blue Donnelly must come to terms with what his future
holds if he can no longer fly, and whether that future
includes a beautiful horse whisperer who turns his life
upside down.

In stores and online June 2024.

MILLS & BOON

millsandboon.com.au

Subscribe and fall in love with a Mills & Boon series today!

You'll be among the first to read stories delivered to your door monthly and enjoy great savings.